OBSIDIAN THRONE

THE LOCHLANN FEUDS

ROBIN D. MAHLE

ELLE MADISON

WHISKEY WILLOW

To everyone who took a chance on a story that started with vodka.
Psst... It ends that way too.

"Meet me on the battlefield
Even on the darkest night
I will be your sword and shield, your camouflage
And you will be mine
Echoes and the shots ring out
We may be the first to fall
Everything could stay the same, or we could change it all…"

Meet Me On The Battlefield
-SVRCINA

the Lochlann Realm

Kingdom of
Socair

Kingdom of
H'Ria

Masach Mountains

Dorcha
Forest

Coair R.

◆Chridhe

◆ Tuath
Towne

◆ Deas
Village

Kingdom of
Rionn

◆ Hagail
Falamh R.

The Bala
Dam

Lake
Morainn

Othach
Village ◆

◆Alech

Kingdom of
Luan

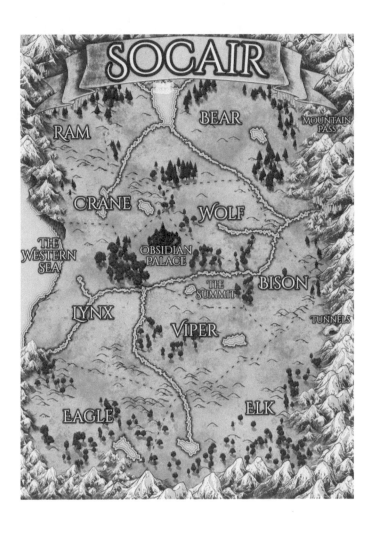

CHAPTER ONE

EVANDER

Fifty-three days.

Fifty-three storms-damned days since I had seen my wife.

We had only spent one insanely perfect night together before I was ripped away from her, forced to come back here to try to salvage the mess my father and Iiro had collectively made.

I suppressed a scowl as yet another wagon ambled along the road to the Bear Estate, full of Lochlannian goods and manned by yet another flame-haired couple.

Just like every time, I couldn't help but scrutinize the faces for Rowan's bright green eyes and mischievous lips.

Of course, she wasn't there.

That thought should have flooded me with relief. That meant she was actually listening to me and sticking to our plan, which was a wonder in and of itself. It meant she was safe, or as safe as she could hope to be right now.

Nonetheless, my chest felt hollow, and I found myself closing my hand around the signet ring I had worn around my neck since I left.

Her ring.

"Is this you *not* looking for her again?" Kirill muttered from his spot at my side.

We were waiting outside with the estate regiment, and he was at my left while Taras stood in his place at my right.

I ostensibly ignored Kirill as I surveyed the newest soldiers taking their turn on farming duty in the distance.

It was part of their training now, a way to ensure we made use of the seeds Lochlann had sent without sacrificing the troops I was beginning to suspect we would need. Only a small portion of it was here at the estate, while the rest had already been distributed to the farmland around the villages.

Kirill gave a chuckle at my lack of response, and Taras huffed out his more controlled version of one.

"I'm only saying," Kirill went on. "You look awfully concerned about someone who, what was it you said?" His features twisted into a semblance of contemplation as he pretended to search for the memory. "You couldn't care less about, so long as it didn't affect the clan?"

He had not been thrilled about me taking the princess captive to begin with, so I had made my opinion on the matter clear.

"Technically," I corrected, my lips twitching, "I said I couldn't care less about her feelings when the clan was at stake."

And damn it all if even that hadn't been a lie.

There was no part about Rowan I could seem to avoid caring about, and now...

Two months was far too long to be away from her. It had been bad enough when I thought she was happy, in Lochlann, moving on with her life.

But now she was mine, and she storms-damned well belonged here. With me. Preferably in my bed.

I was providentially distracted by the memories that always accompanied that particular line of thought when an ostentatious black carriage came into view. It wasn't hard to guess who had finally arrived.

"Looks like the bastard has finally decided to make his appearance," Kirill muttered under his breath.

While Bear's carriages, like everything else here, were accented in white, Iiro had wasted no time in displaying his new correlation to the obsidian throne. The surrounding regiment wore deep purple uniforms with black buttons and no trace of another color.

I clenched my jaw, not sure which brother I was looking forward to seeing the least. Iiro was perhaps one of my two least favorite people in the entire world, tying closely with my dear stepmother.

But I might never rid myself of the mental image of Korhonan's body pressed over Rowan's in the tent at the negotiations, his mouth on her neck, the way she had been flushed with pleasure before fury had made her burn an even brighter shade of crimson.

I decided I would rather see the conniving bastard that had managed to trick my father into helping him become king.

Since I had little choice but to go along with his schemes for the time being, I tucked Rowan's ring inside my shirt, then ordered my men to stand at attention until he exited the carriage. As soon as Iiro was visible, the soldiers dropped to a knee as one.

I sank into a bow that was probably a hair too shallow. Given his relatively new power and the fact that Bear had no fewer than three clans directly allied to us, in addition to Lochlann, not to mention, we were now in control of most of the resources…Iiro couldn't actually do anything about it.

Though he did enjoy every moment of dragging out the time before he gave the order for us to rise.

He stopped a few feet from me, his wife and his brother trailing a step behind. Iiro was an inch or two shorter than I was, but he compensated for that with his new crown.

Or rather, his old crown, since it was either the original or a very close replica. Every history book in Socair had a sketch of the tall, black, pointed spikes that made up the obsidian crown.

"I trust your father is well." His lips tilted up in a taunt. "And your charming stepmother."

"Both excellent," I lied.

"And the princess?" he goaded. "I hear there has been trouble at the border. I do hope she makes it in time."

For all that I had talked to Rowan about self-control, it took everything I had to keep my features neutral at his blatant threat to my wife. Before I could respond, though, Korhonan spoke up in an uncharacteristically hard voice.

"I'm certain she's well, Brother," he said pointedly. "After all, we both have a vested interest in Rowan's safety."

My eyebrows rose of their own accord. The Theodore I knew would never have contradicted his brother, even in private, let alone in public. Begrudgingly, I was forced to raise my opinion of him the smallest increment.

Iiro's eyes flickered irritably to his younger brother, and he straightened to his full height.

"Of course." A mocking smile tilted his lips. "Though, given the girl's penchant for idiocy, I should hardly be surprised if something befalls her of her own accord. Shame, though it would be," he tacked on.

Korhonan stiffened, and even Iiro's wife pursed her lips.

But I had eyes only for him. Everything in me went still, and I let him see the cold, empty, ruthless part of me that had been slowly taking over before Rowan burst her way into my life.

"Speaking of idiocy," I said in a deadly casual tone. "It's awfully bold of you to show up in that crown when I hear that there are still two signatures missing from your coronation docket."

It was a reminder of why he couldn't openly stop mine and Rowan's wedding and risk losing what support he had. A reminder that threatening the heir to the single largest clan in Socair while his reign was not yet secure was, well, *idiocy*.

"An oversight that will be corrected shortly," he said tersely.

"No doubt," I said, my tone implying the opposite.

Finally, I stepped back to usher our party inside, bracing myself for another week of these political games and reminding myself that this was nothing unexpected.

I knew he would try to find an underhanded way to stop this wedding. That's why we were taking these precautions to begin with. Our plan would be enough.

It would have to be.

Because I might have told Rowan there was nothing I wouldn't do for the safety of my clan, but if something happened to her...I would raze this entire kingdom to the ground to get her back.

And I would start with Iiro.

CHAPTER TWO

ROWAN

My breath seized in my chest as we finally rounded the last bend of the mountain pass that led from Lochlann to Socair.

To Bear territory, more specifically.

My husband's territory.

After two weeks of twiddling my thumbs and drinking too much with Davin and trying to enjoy the last of my time with my family while every part of me ached for Evander, the five-week journey here had been excruciatingly slow. Though, the rest of my caravan did make it a little more bearable.

Still, it was seven weeks.

Seven weeks without hearing the word *Lemmikki* on his lips, without seeing his sardonic grin or his tousled black hair. Now, even just the sight of his kingdom was enough to make my stomach flutter with excitement.

I was nearly there now. Nearly to my new home. Nearly back to Evander.

Though that feeling morphed into something darker when I saw the soldiers set up at the border, the ones who most definitely were not from Bear, even if I had been expecting them. My hands clenched into fists on my lap when we heard the first guard call for us to stop.

The wheels grated along the loose stones of the mountain

pass as we slowed our pace, readying ourselves for the border inspection the returning caravans had warned us about.

My vision turned crimson at the audacity of Iiro claiming any rights here. The bastard had declared himself king, and suddenly, he was brave enough to act as if he had a say in the comings and goings of Evander's territory.

I tried to wipe the scowl from my face as my fingers went to the woolen hood of my cloak, pulling it lower. Socairans liked their women demure, something I was decidedly not feeling today.

Or ever, for that matter.

"Tiny, gorgeous girl, the aim is to blend in. Don't draw attention to yourself like this," Uncle Sai cautioned, pulling the hood back where it was.

"Ah, yes," I agreed. "Blend in. Because that's a simple feat for a cursed redheaded princess from Lochlann with a target on her back."

"Aye, but wi' the two o' us around, they wilna be lookin' at you anyways." Uncle Cray tilted his chin proudly, grinning widely to display a row of golden teeth. "Yer only average compared tae yer handsome uncles."

"Exactly," added Sai. "And don't forget to smile for the evil men."

He pointed to my mouth, and I gave him a baring of teeth that was probably as striking as a deranged squirrel.

"That's better, my child." Sai laughed. "The Purloiners of the Perilous Plantation have a reputa--"

"Is there a purpose to this?" Callum interrupted, massaging his temples with his fingers.

The two men had pushed him to the very limits of his propriety and sanity on this month-long trek from Chridhe to Socair.

Mamá had sent me with her personal guard and a few of the people she trusted most, aside from our immediate family. Fortunately for me, not only was it safe, it was hard to stay in a bad mood around my thieving uncles.

They had been a rather welcome distraction from my own

worried thoughts and the ridiculous chasm in my chest that my husband's absence had left.

At least, during the day. At night, there was nothing to chase away the constant ache of Evander being gone. At night, I could still feel the ghost of his body over mine, his warm hands on my thighs, and his lips on my skin.

Stars.

Only a few more days.

"Aye," Sai finally answered Callum, pulling me from my thoughts. "We need to have our stories straight, and we have no chance of that if we all give them a different name--"

"Ach, no Sai," Cray interrupted. "I've told ye and I've told ye. We dinna have a name. We dinna *need* a name. So, stop tryin' tae name us!" He shook his head, his words coming out in a bitter huff of air. "Faeries help us…" he muttered the last part mostly to himself.

Before anyone could respond, the carriage came to a stop, and I took a steadying breath. Harsh, heavily accented voices sounded all around us as each Lochlannian was asked to exit the carriages and line up along the mountain face while *the goods* were inspected.

"Inspectin' the goods, me arse!" Uncle Cray scoffed. "Ye better no' be pilfering any of the Bear Laird's tings. He'll have me head an' then I'll come fer yers!"

I fought back a laugh at his threat while the guards only shook their heads, looking down their noses at him. Which was easy to do, considering he was at least a head shorter than my already minuscule height.

Taking my place in the line between Uncle Sai and Callum, I reminded myself to stay calm and less stabby.

Even if these men worked for Iiro and probably hated me as much as he did. Watching them rifle through our things and push around my people had my fingers itching for a weapon.

A few of their eyes raked over the strands of red hair that had escaped my hood, and I did my best to appear unbothered by it. Each time we had sent a caravan to Bear, we ensured that there were women around my height with varying degrees of red or curly hair to throw them off.

It should feel commonplace by now.

One of the Socairan soldiers in a deep purple uniform came over to speak with the head merchant next to Cray, asking questions about the nature of our visit, how long we intended to stay, and several other inquiries about the goods on our wagons.

But I knew it was all a cover for what they were really looking for.

Me.

Iiro might not yet have the power to stop this wedding outright, but I knew––and Evander had known––that it would be easy to find an underhanded way to…dispose of me before I could make it to our wedding.

My breath hitched when one of the guards started to go down the line, looking at the faces and hair of each member of our party.

My heartbeat pounded in my ears. I had wrangled my hair back into a knot tight enough to make my head hurt, twisting my curls in a bun at the base of my neck.

Anything to separate myself from the wild locks I was associated with before.

The guard glared at me. For a chilling moment, I wondered if I had seen his face before. Had he been one of the men that traveled with us to the Summit? Was he at Elk Estate when I was a prisoner there?

I was suddenly painfully aware of the dagger on my thigh, as well as all of the hidden weapons on the men and women around me.

"What is your name?" the man asked, his accent as thick as Theo's.

"Juliette, mi'laird," I said in the brogue of the villagers, and it wasn't a lie. Juliette was one of my names…

The soldier's eyes narrowed as he glanced between me and a woman standing three spots away, the one whose hair was an even brighter shade of red than mine.

My palms were wet and hot, in spite of the freezing temperatures, and I resisted the urge to wipe them on my dress.

The man took a step closer to me before Cray stepped out of line, speaking up so his voice carried through the mountains.

"Do we have tae stand 'ere fer much longer? I'm freezin' me bollocks off."

The Socairan's attention snapped to him, and my uncle nodded toward the carriages. "Surely I dinna need tae reminded ye again of whose orders brought us here."

"Aye," Callum spoke up. "Not to mention, we would much prefer to return to Lochlann before the pass closes."

The Socairan soldier huffed, calling out to his Captain in their language.

I didn't understand the dialect, but I did catch some of the words. I tried not to let the relief that washed over me show on my features when the Captain told him to let us pass. Or at least, I hoped that's what he said.

When the soldier turned back around to face me, the woman he had been comparing me to ran her hands through her curls to fluff them a little more. A few strands clung to her fingers, and she waved them toward the man.

He practically leapt away before they could touch him.

Thank you for your ridiculous superstitions, I thought as the man made the same sign to ward off evil that I had grown so familiar with, continuing to put distance between them.

Sai bit out a hearty laugh, and soon a few of the others followed suit.

"Are you truly afraid of the cherry-haired women?" he asked. "No doubt, their tempers be terrifying, but other than that, they are fairly harmless."

"But what about that lass from Loch Briste?" Cray asked, and Sai's brows rose to new heights.

"She was an exception, when she be finding me necking with the barmaiden…" Sai trailed off, pulling the collar of his shirt down to show a smattering of white scars against his deep brown skin. "Well, we will just say I did not know you could be maiming a man with only a spoon."

A peal of laughter rang out from our line, and even a few of the Socairans found themselves reluctantly amused.

Here was to hoping that their antics would be enough to distract the soldiers from looking at us too closely. The soldier merely shook his head and started to wave us away when another one came to stand next to him, speaking in low, clipped tones.

My heart thundered in my chest as I met his eyes. Images of the new man in a blue-and-tan uniform came to mind, followed closely by the memory of his bruising grip around my arms as he dragged me up the stairs of the Elk dungeons.

The other soldier had looked vaguely familiar, but this one undoubtedly knew me.

His brown eyes met mine and I looked away, hoping to appear meek rather than cowardly. Both of which I wasn't, but if I had kept eye contact, he would have undoubtedly recognized the defiance in my gaze, not to mention their telltale light-green hue.

"What are you doing?" the new soldier demanded. "We are supposed to be inspecting them, not joking--"

"And we did," the first man cut him off. "*I* did. They can go now."

I waited for him to argue again, to step closer to examine me or call me out. With each breath I took, my fingers inched closer and closer to the false pocket in my skirts that would allow me to access my dagger.

The two men looked us over once again, and the smallest spark of recognition glinted in the former Elk soldier's eye. His lips parted as he tilted his head curiously in my direction.

Stars-blasted everything.

Thankfully, before he could say anything, the fates chose to side with me and a stray strand of my infernal red hair flew directly into his mouth.

He pulled it away, cursing as realization dawned on him of what it was. After that, there was a lot of gasping and gagging and practically running away from us as they tried to ward off our evil.

Cray and Sai laughed outright, and even the corner of Callum's mouth twitched in amusement as they ordered us back into our carriages and to leave as quickly as possible.

It wasn't until we rode away that I allowed my shoulders to sag in relief. My head was spinning with how close I had come to being caught, how close I had come to *not* returning to my husband.

Sai let out a low huff of laughter, patting me on the back. "Well done, little one! If things don't work out here, you always have a home with us in the Thieves' Forest."

I shook my head, letting out a laugh of my own. "Yes, Da' would be so proud."

Cray erupted into a long spiel about why Da' didn't have a leg to stand on, listing stories from their past while Sai swooned over Mamá and lamented that my father stole her from him.

Callum all the while sat back against his spot on the bench, closing his eyes in an attempt to tune out the men.

But I wasn't bothered by their banter in the slightest. With each mile we put between us and Iiro's soldiers, I felt like I could breathe a little more. And eventually the tightness in my chest even began to ease.

Because once again, we were on the road to Bear.

To Evander.

CHAPTER THREE

ROWAN

The next few days were a blur of traveling through the Socairan countryside, stopping only to camp for the night and picking right back up again before dawn.

There were a few tense moments where we passed even more of the Unclanned than I was used to seeing, but we avoided any actual incidents.

The minutes and hours and days crept by with interminable slowness until we were finally driving up the all-too-familiar road to Bear estate. There was no controlling my frantic heart as we passed through the familiar village, winding up and through the same small mountains I remembered all too well.

Finally, when the domed spires of the black and white castle came into view, a hesitant smile stretched across my face. This was still dangerous, a tenuous game we were playing until our vows had been said, but Evander was waiting for me on the other side of those walls.

That was all that mattered.

And I could reluctantly admit that this subterfuge had been necessary. At least, I could admit it in my head. Not out loud to Evander, of course.

His ego would become intolerable.

A slow grin stretched over my lips at the memory of the cocky smirk on his ridiculously attractive face.

Warmth crept into my neck, and I pushed the images of Evander away as we pulled around to the servants' entrance at the back of the castle. Callum moved aside to set my trunk on the floor of our carriage before we came to a full stop.

It was small, and rather cramped, with only a single item inside. The ominous box Rayan had given me.

Pins and needles danced along my spine, like the warning I got before a storm, but this one was different and far more intense.

Most of my things had been sent ahead with the first wave of caravans, but the long, flat rectangular box sat against the wall of the trunk, with just enough room for me to climb in next to it.

As soon as my arms brushed against the sharp wooden edges of the box, those pins and needles raked down my spine even faster.

"Are ye all right, Highness?" Cray asked, his face twisting in concern.

I gave him a quick nod, pasting a smile on my face that was more genuine than I felt.

"It's just a little cramped in here, even for me," I told him.

His shoulders relaxed a little.

It may not even happen. Rayan had said he was being overly cautious. I repeated the thought over and over again, though I couldn't quite bring myself to believe that in my soul.

"Oh, sweet girl!" Uncle Sai said, tucking the rest of my dress into the lined trunk. "If you be needing anything at all, just send word."

"Thank you, Uncle Sai—"

He cut me off by placing a gentle kiss on my forehead. "We've been over this. You can call me Faada, since I am, after all, practically your stepfa—"

"Ach, ye crazy bastard," Cray broke in. "She'll no' be callin' ye anything but a nuisance if ye get us caught because ye couldna haud yer wheesht."

Sai winked at me before he donned an expression of mock offense and argued back. That was always the way with the two of them; arguing to fill the silence in between Sai's proclamations of love for my mother that had me wondering if there had been more between them than my father liked to admit.

Mamá maintained that it wasn't the case, but that hadn't deterred the man for as long as I had known him.

My smile broadened as Cray paused his arguing to give me a kiss as well, while Callum nodded his head at me in respect.

"Be safe," he said fervently.

Then they closed the lid to my trunk, and everything was dark. I felt the presence of the box even stronger as whatever was inside thrummed with energy.

What in the stars-blasted hell did Rayan give me?

There was a small jerk of the carriage as we came to a full stop. Then the door creaked open, and a familiar voice shushed the men around me.

"Is this it?" Taras asked, his tone clipped and distant.

"Ach, no. We kept the very important package with the ones on the back of the wagon. Of course this is it, ye wee eejit," Cray hissed, and I stifled a laugh.

The mere idea of my two worlds colliding this way would have made my head spin only a few months ago. Now, I just wished I could see the look on Taras' face as he tried to form a response.

"Well, then," he said brusquely, and my trunk began to move.

I had the faintest feeling of falling through the air before jerking to a stop and swaying to and fro. The sound of steps on the loose stones morphed into shoes clacking on hard floors.

"Lady Mila's things sure are heavy," Kirill's voice sounded near my feet, his tone teasing.

Taras chuckled. "Indeed."

A smile tugged at my lips. Even though I had left my family behind, I couldn't help but feel like I was coming back to one, too.

CHAPTER FOUR

EVANDER

The day of our wedding was already not going well, in large part due to my father.

He seemed to be especially lucid today, which at least boded well for Ava's frequent attempts to sway him away from allowing this alliance. But it also meant that he was in the mood to issue edicts.

So instead of focusing on preparing for my wedding, I was headed to deal with that. I supposed it provided a nice distraction from obsessing over whether Rowan would arrive safe and on time.

I had barely walked into his sitting rooms when my stepmother intercepted me.

"Mairi," I said the name mockingly now that we both knew it wasn't true.

"Stepson." Her insistence on calling me that was just another way for her to assert control, to try to remind me of the power she once held over me. "Your father isn't up to visitors just now," she said.

I moved to step around her. "I'm certain he's always up to seeing his son."

Sick bastard that he was, he did hold me in some affectionate regard, or at least his legacy.

"I hear there was an Unclanned attack on one of the caravans today," she remarked casually, a familiar cruel glint in her eye.

My blood froze in my veins, and I forcibly reminded myself that Rowan was with skilled men who would die to keep her safe. That she was a fighter in her own right. That Ava had always been a liar, and I refused to give her the reaction she wanted.

"I would be worried if I didn't know how terrified you were of your beloved family coming after you," I said evenly.

She scoffed, but there was fear behind her eyes. "You can't think that threat is effective, when they all know where I am."

"They've always known where you are," I informed her with a shrug. "What they were lacking was information that only someone in Bear could give them."

A cold smile stretched across my face, and she took a step backward. Then she lifted her chin.

"Information can be so dangerous in the wrong hands," she said softly. "For instance, I wonder what your father would say if he knew you had forged his signature on the marriage contract."

My father's pride and refusal to admit his memory failed him made it a reasonable gamble to sign off on things on his behalf, but I used that sparingly, since generally it was easier to actually get him to sign.

I wasn't sure what he would do if he figured that out. But I had learned a long time ago when to show weakness in front of this woman, and now was not that time.

I let out a dark laugh. "By all means, pit your word against mine. After all, I'm only his son, his legacy, the next in line to his clan, while you're the woman he was forced to marry after the wife he chose, the wife he *loved*, died."

Fury flashed across her face, because she knew every word of it was true. Hell, it was why she hated me so much to begin with.

Her hand clenched at her side, and I wondered how much restraint it was taking for her not to slap me, though she had never dared to do anything quite so obvious.

Instead, her features twisted. "I may not be the wife he chose, but would he really choose you if he knew what a coward you were? Remember how you used to beg me not to punish you, even when you knew you deserved it?"

Had she ever possessed an actual soul? If Princess Isla's reaction when she met me was anything to go by, the answer was no.

Times like this, I kept my composure by picturing the way her empty eyes would widen in surprise if I calmly severed her head from her body.

But sadly, it was not to be.

I forced a nonchalant sigh. "It still wouldn't be enough to make him love you more. Or...at all, for that matter. In any event, I doubt you want to find yourself explaining to him how he managed to sign off on the leader of his enemy clan becoming king."

"Like I had any control over that," she spat. "As you know, women are not allowed in the Summit tent. We're lucky he was feeling as lucid as he did then. At least they only believe he is as mad as he ever was."

Hearing that woman refer to us in any sense of the word was galling, but she was right. We were lucky it hadn't been worse.

Iiro convincing the lords there would be a war and taking advantage of my father's never-ending bloodthirstiness toward Lochlann was, in reality, far from the worst thing that could have happened.

Ignoring her this time, I continued into my father's study, shutting the door behind me before she could follow.

He was sitting at his desk, paperwork neatly piled in front of him. For a moment, he looked like he had when I was a child, back before I knew what a monster he was.

I sucked in a breath, and he looked up at last.

"Evander." He said my name fondly, if not precisely warmly. "Did you take care of the issue with the soldiers?"

I mentally reviewed the first edict he had sent out this morning. It was harmless enough, just a stricter version of the laws on storing the clan flags.

"I did." Now, I had to distract him before he remembered the half portions order he had sent along with it. The men's rations were tight enough. They would starve on half.

"Sir Heikkenin arrived this morning from Eagle," I told him.

As expected, my father let out an irritable breath. "I suppose I'll need to take a break to greet him."

Thank the storms for that.

"Speaking of arrivals today, where is your bride?" The silver glinted in his gray eyes, the only physical sign of how he felt about me marrying into Lochlann.

"We thought it prudent she arrive at the last minute. You know how the dukes can be," I explained.

He nodded. "I'm proud you thought of it. You're your father's son."

He smiled like he had complimented me rather than compared me to a man who had ordered countless innocents to be slaughtered in his lifetime, and I forced myself to give a semblance of it back.

"It was a good plan," he went on. "Marrying the girl so it will be easier to attack her family from the inside."

He repeated back the only rationale I had been able to give him when he looked dubious over his signature on this alliance.

"Thank you, sir," I nodded, keeping my features carefully neutral, rather than let him see that hell itself would freeze over before I allowed my wife's family to be harmed.

I hoped my mother at least had not been a sociopath, or there was really no hope for me.

"Very good." He walked around his desk to clap me on the shoulder. "Take the rest of the day off, Son. It is your wedding, after all."

I put a hand on his shoulder in return. "Perhaps we both could, devote our time to making a strong showing. Besides, we should be celebrating."

My father nodded thoughtfully, and I tried not to show how badly I needed him to agree. To forget about the things he was trying to enact this morning.

"True. My son will be the one to finally put Lochlann in its place." He smiled, but there was no warmth in it.

Well, it had been too much to ask that he might celebrate my actual marriage, but at least he wouldn't be killing anyone today.

CHAPTER FIVE

ROWAN

The trunk swayed precariously as we climbed the several sets of stairs that led to the living quarters.

"It's about time, Husband." Mila's throaty, accented tone sounded, and I nearly squealed. "My bath is getting cold, what with it being so close to the wedding."

We moved more smoothly, presumably down the hallway, and Mila continued to chatter.

"Now if you can drop the trunk and hasten out of here, I can *hurry* to get ready for the wedding, since I would hate to be late."

That last part felt pointed. I wondered what time it was and how close I had come to missing my own wedding.

A door creaked open, and the trunk settled on the floor. Seconds later, the lid was open, and Mila was smiling down at me excitedly.

"Scarlet Princess!" She whisper-shouted her title for me while Kirill and Taras helped me out of the cramped space.

"Mila!" I whispered back, my grin stretching to match hers as we threw our arms around each other. "I've missed you so much."

She hugged me back with one quick squeeze before Taras cleared his throat behind us. When I turned to look at him, his eyes weren't on me. They were firmly fixed on his wife.

There was affection in his gaze, and none of the awkwardness that I had seen between them at the cabin months ago.

He moved in to kiss her forehead, and the simple gesture made me miss Evander so much it physically hurt.

"We'll be off, then," Taras told her. "I'll be back to escort you in—both of you—but we need to get to Van."

"Yes," Kirill agreed. "Someone needs to tell him she's arrived so he can stop his fretting."

A small laugh escaped me at my stoic husband doing anything close to *fretting*, like a village granny. Then it dawned on me, what they had said.

"He's not coming here?"

Sympathy flooded Kirill's gaze. "It's too much of a risk, and there isn't time. The ceremony is soon, though, Princess. Then he'll be all yours."

All mine. For good this time, with no more two-month stars-damned separations. Nodding, I tried to focus on that, rather than the sinking feeling at his absence.

Both men nodded to me before Mila shooed them away, pushing me toward the bathing chamber.

A few seconds later, the door opened again, and Taisiya joined me. She had come ahead with Evander's party.

"I'm so relieved that you made it safely, Highness," she said before dipping into a curtsy.

I smiled at her.

"Me too, Taisiya. Me, too."

Before I knew it, I was in the porcelain tub, and she was washing my hair while I scrubbed every last remnant of our travels off of my skin and out from under my nails.

When we were finished, we moved back out to the main room where Taisiya dried my hair with warm towels and began to apply my cosmetics the way the twins had taught her in Lochlann.

The tea table was now covered with platters of finger foods, fruits, cheeses, and several other things that were unfamiliar, including small, round bits of what looked to be pastry, with an assortment of toppings.

"What are these?" I asked, picking up one of them.

It appeared to be dried meat in a shade of pale pink, with a dollop of cream and a sprig of something green. I sniffed it suspiciously. *Dill.*

Mila shot me a questioning look. "Did you really live here for months and never had a chance to try a blini?"

I shrugged, and she made a gesture for me to take a bite.

"This one is smoked salmon with cream--" She trailed off at the dubious expression on my face and laughed. "Just try it."

My traitorous stomach growled in spite of the fish stew memories, and I shook my head before popping the entire thing into my mouth.

To my surprise, it was actually quite tasty. Savory and creamy with a salty and slightly sweet aftertaste. I ignored Mila's *I told you so* expression and went for another one.

"This is delicious," I said after practically inhaling the second one.

"Try the sweet one next," she said, pointing at a blini with cream and a deep purple berry concoction, sugar powder dusting the top.

As soon as the combination brushed against my tongue, I groaned in obscene pleasure. How was this even better?

"Told you," Mila said, wiping away a drop of the compote from her lips. "Now, let's finish getting you ready before they think you're missing in truth."

"Where do the dukes think I am?" I asked her once I had swallowed all of my food.

"They assume Evander has had you hidden away somewhere for weeks." She shrugged. "They just don't know where."

Evander really had thought of everything...

Mila strutted over from the small bar with glasses of chilled vodka. She placed a rather full one in my hand and all but shoved me toward the vanity.

Tipping the cold glass to my lips, I took several long swigs of the crisp, refreshing spirits as Mila helped Taisiya finish my hair and make-up. We kept up a constant stream of gossip and chatter about the last few weeks and everyone who was here.

Mila updated me on the politics of the situation, which were confusing and strained. It was enough to remind me what this wedding was really about.

We were making a point.

My eyes darted from the black dress hanging in the corner of the room to the kohl in Taisiya's hand.

I was more than ready to send a message to Ava that she would no longer have power over me. It was a riskier move with the dukes, but from what I had read on Socairan wedding customs, it wasn't like my wedding gown was forbidden... just, very frowned upon.

But then again, so was I.

Once I was finally dressed, Mila took a long look at me.

Two thick lines of kohl boldly accented my eyes, with a lighter dusting shadowing the creases, and my lips were a crimson shade so deep, it was nearly black.

My hair was pulled completely up for a change, smoothed and twisted back into an elegant bun with a few artful curls escaping. Mila rested a few jeweled combs into my hair, the gems shimmering between black and gray, almost like a stormy sky.

It felt fitting, for the storm that always seemed to rage within me.

And then there was the dress...

"I can't pretend I'm not anxious to see their faces when it comes time to remove this thing," Mila said as she helped me don the customary opaque veil, settling it over my head until it fell in soft waves all the way to my thighs. "Perhaps we'll get fortunate, and one of them will die from the shock of it."

"Or perhaps Evander will..." I added, then I shoved the nervous thought away.

He had, after all, told me any black dress would do.

Here was hoping he didn't want to eat those words.

CHAPTER SIX

ROWAN

I heard the music before I even rounded the corner, and my lungs seized.

This was it.

Mila had talked me through every minute of this ceremony while I got ready. I would walk down the aisle alone, as Socairan women always did, still wearing the stars-blasted stupid veil that practically blinded me.

Leave it to the Socairans to assume a bride being able to see to walk down the aisle was a frivolous desire.

Oh, well. I supposed it would make my reveal that much sweeter.

My heart galloped within my chest, and butterflies danced in my stomach. After several slow, deep breaths, they still hadn't faded.

I wasn't sure what I was more nervous about. Seeing Evander again for the first time in weeks, or what he would think when they took my veil off.

Taras escorted me as far as the main doors, sending Mila ahead, then stopped. "I'll stay on this end of the room to guard your back."

I nodded gratefully, taking another deep breath. His shadowy hand gestured for two guards to open the massive doors to the banquet hall.

This is it.

The short, pointed heels of my black leather boots thudded softly with each step, echoing in the silent room.

It was unnerving, being able to see so little in a room where I knew I was surrounded by enemies. Iiro. Aleksander.

And Ava, of course.

I used that thought to propel myself forward on slow, measured steps. The sound of an organ played my entrance, but I barely heard it over the sound of my breathing.

I reminded myself that I was not at their mercy, especially not *hers.* I would not cower in front of that woman ever again. Not in front of any of them.

An eternity passed before I reached the dais where Evander waited.

In spite of the dark veil, I could still see him, my memory filling in the gaps of my impaired vision. From his pristine, high-collared uniform to the black locks that were swept back at an angle, he was as gorgeous as ever.

I stepped close enough to make out his perfect features, a mask of careful arrogance. I didn't mind.

Today was about the show, and it wasn't hard for me to spot the anticipation that glimmered in his gray eyes.

The butterflies beat their wings even faster, but this time the rhythm was different.

Evander took my hand, and a small breath escaped me at the feeling of his skin on mine, the familiar energy that thrummed between us. His thumb swept over my wrist, a reminder that whatever display of strength we put on today, he was still mine.

I squeezed his hand back, hoping he felt the same from me. The corner of his lip barely twitched up, and relief coursed through me.

I hadn't realized just how worried I was about this moment, that something between us might have shifted in the two months we were apart. We were still tethered together, though, by whatever force had always compelled us toward one another.

Evander turned me to face the back of the room, where the magistrate was already speaking. The man droned on in

Socairan, things about duty and alliances and several more things I couldn't quite translate.

But I heard him clearly when he instructed Ava to remove my veil.

Mila had explained that it was tradition for the mother-in-law to present the bride to her son, which worked out better than I could have hoped for. A wicked smile tugged at my lips.

That meant she would get an unobstructed view…

Ava crept up behind me on slow, pointed footfalls. Her steps echoed through the Hall, drawing attention to her. *Good.*

Icy fingers grazed the exposed skin on my shoulders as she wound her way up to my head and gently removed the veil. Her breath hitched, but she was still blocking everyone else's view.

For now.

I tore my eyes away from Evander's to glance at Ava over my shoulder.

"Admiring your artwork?" I said the words lightly, but my voice echoed through the cavernous room.

Her features twisted in rage, but she had no choice but to return to her seat, fists clenched around the dark veil. As soon as she cleared the way, whispers of confusion and shock sounded throughout the space.

I returned my gaze hesitantly to Evander's.

I had been terrified of Ava for so long, and it was empowering, taking this control back, dismantling this power she had over me.

But I wasn't sure he would see it the same way.

Evander's storm-cloud gaze flitted from the jewels in my hair, down, lingering for a moment on my burgundy lips before finally sweeping to my shoulders, to take in what the room had already noticed.

My dress was demure enough from the front, all black lace and long sleeves with delicate white accents and a narrow waist that cascaded into full black skirts.

But the other side…

It was completely open from my shoulders all the way down to the small of my back. Four thin, woven strands of silver held the fabric together, accenting my angry red scars rather than hiding them.

Evander's lips parted. I had less than a second to wonder if he was upset before his mouth tilted into a savage grin.

"You look ravishing today, as always, Princess," he said in a low tone that nonetheless carried.

I let out a whoosh of air, returning his smile. "And you as well, My Lord."

We both turned back to the magistrate for our vows. Evander went first, echoing the Socairan words in a low, deep tone that had heat flooding through me.

Then it was my turn. The magistrate gave me my vows in the Common Tongue, and I could practically feel the judgment emanating from the room.

So I gave them back in the flawless Socairan I had been practicing every day since Evander left Lochlann.

Well, most of it was flawless. I did stumble over one word, but it wasn't the pronunciation that tripped me up. It was the translation. *Obey* had not been removed from these wedding vows, as it had ours in Lochlann.

Evander's eyebrows rose, and his eyes filled with pride, even as he fought back a smile at my obvious dislike of that part of the vows.

Sadly, there were no kisses in Socairan weddings, probably because they were all hopeless prudes. Wedding rings were also not a part of ceremonies here, though we were both already wearing ours.

After the vows, the magistrate gave his official pronouncement about us being husband and wife, along with a pronouncement that I was now afforded the honor and protection of a Clan Wife.

With that, Evander and I turned to face the room. Distantly, I noted that everyone in the room was holding a drink.

In spite of the crowd of people, faces both familiar and not, it was Iiro who caught my gaze. He sat in a seat of honor at the front of the room. His hazel eyes were so like his brother's, though they held none of the warmth.

I gave him a shallow nod, and he raised his chalice ever so slightly in salute. On the surface, it was a simple gesture, a congratulations.

But the pressure on my spine intensified, and I knew it was more than that.

It was a warning.

A threat.

CHAPTER SEVEN

ROWAN

We were escorted to a small room off the grand hall, a space designed to give the couple a moment to collect themselves while the guests were settled in the ballroom.

Evander guided me in with a single hand on my bare lower back. He didn't look down at me at all, just stared straight ahead, his footsteps measured and his expression aloof.

A guard opened the door for us, and I stepped inside first. I took a single glance around the room, long enough to take in the small couch and the table next to it, already set with two glasses of wine.

Then the door shut behind us, and Evander's hands were on my waist, spinning me around to face him. There was nothing distant in his features now.

His eyes were burning with a deep-seated need that matched my own. He picked me up, pressing me against the black, wooden door and leaning in to support my weight with his solid, muscled body.

He buried his face into my neck, peppering kisses along each bare inch of skin he could find.

"How long do we have in here?" I gasped the words with what little breath I could find.

He chuckled against my skin, sending tendrils of fire flickering through every part of me. "Not long enough."

"Well, that's a shame." It also explained why he was avoiding my face and all the carefully applied cosmetics, which I appreciated, even if all I wanted to do was feel his perfect lips on mine.

Though, this wasn't a bad consolation.

"Der'mo," he murmured into my ear. "I missed you, Lemmikki."

"I missed you, too." My voice was still breathless. "No more plans like that."

"It worked," he argued, not stopping in his ministrations.

It wasn't the answer I was looking for, but we had already fought on our first wedding night. We could argue about this later.

Still, as usual, he read into my silence. He pulled back to look at my face, though he didn't set me down, didn't stop his hands from where they traced maddening patterns along the bare sides of my ribcage.

"You're here," he reminded me. "Safe. And now, with the protection of a Clan Wife. Even Iiro wouldn't risk his tenuous position thwarting one of our most sacred laws." Those last three words dripped with sarcasm.

"Tenuous?" I clarified.

"Arès and Ivan Lusikka from Bison didn't sign."

"What does that mean for us?" I asked.

He finally set me down, though he didn't take his hands off of me.

I couldn't blame him, since my fingers were roaming of their own accord up his biceps, over his shoulders, down his chest.

"It means that there's a chance this won't stand...a chance I plan on actively pursuing, but since my father did sign, we have to make some pretense of...obeisance."

I digested this information. "So, bowing and Your Majesty-ing?"

He blinked irritably. "Unfortunately."

"Well, it's a good thing we're both so good at pretending," I smirked, though it occurred to me that really only one of us was when it came to things like this.

It apparently occurred to him as well, because he returned my expression with a somewhat dubious look of his own.

"Indeed," he said drily. Then he studied my features. "Speaking of which, it's important that my father not understand that there is...actual affection between us."

I almost laughed at how hard that was for him to say, but his face was serious enough that I refrained.

"Why?" I asked instead.

"It's best if he believes he has control of a situation," he explained, his eyes searching mine.

Was he worried I would be upset?

"For that matter," he went on, "the dukes tend to pounce on any perceived weakness as well. Things will be easier if they believe this is nothing more than a political alliance."

I sighed. "Ah, yes, the dukes. Well, we're in this together now, so I suppose I should do my part. Shall I assume it would be prudent for me to dance with all of them, as I did at the Summit?"

Evander's gaze darkened. "You don't have to dance with *all* of them."

I narrowed my eyes in confusion before comprehension dawned on me. If Iiro was king...Theo was a duke.

"Jealousy, Evander?" I teased. "On our wedding day?"

"You know I don't like other people to touch what's mine," he growled, and the sound tugged at things low in my abdomen.

I shook my head. "I'm sure there are points to be made."

"You've made a hell of a point already," he pointed out, looking significantly at my dress.

I shrugged one shoulder. "They were calling me the Lochlannian whore, regardless. Now that they know how little I care, maybe they'll find something more interesting to talk about."

His features darkened on the word *whore*. "Rest assured, Lemmikki, they weren't saying it where I could hear it."

"The dances..." I reminded him.

He sighed. "Yes. It would be *prudent* to dance with the dukes, but this won't be like the Summit. If a single one of them puts their hands where you don't want them, it will be completely within my rights to end them. A right I will take full advantage of, with pleasure." The ruthless flash in his eyes sent a small thrill through me, and I nodded.

"Well then, we can hope Mikhail struggles to control himself," I said.

The corner of his lip tilted up. "One can dream."

The ballroom was a whirlwind of standing at Evander's side while he accepted our congratulations with a haughty tilt to his chin and a proprietary hand around my waist.

He hardly glanced in my direction, but every once in a while, his thumb would brush underneath one of the chains of my dress, stealing my breath and sending bolts of lightning throughout my entire body.

It was a stark contrast to our wedding in Lochlann, where he had openly shown affection and laughed with my cousins. Here, he was the brutal heir to the most powerful clan in Socair.

So I tried to follow his lead, giving little away, letting my dress and my cosmetics be a shield for me.

Even Mila was more on guard than I usually saw her, making her way around the room at Taras' side with none of the warmth I had witnessed between them earlier.

And then there was Theo, whose features could have been carved from stone as he offered Evander and I both a congratulatory nod. I hardly had time to respond before the string quartet started up, and it was time for the dancing to begin.

Evander led me out to the floor, taking one of my hands in his. Tension zapped between us at every point of contact.

It was still surreal that we were finally here, together. We had been given so little time together before we were separated that I had half-expected things to be awkward once I was here, but standing in his arms felt...perfect. Right.

Just as it always had.

I savored the several minutes of the song in his arms, of us moving around the dance floor as if we were one singular person. My body instinctively responded to his, following his lead fluidly.

By the time the music stopped and a muted applause sounded around us, I wasn't ready. Our dance was over far too soon, leaving me to face the room at large.

As if he sensed my disappointment, or perhaps shared it, Evander rubbed a small, comforting circle between the thin layer of my gown and the sensitive skin on my lower back.

Fire ran through me, and I saw it reflected in his eyes just as he released me to make my way around the room.

Worse yet, I realized if I needed to dance with all the dukes, that included...Aleksander.

The man in question strode over, offering me his hand. His eyes were clearer than I was used to seeing them, the same exact shade of gray as Evander's, but the look in them was even more calculating.

It struck me that this version of him was far more terrifying than the unhinged man I had seen in the breakfast room. What would have happened if he had felt this way the day I walked into his rooms?

I suppressed a shudder, taking his hand while Evander watched us warily from the corner of his eyes.

"I finally meet my son's new bride," he commented.

His voice was almost too casual, and the resemblance to Evander's tone was startling. At least he truly didn't remember meeting me, unless this was part of a game he was playing.

It wasn't a question, so I didn't respond.

"Good." He nodded his head. "I had worried when I saw that dress that you would be difficult, like your grandmother was. She fought hard, for all the good it did her. But you won't be difficult, will you?"

The nonchalant reminder that he had strung up my mother's parents outside their own castle for the world to see had the blood draining from my face. I glanced at Evander, who was dancing with Ava.

His features were still perfectly neutral, but his eyes were fathomless pits of ice. They grew harder still when he caught sight of my expression, and I willed it into something more unaffected before he intervened.

I wanted desperately to tell the duke I took more after my father, the man who had closed the tunnels over hundreds of the duke's men, including his brother. I wanted to remind him that my family won that war, and I was no one to be trifled with.

But I had told Evander I would do my part to help, not make things worse. So I gritted my teeth.

"No. I won't be."

Aleksander smiled in a patronizing way. "Good girl."

I averted my gaze before he could see the fury flashing through my eyes, and I wondered vaguely how many of these days he had.

At least Evander and I could face it together, this time.

CHAPTER EIGHT

EVANDER

My stepmother's claws gripped my hand and shoulder more tightly than was necessary, ten pinpoints of revulsion I had to fight not to shake off.

But there were appearances to be made.

A fact I very nearly let myself forget when I caught sight of Rowan's face. Her porcelain skin was even paler than usual, her mouth set into a hard line...all because of something my father had said to her.

Her eyes flicked to me, and she rearranged her features into something resembling neutrality, or at least, closer to it than she usually managed. Then he turned her, and I couldn't see her face anymore.

I reminded myself that she was fierce, and that he wouldn't physically hurt her now that she was a Clan Wife. *My* Clan Wife.

My gorgeous Clan Wife, I amended, taking a moment to rake my eyes over the crimson curls that were artfully arranged, the subtle muscles in her back and her slim waist.

And the scars that she had put on display for the entire court to see.

I wasn't sure how to feel about that.

In the few times we had played Dominion with her family,

Rowan had occasionally managed to get an edge with the sheer nerve of her bold, unexpected moves.

But sometimes, they were reckless as hell. Sometimes, they cost her more than she could afford to lose.

On the other hand, I had been worried that she was afraid to return to the castle where Ava resided. Instead, Rowan began her life here by rattling my stepmother in a way few people were capable of.

Even now, Ava looked at her silently, her usual sneering remarks noticeably absent.

And for that, I couldn't help but be proud. Even if that pride was edged with concern for what underhanded method Ava might use to retaliate.

The dance finally ended, and so did that line of thought. Rowan was passed off to Mikhail, who was only marginally preferable to my father. That would have normally left me with Lady Galina.

I barely suppressed a sigh. The girl was terrified of me, evident by the way her pale-blue eyes widened and her hands trembled every time we had danced in the past few years.

Relief coursed through me when I saw she was occupied, talking to Korhonan, and I took my opportunity to speak with Arès instead. He was one of the few dukes I actually liked, a feeling I suspected was mutual, but he had made his unhappiness with me clear since I returned.

I had been too focused on this wedding and Rowan's arrival to deal with that. He was leaving in the morning, though, so I approached him now. The way he was standing alone by the refreshments table made me think that was exactly what he intended to happen.

"I hope you're devising a way to fix this in that clever brain of yours," he said without preamble.

That was fair, all things considered. And I was, slowly but surely, thinking of solutions.

"An alliance with Lochlann isn't a bad start," I pointed out.

He shook his head. "An alliance you could have procured while she was still here, or by sending a bird when she left, rather than gallivanting off to Lochlann for four months and giving that bastard his opportunity to move in on the throne."

It was the closest he had come to admitting that he knew my father wasn't the one in control of Bear.

I thought of the responses I could give him.

Because I wasn't sure she wanted to marry me. Because I would rather have had no alliance than feel like I tricked her into one or took advantage of the power I had over her.

"It didn't honestly occur to me that he would do that," I said instead, referring to both Iiro and my father. "I thought by leaving I would ensure he *didn't* get the alliance."

Arès gave me a look that clearly said, *Don't treat me like an idiot. We both know why you ran off to Lochlann.*

But since he didn't say it out loud, I didn't bother to respond.

When I glanced back at Rowan, the dance had ended, and Korhonan was taking Mikhail's place.

I suppressed a sigh.

He stared at her like he hardly recognized her, but that was because he had never understood her to begin with.

The woman with the scarlet lips and the backless dress was exactly who Rowan had always been. And though I had been appreciating that dress a moment ago, I was markedly less enamored with it when it allowed him to put his hand on her bare skin.

I felt Arès' gaze, somewhere between amused and aggravated, and I took care to school my features. Just as I was contemplating the many ways I might interrupt this dance, Iiro sauntered up to us.

"Sir Iiro," Arès intoned.

Iiro raised a single condescending eyebrow. "Don't you mean *Your Majesty?*"

Arès met his eyes solidly. "Not *my* majesty."

The almost-king's eyes flashed with murder, and I lifted my drink to my lips to hide my smirk.

"I'm certain that you'll be...influenced to come around in no time," Iiro said with a pointed glance in my direction.

So that's how he's going to play this. He wanted my help in turning the two remaining clans in his favor, which meant he believed he had some sort of leverage over me.

I made a noncommittal noise in the back of my throat, and Iiro left with an expression entirely too calculating for my liking. I turned back to Arès, a muscle clenching in my jaw.

"Yes," I answered his first question again. "I will find a way to fix this."

CHAPTER NINE

ROWAN

I had been worried that my dance with Theo would be uncomfortable, but his presence was as steady and calming as ever. I wondered if we would ever get to the point where we considered each other friends.

"How have you been?" I asked him.

He gave me a small smile. "You mean now that my brother has proven Evander right and upset half of Socair?"

"Only half?" I raised my eyebrows, and he let out a reluctant chuckle.

"It's been...interesting." Theo cast a sideways glance at his brother. "I would tell you to be careful, but I'm certain it would be pointless."

His gaze roamed from the thick lines of kohl around my eyes to the dark color of my lips, then down to where my dress abruptly cut off at the shoulders. I got the sense he was seeing me in a way he hadn't before, and possibly in a way that made him grateful things hadn't gone differently with us.

Would he have died on the spot if I had shown up to our wedding this way? Would he have understood?

"Sometimes, bold moves are in order," I told him.

He nodded hesitantly. "Sometimes. I just hope you know what you're doing."

That makes two of us.

When the music ended and the dance was over, Theo dipped his head in a respectful bow. I returned the gesture before excusing myself for a refreshment break while he moved to ask Lady Andreyev, Inessa's mother, to dance.

My shoulders sagged in relief when the only person near the table full of food and a steaming bowl of medovukha was the servant in charge of the food. I enjoyed my break from the court while the man ladled the drink into a chalice made of polished silver with what looked like the claws of a bear grasping the cup.

I shivered after the first sip, warmth flooding through me before I filled a small plate with more of the blinis that Mila had shared with me earlier. However, I staunchly avoided the caviar and raw beef on crisps that the other Socairans seemed to favor, remembering the joyous experience of nearly spitting one out at the Summit.

I was contentedly snacking and watching Evander dance flawlessly with Sir Nils' wife when Inessa walked over to me.

"Your Majesty," I said after swallowing the large mouthful of smoked salmon and cream, giving her a deep nod.

She seemed rather surprised at my acknowledgment of her new title, but I wasn't about to refer to her as anything else. Evander had said we needed to play this game for now, so I planned to do just that.

Besides, I seriously doubted, given the nature of their relationship, that Inessa was in on whatever Iiro's plans were.

"Lady Stenvall," she greeted in response, and I couldn't help the smile that tempted the corner of my mouth.

Lady Stenvall.

"I had begun to hope you would be Lady Korhonan one day," she said quietly. Then she looked to where Evander stood several feet away, his eyes still fixated on me even as he moved around the floor. "But I see it was not to be."

"No," I shook my head. "Even if everything else hadn't happened...my name would have been Rowan Korhonan."

When said in the correct Socairan accent, with the silent *h* and the long O, the names most definitely rhymed.

Inessa let out a small, startled laugh before she covered her mouth. "I can see where that would have been...unfortunate."

Then her face turned serious once more. "Regardless, I hope that you have found contentment."

I gave her crown a pointed look. "And you as well."

Before either of us could say more, Lord Luca walked over to where we stood, Mila at his side. Inessa glanced between the three of us before politely excusing herself.

"I was quite devastated when you turned down my proposal, you know," Luca said by way of greeting, but his tone was teasing.

He certainly wouldn't have been a bad consolation prize, had there been no Evander and no Theo. With Mila's high cheekbones, tan skin, and chocolate-colored eyes, not to mention the same warmth and humor, he was definitely going to be a catch for someone else.

Mila subtly elbowed him. "Oh, you were not."

He chuckled. "Perhaps I just believed Evander needed more incentive to pull his head out of his arse, then. Though, I'll confess, I didn't realize he would actually go all the way to Lochlann himself."

I raised an eyebrow, and he gave me a knowing smile that was reminiscent of his father.

"You know," he said in a conspiratorial tone, "I came to that cabin prepared to refuse his offer when he was unwilling to marry Mila himself, but it took me fewer than five minutes to realize why his hand wasn't in the running."

A flush rose to my cheeks.

"And what would you have done if I had accepted your proposal?" I demanded.

Mila covered her laugh with a light cough. "She's got you there, Brother."

But Luca only raised his eyebrows. "I think we both know there was never a danger of that. Perhaps he wasn't the only one I wished to incentivize."

"Why would you bother to do that?" My tone was curious.

He studied me over his drink before answering.

"Because I know what people think of Evander, but I also know what I've observed of him," he said more quietly. "And I believe he'll make a strong leader, one who helps effect necessary changes, not only in his own clan. My father thinks so, too. That's why we decided to ally with him at all."

He met my gaze solidly, as if he was weighing his next words more carefully. Whatever he saw in my features made him decide to go forward. "But before you came along, that strength was starting to harden into something else...and no one needs another Aleksander."

Mila nodded so fervently that I wondered what exactly had transpired in my absence, but now hardly seemed the time to ask.

Instead, I took a moment to digest what Luca just told me about my husband, warmth surging through my veins.

"Thank you," I said at last. "For telling me that."

"Thank *you*," he said. "For not accepting my proposal."

I suppressed a laugh, feeling a small stab of regret that Luca didn't live here also. He reminded me of Davin, with his easy charm and clear lack of interest in settling down.

A smile spread across my lips. "Any time you need someone to ignore your overtures of marriage, Lord Luca, I'm happy to oblige."

An eternity passed before Evander announced the last dance, his eyes boring into mine with a heated promise that made my knees threaten to give out.

I knew from what Taras had told me that this one should have been for Evander and me, but it didn't surprise me at all when Iiro asked for it himself.

He was all about power plays, after all.

Evander nodded, his face impassive but for the smallest twitch of his jaw. "Of course, Your Majesty."

Iiro held a hand out, and I took it with all the graciousness I could muster, though I knew I wasn't half as good at concealing my expression as my husband was.

It was a stately dance, easy to make the motions and leave room for talking, something I was not eager to do. I wondered if that was half of why Iiro picked it, since he didn't take long to start speaking.

"For whatever it's worth," he said evenly, "I never meant for you to get hurt."

Shock parted my lips. Was that...an apology?

His hazel eyes flitted toward the lash mark on my shoulder, and I suppressed the urge to scowl.

"What did you intend?" I couldn't help but ask. "Why not just ask my father about a marriage alliance, if that's what you wanted?"

He raised an eyebrow. "Didn't he tell you? I did ask, and he declined."

I supposed I shouldn't have been surprised, given how Da' felt about me being in Socair, even now. But the idea that he hadn't taken no for an answer and had manipulated the situation to try to force my hand made my stomach twist in knots.

"Knowing my brother as I do," Iiro continued, "I knew that once you were here, it would be an easy matter to pair the two of you together."

"And what if it hadn't worked?" I asked, careful to keep the ire from my tone.

"It very nearly didn't." He shrugged like that was of no consequence. Like it would have been an easy price to pay, if I had accidentally died.

"No one was more shocked than I was when the Summit was ready to set you free." Iiro's tone was dry, with a bitter aftertaste. "Though, if Aleksander had come, that wouldn't have been an issue. I suspect Evander was largely responsible for staying their hands, since I doubt seriously it was your...*charms*. But fortunately, your little outburst solved that."

My eyes went to Evander, recalling his frustration when he told me if I had just kept my mouth shut, I would have been fine. Because he was working, even then, to keep me safe.

Whether or not he had his own goals in mind, the thought warmed me. Until I glanced back at Iiro.

I thought about the way Mikhail had goaded me into my outburst that day at the Summit and cursed under my breath.

"That was your doing," I said aloud.

He shrugged again. "Fortunately, you can always be counted on to do the inappropriate thing."

Iiro looked pointedly at my dress, and I clenched my jaw.

"And what if the Summit had voted to kill me and refused to let me marry Theo?" I gritted out.

"That was a small risk," he said with less nonchalance than I was expecting, a small frown creasing his brow. "One I didn't expect to bother me."

It was my turn to raise an eyebrow, and he gave another long-suffering sigh.

"I will admit, Princess, that I was almost beginning to not hate you, at the end." His face darkened. "At least, until you turned my brother against me while simultaneously humiliating him."

I shook my head, guilt over what happened with Theo warring with my general disdain for Iiro until the latter won out.

My lips pulled into a smile that was more a baring of my teeth. "And I was almost beginning to not hate you, until I found out you trapped me in the tunnels and manipulated me and nearly got me killed all in your quest for power."

He raised both of his eyebrows, whatever momentary hint of humanity he had shown effectively dissolving in the wake of my comment. "Initially, I was upset when you turned my brother down, but I don't believe I envy Lord Stenvall trying to keep you in line."

I thought about telling him I wasn't something to be kept in line, but he would never believe that, and I was tired of this conversation already. *Let him believe what he will.*

"That's why I chose to allow this union to continue," he added.

I barely, *barely* suppressed a snort. I didn't know everything about this situation or Socairan politics, but I knew that if Iiro could have stopped this wedding, he would have. I knew that he had tried, in his duplicitous way, and that doing so overtly was not an option for him.

But there was nothing to be gained by saying that, so instead, I nodded. "Most gracious of you."

Could he hear the mocking edge to my tone?

The music came to a slow lull, finally signifying the end of the dance. Giving him a small, very Lochlannian curtsy, I walked away before he could respond.

CHAPTER TEN

ROWAN

The room raised their glasses in a toast to us again, and I was grateful for the much more subdued send-off than the one we had endured in Lochlann.

Not that I would have cared tonight.

Not that anything could have robbed me of the heady sense of anticipation as Evander scooped me in his arms and carried me out of the room. That was one tradition I didn't mind, especially when he cradled me possessively against his body.

Tension thrummed through every part of me. I resented every measured step up the grand staircase, down the unfamiliar hallways.

"Where are we going?" My voice was breathless, and he chuckled down at me.

"Impatient, Lemmikki?" But the way his hand tightened around my thighs told me I wasn't the only one.

"I have been patient for seven stars-damned weeks," I reminded him.

It was a lie. Every single day of that had been torture.

"Well, that makes one of us," he growled.

Finally, he pushed open a door and carried me through it. I barely had time to see that the room was even bigger than Evander's spacious suites, that it had textured black walls and an enormous bed with a gauzy white canopy, situated in a turret with floor-to-ceiling windows.

Then he all but threw me on that bed, and I stopped caring what the room around us looked like.

He had been gentle our first wedding night. Patient, and almost maddeningly slow.

He was none of those things now.

Our mouths met in a clashing of lips and teeth as we all but devoured one another. I fisted my hands in his hair, pulling him even closer to me. He made a sound low in his throat that thrummed through my insides before skating his lips down my neck, his teeth nipping lightly along the way.

I tugged at his shirt, and he removed it in one fluid motion, revealing every muscled inch of his glorious chest. My lips parted, and the corner of his mouth tilted up in the arrogant smirk I had missed so, so much.

He went to pull my dress down past my shoulders, and it caught at the top chain. Without hesitation, he pulled at the sides until the delicate silver strands snapped, giving him the leeway he needed to remove it.

If I thought his face was intense before, it was nothing compared to the way he looked when he realized I had nothing underneath that dress. Which should have been obvious, given that it was backless, but judging by Evander's slack features, it was not something he had considered.

"Der'mo," he murmured.

It was my turn to smirk, though that expression faded quickly when his lips met mine once more. There was no more talking after that, no teasing. Just a profound feeling of rightness when our bodies finally came together again.

I had been empty, untethered, and fractured for weeks. But now...now I was whole again.

CHAPTER ELEVEN

EVANDER

"**A**re you going to tell me where we are now?" Rowan's lips moving against the skin of my chest were enough distraction that it took me a moment to answer.

"Our room," I told her.

"I just assumed we would move into your rooms," she said, looking up at me.

I could usually read her fairly well, but her tone wasn't betraying whether she was disappointed or merely curious.

"These are bigger," I said evenly. Then, forcing myself to give her more truth than that, I admitted, "I thought...we could use a new start. In a space that's ours."

At least, I could.

I didn't want to stay in the rooms where I had spent two months after she left wondering if I would ever see her again. The rooms where I had almost watched her die.

Rowan surveyed the room thoughtfully.

There were several extra sets of suites since the castle had been built to house lords and their families, but this one gave a stunning view of the mountains she spent so much time looking at.

Sure enough, her green eyes sparkled in the light of the low lantern when they landed on the windows.

"It's perfect," she said, looking back at me. "I love it."

"And I love you, Lemmikki." I tried to focus on the simple perfection of this moment, not this persistent, portentous feeling of waiting for something to go wrong.

Not this knowledge that with Iiro in some form of power and my father using up all his lucid moments to profess his hatred for my new bride, all of this felt tenuous. Temporary and not quite real.

Rowan shifted her body until she was laying on top of me, her soft curves pressing into my solid chest, and the feeling grounded me.

She leaned down to press a kiss against my lips. Her mass of crimson hair spilled all around us, cocooning us further into this world that was just ours and pulling me from my morbid thoughts.

Not wanting this moment to end, I couldn't help but tease her.

"I especially loved you in that dress tonight, though I have to say, I much prefer you out of it."

One of the many, many things I adored about my wife was that she didn't bother to pretend to be shy.

"Oh?" She gave me a wicked little smile, sitting up and shaking her hair behind her while she stretched her arms over her head. "I think I prefer that as well."

Again. She had no issues with shyness.

My mouth went completely dry. She was, without a doubt, the single most exquisite thing I had ever seen. It was still hard to believe she was here.

Here at the estate.

Here in my bed.

Here in my arms.

"Have I told you lately how gorgeous you are?" I murmured, leaning up to press my lips against the space just below her collarbone.

"Hmmm," she mused. "I believe you've told me...never."

My eyes snapped up to hers. She didn't look particularly bothered by this fact, but neither was she lying.

That can't be right.

I had thought it every waking minute of every day she was in my rooms, even when she was being infuriating. Especially then, the way her eyes would burn in defiance or sparkle with amusement when she argued with every storms-blasted thing that I said.

But I had put so much effort into concealing those feelings, it hadn't occurred to me that I never actually told her.

"Well, allow me to remedy that," I said, running my hands along the creamy skin of her shoulders, down to her waist. "You, Rowan Stenvall..." *Der'mo*, I loved the way that sounded.

"Are irresistibly..." I pressed a kiss against her jawbone.

"Insanely..." I kissed closer to the spot below her ear, the one I knew would elicit a gasp from her.

Sure enough, it did.

"Beautiful," I whispered in her ear.

I expected her to make a cheeky remark in response, but when I backed away to look at her face, her eyes were wide, and she swallowed.

This meant more to her than she had let on. For all her jokes and her confidence, it mattered to her. I gave her another piece of the puzzle, something to solidify the truth of my words in her mind.

"Why do you think I came over to talk to you that first day?" I raised an eyebrow.

Her lips parted in surprise. "I...never really thought about it, since you wound up being such an arseling."

That was fair enough, but only because I had put together that she was from Lochlann once I saw her green eyes and suspected a scheme.

Before that, though, I had seen the profile of a pert nose, soft lips, and her stubborn chin. I had seen a girl standing unflinchingly in a sea of men who towered over her while she followed every blow of a fairly brutal fight.

And I had been drawn to her by an invisible string that I never could quite seem to sever.

Whatever she saw in my expression made her lean her head

down for a slow, purposeful kiss that left no doubt of her intentions.

"You know, for all your jokes about my stamina, you certainly do seem to be testing it now," I murmured against her lips.

I was only half-joking, but I certainly wasn't complaining. I felt it, too, this constant, compelling need to consume and be consumed by one another.

Rowan smiled against my mouth, her teeth nipping at my bottom lip just long enough to drive me insane.

"Well, if it's too much for you..." She pulled away with a dramatic sigh, and I tugged her back toward me firmly.

Maybe this feeling of foreboding was valid, and maybe we were hurtling toward something that would tear all of this apart. But I had her now, and I damned sure wasn't going to waste a minute of that.

CHAPTER TWELVE

ROWAN

Eventually, I did get around to inspecting *our* room. A thrill went through me at the thought.

Our bed sat in the circular portion of the room, poised to be cordoned off by a set of thick drapes hanging from the ceiling. The rest of the room was an elegant sitting area, with a small breakfast table off to the side and two expansive doors leading to a wide balcony.

Boris' bowls were on the floor in the corner, though the cat himself had not yet made an appearance. There were two lavish privies and two bathing chambers, each with an enormous bronze tub.

A large set of double doors led to Evander's study, already filled with his massive desk and several shelves of books.

Instead of armoires, there were spacious closets. Mine was already filled with dresses, some that I had brought with me, and others that had been made here.

And the box, of course, sitting on a low shelf. Taisiya must have brought it in, though I had instructed her not to open it.

Everything else was neatly unpacked, so it stood out in stark contrast. I stared at it, the same awareness prickling along my spine.

Evander studied my features, following my gaze.

"What is that?" His tone was almost too neutral.

"Something Rayan gave me," I told him. "Something he said not to open until I knew I needed it."

"How will you know if you need it if you don't know what it is?" He said the words quietly, like he sensed the foreboding as well as I did.

"That...that is the question." I didn't want to mar the perfect space of my and Evander's new rooms with this conversation, so I cleared my throat, going to examine the rest of the closet.

"You never did tell me where those dresses came from," I mused aloud.

"I would think that's obvious." His tone was amused.

I shot him a look. "I meant that they don't look like any other Socairan dresses I've seen."

"Well, those seemed highly impractical, as you aren't like any Socairan women I've seen," he said, stepping closer to me.

"So you designed them?" I raised a teasing eyebrow, running my hands over the soft fabrics in the closet. "I never knew you took such an interest in women's fashion."

He narrowed his eyes. "I can assure you, I do not. I merely explained to the estate seamstress the kind of things you would be doing, that you would need the use of your hands and the ability to ride a horse and dress yourself. After she recovered from fainting over the impropriety of it, *she* designed them."

"And do you?" I asked quietly, my hand dropping to my side.

He gave me a questioning look.

"Faint from the impropriety of it?" I clarified.

"I'm really not the fainting kind." He chuckled, then seemed to sense that the answer mattered to me.

Taking a deep breath, he locked his eyes on mine.

"I won't pretend that your outspoken nature doesn't present some concerns in the context of Socairan politics," Evander said carefully. "Things are...freer in Lochlann. There, you give your opinion and someone else gives theirs, and you both move on. Here, everything we do and don't say is scrutinized and hoarded away to be used as a weapon."

"Oh." I tried and failed to keep the disappointment from my voice.

He put a finger under my chin, guiding it up until I was looking him in the eye.

"But if you're asking whether I would have preferred a quiet wife who rode sidesaddle and didn't have an incredibly inappropriate dagger stashed on her person at all times, the answer is a resounding no." He bent to kiss me, his tongue teasing at the seam of my lips.

Tiny sparks of pleasure coursed up and down my skin at the touch. I leaned into it, sliding my hands up his bare chest before wrapping my arms around his neck. I stretched up on my tiptoes to be closer to him, and his hands came around to grip the backs of my thighs. He picked me up to carry me to the bed, deepening our kiss.

It was almost terrifying, the intensity with which my body craved his.

My only consolation was that at least I wasn't here alone. Evander matched every bit of my need with his own.

He might have quipped about me testing his stamina, but he certainly didn't seem inclined to stop now.

CHAPTER THIRTEEN

ROWAN

The next morning, we were awoken by a knock on the door.

It was so reminiscent of our first wedding night that my first thought was to panic, before I realized it was probably just breakfast.

"Enter," Evander called, looking at me warily for some reason.

The man who came in was not dressed as a servant, nor did he have a breakfast tray. Something tugged at the back of my memory, but I didn't put the pieces together until I heard his voice.

"Lord Stenvall. Lady Stenvall." He nodded at Evander, then me.

It was the medic who had seen to me during my fever. Which meant...

"I trust you're ready for the examination," the man said.

I didn't say anything, too busy focusing on keeping the blush from my cheeks.

"Of course," Evander answered. "If you'll allow my wife a moment to dress."

The medic turned around.

"Well, that feels rather pointless, but..." I muttered, and

Evander gave me a wry look, stepping out of bed to hand me a black silk robe.

I put the robe on and told the man he could turn back around. Then we began the awkward business of me lying back for his not remotely invasive examination.

For all that Evander had pretended this was no issue, he stood glowering at the foot of the bed, watching the man's every move. Which, naturally, made this at least seventeen times more uncomfortable.

"You can feel free to be literally anywhere else, you know," I told him.

"No," he said shortly.

Well, then. I averted my gaze, sure my face was crimson by now, and tried not to shift in discomfort. After about fifteen seconds of this fun, Evander let out an irritable breath.

"I'm certain you have what you need by now," he said in a curt tone.

"I do," the medic said with a long-suffering sigh, like he was used to overbearing Socairan men overseeing this process.

But my sympathy for him was limited, since no one was examining *his* body right now.

He stood up and moved to walk out of the room. "I'll go make my report now."

I glowered at his back, burrowing into the blankets. "Yes, please do enjoy telling everyone about the state of my--"

"Lemmikki." Evander's eyes sparkled with amusement, though his features were otherwise stoic.

I declined to finish my sentence, and the medic left without further conversation. Once he was gone, I still found it difficult to look at Evander. The exam wasn't his fault, but it still rankled that I had to be subjected to it at all.

Besides which, it had been humiliating.

"Lemmikki," he said again, his tone softer this time. "I asked for biscuits with breakfast."

"Ya ne khochu vash pechen'ye." *I don't want your biscuits,* I told him in Socairan, though it wasn't strictly true.

He let out a slow breath. "While your Socairan is improving

at an impressive rate, your lying skills are not. And you always want biscuits."

Evander settled on the bed next to me, but he didn't get under the blankets, like he knew I was using them as a form of armor.

Leaning over, he tucked a stray hair behind my ear. "I *am* sorry, Lemmikki."

I looked at him in surprise, sure it was the first time I had ever heard him actually apologize.

"If I could have taken your place, I would have," he said. "But this legitimacy is what gives you the protection of a Clan Wife. It's what keeps you safe."

I sighed. "I know that. But who exactly is he making a report to?"

Evander's expression came closer to a wince than I had ever seen it. "The...gathered dukes."

"Oh. Perfect." My cheeks flamed once more, and I crossed my arms over my chest. "I hope you at least ordered honey with the biscuits."

He scoffed softly, like that was obvious. "Of course I did."

That was something, at least.

It wasn't long after that we were required in the courtyard to send off the wedding guests. The noonday sun bore down on us from a cloudless sky as we bid the dukes goodbye, with me doing my best to avoid direct contact with any of them.

Ram, Crane, Bison, Viper, and Eagle had already left, leaving only Lynx, Elk, and Wolf lingering in the courtyard. Along with the royal envoy, of course. Iiro couldn't possibly leave quietly, or less annoyingly.

Mila stood quietly off to the side, talking with her father in what appeared to be a tense conversation. Sir Nils, predictably, left without saying a word to me, and Evander reluctantly followed to make sure they parted on peaceful terms, though his eyes flashed irritably.

Wolf was one of Bear's longest-standing allies, and arguably the most important, due to their large, shared border.

Which left me in the uncomfortable position of saying goodbye to Theo while Evander took off after the Duke of Wolf.

"Sir Theodore," I greeted awkwardly as he dipped his head in a small bow.

I tried to tell myself this was no different than our dance yesterday, but knowing he had heard the...report this morning certainly made it feel that way.

"Princess," he returned, his voice quieter than normal.

I finally met his eyes and saw the hesitation dancing within them.

"Theo--" I began before he stiffened and cleared his throat.

Taking my hand in his, he leaned down, pressing a kiss to my knuckles before whispering so quietly I nearly missed it.

"Be careful, Rowan."

This was now the second time he had warned me, and it sent tendrils of fear raking down my spine. They only intensified as he turned to walk away, leaving me to face the too-familiar voice behind me.

"Lady Stenvall," Iiro greeted, and I spun around to face him and Inessa. "What a lovely wedding."

Though a thrill usually went through me at the name, hearing it on Iiro's lips felt like a snake slithering down my spine. I dipped my chin into a deep nod, mostly to hide my expression.

When I looked back up, I had managed to school my features until they resembled something closer to boredom.

"Your Majesties, what a pleasure it was to have you here." I grinned, and Iiro narrowed his eyes.

"Indeed." His lips parted to say something else when he sighed instead.

A warm, comforting touch rested against the small of my back, and I turned to see Evander at my side.

"Apologies, My Lady," he said, addressing me first. "Your Majesties, thank you for honoring us with your attendance."

Evander's voice was smooth, and his expression was

perfectly neutral, making me wonder if it was only me who could hear the murderous undertone in each word.

"But, please, I didn't mean to interrupt." He added in his next breath, urging Iiro to continue with whatever he was saying.

The corner of Iiro's mouth twitched before he opened his mouth to speak.

"I'm looking forward to seeing you both at the Obsidian Palace soon," he said, looking back at Evander.

There was an undercurrent to the words, a threat veiled by an innocuous invitation.

"Of course," Evander said, his eyes locking on Iiro's. "We'll send word once we look at our schedules."

A condescending laugh pulled my attention back to the new king.

"I've already discussed it with your father, and he's assured me that five weeks will be sufficient time." Though his tone was pleasant enough, his eyes were cold and calculating. "Reestablishing the Obsidian Throne will benefit us all, but in order to rebuild, we first need to discuss taxes."

Iiro looked pointedly at the supply wagons before continuing.

"Of course, Sir Aleksander is welcome to come by himself. I could use his support on a few--"

"We'll be there," Evander said flatly before Iiro could finish.

Iiro's smile widened, and Evander's fingers tightened on my waist.

Then the self-proclaimed king made a show of a polite farewell before turning to go. Inessa met my eyes with an inscrutable expression before dipping her head and following after her husband.

"Taxes?" I asked quietly, as we watched their carriage leave. "Will the gold be a problem for Bear?"

Logically, I knew the value in having them, but considering that each clan already had a system in place, adding more for Iiro's new position felt...excessive.

"No." Evander gently pressed his hand against my back, leading me back into the castle. "Money is no object for any of the clans, really, but least of all, Bear. He's referring to food taxes." A muscle ticked in his jaw. "And I won't starve my people just so he can better feed his new army."

I thought of the food that my parents had sent as part of my dowry. Even Lochlann's food stores were limited. Trade or not, they hardly had the resources to feed all of Socair.

How far would it go within Bear and our allies? And what would happen when that supply ran out?

CHAPTER FOURTEEN

ROWAN

The next several days were a blur of Evander and me, interspersed with an occasional report from Taras, Kirill, or Yuriy.

There were likely a thousand things for us to do, for the clan, for the estate, to prepare ourselves for whatever Iiro had planned...still, I was grateful when Evander locked the door behind us, keeping the rest of the world at bay.

We spent our days losing ourselves in one another and making up for all of the time we had missed. There wasn't a single part of me that stopped craving him. His nearness, his touch, the gentle sounds of his breathing as he slept.

I wanted it all. All of him.

After a week of mostly hiding in our rooms, though, Evander announced over breakfast that we would need to return to normal life, or the new normal of being married to the Clan Heir.

Which, in my case, seemed to consist of learning how to navigate the politics of my new clan and getting to know the people in my court.

I shot him a bitter look and consoled myself with another piece of the maple bacon that was so popular here. It had nearly been ruined for me in the days I had spent eating with Aleksander, but these past couple of days, I had come to truly appreciate it again.

"Lemmikki." Evander's voice was a mock warning as I dutifully ignored him, savoring the sweet and salty taste of the bacon, the heady flavor of the sticky maple syrup coating each piece, and the kick of pepper that added just the right amount of spice.

I groaned, licking my fingers as my eyes rolled to the back of my head.

A soft laugh escaped Evander's lips as he crept across the bed and slowly kissed me, savoring me as much as I had the bacon.

"Did you know that you make that same face when..." He raised his eyebrows suggestively as I threw a pillow at him to shut him up.

"What can I say? Food is delicious, you're delicious, the way you make me feel is del--" He interrupted me by pulling me further into his lap, and a giggle escaped my lips. "I appreciate delicious things."

A low growl emanated from the back of his throat that solidified my desire to never leave this room again.

A desire that had nothing at all to do with the way I dreaded the idea of meeting with the other ladies for tea or lunch. Or the fact that it also meant Ava would be present.

Here was hoping that she neglected her responsibilities more than I intended to.

At least that wasn't for several more hours. I had more appealing plans for the rest of my morning.

"Is there somewhere I can spar this morning?" I asked, turning to face him.

He finished taking his sip of coffee, setting the mug down on the breakfast tray beside him before assessing me.

"I'm sure that can be arranged."

Boris leapt onto the bed with an irritable half-meow, settling his fluffy ginger mass on Evander's pillow behind us, which elicited narrowed eyes from my husband.

With a low chuckle, I shared the last, precious morsel of bacon with the cat, who purred as he inhaled the delicious bite.

Then I reluctantly pulled myself from bed to ready myself for the day.

After washing up, I chose the black dress Evander had commissioned for me from my closet, before moving to the vanity to fix my hair and cosmetics.

I had considered going with one of my more traditional Socairan gowns, but they were impossible to move in. *Even more impossible to spar in.*

And the reality was, I didn't want to dress like that for the rest of my life, so I aimed to start a new trend. Between Mila and me, I hoped that wouldn't be too difficult.

Evander gave me a look of approval when I emerged, having finished pinning the stray curls back away from my face.

A *heated* look of approval, one that delayed our departure by several minutes and forced me to re-pin the wayward locks.

Finally, though, we were on our way.

"Are we going to a private sparring ring?" I asked him, an extra bounce to my step as we made our way across the courtyard.

There was no real chance I could beat Evander, but facing off against him was still exciting. Sparring, period, was something I enjoyed, and it had been a couple of weeks since Callum and I practiced on the road.

"No," he said simply.

"Surely the men will resent it if you make them leave," I said.

Resent *me*, I meant.

When Evander had brought me here before, he had ordered the men out as soon as we got there. I couldn't imagine that going over well every single morning.

"They probably would," he agreed a little too amicably, his usual smirk tugging at the side of his lips.

Before I could push him further, we were at the training grounds.

The sound of unsharpened blades clanging and the grunts of men training rang out as soon as Evander opened the massive doors to the sparring ring.

Just like the last time, the noise quieted when the men caught sight of me.

I waited for Evander to dismiss them the way he had before, but instead, he was silent as we walked toward the center of the room.

Yuriy met us there, and my husband sized up the two of us, nodding his head in approval.

"Perfect. You can start with Yuriy."

Yuriy subtly glanced around at the room full of men, his face a mixture of confusion and apprehension. The other soldiers looked nonplussed, their eyes darting between Evander, Yuriy, and me.

"I'm not sparring with you?" I asked, quiet enough that only Evander could hear me.

"I'm sure there will be time enough for that later, Lemmikki," he responded with a wink, implying that he had a different kind of sparring in mind.

Yuriy awkwardly agreed, and I took a moment to stretch. It wasn't lost on me that Evander had put me on display in the middle of the room, clearly making a point.

While I warmed up, he moved around the room, giving feedback on the form of the other fighting men. A few minutes later, he returned with one of the sparring swords, handing it to me before telling us to begin.

We took up our fighting stances, though Yuriy was still hesitant. Many of the men around us stopped to watch, but I refused to let that bother me.

Isn't this what I wanted? To be able to openly spar in Socair the way I did in Lochlann?

Instead of standing and waiting for Yuriy to strike, I went on the offensive, throwing myself into an attack. He deftly maneuvered backward, blocking my sword, but made no move to attack.

"Stop holding back, Yuriy." Evander's voice was low, but it still reached us over the sounds of our blades clashing.

Yuriy gave the smallest shake of his head, then made a single offensive strike, which I parried efficiently. He frowned, looking at Evander once more. Whatever Yuriy saw on his cousin's face must have been enough, because the next thing I knew, we were sparring in truth.

Evander circled us as he critiqued us both.

"Lemmikki, remember to lift your elbow."

"Yuriy, on your guard. She's taking advantage of your weakness with your left."

"Your footwork is sloppy, Lemmikki."

And finally, "Are you really going to let a woman beat you, Cousin?"

I practically growled at him for that one, but when I caught his eye, there was a gleam of mischief dancing there. He knew exactly what he was doing.

Sure enough, Yuriy unleashed a flurry of attacks, fast enough that I had to employ a series of ducks and twirls to evade him. As I danced out of the way of his blade, though, I watched carefully for my opening.

And he gave it, on his left, just as he had been doing all along.

Instead of dragging this out any longer, I flew through the next several movements, bringing my blade down on Yuriy's with more force than necessary.

Once he was where I wanted him, I feinted to the right before stepping in between his legs to throw him off balance, then shoving him the rest of the way to the ground.

With my blade at Yuriy's throat and his hands in the air, Evander called the match.

"Now," he said to the stunned men around us. "Who can tell me what they did wrong?"

CHAPTER FIFTEEN

ROWAN

I t didn't take long to realize what Evander was doing. By critiquing my movements and Yuriy's, his cousin and third in line for the dukedom, he had put us on equal footing.

The others were hesitant to offer feedback--on me, specifically--but one look from Evander had them quickly coming up with something constructive to say.

Once that was done, I sparred with two other soldiers, winning one match and losing the other. By the time we left, I felt a little more grounded and insanely satisfied.

Maybe we really could do this.

Sure, there would still be plenty of Socairans who despised or feared my hair, but I hadn't missed the way a few more had softened to me today.

Taisiya had a bath drawn for us by the time we returned to our room, and we took our time cleaning up before we were both required elsewhere.

While Evander went to discuss clan matters with the local lords, I met Mila and the other ladies of Bear court for a late luncheon.

Fortunately, Ava wasn't in attendance, just as I had hoped earlier, so the meal went relatively smoothly. I tried to make conversation with each lady in attendance, learning about who they were, how long they had been staying at the castle, and what part of Bear they lived in.

Most of the ten in attendance smiled and politely responded, even if some of that felt forced. Some of them were even more talkative than I expected. But there was one who clearly wanted nothing to do with me.

Lady Katerina was impeccably dressed in an elegant pale-pink gown that offset her light brown skin, with her dark hair swept into a smooth chignon. According to Mila, she was one of the more prominent ladies at court, but also one of the nicer ones.

Except, it would appear, toward me.

She wasn't precisely hostile, nor did she seem afraid, but any time I tried to speak with her, she was suddenly very interested in her finger sandwiches or scones.

Odd.

By the time lunch was over, we all went to take our tea in the drawing room, and I finally had an opportunity to talk privately with Mila.

Most of the ladies took a spot at one of the round tables, playing some sort of card game that didn't look nearly as fun as Kings and Arselings, while two chose corner seats and picked up their knitting to work on alone.

I felt like I had done my share of my forced socializing for the day, so Mila and I sat on a small, secluded couch that faced the large bay windows near the fireplace. It had the perfect view of the snowcapped mountains.

Or, it would have been, if my eyes didn't keep going to Lady Katerina.

If Mila didn't shift uncomfortably when she followed my gaze.

I darted a glance back at Katerina, and something twisted in my gut.

Because I had finally identified the expression hiding behind her eyes. It wasn't the usual fear of my cursed Lochlann hair, or even the derision that came from my being the enemy.

It was jealousy.

"Mila," I said in a low tone.

My friend's brown eyes met mine, an uncomfortable sort of guilt stirring there, confirming everything I was already suspecting. The several scones I had consumed for lunch were threatening to make a reappearance right about now.

"Mila," I repeated her name more firmly. "Tell me that Lady Katerina is looking at me like that because she hates me for being me...and not because she has some *attachment* to my husband."

She winced. "Wish that I could, Scarlet Princess."

I groaned, hiding my face behind my cup of tea.

Of course, Evander hadn't been...chaste, before me. I knew that. I had a past and, logically, I knew he did, too. But it would have been nice to be prepared.

"From what I've heard, it wasn't serious," she whispered consolingly, smiling over at Lady Sidorov. "She's actually one of the less uptight ladies of court. She'll warm up to you."

"Great," I hissed back. "Perhaps we can start swapping stories and compare notes on the Bear Lord."

Mila laughed loudly before trying to cover it over with a cough. The attention in the room shifted to us as I patted her on the back, helping her work through the amusement that had lodged itself in her lungs.

She held up a hand, thanking me and assuring the room she was fine. When she looked back at me, though, her eyes still held the same level of diversion as before.

"If it makes you feel any better, Lady Sidorov has a history with Taras," she nodded subtly toward one of the women knitting in the corner, the one she had smiled at a moment ago. "Only theirs was an actual courtship."

"Twisted though it may be, that does make me feel a little better." Whether it was the commiseration or the reminder that we all had our own histories, something inside me eased a bit. "Thank you, Mila."

She raised her cup of tea in salute before taking another sip. "I am happy to oblige."

After that, she went on to catch me up on all of the gossip

she'd been hearing, filling me in on the politics at court, the newer fashions, the noble families of Bear that were clashing, and anything else she could think of.

By the time we left to prepare ourselves for dinner, I had a more insightful look into so much more of Bear than I expected. Along with a few etiquette and dinner tips that would hopefully push me over the edge of being the lowly Lochlannian royal to a proper Lady of Socair.

Well, as proper as I would ever be.

CHAPTER SIXTEEN

ROWAN

I promised myself I would not bring up Lady Katerina.

But in fairness to me, I knew it was a lie, even before Evander walked in and asked how my luncheon went.

"It was interesting," I said, unable to keep the bite from my tone.

He raised his eyebrows, turning slightly to uncork a bottle of whiskey from the bar.

"I especially enjoyed meeting Lady Katerina." Sarcasm laced my tone.

Evander froze with the bottle halfway tilted.

"A warning would have been nice," I added in a more serious tone.

His gaze slowly met mine, a cautiously neutral expression on the stupidly perfect features that I was currently picturing Katerina running her elegant fingers along.

"It was a long time ago, Lemmikki," he said, somewhat defensively. "And when exactly was I supposed to bring that up? Did you want me to casually mention it this morning on the way to the sparring ring, or perhaps while we were in the bath?"

"At literally any point before I had to figure it out at this luncheon would have been preferable," I shot back. "Honestly, how would you have felt in Lochlann if you had been sitting down to cards with the lairds and happened upon the realization that the one sitting next to you had bedded your wife?"

His features darkened, and he looked away. "Fair point."

I sighed. "I'm not complaining that you have a past, Evander. But in the future, perhaps you could just...let me know what I'm walking into."

He nodded, and I gave him a more pointed look. "I'm giving you the chance, right now, before another luncheon tomorrow."

Evander leveled me with a look. "I'm not Davin, Lemmikki. It's not as though I've been with half the court."

"I'm sure he'd be offended that you think it's only half." A smile tugged at my lips, though it was bittersweet as I realized just how much I missed my cousin. These were exactly the kinds of situations he always helped me to navigate.

Evander's mouth tilted into an amused smirk as he set the bottle down and stepped closer to me. "If it matters to you, I will make sure that you are...informed, should the situation arise."

"Yes, it matters to me," I said, peeking up at him through my lashes.

My hands went to run along his chest, and I stood up on my tiptoes to whisper in his ear in the same low, possessive tone he had used with me the day he arrived at the Lochlannian Court. "Or did you forget that I own you, Evander?"

He let out a chuckle at the echo of his words. "I could never forget that, Lemmikki."

Dinner with Mila and Taras was a welcome break from thinking about the politics of my new life.

"I am so ready to bring these new dresses in style with you," Mila gestured toward her pale-yellow gown, which was a similar design to mine. "I may not fight or ride a horse the way you do, but they're comfortable. Besides, anything is better than southern style clothing."

She gave a visible shudder, and I joined her.

"I don't know," I said. "Evander was rather fond of those

nightgowns. He found them to be quite...provocative." I used his word from the first night we had been forced to share a bed at the inn.

Taras shook his head while my husband choked on a small chuckle.

"Indeed, I did," Evander agreed. "I'm not sure how I kept my hands off you then, what with the seventeen layers of irresistible ruffles."

Mila laughed out loud, a rich sound that permeated the room. "I'm fortunate that my father was more lenient than most dukes. I was never forced to suffer those."

"A fact for which I am grateful," Taras added.

"Speaking of your father, he looked...displeased as he was leaving the other day," I commented.

Mila exchanged a look with her husband.

"Yes, well, Iiro is pressuring him to sign. And he isn't thrilled that as Bear's ally, it's harder for him to stay neutral. But neither was Evander here to prevent this from happening," she said quietly.

Evander went still, but not in the way that this was a surprise to him. More in the way that he was waiting to see how I took it, the realization that by coming to me in Lochlann, he had upset not one, but two of his allies.

And allowed Iiro to become King, or whatever version of it he was currently playing.

Something apparently everyone at this table had known but me.

When I didn't respond, Evander spoke up. "Well, we're working on that."

"How?" I asked.

"Slowly," he responded. "And carefully. We're trying to find diplomatic solutions, and if not..."

He trailed off, leaving me to fill in the blank.

"And if not, there will be war," I finished for him.

He nodded tersely.

"How would that work, with your father supporting him?" I asked.

Evander's features went tight, but it was Taras who responded.

"It's an unlikely outcome, given the odds, because...Bear would have no choice but to fight for Iiro."

My jaw dropped, and Mila clenched her fork tighter in her fingers, the last bit of her noodles dangling from the prongs.

Silence descended on the table the way a blizzard hits, unexpected and impenetrable.

I stared at my plate and forced myself to take another bite of the stroganoff, knowing how important it was not to waste food here, even if it tasted like ash in my mouth now.

Evander's hand came to rest on mine, but it was Mila who broke through the hush.

"All right," she said in a deceptively light tone. "I hereby ban further discussion of politics this evening. We need...a night in the sauna. Perhaps my husband can win another butt imprint contest."

"One can dream," Taras intoned, and a small smile tilted my lips, in spite of myself.

She was right. We did need this.

And somehow, I suspected there would be more than enough talk of politics and war in the weeks to come.

An hour later, we found ourselves venturing out toward the sauna. One of them, anyway.

The estate apparently housed several, but of course, this one was reserved for the immediate Stenvall family.

It was nonetheless a large building, and since we had sent word ahead, there was already smoke coming from the small stone chimney.

We walked around to the entrance just this side of the river, passing several guards who were stationed around it until we came to the small divided changing area.

Thank the stars for small mercies.

As much as I tried to be less prudish than I was, going

through the act of taking off my clothes in front of my friend's new husband felt wildly uncomfortable. Mila and I quickly disrobed, neatly lying our dresses on the given tables.

Finally, I took off my dagger and sheath, tucking them underneath my dress.

When we got into the steamy room, Taras and Evander were holding two ales each. They held the extras out to us, and we settled on the bench across from them.

I wasn't complaining about that, since it gave me a spectacular and unobstructed view of Evander's perfect, muscled body. My eyes lingered on the way he casually balanced his mug on his thigh, drifting up to his perfectly sculpted abdominals and finally to the smug expression that somehow made him infinitely sexier.

This time I didn't have to worry about what others thought of my appreciative glances in his direction, because he was mine. Besides, Mila wouldn't judge since she was doing the same thing with Taras.

Unlike dinner, our time in the sauna was spent laughing and talking. It was nice to leave the grim feeling behind for a while, soaking in this feeling of friendship and the life we could have here if things ever calmed down.

I got up to pour more water over the stones, releasing a fresh wave of steam, but instead of going back to my seat, strong arms wrapped around my waist, pulling me in the opposite direction.

Through the steam, I watched as Taras moved to sit next to Mila before turning my attention back to Evander. He pulled me down next to him, refusing to release the arm he had around me.

I wasn't about to argue with him. We stayed for another ten minutes that way, continuing to talk and laugh as Taras and Mila shared stories about their wedding and the awkward dance she'd had to endure with one of Sir Heikkinen's sons.

Apparently, the much younger grandson of the Duke of Eagle had confessed his love for her and had forced her into three uncomfortable dances before Taras and the boy's father had to order him away.

I laughed hard at that. Despite the awkwardness of our wedding, at least no one had done that with me.

We were all more than relieved when Evander suggested it was time to rinse off in the water. I had been distracted with the story but even more so with the slow, tantalizing circles Evander's thumb was drawing on my thigh, the way my breath hitched each time he repeated the pattern. I hadn't realized how long we had been in the sauna, or that my lungs were desperate for fresh air.

There was a direct, secluded path from the sauna to the river, and I resisted the urge to don my robe. Once again, the moonlight illuminated my pale skin, contrasting sharply with the varying shades of light brown that Mila, Taras, and Evander all had.

My husband walked next to me, his hand on the small of my back and a relaxed smile on his lips. He had needed this, too, I realized, a break from all the heaviness around us.

When we got to the edge of the river, Mila and Taras jumped right in, but I hesitated.

Was it just me, or did the water look extra freezing today?

Before I could think too long about it, Evander's warm arms came around me...and promptly lifted me to hurl me into the river.

Ice shot through my veins, paralyzing me for a fraction of a second before I kicked my way to the top.

I was right. It was extra freezing.

I felt movement next to me, and the arseling had managed to emerge at the same time I did, probably because, unlike me, his feet touched the ground here.

"You. *Aalio*," I said through chattering teeth.

He threw his head back and laughed. "You were overthinking it, Lemmikki."

His stupid teeth weren't chattering at all. In fact, looking at him, Mila, and Taras, you would think they were all here for a leisurely evening swim.

I splashed water at him, which only made him laugh harder. He pulled his arms around me again, tugging me next to him and lending me some of his warmth before pressing a wet, sloppy kiss against my lips.

I stuck my tongue out, and he nipped at it playfully before carting me out of the river for another much-needed round of sauna.

After a few more rounds of this, we finally went to dry off and get dressed.

I was so caught up in the fun we were having that it took me a while to realize something was off, and even longer to place what it was.

My dagger, which I had tucked carefully under my dress, was now sitting out in the open on the bench, halfway out of its sheath.

Evander had said the only people allowed here unescorted were the duke and his heir...and their wives. There were guards outside ensuring no one broke that rule, not that anyone would dare.

Ava.

What was she doing here? And what did she want with my things?

CHAPTER SEVENTEEN

ROWAN

Another week passed in much the same manner.

We sparred in the mornings. Then in the early afternoon Evander conducted business with the lords or occasionally, his father, and I made an effort to get to know the ladies.

All the while, there was an undercurrent of tension as he worked very subtly on whatever he was doing to undermine and dethrone Iiro, even as the threat of food taxes grew ever nearer.

At least Ava still made herself scarce, thank the stars.

When Evander wasn't working, he still spent a great deal of time at his desk, the muted scratching of his quill traveling through the open door. Each time I joined him in his study, he took the time to explain what he was doing, which generally involved reports of some sort.

Whether it was about laws, trade, coffers, or the soldiers, he seemed to have a hand in everything that went on in Bear. When he wasn't directly responding to someone, he pored over a number of charts and maps, making notes and drawing arrows as he went.

"What are those?" I asked curiously.

"Plans for reallocating resources in a way that might actually address both the famine and the population issues. Not that Iiro will ever listen," he muttered irritably.

"That's why alliances are so important to you," I pointed out.

Not just for the militant aspect, as I had suspected—as Iiro had assumed—but for this. I wasn't sure why it surprised me when he planned for literally everything else, but I had only ever seen him focused on his soldiers.

He nodded. "A united Socair wouldn't be the worst thing, if it were under someone who actually gave a damn. Unfortunately, the only one I could be reasonably certain meets those requirements is Arès, and after keeping to himself for so long, I doubt he could garner the support even if we could rid ourselves of Iiro."

Evander sighed, but the arrival of yet another report via Kirill stopped any further discussion on that.

The following morning, his gaze lingered on me, and a happy, purring Boris snuggled against me in our bed, as he dressed for the day.

"I have to act in my father's stead at a meeting with the lords in our territory," he said, casting me a speculative glance. "It would be a good idea for you to accompany me."

"Are women allowed at these meetings?" I raised an eyebrow.

"Not generally," he admitted. "But this is the first one since our wedding. It might be prudent to start as we plan to go on."

A smile spread across my lips. Somehow his invitation to something as mundane as a meeting with the lords was, dare I say, *romantic*.

"All right, then," I said, narrowly avoiding Boris' spiteful nip at my decision to leave the bed.

He went into my closet and emerged holding a dress that was similar to the style I usually wore, but in a more formal, brocaded fabric. "Wear this."

I raised an eyebrow but obliged him. Taisiya came to help me with my hair, then Evander and I were off.

I could tell this was different from Lochlann's council before

I even sat down. For one thing, it was, predictably, all men. It was also all lords, with no one to represent the common people.

Where the Lochlannian Council had long since ceased to rely on ceremony, everyone at the rectangular table stood to offer a bow when we entered. Evander nodded back, his face a mask of arrogance.

Not one of them dared to question what I was doing there, but they cast me dissatisfied glances all the same. All except for Taras, who merely looked...wary, as he gestured for the lord closest to the head of the table to move down.

With obvious disgruntlement, the entire right side of the table shifted, and I took the proffered seat. That was my first misstep, apparently, given the looks I received.

No one else sat until Evander did.

I examined my husband's features, noting how well he played this part. It was hard to believe he was the same person who had been in our bed this morning. There was no trace of softness on his features now, but then, I supposed that's what being a ruler in Socair was.

In any event, at least he didn't appear to be fazed that I sat down before him.

Evander called the meeting to order, and the lords brought various issues to his attention. He considered them all with that same aloof face, asking pertinent follow-up questions before giving a decisive response.

It was impressively efficient, and I had to wonder how he felt about Lochlann's council style of rule. Things that took days of discussion to decide on there, were settled in a matter of minutes here. From what I could see, Evander's judgements were fair, if a bit...exacting.

Most of the conversations surrounded food distribution, though a few touched on disputes with one another's lands. Taras' father, Lord Lehtinan, brought up issues with the Unclanned and a few instances of theft, while another lord mentioned raids on food stores.

I followed along, trying to glean any information I could

about my new home and the people I would be partially responsible for, the same way I would have my holdings in Lochlann.

A couple of times I voiced a quick, clarifying question, and
Evander would give me the barest approving nod before
answering. Other times, he or Taras offered a low explanation
before I even needed to speak up.

All in all, the meeting was going better than could be
expected until the lord next to Taras spoke up.

"My Lord, we have a situation with three dissenting soldiers."

Evander gestured for him to go on.

"They were firstmen, ages fifteen, fifteen, and sixteen." He
paused, irritation flashing across his features. "They set fire to
piles of gunpowder, frightening the ladies nearby and destroying
some of the shrubberies."

He looked a little uncomfortable using the word shrubberies.

"Was anyone harmed?" Evander asked coolly.

"No, My Lord. The noise was what frightened the women."

It sounded like something the younger lairds in Lochlann
would do. Something meant to cause a stir and be shocking, but
not to actually hurt anyone.

My husband considered for several seconds, deliberating for
a bit longer than he had on the others. He cast me the briefest of
sideways glances before he gave a sharp nod. "Fifteen lashes
each."

"What?" The word escaped my lips unbidden.

Surely, I had misheard him. I had been given thirteen lashes,
and it had nearly killed me.

Evander's head turned slowly to me, his features inscrutable.

"Fifteen lashes for children playing a prank?" I said the words
quietly, but they nonetheless carried. "Surely that's excessive."

He blinked, and the muscle in his jaw ticked, the one that
either meant he was fighting back amusement or fury. And I was
fairly certain he found nothing amusing about this situation.

Which made two of us.

"Twenty lashes is standard for disobedient soldiers," he
explained in a deceptively neutral tone. "Given the potential

consequences. The *leniency*," he stressed the word, "is because of their age."

The room was deadly silent and thick with tension, with offense that a woman would dare to contradict their precious lord.

"Leniency," I repeated, disbelief evident in my tone.

He nodded, a single, sharp dip of his head.

My lips parted in disbelief. "Well, then. I suppose I can be grateful Lady Mairi was even more *lenient* with me."

His eyes lit up with something like a warning, but it was Taras who spoke.

"I'm sure their families will appreciate the concession," he said in a quiet voice that was nonetheless pointed. "Is there anything else, Lord Juto?"

Evander tore his gaze from mine, returning to his meeting like nothing had happened. I hid my hands in my lap before any of the lords could see the way they trembled with fury.

"No," the man said shortly.

He cast me a baleful glance until Evander cleared his throat pointedly.

I ignored them both, and the rest of the room, after that, fixing my attention on small details on the walls, focusing on taking even breaths.

And counting down the minutes until I could get out of this room.

CHAPTER EIGHTEEN

ROWAN

W hen Evander finally called for a break for lunch, I couldn't leave fast enough.

Kirill waited outside the council room for me. I wasn't sure if he was more guarding me at this point or just making sure I knew my way around when Evander was busy, but either was appreciated.

His usually affable features faltered when he caught sight of mine.

"Is everything all right, My Lady?" he asked cautiously.

All of the men had taken to calling me that, because being a Clan Wife of Bear was a higher honor than being a princess of a foreign land.

"Perfect," I spat out, forcing myself to walk at an even pace toward the stairs.

Of course, that meant Evander caught up to me easily, dismissing Kirill. I ostensibly ignored my husband, though there was no real escaping the waves of ire emanating off him.

Still, we walked in silence to our rooms, neither of us speaking until he carefully shut the door behind us. It wasn't hard to see what an effort it was for him not to slam it, and his fury only further ignited my own.

"What exactly are *you* upset about?" I demanded. "It's not like you were just demeaned in front of the entire council."

He shot me a look of disbelief. "It *is* like that, as a matter of fact."

A scoff escaped my lips. "Surely, you didn't expect me to just sit there in silence while you--"

He interrupted me. "That's exactly what I expected you to do."

Rage burned through my veins, punctuated by each thunderous heartbeat echoing in my ears.

"Well, perhaps you can bestow a barbaric punishment upon me, as well." I put a finger to my lips, pretending to think. "Let's see, if fifteen lashes is standard for mischievous boys, whatever would a disobedient wife rate?"

Evander took a deep, furious breath through his nose, apparently too angry to respond to that comment.

"Why did you even invite me if you didn't plan on listening to a damned word I said?" I demanded.

"Well, I confess," he began sarcastically, "it didn't actually occur to me when I asked you to go that you wouldn't have the basic common sense to refrain from criticizing my decisions in front of the entire Council of Lords, regarding a law that you know exactly nothing about."

My jaw dropped in fury. "Funny, because it didn't actually occur to *me* that you would be sadistic enough to subject someone else to the same form of torture that you've experienced yourself, that nearly killed your wife."

That admonitory expression entered his eyes again.

"Lemmikki," he growled. "These *boys* are twice your size. Fifteen lashes won't kill them, especially when the whip isn't being wielded by a man like Samu. It will, however, deter them and everyone watching from disobedience in the future that would get them or their fellow soldiers killed."

"And this is the only way to accomplish that?" I demanded. "Scarring them for life?"

"It's a known, effective way of accomplishing that," he gritted out. "And again, this is *not* what happened to you. One standard lashing isn't likely to leave them mutilated."

"Likely?" I echoed, blinking slowly. "Well then, what could I possibly have to be upset about, as long as the boys are *likely* not going to be mutilated?"

"We're very possibly teetering on the brink of a war, and you want to argue with me about the way I discipline my soldiers?" Incredulity coated his tone. "A job that, by the way, I was doing back when your biggest concern in life was which tiara to wear that day."

A whoosh of air escaped me. *Aalio.*

"No, of course not, My Lord," I said in a simpering tone. "I wouldn't dream of having an opinion about something so bold as politics or warfare. Perhaps you could find me something to knit instead."

"Perhaps I should." Evander was closer to yelling now than I usually heard him. "If the alternative is you making arses of both of us in front of the people we need to respect us most."

A bitter huff of air escaped me. "Respect *you*, you mean."

He squeezed his eyes shut, his nostrils flaring.

"As much as I would love to stand here and debate every aspect of Socairan law and custom that you haven't bothered to learn or understand, I have to get downstairs for lunch with the lords to smooth over the damage *you* caused in the council meeting." He gestured toward the door with a flourish. "But you are welcome to join me."

"I'm sure I wouldn't want to risk further *damaging* the fragile egos of any Socairan lords," I said pointedly, ensuring he knew exactly whose ego I was referring to.

Evander clenched his teeth, and I couldn't help but follow the line of the muscle that ticked in his jaw to the furious set of his mouth, the same mouth that had been on mine only a few hours ago.

He tracked the movement of my eyes, a different sort of heat entering his features.

My feet moved of their own accord until I was standing in front of him, my hands acting without my permission to shove him back against the wall as I stretched up on my tiptoes to crash my lips against his.

He didn't resist, instead returning my kiss with a bruising impact.

His fingers came around my waist and then he was flipping us, lifting me up until I was eye level, his body pressing me solidly against the textured wall.

My anger hadn't dissipated, by any means, but it morphed solidly into a different kind of passion. All of my body pulsed with awareness, my heart beating a frantic staccato that demanded to be satiated.

I clamped his lower lip between my teeth, returning his fury with plenty of my own as I wrapped my legs firmly around his hips. He groaned, moving his mouth over to my neck.

"A sadist?" He growled in my ear. "I think masochist might be closer to the truth, considering my choice in bride and what an enormous pain in the arse she is."

He bit my neck hard enough to leave a mark, which I was sure was intentional. I let out a gasp.

"Whereas my choice in husband is just an enormous arse," I breathed, though my voice was less steady than I wanted it to be.

Evander's lips returned to claim mine, and for all his talk of needing to get downstairs, he didn't seem in any particular hurry to do that now.

I still didn't accompany Evander to his ever-important lunch. In fact, we didn't get any more talking at all accomplished.

Once he went downstairs, I asked Kirill to escort me to Taras and Mila's rooms. He looked at me uncertainly for a moment before nodding.

I stormed through the halls until he raised his eyebrows, then I forced myself to walk more slowly.

"I take it the council room meeting did not go well," he observed gently.

"Well, I don't call him *Lord Aalio* for nothing," I muttered.

Kirill chuckled under his breath, reminding me of when he

had been the closest thing to an ally I had in Clan Bear, when Evander first took me.

"Can I ask you something?"

He nodded, curiosity sparking in his dark eyes.

I looked up at him. "Seeing the way everyone defers to Evander, I'm curious why you were willing to supply me with that nickname."

He laughed again, more loudly this time. "Because I hadn't seen anyone even tempt Van into a smile in such a long time. It was worth it to see his reaction." In a more serious tone, he added, "And I knew he wouldn't be upset, not truly."

"Nor did he punish me for it, even as his prisoner," I mused aloud. "So, it's only his wife who can't speak up in front of others."

The words were more bitter than I intended them to be, and Kirill shot me a sympathetic glance.

"For what it's worth, I'm not sure he ever actually thought of you as his prisoner." Kirill grinned then. "Unless I've been willfully oblivious to the endearments he gives the rest of them."

I flushed then, realizing that all of the soldiers and literally everyone else knew he was calling me *darling*. We arrived at Mila's rooms before I could respond to that, though.

"You won't..." I trailed off, not sure if it was acceptable for me to ask Kirill not to tell his lord what I said.

"Oh, you couldn't pay me to bring this up to Van." He gave me another of his easy smiles, and I returned it this time, even if my own was strained.

Then I turned to knock on Mila's door.

"Do you have any vodka?" I asked without preamble when she answered.

"Obviously," she replied, stepping back to allow me entry.

She didn't ask what happened, which didn't surprise me. Even if her husband hadn't been in the council room, Mila seemed to have a way of knowing everything that went on.

She poured two sizable glasses, adding a large, round ice cube to both before sitting down in one of the chairs and gesturing for me to sit in the other. Her gaze traveled to my neck with a smirk, and I bit back a curse.

I knew that *aalio* had left a mark.

No wonder Kirill had hesitated before walking me down the hall. He probably wanted to tell me to don a scarf and then decided I was angry enough already, or at least that the halls in the family wing were empty enough for it not to matter.

"It looks like your day wasn't all bad, at least," she commented.

"It was...a mixed bag," I said, taking a deep drink.

"Want to talk about it?" she offered.

I lifted a shoulder in a shrug. "What is there to say? Evander treats me like an equal one minute, acts like he wants others to do the same, but I have to wonder how deep his Socairan ideals run if I'm not even allowed to speak up in the council room."

Mila eyed me over her glass, her expression thoughtful. "Things must be very different in Lochlann."

"They are," I muttered. "My parents rule equally, and my sister is poised to take the throne. Even now, if I find myself at a council meeting, I have a voice."

She nodded slowly, and I sensed she was holding in her commentary for a rare change.

"What?" I asked.

She took a deep breath. "You know that the hierarchy here is...very strict."

"I have gathered that," I said drily.

"It's unprecedented, really, for an heir to be granted the kind of authority that Evander has." Mila met my gaze, and I nodded my understanding, though I wasn't sure where she was going with this.

"I've been here long enough to see the way things are with the duke," she said carefully. "It might be different, if Evander's authority were like Aleksander's, unquestionable, but with the work he has put into gaining the respect of the lords..." She trailed off, waiting for me to put the pieces together.

"So if the lords don't respect him, there's no solid reason to obey him?" I clarified.

"Then the running of Bear would fall entirely to Aleksander, and, through him, that horrible wife of his," she added darkly.

I shook my head, frustrated by the entire situation.

"So I should just, what?" I gestured vaguely with my cup. "Sit back and let him order what's essentially torture on young boys and keep my mouth shut? You said yourself that flogging is barbaric."

Mila took a long sip of her drink, chewing the inside of her lip. "I did..."

"But?" I prompted.

"But..." she answered thoughtfully. "The clans have been separated for less than twenty years, so most of them have the same laws. I can't be sure about Bear, but in Lynx, even one instance of disobedience in a soldier is an Unclannable offense. So by giving them lashes, fewer lashes, even, than what the law calls for..."

Again, she waited for me to fill in the blank, and it didn't take me long.

"He really was being lenient," I said quietly.

She nodded. I had to wonder why Evander hadn't explained any of this, but then, my husband was neither used to explaining himself nor particularly fond of it.

And, I could admit, I hadn't really given him the chance.

"If it makes you feel any better," Mila said, a small smile playing on her lips. "Taras and I come from the same kingdom, and our first month of marriage had plenty of...disagreements."

"Oh?" I raised an eyebrow, inviting her to share.

"Well, he's very..." She cast around for a word. "Disciplined."

"Well, you can't just leave it there," I said. "I'm going to need some specifics."

She giggled, finally caving.

"The man folds his underthings before he puts them in the soiled basket. Which would be nothing more than an oddity, except that he apparently expects me to do the same because it *looks neater that way*." The last few words were in a hilariously accurate imitation of Taras' voice, and I laughed out loud.

I thought about Evander's absurdly tidy side of the room, and the way he frequently cast glances at my less than organized side.

"It must run in the family," I muttered.

Mila giggled again, taking another swig of her vodka before launching into a series of stories about Taras' habits and idiosyncrasies both in life and, even specifically, in the bedroom.

By the time I left her room I was both amused and...far more informed than I wanted to be.

CHAPTER NINETEEN

EVANDER

L unch with the lords went exactly the way I expected it to, with a number of thinly veiled insults directed at Rowan, some at me, and not a few insinuations that perhaps my father should resume the leadership of the Council of Lords.

Der'mo.

I knew that things were different in Lochlann, though admittedly, I hadn't understood just how much until she had referenced stud services in the middle of that council.

But could she honestly not see the difference in her people and mine?

Or take five storms-blasted seconds to think about the consequences of the things she said?

Taras walked with me toward the stairs that led to the wing we both stayed in. He eyed me warily, taking in what I was sure was my thunderous expression.

"Remember that she is new here and not experienced with the way we do things," he said in his usual quietly firm tone.

"Which is precisely why she should have refrained from commenting," I responded, my voice far calmer than my mood was.

"Did you tell her that before she came?" His deceptively mild inflection said he knew I didn't.

I had, admittedly, expected her to know.

"Is that something that needs to be said?" Sarcasm crept into my voice, though my defensiveness was evident as well.

Taras sighed. "To a Socairan woman? Probably not. To a woman from Lochlann who is used to saying every last thought that creeps into her head?"

He glanced over at me. "Honestly, I thought she showed remarkable self-restraint for the first half of the meeting, considering. She didn't bat an eyelash when my father talked about executing the men who broke into the food stores, though I can't imagine that punishment is standard for Lochlann."

"If you thought she was so remarkably restrained, why did you take my side?" It was an unfair question when I knew the answer, but I was unreasonably irritated by the entire situation.

My cousin sighed. "Besides the obvious? Because I know what she doesn't about the laws. I didn't say she was right, just that it was understandable. But..."

Taras trailed off, and I paused at the top of the stairwell, looking at him.

"When we traveled to the negotiations together, we all slept in that farmhouse," he finally said.

I nodded impatiently, trying to follow his uncharacteristic non sequitur.

"She had been trapped in the tunnels at that point," he explained. "Put on trial for her life. Kidnapped by a man she only had reason to fear. And she was laughing, teaching the men her ridiculous card game, and *mocking* you, for storm's sake." He let out a low chuckle that almost sounded impressed. "I took a guard shift that night, and she didn't stir in her sleep, even in the middle of a room full of soldiers."

I remembered. Half the kingdom was terrified of me, but not this tiny slip of a princess who actually had reason to be. It had been...infuriating. *Intriguing.*

"I'm sure the vodka had something to do with that," I muttered. "But it's not exactly evidence of her discretion. If anything, you're proving *my* point."

He gave me a look that said I was being deliberately obtuse, and I raised my eyebrows.

"The point is that she was more resilient than you could expect anyone in her situation to be. But after Samu got a hold of her..." Taras' eyes darkened. "Van, she didn't leave that bed for weeks. She barely smiled. In the limited time we spent in your study, even I heard her cry out in her sleep, so I'm sure that wasn't rare."

I could hardly stand to think about those days.

The way she tried to hide the constant pain she was in whenever she moved. The way she had gone from talking and laughing and hell, even yelling, freely, to shutting herself silently inside the black canopy of my bed for days on end.

And the nightmares.

"No." My voice was quiet. "It wasn't."

"And that's not even including the injuries themselves," he reminded me.

Even if the entire wedding hadn't seen her scars by now, Taras had helped me carry her to my rooms the day it happened. That was another image I would never get out of my head.

Rowan, chained to a post, the top half of her dress ripped away and blood pouring from the deep gashes in her pale, perfect skin.

"Can you honestly not see why the subject of flogging might have been too much for her to stay silent on?" he pushed.

I thought about the words she had hurled at me earlier, when I had been too angry to take them into account. Words like *torture*.

The reminder that she almost died.

"You've made your point," I said shortly.

"Good," he said simply. "Then I'm going to get back to my own wife."

We parted ways, and I continued down the hallway, trying to tame the whirlwind in my head before Rowan and her temper no doubt added to it.

CHAPTER TWENTY

ROWAN

I was pacing the room when Evander finally walked in.

He froze in the doorway, assessing me with an unusually hesitant expression.

I hated this. Fighting. Seeing that guarded look on his face instead of the open one he had been wearing this morning.

But even with everything Mila had said, I couldn't quite shake this feeling of frustration. There was understanding too, though.

With a sigh, I went to the small bar and poured us both a glass of vodka, handing one out to him. He eyed it warily, but took it, his fingers lingering on mine long enough to steal my breath, in spite of everything.

Finally, he gestured to the chairs for us to sit.

We stared at each other for a long, tense moment, until I reluctantly broke the silence.

"I can acknowledge that I was, perhaps, not entirely in the right for speaking up in the council room today," I muttered.

He raised his eyebrows, a hint of surprise showing on his features.

"You understand that it's not that I want you to be silenced," he said evenly.

"Yes and no," I answered.

He started to argue, but I held a hand up to stop him. Taking a breath, I tried to explain.

"I do understand that your authority here is..." *sexy*, I thought irrationally, remembering our afternoon.

Judging by his raised eyebrow, he knew exactly what had crossed my mind. I hastened to go on.

"Necessary," I finished. "And hard won. On the other hand... When I was going to marry Theo, I had resigned myself to a life of having no voice. I didn't expect that here."

Evander ran a hand through his hair, sighing. "I hear what you're saying, but have you considered that this has nothing to do with the fact that you're a woman, and everything to do with the fact that you have exactly no experience with any of this?"

I bristled. "Are you going to make another tiara comment now?"

"No. I...shouldn't have said that." It didn't escape my notice that he didn't actually take it back or say it wasn't true. "But I will say that I didn't speak at my first council meeting. Storms, I didn't speak at my first ten council meetings. I *listened*."

"And that's what I was doing, too, until--" I tugged at my curls, taking a breath to ease my temper. "You say you want to start as we plan to go on, then you're upset because I dare to have an opinion."

He released a frustrated breath. "It was not your having an opinion that was upsetting, Lemmikki. It was the manner in which you chose to express it."

"And if I had waited, your judgment would have already been passed," I said. "So my options are..."

He searched my features, though for what, I wasn't sure.

"Is it so difficult to fathom that while you are learning about Bear, in the meantime, you might simply...trust my judgment?" There was more in his expression than frustration now, enough that instead of shooting back a response, I took a small step back.

"I know that today, with the...flogging." Why was that word still so hard for me to say? "I realize that you were being lenient. So yes, I should have trusted you."

He took a sip of his drink, swallowing it slowly like he was weighing his next words carefully.

"And what if I hadn't been?" His gaze bored into mine.

"If you hadn't been right?" I clarified.

"If I hadn't been lenient," he responded. "That is not always a luxury I have, Lemmikki. In fact, it rarely is."

He wanted to know if I could trust his decisions, even when I didn't understand them. If I could trust *him*.

And it was clear that the answer mattered to him.

I thought about Evander, who he had always proven himself to be. I thought about what was at stake in his territory, the careful power plays he had to make, and the way he expertly maneuvered his way through them.

More than that, though, I thought about *my* history with him. And finally, I knew what to say.

"At the negotiations," I began slowly, "I wasn't going to make my counteroffer."

"What?" he asked sharply.

Even now that we were married, my heart beat faster in my chest with this admission. The exposure of it.

The guilt of it.

"After I found out what Iiro had done," I continued, trying for a matter-of-fact tone, "I was going to let the negotiations fizzle out, even though I knew it meant coming back to Bear. Because...because I felt safest with you."

His lips parted. "Then what changed your mind?"

"You said you were eager to get rid of me," I reminded him drily.

He raised his eyebrows. "After you called me a child murderer."

My cheeks warmed, but I remembered all too well what had precipitated that particular burst of fury. "After you said your life would have been easier if I had never come here."

Evander's brow furrowed, and I suspected he was putting the pieces together that I hardly liked to admit to myself. How deeply I had cared what he thought of me, and whether he wanted me around, long before I should have.

How much I had trusted myself with him above everyone else.

"If that's true, why were you so upset when we returned?" he asked quietly.

A disbelieving puff of air left my lips.

"Because you said it was a punishment keeping me around," I said somewhat forcefully. "And then I was here, where I knew you...didn't want me."

The truth of that statement hit me. I had lied so thoroughly to myself, even after I got back.

But Theo's breakup hadn't hit me half as hard as being at odds with Evander had. I wasn't sure I wanted to think about what that said for me or my fidelity, or whether it was just like Theo had said...that Evander and I were always inevitable.

Evander's eyes widened, but he didn't respond.

"Anyway--" I cleared my throat. "The point is that I do trust you. I always have. Today was just..."

"Not entirely your fault," he cut in. "I should have prepared you better, especially for that."

That had been, frankly, more than I expected him to give.

"Well, in fairness, you did expect me to have, what was it you said, basic common sense?" I gave him a small smirk.

"Another error on my part," he said sardonically, his own lips tilting up. "And Lemmikki?" He waited until I met his eyes again to go on.

"Make no mistake about it, it *was* a punishment keeping you around." I went still, and he leaned forward, tucking a stray curl behind my ear. "It was a punishment when I knew you could never really be mine."

I rearranged my memories of that day with his words in mind, realizing that they soothed some of the old wounds I hardly let myself acknowledge.

"Another error on your part," I said quietly, purposefully leaning closer to him.

His gaze dropped to my neck, then roamed lower, to my corset laces. I set my drink down, preparing to cross the small distance to him.

Before I could make the move to climb into his lap, his hands darted out to my waist, and he pulled me on top of him. Using his teeth, he tugged at my laces until they came completely undone.

A soft groan escaped his lips as he pressed them against the newly exposed skin. The warmth of his mouth contrasted with the cool air of the room, and I sucked in a sharp breath.

I wondered if I would ever get used to his reaction to me, or mine to him, for that matter. It didn't seem likely.

Especially not when he slid his tongue up to my neck, taking time to trace the outline of the mark he had left earlier, before continuing up to the delicate skin of my ear. There was ownership in everything he did, but I couldn't blame him, not when I felt it, too.

I expected him to move us to the bed. Instead, all he did was lift me up with one strong arm while he used the other to rid us of any fabric that was between us.

Being over him on this chair put my face level with his for a change, if not a little higher. Evander seemed to be singularly enjoying this fact, taking advantage of his easy ability to move his lips between my face and my exposed curves.

Wrapping his free hand in my hair, he tugged my head backward to give himself better access, and I had a split second to reflect that fighting wasn't so bad if this was how we made up.

Then he shifted me closer to him, and I lost my ability to think at all.

To breathe.

To speak.

All I knew was that we had come a long way, because it wouldn't have mattered if we knocked his glass from the table next to us. If the whole stars-damned bottle fell over. If it shattered into a thousand pieces as I was sure to do at any moment.

There really wasn't anything I would have let stop me from being with Evander now.

CHAPTER TWENTY-ONE

ROWAN

The next few days were back to whatever semblance of normal we had created.

As Mila predicted, Lady Katerina did gradually warm up to me. And I had the immense relief that no more *warnings* had been required from Evander, at least so far.

More ladies of the court were ordering dresses like mine and Mila's, so I stood out less and less as being *other*, although my hair would always mark me as Lochlannian.

Every morning, I sparred with the men and they, too, became accustomed to me. Ava and Aleksander were conspicuously absent, but I learned from Mila and the whispers around court that there was nothing unusual about that.

Still, it gave me the oppressive feeling of waiting for the other shoe to drop.

Sure enough, I was lying in bed with Boris, nursing a particularly bad set of moontime pains when Evander came in wearing an expression a shade too neutral to be a good thing.

"What?" I asked, not bothering to hide the whine in my tone.

He surveyed me before answering. "Our presence is required at an estate dinner tonight."

That could only mean… "Required by your father?"

He nodded.

"Wonderful," I muttered, thinking of how very unappealing the idea of squashing my abdomen into a corset sounded.

As it was, I was wearing one of Evander's shirts instead of my own more-fitted nightclothes. Briefly, I considered whether there was a way out of this, but my husband's face was enough to tell me there was not.

"How did you get away with missing so many estate dinners and council meetings and, well, everything when I was here before?" I asked.

Evander smirked. "I told everyone I was...preoccupied with my captive."

My jaw dropped. "You *aalio*."

He shrugged without a single shred of remorse. "I did what I had to do to keep you safe, Lemmikki. It was the most believable lie."

"Well, at least now I know where the rumors came from," I muttered.

"Yes, because no one would have said a word about you sleeping in my rooms and sharing a room at the inns with me otherwise," he replied wryly.

Fair point.

"Well, I suppose I can't be too upset since it wouldn't have been a lie if I had been given a say." I grinned at him wickedly, and heat entered his gaze.

But when he sank on the bed next to me and pressed his lips against mine, a sharp pain in my abdomen reminded me that we couldn't take this any further today.

Which was just great, considering we also had this wretched dinner to attend.

Evander noticed my uncharacteristic hesitation and pulled back, examining my face.

"Lemmikki?" he inquired.

"We...can't," I said irritably.

"Why not?" He looked more confused than unhappy.

"Because..." *I am an adult, and my cheeks will not redden.* "I actually do have pressing feminine needs at the moment."

Understanding dawned on his features, and he moved his

lips to my forehead instead. "I see. Well, at least we know the herbs are working."

He settled in next to me, and I leaned into him, hissing through my teeth at the movement.

"Are you in pain, Lemmikki?" The concern in his voice was...frankly adorable.

"Nothing I can't handle," I assured him.

Still, his hand went to my abdomen. The pressure eased some of the discomfort, and I sighed in relief, snuggling farther into him.

Then his other comment resonated with me, and I realized there was something we should probably talk about sooner rather than later, in the event that the herbs did not work.

"You realize that...if we decide to stop using the herbs, or they don't work…" Again, I forced a blush from my cheeks. "Any children of ours will have my blood."

A beat of silence passed before he responded. "I am aware that's how these things work."

"My fae blood, I mean," I said, my tone laced with exasperation. "And we don't know how that manifests. Avani, when she was younger…it was difficult to hide the way the animals would all kind of flock to her. On the other hand, the twins had no trouble hiding their communication. But there would be some level of danger."

Evander moved his thumb in small, comforting circles on my stomach, taking a moment before he responded.

"Well," he said cautiously, "we've never shied away from a challenge before. As long as we wait until things are in order here, I'm sure it's nothing we can't handle."

My shoulders eased in relief. I hadn't realized how much I worried that would be a deterrent for him...or how badly I wanted children with him one day, until I heard him confirm it.

As always, he weighed my reaction carefully. He took a deep breath before he responded to it, though.

"I won't pretend to know anything about having a real family, Lemmikki, but never doubt that I want that with you, in whatever capacity you are willing." He pressed his lips against my hair. "If you wanted our family to stay a family of two, that would be all right. But if you want to be like your parents and have a whole brood, we can do that, too."

His rare sincerity sent warmth blooming through every part of me.

I laughed softly. "Let's just start with one, once things calm down. Or two," I amended. "Since twins run in the family."

"Storms help us all if we have two of you." He chuckled.

I elbowed him playfully. "Oh, but two of *you* would be a picnic?"

As soon as I said it, I couldn't help but picture it.

Two gorgeous dark-haired boys with his light-brown skin and my pale green eyes, both smirking mischievously. It filled me with a curious mix of excitement and dread, because I wasn't sure I had ever wanted anything as much as I wanted this life with Evander.

But I couldn't shake the ever-present tingling in my spine, the constant feeling that something was waiting to take this away from me. I wasn't sure if it was residual apprehension over what happened with Avani and Mac...but it felt like something more.

It felt like something was coming that we wouldn't be able to stop.

CHAPTER TWENTY-TWO

ROWAN

I chose another black dress for dinner, this one crushed velvet with full skirts and long, fitted sleeves. The bodice buttoned all the way down in the front. It was a combination of the traditional Socairan style and my more comfortable gowns, allowing for easy movement but still on the formal side.

Instead of a tiara, I wore a black silk headband over my braided updo, courtesy of Taisiya.

"Will I do?" I asked Evander.

The question was cheeky, but his features remained tight.

"You look perfect," he said shortly.

"Why do I feel like there's a *but* coming?" I asked.

"Just remember that tonight is about the show." He sighed. "My father is still dangerous. He may not be able to kill a Clan Wife, but that doesn't mean he can't find ways to be...problematic, and we certainly can't rely on his sanity or rationality most days."

It was the first time Evander had outright spoken of his father's illness.

"Has he always been this way?" I asked cautiously, remembering his reaction the last time I brought up his father.

"A bastard?" Evander returned darkly.

He had not taken well to my recounting of my conversation with the duke at our wedding.

I leveled a look at him.

Evander sighed again. "His mind started going several years ago, around the time I joined the military."

"When you were fourteen?" I clarified.

He nodded.

"So, you've been more or less leading Bear since…"

"It got unmanageable around the time I turned seventeen." His eyes churned. "The things he would order...and the soldiers had no choice. So I started to find ways to intercept him, and eventually, to replace him. He allows it, because even on his worst days, he seems to recall his pride."

For six years, since before he was even really an adult, Evander had been playing these games. Successfully, at that.

I leaned up on my toes to kiss him. "You really are incredible."

His eyes widened before his mask took over once more. "Just remember that at dinner tonight."

On that ominous note, he ushered us out the door.

Evander's directive was not in vain.

We sat at a table with only Ava and Aleksander, at the forefront of the vast dining hall. Mila shot me a sympathetic look from her spot next to Taras at a table that looked at least marginally more fun than ours.

Then again, wrestling a rabid mountain lion would have been more fun than sitting at our table.

Tonight was not one of the duke's lucid nights.

"My dear," he greeted as I approached the table.

He gestured to the chair next to him, then blinked in confusion when it was already occupied by Ava, who looked at me with nothing but hatred in her soulless eyes.

Aleksander shook his head, looking at Evander. "Konstantin. Have you met my new bride?"

Once again, he gestured toward me. Evander blinked once, then twice, looking between Ava and me.

"I have not," he said at last, inclining his head to me.

I understood why he didn't argue. The healers had told us with Grandmother Bridget that it was better, usually, to let their mind rest wherever it took them.

Taking Evander's lead, I nodded back.

The duke sat down, ignoring me after that. For the first time, I was grateful for the Socairan outlook on women, as it allowed me to eat in silence. Though, it didn't stop me from hearing Aleksander's stream of increasingly vicious war plans.

Konstantin must have been the brother he had lost in the tunnels...the one my father had killed, if he was mistaking Evander for him.

"So you'll lead the forces through the tunnel with the second wave, after I've taken care of the H'Rians. Mairi has told me the best way in through the gates." He nodded at me, and my gaze went sharply to Ava.

She had a small, victorious smirk playing on her lips, like the memory amused her.

Evander pressed his leg against mine, and I carefully speared a piece of my beet salad with my knife, as Mila had shown me, forcing myself to ignore the conversation.

Then, thank the stars, the duke fell silent. His eyes went distant, and we made it all the way to the soup without further unpleasantries.

It was creamy, full of potatoes and mushrooms. I was actually doing a phenomenal job of losing myself in the first not-disgusting soup I had eaten in Socair, when Aleksander spoke again.

"I see you've brought the Lochlannian whore at last," he said, eyeing me critically.

Your wife has been here all along, I very deliberately did not let myself say.

"I brought my new wife to dinner, as you requested." Evander's entire body was ostensibly at ease, his usual arrogant smirk gracing his lips.

But his jaw gave a telltale twitch, a single sign of his fury.

Aleksander sighed, like Evander was being a difficult child. "I was concerned when you practically begged me to keep her as your pet that you might develop an attachment to her."

"Begging, Evander? Again?" Ava shot him a cruel smile, brushing a strand of her pale white hair behind her ear.

My heartbeat roared in my ears, rage parting my lips.

Slowly, I turned my head to look at her, wishing that my fae blood had given me the ability to set fire to someone with my stare instead of sensing the weather. It wasn't hard to figure out that she was referring to the many, many times she had abused him.

She was too busy looking for Evander's reaction to notice mine, though.

"Your mother was like that." Aleksander spoke with a curious mix of affection and disparagement. "Always taking in strays."

"You know I take more after you, Father," Evander said smoothly. "Though, you always did tell me Lochlannian women were good for a passing diversion."

He nudged his leg against mine under the table in apology, and I resisted the urge to kick him. I would show him a *passing damned diversion* later. It was almost worth his remark, seeing Ava's face go flat with rage.

Still, I knew what he was doing, and I didn't blame him for it. Much.

It seemed to work, in any event. Aleksander gave him a nod as if to say, *good man*, and the entire issue was forgotten.

For now.

CHAPTER TWENTY-THREE

ROWAN

When the main course of dinner came around, I found myself suppressing more than a few gags at the gelatinous pile of goo on my plate. Arranged in a small, wreath-like design was some sort of jelly-coated meat that smelled like the vat of grease the cooks kept for baking.

Sprigs of herbs were artfully placed around the circle, along with roasted potatoes and carrots, as if that would detract from the awfulness of the slimy mass or make it more appealing.

As everyone else dug into their cold, grease-coated meats, I found myself longing for the simpler days where I thought borscht was the worst thing I had ever been forced to eat.

I was a child then…young, naïve, and unaware of the other Socairan horrors that awaited me.

Evander seemed to be enjoying his meal as well as everyone else.

Even Mila and Taras were happily eating away at their table like some sort of masochistic monsters who probably would have loved the disgusting fish stew I had choked down.

A shiver ran through me as I moved my shaking hands toward my fork and knife, holding them the way everyone else did. I slid the knife through the goop, gagging as the jelly moved around the solid pieces of meat.

Then, I promptly chickened out and took a bite of roasted

potatoes instead. At least they were warm and well-seasoned, salty and delicious. I eyed the jelly again, sneering at the way it wobbled like leftover stew that had sat out for too long and congealed.

"Lemmikki," Evander all but whispered beside me. "Is there a problem? Kholodets is traditional Socairan food. Everyone here loves it."

That last part was said pointedly, his subtle way of letting me know that my face was giving me away...and was offensive.

I felt the duke's eyes on me, assessing and cold. And his weren't the only ones. This was our first court dinner together, and I couldn't afford to make mistakes.

"Then everyone here clearly hates themselves," I mumbled back, and he chuckled under his breath.

But I did fix my face.

"Try eating them together next time," he said quietly. "That may help."

Again, his words were carefully directed to remind me that *not* eating this was not an option. Even were there not food shortages, Mila had informed me that it was a longstanding rule of etiquette to finish your plate in Socair, one they had always taken seriously.

Remembering the way Evander had choked down every last bite of puddings and pies and cakes in Lochlann, despite having an aversion to desserts, I gave a determined nod.

Once again, I faced the nemesis on my plate.

This time, I sandwiched a bit of the gelatinous monstrosity in between a potato and carrot. I held my breath, shoveling it into my mouth before I could think too hard about it.

The first flavor that spread across my tongue was of the warm, delicious potatoes, followed by the sweet and savory taste of the carrots. But then... there was nothing but jellied meat.

Perhaps holding my breath had helped, because there was only the faintest memory of beef-flavor that lingered in the fat, but overall, it was as atrocious as I had imagined.

And cutting back on my sense of smell did nothing for the texture.

Cold and slippery, like the lard we used for baking and cooking back home, only firmer and more…jiggly.

My corset was already too tight, my stomach unsettled from my moontime cramps, and this…this was going to do me in.

Again, I felt the weight of stares around the table, and Evander's subtle pressure on my leg.

Was I turning green?

Was my gag audible this time?

I swallowed back the bite, chasing it down with a good bit of wine. Then I looked with renewed horror at the entire ring still left on my plate, save the one tiny bite I had taken.

It quivered like it was alive and taunting me.

Still, I knew I had no choice but to keep going, and I would… at least try several more bites before hiding the rest in my napkin.

I steadfastly continued the same sandwiching method until my potatoes and carrots were gone, but there was still half of the ring left. My eyes watered from the effort of not forcibly reuniting the first half of the wreath with what was left on my plate.

Fortunately, Evander took his very last bite of meat at that exact moment.

Waiting until Aleksander and Ava were focused on one another, he discreetly exchanged our plates. His had no more than a few carrots left on it, and a sigh of relief escaped me.

I nudged his leg beneath the table in thanks.

"You did well," he said under his breath.

It occurred to me that he was lying, but a quick glance around the room seemed to back up his praise.

No one was looking in my direction with any more malice than usual. In fact, when they spotted my empty plate, they almost seemed impressed. Apparently, it was expected for the Lochlannian princess to be too spoiled to finish her food.

Which made me feel somewhat ashamed of myself, as it had proven to be true. But not ashamed enough to make me wish I had eaten any more.

As it was, only polishing off a second glass of wine allowed my stomach to settle into something resembling calm.

I was beyond grateful when we were finally excused from dinner. At least, until Aleksander requested that Evander stay behind.

Not wanting to infuriate the duke by hesitating, I only nodded, heading toward the hallway. Kirill was at my side in seconds from wherever he had been in the dining hall.

Unfortunately, he wasn't the only one. I had no sooner emerged in the hallway than Ava's spider-like hand sank into my arm.

"I'd like a word with my new...daughter-in-law," she said, not looking away from my face.

"Lord Stenvall has ordered me to stay with Lady Stenvall," Kirill said respectfully, though a rare undercurrent of disdain dripped from his voice.

She looked sharply at him. "And the duke has ordered me to have a private word with her."

It was a lie, but not one he could reasonably call her on.

"Of course," I said quickly, before he could get himself into trouble.

"I'll just be down the hall, then," he told me, turning to go.

Ava glared at me, hatred twisting the aging lines of her face. "If you think you can manipulate my husband into--"

"I think we both know the only manipulative one here is you," I interrupted her.

She opened her mouth to respond, but all I could hear was her taunting Evander. My heartbeat thundered in my veins, my fists clenching with the kind of rage I only seemed to know when it came to this single despicable woman.

I cut her off again.

"All this time," I said quietly, "you've been so worried about my family in Lochlann. But they're on the other side of the mountain." I met her eyes solidly. "And I'm here."

Uncertainty flashed in her gaze.

"You know that Clan Wives are untouchable," she said.

"Are they?" I shrugged, a cold smile creeping across my lips. "I'm so new here, I'm always forgetting custom."

"You'd be killed," she spat. "Or worse."

I took a step closer to her, my voice filled with the kind of lethal quiet I usually only heard from Evander. "But you would be just as dead."

She clenched her jaw, but I saw fear trembling through her as well. She was used to dealing with Evander, who had grown up surrounded by Clan Wife laws and had to worry about protecting his entire clan.

But here, I only had to worry about Evander.

I let her see every bit of truth in my eyes, in the fact that I would find a way to kill her one day.

She adjusted her skirts with false bravado. "All I have to do is open my mouth to have every soldier in this estate come running."

"I was trained by my father, *Mairi.* You wouldn't even last until they got here." I took another step forward, and this time, she took a step back. "Remember that, the next time you even think about *my* husband. Don't look at him. Don't speak to him. As far as you're concerned, from this point forward, Evander doesn't exist."

Maybe it was stupid to threaten her, but I didn't think so. At her core, Ava was a coward. She wasn't a fighter, not physically or otherwise.

But I was.

CHAPTER TWENTY-FOUR

EVANDER

"You insult the men by allowing her to spar with them," my father said the second Rowan stepped away.

Samu must have gone tattling. Fortunately, lying to my father or twisting the truth to stay his hand was as easy as breathing these days.

I gave a long-suffering sigh. "There are only a handful of ways to keep her mouth shut, Father, and fewer still that are appropriate for public places. The men will get over it if the heir to their Dukedom decrees it."

A misdirect on Rowan, and a play at his pride. My stomach twisted at the necessary lie, but I would rather him think I hold no respect for my wife than that she poses a threat to him.

He gave a dark chuckle, just as I knew he would. "Very well. I'll tell Samu it's with my approval. Have you made any headway?"

He meant on my plan to destroy the Lochlannians from the inside out.

A plan that began and ended with Rowan, as far as he was concerned.

I made up a few things until his mind trailed off again, which fortunately, didn't take long. Then I left him in his semi-lucid state, celebrating with a glass of chilled vodka as he congratulated himself on the success of his son.

A bitter taste filled my mouth as I headed out to the hall where Kirill was standing. His usually easy expression was pinched in concern.

"What's wrong?" I asked, and he tilted his head toward the intersecting hall.

Before I could take another step, Ava's gray-headed figure angrily rounded the corner, giving both of us a wide berth.

For once, she didn't stop to make some scathing remark or a threat that she could no longer substantiate. I groaned internally, already suspecting what might have accounted for my stepmother's mood and her unusual silence.

Sure enough, standing in the other hall was my wife. With a look, I dismissed Kirill for the night. He gladly obliged, leaving me to face whatever had just happened with Rowan.

There was an icy calm on her face, a tight set to her shoulders that reminded me of the rare occasions when I had seen an unexpectedly ruthless side of her.

When she noticed me approaching, her light-green eyes snapped up to mine, and her expression turned just a hair too innocent.

"Lemmikki," I began. "Do you care to explain what happened?"

I didn't need to gesture to where Mairi--or Ava--had stormed off. Rowan's gaze followed the length of the hall anyway.

"Nothing much," she claimed. "We were merely discussing the many Socairan delicacies I have yet to be subjected to."

I shot her a disbelieving look, sighing. "Didn't we discuss not provoking violent sociopaths for the time being?"

Rowan shrugged one slim shoulder, giving me a sideways glance. "I feel like an explanation is an awful lot to ask from a...what was it you said? A passing diversion?"

Storms. I knew I would pay for that one. At least she hadn't heard what I said to my father after she left.

I opened my mouth to explain when she shook her head, a wry smile tugging at the corner of her lips.

"You really don't have to concern yourself with offending my delicate sensibilities every time we have to play this game," she said. "I know this situation is...tenuous enough to navigate."

Unexpected relief coursed through me. I hadn't realized how much I needed her to understand that until she did.

Then a trace of mischief entered her gaze. "Besides, it's only fair since I told the entire Lochlannian Court I was only using you for your very capable hands."

Amusement and desire warred in my mind until the latter won out, my mind wandering to the way her body felt in my apparently *very capable* hands. It must have shown on my face, because her smirk turned into something far more wicked, and she let out a low laugh to accompany it.

For all that I had told her it would be frowned upon to be openly affectionate, I couldn't look away from her in that moment. Her face. Her lips. Any of her.

I had meant what I told her in the cabin about marriage being an inevitability. It had always been assumed that someday, I would marry for the benefit of my clan...but I had never expected to find someone who was prepared for the challenges that being married to me presented.

Yet here she was.

All five feet of her, with her wildly intoxicating wit, her fierce, stubborn bravery, and her wonderfully clever mind, all wrapped in this gorgeous shell that was uniquely *Rowan.*

I settled my hand on her lower back as we made our way up the stairs, satisfaction coursing through me when she shivered at the contact.

Not for the first time, I realized I had done nothing in my life to deserve her, and that nothing I could ever do would change that fact.

And I didn't care.

Because every part of her belonged to me.

Just as I belonged to her.

CHAPTER TWENTY-FIVE

ROWAN

The next morning, we were in the sparring ring.

We were alone this time since the soldiers were doing outdoor training today. Evander was teaching me to fight the way he did, with both swords.

Fia had always stressed the importance of being adept with either hand, but my left was still significantly weaker. It was an effort to engage both at the same time.

I cursed in frustration as his blunted blade tapped against my side.

"It takes time, Lemmikki," he said, a bit of amusement coloring his tone. "With one blade, you can rival at least half of my men. This will only enhance that."

I glanced up at him in surprise. "Do you mean that?"

He nodded.

"Remember that the Unclanned were all soldiers at one point, and you've taken down your share of them." Evander peered down at me curiously. "Why did you think I gave you a sword at all after we sparred the first time?"

"Well, in fairness," I countered, "all you said back then was, *watch your footwork* and *you're dropping your elbow.*"

He shrugged, managing to make even that look graceful and masculine.

"Both of which were true. I wanted you to be as prepared as

you could be," he said seriously. Then, a smirk graced his lips. "And that delightful blush you get when you're angry might have been a welcome bonus."

He trailed a finger from my chest, which was slick with a sheen of sweat, up to my cheeks. I glared at him, irritation making that very thing happen. Well, it was at least partially due to irritation, anyway.

"That's the one," he remarked. Backing away, his features turned serious once more. "You have definitely honed your skill since your time in Lochlann, though."

"Well, I had a lot of anger to work out," I muttered without thinking.

When he went deadly still, I wanted to take the words back. It came close to things we rarely referenced, the months we both thought we might never make it here.

"And now?" His tone was carefully neutral.

He was asking whether I still blamed him for that. It was a loaded question, because the simple answer was *no*. I was just happy we had gotten where we were now.

But there was a part of me that couldn't help but notice that he still didn't see anything wrong with the way he had made the decision that I needed space for both of us.

Since I didn't have a good answer, I thought about his question more literally. Between Ava and our upcoming meeting with Iiro, there was still plenty to be angry about.

"And now," I responded, picking up the sword I had dropped during our last match. "I'm sure our impending trip to the Obsidian Palace will give me sufficient rage to pull from."

And the fact that Iiro would find a way to starve our people when we got there.

Evander's face darkened. "Speaking of which, we leave at first light in three days."

"So soon?" I asked.

"We'll need to take a carriage, and we'll be staying with the lords and at Wolf Estate instead of in the inns, so...it will be slow going."

"Wonderful," I intoned. Then I opened my senses up, letting

myself feel the elements around me. "Although it will be cool enough that at least we shouldn't bake inside the carriage."

"I'm sure there are plenty of advantages to being shut up in a carriage, with the curtains drawn..." He let that thought dangle in the air, then went on the attack without warning.

"*Aalio*," I muttered, dancing out of the way.

"Good." He nodded.

And though I told myself I didn't care about that small sign of approval, the reality was that Evander was grace and speed and power in motion. On top of that, he was an obnoxiously good teacher, his watchful eyes constantly assessing and correcting.

We had sparred nearly every day since my arrival, and I had come further in those three weeks than the two months I had been training constantly in Lochlann.

"I want you to wear a sword while we're on the road." He interrupted my thoughts, not remotely out of breath from the exertion.

My eyebrows rose as I deflected one of his blows automatically with my right hand. He came in from the left, easily landing a hit, and I scowled.

"You distracted me on purpose," I accused.

"Deflecting an attack on that side with your left sword needs to be your instinct, not something you think about. Again."

We started again, and he waited a few moments before speaking. "I wasn't just distracting you, though. There are more Unclanned gathering now that Iiro has driven away the bands near the Obsidian Palace, so we need to be careful."

He attacked again, and I deflected from the correct side this time, eliciting another nod.

"How will the lords take me being armed?" I asked, going on the offensive.

His features went cold. "Like their future duke told them to get over it."

Evander countered my strikes with a frustrating ease. "Politics is one thing, Lemmikki, but I won't play games with your safety. I'm sure Iiro won't allow you to carry a weapon in his palace, and Sir Nils will probably take issue, but on the road and while we're in Bear, there's no reason for you to go unarmed."

With that settled, he launched into a true attack. There was something incredibly alluring about the way he held back less and less, always testing the furthest bounds of my capabilities.

It was easy to feel like we could accomplish anything together.

But remembering Iiro, and the Obsidian Throne, and that cursed damned box, I couldn't help but feel like that belief was the most dangerous of them all.

CHAPTER TWENTY-SIX

ROWAN

We awoke to a pounding on the door.

Evander flew out of bed, wrapping his plush black robe over his bare skin before going to answer. Taras' voice carried through the room, his tone edged with frustration.

I stumbled out of bed and threw on my own robe before rushing over to them. Taras' features were tight, and his entire body was wrought with tension.

Evander felt it too. That muscle in his jaw twitched and his hands were clenched into fists at his side.

"What happened?" I stepped up beside him, placing a hand on his arm.

Taras looked at his feet, exhaling slowly.

"A soldier defied my father's orders," Evander said, his voice devoid of any emotion.

He nodded his head toward the door, and Taras spun on his heel and left. Evander ran a hand over his face before turning toward me.

"I need to go take care of this," he said. "There will be a sentencing later this morning. You will need to be there."

His tone was laced with defeat.

"Of course." I tried to reassure him, though snippets of the last council meeting came back to mind.

Evander hesitated, not quite meeting my eyes. "You should know, the punishment is carried out at the time of sentencing."

Flogging.

Would I be able to stand there and watch it happen? Would Evander be the one to deliver the blows?

Meeting his churning gray eyes, I knew I didn't have a choice. He wouldn't have told me to come if it wasn't necessary.

"All right," I said quietly. "Thank you for warning me."

Evander nodded, his lips forming a tight line before he pressed a kiss to my forehead. He turned, walking over to the closet. Within moments, he was dressed and striding out the door to meet Taras.

It was still early. The sky was dark and full of stars, but I was wide awake. I climbed up into the window seat behind our bed and stared at the mountains, my mind drifting over them to my family in Lochlann.

Had Avani already been forced to make the kinds of decisions that Evander did, and I had only, as he said, been too preoccupied picking out my next tiara to notice?

A selfish part of me missed that now, but another part rose to the challenge.

Little by little, we were changing things, and someday, I was determined that Evander wouldn't have to face these things alone.

Kirill led me to where Evander was waiting. If I hadn't known already that this would be a somber affair, the uncharacteristically grim line of Kirill's mouth would have told me.

He left me with Evander just outside of the Great Hall, where everyone was already waiting on the other side of the massive oak doors.

Tension rolled off of my husband, practically choking the air in the small space, but his face was impassive, as usual. I linked my arm in his, squeezing his bicep in a small show of support.

He rubbed a hand over mine, though his features didn't twitch.

When the doors opened, I put my own mask of steely resolve in place, doing my best to keep any emotion at bay.

In spite of the warmer temperatures of the day, heat poured through the doors from the roaring hearth at the far end of the room.

Rows of soldiers in black and white were lined up along the walls, along with a woman who was sobbing and cradling her swollen belly. Each of them faced a tall, broad man standing in the center.

His wrists and ankles were bound together by shackles and a chain as he stoically faced the massive throne-like chair at the head of the room.

Evander moved forward to take his seat near the fireplace.

I took my place next to him, as he had instructed me, standing on one side while Taras stood on the other. I wasn't the only woman here, either. Though Ava was absent as usual, Mila and a few of the other ladies stood around the edge of the room.

My friend met my eyes, something between sadness and caution in her own. And already, I knew that whatever was happening would be even worse than I had anticipated.

When one of the soldiers stepped forward, it was an effort not to scowl.

Samu.

"Speak," Evander said in an icy tone.

Samu dipped his head before launching into the crimes the man was guilty of. "...namely, treason against the duke himself while out on assignment."

"What were the orders?" Evander asked.

The soldier in question winced, the movement nearly imperceptible, and the crying woman in the corner began sobbing even harder.

"To rid the village of Boldegu of any remaining rebels-- regardless of their age," Samu answered flatly.

Remaining rebels...

I thought back to what the duke had ordered that day in his rooms.

Were there truly rebels there? Or had he made the order when his mind was living in the past, like he had when he accused me of being a spy?

Then the last thing Samu said struck me.

Regardless of their age.

The horror of it washed over me, and I wanted to be sick.

Long before I knew anything about Bear or Evander, Mila had mentioned the rumors. The slaying of women and children.

I thought of the question I had hurled at Evander... *Murder any children lately?*

I forced myself not to flinch at the words and the haunted look in his expression when I had said it. The dark reminder that this was something that Evander and his soldiers would actually be forced to do. Had been forced to do.

That they would have been punished for if they disobeyed.

What was it that Mila had said? Lashes were standard, but it could also be worse. Unclanning.

Yet, this soldier had refused.

Was it worth it, I wondered, when his family would pay the price?

That choice wasn't a luxury Evander had ever been given, not when he was the only buffer between his sadistic father and the people of Bear.

"Were there any witnesses?" Evander asked coolly, and Samu nodded.

"I witnessed his disobedience myself, along with several other soldiers in his regiment."

My husband's knuckles went white around the armrests of his chair for a fraction of a second, and his jaw clenched. Still, he kept his impassive eyes fixed straight ahead.

"How do you plead?" he finally asked in that same empty tone.

The man swallowed hard before looking up to meet Evander's gaze.

"Guilty," he said, his voice breaking slightly.

Evander sat still as a statue, his features too neutral when he spoke again.

"You understand the punishment for directly defying the orders of your duke?"

The man squeezed his eyes shut against the cries of protest coming from the woman I assumed was his wife, before giving one solid dip of his head.

Evander returned the gesture, sitting up straighter in his chair.

My eyes drifted over to the roaring hearth and the soldier there holding an iron rod over the flames as Evander's voice filled the room once again.

"The sentencing is as follows: Vasily Lenkov, you are hereby stripped of your title, your estate, and your affiliation with Clan Bear. You will live out the rest of your days *Unclanned.*"

He rose from his chair and walked toward the flames, slipping his hand into a thick glove before grabbing the iron rod. The muscles in my stomach clenched, and I sucked in a breath.

He turned back to the soldier with that same cool, unaffected mask he always wore, but I saw the strain in his gray eyes. The slight flare of his nostrils and the stiff set of his shoulders that belied the calm way he spoke.

"Your household can choose to follow you," Evander continued in a cold voice. "Or depend upon the hospitality of relatives, but they are no longer welcome at your estate and will be stripped of their titles and belongings as well. Do you understand this sentencing as it has been laid out before you?"

The man nodded again, and something inside of me broke at his calm acceptance.

Evander gestured toward Vasily's wife, and two soldiers stepped forward to restrain her. My eyes snapped back to my husband. He was now standing in front of the soldier, who had sunk to his knees.

With no outward sign of hesitation, Evander raised the brand and pressed it to the man's forehead.

A sizzling sound filled the air before cries of pain followed.

Bile crept up my throat, and I swallowed back the nausea assaulting me.

Theo had once described Unclanning as a fate worse than death. If the branding wasn't enough, the entire family was also affected--shamed or shunned--no matter their role in the action.

The soldier's wife was pregnant.

Did they have more children at home? Did their parents live there, too? Who all would suffer because of his disobedience?

I forced my hand back to my side, straightening my back and steeling my features.

Evander turned around without another word. He handed the iron brand to the soldier by the fire once again before facing me.

He took several steps closer, closing the gap between us, and my mind filled with images of his face from this morning. The defeat that had settled over him before he even left the room, the pained expression in his gaze as he kissed me goodbye.

Our eyes met in a silent conversation, a thousand questions filling the space between us in those two heart-stopping seconds.

Would I forgive him for this? Would I understand? Would I accept this?

The cries of the woman grew louder as she ran over to her husband, throwing her arms around his neck. Tears stung at the back of my eyes as I looked away, keeping my face a mask of neutrality.

Then I linked my arm in my husband's, giving it a small, reassuring squeeze just as I had done on the way into the room. Again, his hand came to cover mine, his fingers squeezing mine this time.

Every fiber of my being felt hollowed out, but I could feel that same emptiness emanating from Evander as we left the Great Hall.

I knew there was no part of him that wanted to do this. I knew that he hated himself in this moment.

And I would not make this worse for him.

CHAPTER TWENTY-SEVEN

EVANDER

The woman's screams echoed in my head the rest of the day. Her husband's, too, for that matter.

I got through the motions of training with my men and finishing up business around the estate before it was time to head back to my and Rowan's rooms. When I reached our door, I paused for a moment, bracing myself to face her again.

She might have stood publicly by my side earlier, but she had also watched me exile and brand a man for the egregious crime of refusing to murder children. I wasn't sure how I felt about his choice.

The children had died anyway, and his family had paid for his conscience.

But part of me was almost jealous, in spite of the branding and the pain and the life I knew he would have to live now, because it was a stand I had never been able to take.

Who knew how many more innocents my father might harm if I weren't here to stay his hand? Even in Lochlann, I had worked constantly to subtly counteract his orders, though this one had obviously slipped through the cracks.

I supposed I could just add the screams from today to the rest of those that haunted me.

"Van?" Yuriy's voice cut into my thoughts.

Kirill must have gone home to his wife for the day.

I gave my cousin a tired look, and he returned it with one of understanding. We had all been forced to make decisions that ate away at our souls, even Yuriy, at only seventeen.

Nodding in return, I finally pushed open the door.

Rowan was sitting in the window seat near our bed, staring out at the mountains. Her crimson curls fell freely down her back, and she was wearing her black-and-white tartan night-clothes.

She turned when I entered, her green gaze assessing me. Wanting to talk about literally anything but what happened earlier, I gave her outfit a once over.

"Interesting dinner attire," I commented, though even I heard the hollow sound to my voice.

"I thought perhaps we could have dinner sent to our rooms?" Rowan mentioned in a neutral tone.

I raised my eyebrows. "As tempting as that sounds, we have--"

"Dinner with the lords," she finished, a ghost of a smirk on her lips. "Taras told me. He also said it wasn't completely neces-sary, so... I could ask him to convey our regrets. And we could relax here."

I opened my mouth to argue, then closed it. I didn't really need to have dinner with the lords tonight so much as I hadn't been prepared to face Rowan's judgment about the Unclanning.

But she didn't appear to have any.

"That...would be preferable," I admitted.

She nodded, then went to the door to tell Yuriy while I unbuttoned my coat. I hung my clothes up one by one, and Rowan shook her head.

"You know, you could just put them on the chair for now."

I looked over to where her dress from earlier was flung casu-ally over one of the sitting room chairs, her shoes kicked haphazardly next to them.

"Why does your *for now* always seem to stretch on into forev-er?" I asked, though I couldn't quite inject my usual amount of amusement into my voice.

She played along, but her subdued tone told me she read my

mood accurately. "You told me you wanted my clothes on your bedroom floor."

"That part didn't count, because we both knew I was lying." My lips tilted up at the corners, barely.

"But you said you would put up with it," she said in a singsong voice. Any lingering amusement vanished when she took in my features again. "You've been up for hours, Evander. Come lie down before dinner."

It never ceased to strike me, how well she could read me when so few people could. I *was* tired. For that matter, she looked like she could use a nap, too. Her skin was pale enough to make out bluish circles underneath her eyes.

So I obliged her, joining her in our enormous bed. Neither of us spoke for a moment, but she slid closer to me, putting a tentative hand in my hair.

"When I would have a bad day," she said quietly, running her fingers through the short strands. "My mother would always bring pastries, and then she would comb her hands through my curls, like this."

Back and forth, she wound her fingernails in different patterns on my head. It was oddly and unexpectedly comforting, a comfort I knew I didn't deserve today, but I couldn't bring myself to tell her to stop.

"I know how you feel about pastries, though." She gave a small smile, but it faded quickly.

Her fingers came down to my shoulders, running along my chest. I wasn't sure anyone had ever taken care of me like this.

I didn't remember my mother at all, and my father was hardly the nurturing kind. Ava...didn't bear thinking about. Taras' and Yuriy's mother was kind, but distant, even with them.

And today, of all days...

"Why today?" I couldn't help but ask her.

She leaned over, pressing her lips against one of the scars that crept around my shoulder before she answered.

"Because I know, even though you'll never say it, how hard that was for you."

"Not as hard as it was for Vasily," I muttered.

"Maybe not," she allowed. "But that doesn't change the effect it had on *you*."

I shook my head in bewilderment.

"What?" she asked.

"I suppose I should be grateful that you watched me brand a man today and you care in spite of that, but it's...surprising." To say the least.

"Is that what you think?" She lifted her head, her questioning gaze boring directly into mine. "That I love you in spite of what you had to do today?"

I stilled, not sure where she was going with this.

"Evander," she said earnestly. "I don't love you in spite of who you are or who you've had to be. I love you *because* of those things. I love you for the strength you have to make difficult decisions for the good of your people, even when it kills you. It's what makes you a good leader..."

She paused, discernment bleeding into her features. "Even if it doesn't feel that way on days like today."

I was stunned into silence.

I hadn't realized how badly I needed to hear her say that until she did.

All this time, some part of me had believed, especially since she got here, that she had fallen in love with the version of me at the cabin, or even in Lochlann, with the person I didn't have the luxury of being at the estate.

That she was...disappointed at the husband she wound up with, compared to the one she expected.

But once again, I had managed to underestimate her.

She pressed another kiss on my shoulder, against the scars that I rarely let anyone see, let alone touch, before she spoke again.

"I'm not going anywhere, even when things are difficult and complicated." Rowan moved then, lying next to me, her hand once again going to run through my hair. "We're in this together now, right?"

I brought my hand up to her face, tracing the outline of her rounded cheekbones to her pointed, stubborn chin. She kept saying we were in this together, but after a lifetime of handling things alone, I hadn't really let myself believe her.

I was starting to now.

"Yes." My voice came out a quiet rasp. "We're in this together."

"Promise me you'll remember that." Her face was close enough to mine that our breaths were mingling together, her eyes shining with rare sincerity instead of the cheeky mischief that was usually there.

And there was nothing I could have denied her in that moment.

"I promise," I told her.

More than anything, I wanted that to be true.

CHAPTER TWENTY-EIGHT

ROWAN

E vander had fallen asleep in my arms for a change last
night.

After dinner, he had lain next to me while I trailed
my fingers in soothing motions up and down his back, in his
hair until he finally drifted off.

But by the next morning, I awoke cocooned in his arms, the
way I always did. My head was on his muscular bicep, and his
other arm was around me in a protective iron grip, like he could
keep me safe from the many things that were trying to harm us
through the sheer force of his will.

And maybe he could, at that. Stars knew he was stubborn
enough for it.

When we finally got out of bed, it was a flurry of packing and
preparing to leave the next day. I was in my closet, adding a few
things to my trunk, when my eyes once again landed on the box.

Every time I drew near it, my spine tingled with the threat of
a particularly brutal storm. Awareness prickled all the way from
the base of my neck down to the small of my back, intensifying
as I picked up the wooden case.

Rayan had said I would know if I needed it, and though I
couldn't explain exactly why, that didn't feel true yet. But he had
also said to keep it close, so I carefully placed it among my
dresses in the spacious trunk.

Evander eyed me from the doorway of my closet, storms brewing in his silvery gaze.

"Just in case," I said quietly.

He nodded.

I could tell it was killing him not knowing what was in that box. He was a man who liked to plan for every eventuality, account for every resource, but he had thus far respected my decision.

The day passed quickly, and we had a goodbye dinner with Mila and Taras before heading to bed early.

I was in no way prepared to be dragged out of bed before dawn, but somehow, I managed to be functional all the way through getting dressed and walking to the carriage.

At which point, I promptly curled up with my head on Evander's lap.

"Wake me if we get attacked."

He chuckled softly, pulling his arm solidly over me to keep me from rolling off the bench.

At least we didn't have to share a carriage with Aleksander and Ava. The duke insisted on traveling separately so that both he and the heir weren't at risk at the same time, which I had to admit made sense.

But even if it hadn't, I would have been grateful for it. I wasn't sure I could refrain from stabbing either of them for an entire week in close quarters.

The first half of our journey was as uneventful as you could expect, considering we were likely walking into a trap and being forced to give up resources the people of Bear needed.

But, as Iiro's letter reminded us, it was a privilege to do so.

Bastard.

In between our brief stops at estates of the lords, the only other people we encountered were the *Besklanovvy*. Though we saw far more than we usually did while traveling, they gave us a wider berth than they had in the past.

That was only slightly confusing considering how Ava despised me and how she had used the Unclanned in an attempt to kill me more than once.

So why would she give up now?

Was she being more careful since she was traveling only a few carriages behind ours?

Did she not have sway over these particular bands? Or did she just have something else planned?

Evander's brow furrowed, and I didn't have to wonder for long if he was thinking the same thing.

"She has to be up to something," he muttered.

We passed another band of Unclanned, and my fists clenched around my skirts.

How many lives were lost in her failed attempts at killing me?

She had preyed on their basic needs and pitted them against one another, all because she was a coward who didn't care whether or not they lived or died.

I scanned the faces of each group we passed, looking for Vasily or his wife, wondering if they had decided to join up with one of the bands.

Would they fall prey to Ava's false promises? Would she have someone there to help her deliver the baby? Would they survive the harsh winter?

My stomach twisted with the weight of those questions, the churning realization that they were hardly the only people in those circumstances.

"Do you think she's given up on the Unclanned doing her bidding?" I wondered aloud. "Or is she just biding her time?"

Evander's answer came quickly enough that I knew he had considered it already. "She isn't bold enough to make a move herself, so I wouldn't count the Unclanned out yet. Regardless, we need to be on our guard at the palace. Ava is hardly our biggest concern at the moment."

"What *are* we going to do about Iiro?" I asked quietly. "And these taxes?"

"Arès and I are working on the problem in general, but as far as right now goes..." He ran a hand through his hair, looking out the window. "Honestly, Lemmikki…I don't know yet."

I knew what it had taken for him to admit that, and there was nothing else to be gained by discussing it to death, so I didn't push him. Instead, I leaned over and pressed a kiss along his jawline.

"How long did you say until we stop again?" My tone was deceptively casual, even as I dragged my lips across to his ear.

"At least a few—" His breath caught in his throat when my teeth grazed his skin. "—hours," he bit out.

"Well, I suppose that will have to do," I whispered cheekily, reaching across him to pull the curtains closed.

And it turned out this was another thing Evander had been right about. There *were* advantages to being trapped in a carriage with the curtains drawn.

On the fourth day, we arrived at Wolf Estate, where Sir Nils did a valiant job of pretending I didn't exist for the entire evening. Which was just as well, considering the things he tended to say when he did acknowledge my presence.

The rest of his family seemed to share the same bitter feelings about me and my people, so I spent the majority of my mealtime making sure that I went above and beyond to prove to them that I wasn't the Lochlannian barbarian that they thought I was.

Though, they were at least less hostile than before, which might have been due in part to the fact that their larders were fuller thanks to the supplies we had given them.

Still, it was almost a relief to leave the next morning, until I remembered where we were going and that Iiro was even worse than Nils.

To be fair, Iiro was worse than most people.

CHAPTER TWENTY-NINE

ROWAN

Pressure built in a steady incline along my spine over the next couple of days, intensifying as we drew closer to the Obsidian Palace. I couldn't shake the feeling that it was from far more than the impending windstorms that were rolling in.

Evander felt it too, growing quieter with each mile until I finally couldn't take it anymore and needed to break the tension.

Stars knew we would have enough stress to deal with once we were at the palace. We didn't need to be miserable the entire ride there.

It struck me just how little I knew about my husband, small things that were harder to observe in our day-to-day lives. We had never filled the silence with the kind of fluffy conversations that courting couples usually had, so I didn't bother to ease my way into it.

Instead, I just blurted out the first question that came to mind. "What's your favorite food?"

He cast a startled glance my way. When he saw that I was curious, his lips quirked in a considering way.

"Beef stew." Somehow, that wasn't surprising. "Yours?" he asked, almost hesitantly.

This was new to us both.

"Cranachan," I answered without delay.

He raised an eyebrow, and I went on to explain the parfait-like dessert with layers of sweet cream that H'Ria was known for, and whiskey-soaked, toasted oats and raspberries. Evander made a dubious face, eliciting a chuckle from me.

"Yes," I confirmed. "You would probably hate it nearly as much as I hated the meat goo."

"I confess," he said, wincing, "there was a moment I thought you might actually vomit at the table."

"There were several moments I thought so, as well," I assured him before moving on to my next question.

I should have taken a moment to think about it, but of course, that wasn't my way. So, what came out of my mouth was, "Were you really going to marry someone else in Lochlann if I had said no?"

His eyebrows shot up to his hairline. "That was quite the escalation from food."

I shrugged, like I had no regrets about asking, even as my insides churned.

"No, Lemmikki," he said plainly. "I just wanted to see how you reacted when you thought that was a possibility. If I'm being very, very honest, I wanted *you* to see how you reacted."

My lips parted in aggravation, but I thought back on that day. I had been keeping my composure reasonably well until he brought that up.

Reluctantly, I had to admit his tactic was sound, if an *aalio* one. Shaking my head, I opened my mouth to ask another question, but he held a hand up.

"No, it's my turn."

I closed my lips dramatically, gesturing for him to go on. He searched my features for long enough that I knew it wasn't going to be a lighthearted question.

"How long did it take you to stop hating me, after I took you?"

My mind raced back to our furious discussions when we danced, the way his eyes burned into mine. To his hands on my waist as he lifted me onto my horse, and the muscle that ticked in his jaw--the one I now knew meant he was biting back a laugh--when I mocked his men about eyeing my chemises.

I thought of how warmth had spread from his fingers to mine, as early as when he handed me that sword, the means to defend myself.

A small, residual, prideful part of myself wanted to lie, wanted to give him a date or an event or a moment. But this question mattered to me, and we had come so far from all of that.

"I never hated you," I admitted. "Even when I should have."

Evander studied my face, as though he was searching for the lie, so I let him see the truth blazing in my gaze. Slowly, his shoulders eased, and I wondered how long he had been carrying that around.

Though it should have been awkward, conversation continued more easily from there. We continued with our back-and-forth questions, some silly, some serious, until I sensed an oncoming windstorm and we called it an early night.

The next few days alternated between questions and comfortable silences, and other decidedly appealing ways to pass the time.

It was almost enough to forget what awaited us on the other side of this journey.

But not quite.

The final morning of our journey dawned windy and rainy, but it was nothing that delayed us. Unfortunately.

"Have you ever been to the palace?" I asked him once we were well underway.

He arched his brow, turning to face me from where he had been staring out the window.

"Once," he offered. "Though, I don't remember it. My father claims that he brought me there as an infant to be blessed by the king and queen."

I nodded, wondering how strange this must feel for him--for

all of Socair, really. To go without a monarch for two decades, only to have it seemingly resurrected overnight.

Would it be in shambles? Decayed from years of disuse? Knowing what I did about Iiro, I could hardly imagine that he would live in squalor for any amount of time. More likely that was the first thing he did.

"Nearly there, My Lord." Pavel's voice carried into the carriage, and I leaned away from Evander to peer out the window.

In the distance, imposing midnight spires stretched high into the air. It was different from the estate at Bear, though. The palace itself looked as if it was made from the same obsidian crystals that were in the hilt of Evander's swords.

The sunlight reflecting off of the stones cast an array of colors onto the ground and in the air around it. Brilliant shades of purple and green and blue cascaded in rippling, shining patterns onto the trees and manicured grasses that framed the courtyard and even to the large stone and iron gates that surrounded the entire thing.

This was the palace that half of Socair wanted left abandoned, and the other half was desperate to conquer.

"We need to keep on our guard," Evander said, his eyes fixated on the looming castle ahead of us. "Iiro is endlessly conniving."

He didn't have to add that having Aleksander with us would be another challenge all together. We both knew how ugly things could get if and when he lost his lucidity... Or hell, even when he retained it.

"Do you think this is about more than the food taxes?" I asked after a moment.

It wouldn't have surprised me that this was mostly for him to flex his newfound power over the dukes, just because he could.

Evander's expression was thoughtful, his brow furrowing before he answered. "I don't know yet."

It was several beats later that I asked the question I'd truly been concerned about.

"Do you think he knows what you've been planning?" I asked, my voice barely above a whisper.

Evander stiffened beside me, his eyes going distant as he considered it.

"Storms help us if he does," was all he replied

I slid my hand into his, intertwining our fingers and giving his a quick squeeze. He lifted our joined hands to his mouth, pressing a soft kiss to my knuckles just as the carriage came to a stop.

The loud groan of castle gates rang out all around us, easing open for us to pass. Within minutes, we were moving again, and that same feeling of dread sat low in my belly.

Were we walking into a trap? A war?

I couldn't shake the feeling that we were like sheep being herded for slaughter, especially when the castle gates slammed shut with a thundering roar, effectively locking us in at Iiro's mercy.

CHAPTER THIRTY

ROWAN

We were met at the castle doors with an excess of fanfare.

Rows of servants lined up, awaiting our arrival. As soon as our carriage came to a stop, they rushed to take our things to our assigned rooms without so much as a word of greeting.

The only person who did speak was the head servant who ushered us inside, directing any of the few words he addressed first to the duke, whose eyes were too distant, confusion coating his expression.

Evander spoke up to cover for his father, his face a mask of calm indifference. If the servant noticed anything amiss, he didn't comment on it.

Instead, he focused his attention on him from that point forward. And in spite of the way my arm was linked in Evander's, the servant was impressively skilled in the art of ignoring me.

He directed us toward the imperial doors to the palace, and we waited for Ava and Aleksander to enter first before following them.

My mouth nearly fell open at the sight that greeted us in the foyer.

As imposing and grand as the palace had been on the outside, the inside was even more so. Kirill let out a low whistle just behind us, while Henrick's and Pavel's jaws nearly hit the floor.

Luxury dripped from every corner, from the gold tasseled curtains to the jeweled eggs that sat in display cases, and the giant marble statues that stood like sentries all around the room.

Ornate tapestries hung over the expansive walls, interspersed with the castle banners, a silver horse on a deep purple background.

We followed a trail of lush fur rugs into the Great Hall, lit by crystal chandeliers that probably cost more than the entirety of Castle Chridhe. A massive oak table sat in the center of the room, laden with more food and drinks than the amount of people here accounted for.

You would never have guessed Socair was dealing with food shortages, given the way Iiro had set so much of it on display.

Kirill and the others weren't allowed into the room, and instead were directed down a different hall.

"They will dine with the other soldiers in the barracks," the man said, gesturing dismissively at the men.

"Are they expecting all of the clans?" I asked Evander in a hushed tone as we were led to our spot at the table.

Evander tensed beside me, his eyes roving over the excess of food as well before he shrugged.

"Knowing Iiro, probably not," he whispered before we took our seats. "Though, he's nearly halfway there with the four of us."

Theo dipped his head in greeting from across the table. Next to him were the Duke and Duchess of Viper. Galina sat across from him with her head low while her uncle, Sir Mikhail of Ram, spoke to her in low tones.

My heart sank a little, wondering whether they were once again trying to throw her at Theo, and how miserable it must be for her.

"Duke and Duchess," Inessa's father greeted, pulling my attention back to them. "Lord and Lady Stenvall," he added, looking at us.

A small shiver raked through me. Though his words were

clipped and suspicion lined his features, I wasn't sure I would ever grow tired of being called by Evander's name.

"Sir Andreyev, Lady Andreyev," I returned with a smile. "When did you arrive?" I asked.

Before he could answer, though, the large doors on the other side of the room groaned open.

Iiro stepped through them dressed in long brocaded robes much like the one that he had worn when I first met him, only these were the same deep shade of purple as the banners.

To top it off, he wore the massive crown that he had on at our wedding.

Inessa followed at his heels, wearing an extravagant crown as well, though she appeared to be uncomfortable with the weight of it.

"Welcome, Clan Bear," Iiro greeted us, a wide grin pasted to his mouth as he surveyed the room.

It was an effort not to snort at his choice in words, as if he hadn't threatened us to attend. Aleksander looked up from the table, his eyes still far away as he lived through a different moment in his history.

But as soon as they settled on Iiro, or more likely, his crown, his features stilled, and he dipped his head in respect.

"Your Majesty," he greeted with far more respect in his tone than I would ever have expected from a man like Evander's father.

The corner of Iiro's mouth tugged into a knowing smile.

"It's a pleasure to have you all here. I am sure your journey was tiring, so let us eat first," he said, gesturing at the piles of food on silver plates. "Business can wait until tomorrow."

There was nothing overtly threatening about the words, nothing that should have given me pause.

But the way Iiro glanced at Evander from the corner of his eye made me feel like someone was walking on my grave.

Or worse, my husband's.

CHAPTER THIRTY-ONE

ROWAN

The next morning, Evander woke up at his usual ridiculous hour. I groaned, dragging myself out of the plush bed as well. It wasn't as comfortable as ours, but it was still rather heavenly, especially after a week of travel.

"You may as well rest," Evander advised. "You know Iiro won't allow a woman in his council room."

In my time at Bear, I had managed to let myself forget how very uninvolved women were everywhere else in Socair.

"Stars, he's such an arsehat," I muttered, settling back into the deep purple covers. "Whatever shall I do with my day then?"

Evander shot me a glance that had me tensing in suspicion. "I believe there's a brunch this morning with the ladies."

"Ah. So while you're in the council room making actual decisions, I'll be enjoying brunch with Ava and Galina, who most certainly despises me?" I narrowed my eyes at him, a different sort of suspicion overtaking me. I had always assumed she didn't like me because of Theo, but... *"Der'mo,* Evander. Not her, too."

He chuckled, an infuriatingly arrogant sound, then crossed over to settle on the bed next to me.

"Have I told you how endearing I find this irrational jealousy, Lemmikki?"

"I like to consider it more of a completely rational territorialism." I peered up at him. "Also, that's not an answer."

He shook his head, leaning down to kiss me on the forehead. "No, not her. As I have told you several times now, my...encounters were few and far between, and not generally at court."

I wasn't sure whether or not I should be pleased by that admission, but at least I didn't have to worry about an added complication.

Evander left after that, and I ordered a bath, trying to prolong the inevitable. I took my time both in the tub and slowly drying my hair before I finally went to get dressed.

As always, I started with my underthings, then my weapon. Or, I would have.

My thigh sheath was right where I left it the night before, on the dresser next to the bed.

But the dagger was gone.

In fairness, Evander and I had been...rather spirited the night before. It certainly wouldn't be the first time we had knocked something off furniture. Just last week, I had lost my wedding ring for two days behind the side table.

I dropped to my knees with a sigh, looking under the bed. The wooden frame was massive, though, and it was impossible to see behind.

Cursing, I got to my feet. Since I couldn't very well tell anyone else I was missing the dagger I wasn't supposed to be wearing, I would have to wait until Evander got back to help me move the furniture.

And if he needed help, he could always claim it was his dagger, large bare breasts and all.

The thought made me smile, and it was almost enough to forget that I would be walking around Iiro's castle unarmed.

Unprotected.

Vulnerable.

CHAPTER THIRTY-TWO

EVANDER

My father had not yet shown up to the council room meeting, which already didn't bode well for the day. Mikhail was sure to comment on his absence, sure to needle at every possible reason behind it, too.

Not for the first time, I wondered what exactly he and the others suspected or knew about my father's condition.

The morning became even less fun when the pseudo-king himself strode in, still wearing his ridiculous ostentatious crown, along with another set of purple robes.

He took his time settling into an ornately carved chair at the head of the table before giving the rest of us permission to sit, and I swear, even his brother suppressed an eyeroll.

The long, elegant table was laden with decanters of vodka, each of them a mix of crystal and polished silver shaped like the animals of the clans that were present.

Instead of helping myself to the bear decanter, I reached forward and grabbed the long narrow one in the shape of a snake that Andreyev had just served himself from, pouring some into my own chalice.

I was well aware of the distrust in Iiro that it showed, the insinuation that he would try to poison me, but I wasn't taking any chances.

Iiro glanced at me with something between glee and malice,

making the space between my shoulders itch. I didn't trust him or that expression.

And it hadn't escaped my notice that I was here with only Iiro's allies and none of my own. And that he had effectively separated me from Rowan.

For at least the thousandth time since I sat down, I reminded myself that she was armed and not half as reckless as she used to be. He wouldn't touch a Clan Wife, even with only his own allies around.

She was safe.

Still, I was already on edge when he began to speak.

"I have different matters to discuss with each of you, but certainly the most pressing is taxes on imports."

A muscle twitched in my jaw. I had wondered what form his attack was going to take. The only clan importing anything was Bear, so clearly, this was targeted. Iiro met my gaze, the corner of his mouth lifting.

"There will now be a forty percent tax on goods that come through the pass. Naturally, this applies retroactively to the goods you have already received."

I fought to keep my expression neutral, though fury burned through my veins. "Those weren't all traded goods. Much of that was the princess's dowry."

"Nonetheless, I would hardly be a fair ruler if I allowed Bear to hoard the resources our united kingdom so desperately needs."

"We are hardly hoarding them," I gritted out.

It was true. We had already sent substantial amounts to at least four other clans.

"But it is well within Bear's purview to oversee their distribution, as it is any future goods that we negotiate the purchase of." My tone settled into a better imitation of its usual nonchalance. "The crown is, naturally, free to pursue its own negotiations."

"That sounds rather like an un-unified clan position. We must start seeing ourselves as one," he said sanctimoniously, making an encompassing gesture. "And you know as well as I do that even Lochlann's food sources are not limitless. Once they give preferential trade to Bear, are the rest of us to starve?"

There were murmurs of agreement among Mikhail and Andreyev, though Korhonan's features gave nothing away.

"Again, I'm sure negotiations can be made." My voice was icy calm. "But Bear will not be agreeing to donate forty percent of its goods, under any circumstances."

Iiro looked far, far too satisfied, considering I had just publicly disagreed with him, and his power was by no means secure enough to punish me for that.

"Your father has already lent his support of my initiatives." He let that statement linger in the air before he went on. "Telling you here was a mere courtesy. He sees, as I do, that it's more important for the whole of Socair to stay strong than to feed a few stray villagers."

Meaning that the food would go to the armies, as I had suspected, rather than the starving women and children who needed it.

Was he lying? It was impossible to know what my father had agreed to at any given point.

But I could hardly voice that aloud, nor could I disagree with the duke of my own clan. For all the times Rowan had been furious about not having a voice, she certainly wasn't the only one.

"He has signed off on this law?" I asked.

Iiro still needed the support of the dukes he was making laws for, at least until the other two clans accepted his rulership.

"I have no doubt that he will, as soon as he makes his appearance," Iiro said smoothly. "Lady Ava says he is unwell this morning. I do hope it's nothing serious."

"I'm certain he'll be fine in no time." *Unfortunately.*

Since my father's illness set in, the healers had been saying his lifespan would be shorter, but he seemed determined to hold on.

What did it say about me that I wished regularly that he would hurry things along?

Especially times like these.

When we finally stopped for a midday break, I wasn't surprised to see Korhonan approach.

The others filed out of the room while he stayed behind to talk to me.

I tried to keep my features civil since he had been by far the least obnoxious person at the meeting, but it was difficult when he still looked at my wife like she should have belonged to him.

It was all good and well to tease Rowan about her jealousy, but I wasn't sure I could have stood here at all if things had gone any further between them than they did.

"I know my brother's method of communication leaves much to be desired, but I believe that he truly does want what's best for Socair." Korhonan sighed. "He just...is extreme in his methods."

I squeezed my eyes shut, not sure how anyone could be so incredibly oblivious to what was right in front of them.

I might have envied that kind of blind loyalty, since I hadn't had the luxury of thinking anything half that decent about my own family in years, except that his idiocy was going to affect my clan.

Again.

"You know that like you knew he didn't want to be king?" I finally asked him, opening my eyes.

He leveled a look at me.

"I said he didn't want to go to war for it, not that he didn't want the throne. He wanted to get it peacefully, and that's what he did. Now we have a chance to put our kingdom back together." He shook his head. "I know who everyone thinks you are, but I also know that there's more to that, so I'm surprised that doesn't appeal to you."

I stilled, but I supposed it made sense if he was obtuse enough to believe there was goodness in Iiro, he thought it of me as well.

Korhonan went on. "The only thing I can think is that this is about you once again holding a grudge."

My jaw clenched. He might not have known the consequences of blabbing to his brother, but Iiro had certainly known what he was doing when he went to my stepmother about my plan to…remove her from the picture.

"Though I do despise your family," I acknowledged casually, "this isn't about a grudge. It's about the fact that I wouldn't trust your brother with the wellbeing of my cat, let alone my people."

He met my gaze unflinchingly.

"It's not like it would be the first time you let your feelings interfere with your judgment, for all you pretend not to have any." It wasn't hard to guess what he was referring to.

Perhaps it was because he walked away stoically from Lochlann, or perhaps it was because I knew he had defended Rowan since then, but I felt compelled to offer him a small bit of truth.

"I didn't take her that day to get back at you," I admitted. "I did it to protect my clan."

He raised a skeptical eyebrow. "You might not have taken her to get back at me, but you didn't do it for your clan either."

I opened my mouth to argue, and he held up a hand. "Or at least, that wasn't the only reason."

"Then why aren't you angrier?" I couldn't help but ask.

Even in Lochlann, he had been frustrated when I got there, but not nearly as hostile as I would have been in his situation.

He held my gaze for a long moment, then shook his head slowly. "Because if Rowan looked at me the way she looks at you, there is nothing I wouldn't have done to keep her."

He turned to go. For the first time since all of this happened, I reluctantly forced myself to consider this situation from his perspective.

And for the first time in years, I couldn't quite bring myself to hate him.

CHAPTER THIRTY-THREE

ROWAN

My day was marginally less unpleasant than I thought it would be, if only because Ava stayed in her rooms with Aleksander.

Galina seemed to dislike me less than before, and she showed a quiet, surprising wit, now that she wasn't busy glaring at me.

Still, I was more than ready to escape to the solitude of my rooms, and readier still for Evander to join me. His face was grim when he entered.

"Fun day with the council?" I asked from my spot lounging on the bed.

"Isn't every day fun with Iiro as an almost king?" he asked.

His eyes landed on me, then, assessing me with something unusually close to hesitation. "You never did tell me...what happened...with Korhonan."

I raised my eyebrows. "I told you what *didn't* happen. I wasn't aware you wanted details of the rest."

Darkness flashed through his gaze. "I can assure you, I do not. I meant when he left Lochlann."

"Oh." I examined Evander's features, wondering where this question was coming from. "I asked him in so I could tell him what I had already decided, but he got there before I did."

Evander nodded, but he clearly wanted more, so I relented.

Sharing pieces of myself may never come easily for me, but I would try, for his sake.

"He said that you and I were inevitable...that he could see it from the first time we danced," I added, not quite meeting his eyes. "Which is...ridiculous, obviously."

Evander crossed over to me, putting his finger under my chin and forcing me to meet his gaze. "Is it?"

All of the breath left my body, my lungs refusing to cooperate with me when I was looking into his perfect, unusually sincere gray eyes.

Whatever he saw in my features must have been all the answer he needed, because he brought his lips against mine. Warmth spread through me, burning hotter as it scorched through every part of my body.

He ran his hand along my side, and I arched toward him, wanting more, as I always did from him. And as always, he was more than happy to deliver.

His lips were on my neck and his fingers trailed possessively down my waist, along my hips and down to my thigh...where he abruptly froze.

"Where is your dagger?" He lifted his head, looking at my face.

"Um…" I tried to make my brain work well enough to think of anything but Evander's hands and his mouth and his body on mine. "I think we knocked it behind the dresser."

"You were unarmed all day?" He looked toward the dresser, and I shuffled my feet impatiently.

"By necessity, yes. And a few more minutes won't make a stars-damned difference." There was a definite edge to my voice.

He returned his attention to me, his cocky chuckle tugging at things low in my belly.

"You would think," he said, kissing me again. "That I had been neglecting you."

"I feel very, very neglected," I assured him. "It has been…" I mentally tallied the time. "Eight whole hours since you show-ered me with any sort of attention."

"Well, we can't have that," he murmured against my mouth.

So for a while, we lost ourselves in each other, ignoring this entire cursed castle and the myriad of problems within it. Of course, at some point, we had to come back to reality and get ready for what was sure to be a charming dinner.

Evander moved the dresser aside while I unabashedly watched his muscles strain with the effort. I peeked behind it, already half crouched to retrieve my weapon.

But my dagger wasn't there.

"The bed?" I asked.

He looked at it dubiously. It would have been difficult to knock the dagger all the way from the dresser back there, but not impossible.

Still, his features were wary as he pulled it out from the wall. Sure enough, the dagger wasn't there, either.

We exchanged a glance.

"If someone wanted to steal it--" he began.

"There are plenty of valuable things in this room," I finished. "Stars, in this castle."

"So, they wanted your dagger specifically." His face was pure murder.

"So I would be unarmed?" I guessed, a tendril of fear shooting through me in spite of myself.

"Perhaps," he said, though he didn't sound convinced. "I'll make sure you have a replacement by tomorrow. In the meantime, you don't leave my side."

I might have argued with his commanding tone if I didn't agree with him.

And if there wasn't just the slightest edge of panic in his eyes.

CHAPTER THIRTY-FOUR

ROWAN

For someone who claimed to want to distribute food, Iiro was doing a damned good job of wasting it tonight.

Once again, there was easily enough here for thirty people, rather than the twelve who were in attendance. Evander's jaw clenched, though I wasn't sure if it was about that or if he was still upset about my dagger.

Both, likely.

Besides which, Aleksander had made it to dinner, but today was clearly not one of his lucid days. He had a faraway expression on his face, and Evander didn't have to tell me how bad it would be if everyone here understood the extent of the duke's illness.

The new king was pressing plenty of advantages, as it was. If Bear was seen as vulnerable to attack from all sides…

I shook the thought away, settling into the seat next to Evander. He and Ava sat on either side of the duke, effectively boxing him away from people.

We would just have to hope it was enough.

It was an effort not to laugh, or gag, at the first course. Despite the food-laden table, servants came by to ladle soup into each of our porcelain bowls, as if the roasted pig and chafing dishes filled with mashed potatoes, gravy, biscuits, and more weren't enough.

No, he had to give us more.

And it had to be borscht.

I glanced up from the bowl of cold soup and caught Theo's eye. He raised his hands slightly in a gesture that said he was innocent, and I chuckled. Of course, Iiro wanted to make me squirm, knowing I risked offending the others at the table by not finishing the soup he knew I hated.

But the joke was on him, because after the jellied meat, this borscht would be downright delicious. Or, at the very least, not quite as bad.

Bracing myself, I kept my features neutral and went for it.

I was wrong. It was still horrid. Each bite was a little worse than the last, and my eyes watered from what I could swear was an extra helping of vinegar.

Evander smirked beside me, entirely unbothered by it.

"At least it isn't fish stew," he whispered, making me laugh.

"This is true. I do prefer my food not to stare back at me." I cast a glance at the roasted hog. "Other than delicious little pigs, of course."

"Of course," he agreed, and the grin that stretched over his mouth was intoxicating.

Mila would have been proud. I successfully finished my bowl, to the surprise of at least three people at the table, four if I included myself.

No sooner had we started on the next course than Iiro cleared his throat.

"I thought we had a rather fruitful discussion today on the necessity of sharing our resources." His pompous tone was far too satisfied, and I knew, somehow, this was directed at Evander. Sure enough, he glanced at my dear father-in-law.

"Of course," Iiro continued. "Sir Aleksander and I had discussed it before, so I'm sure he will be more than prepared to sign on the new law tomorrow."

He shot a politely questioning look at the duke in question.

"Isn't that what you said, Sir Aleksander?"

Der'mo.

My husband subtly tensed beside me, and Aleksander

blinked several times. He looked from Iiro to his crown, then at the rest of the table.

Evander had said the only thing his father held onto was his pride, that it was how he had managed to cover for as long as he did.

Sure enough, Aleksander nodded confidently. "It is as you say, Your Majesty."

A muscle ticked in Evander's jaw, and he glared at Iiro with thinly veiled suspicion. The other Dukes, even Theo, looked warily between Evander and his father.

What in the stars-damned-hell had just happened?

Theo cut in to smoothly change the subject, and the moment, whatever it had been, passed. At least, it did for everyone but Evander, who, for the first time since I had met him, actually had to put his hands under the table to conceal the way they trembled with rage.

Whatever Iiro had just done, it did not bode well for us.

After dinner, Iiro requested Theo's presence in his drawing room, effectively dismissing the rest of us. It was probably the only decent thing he had done today.

Or ever.

Everyone slowly trickled out of the dining hall into one of the parlors or their rooms. Evander and I chose the latter after making sure Aleksander made it to his without any issues.

As soon as the door closed behind us, I turned to Evander.

"Do you want to tell me what the hell just happened?"

He met my eyes from where he was already pouring us both a glass of vodka. "Iiro sowing seeds of dissension. He wants to tax forty percent of the food, including your dowry."

"What?" I said sharply. The people needed more than that. "Can you say no?"

He crossed the space between us, handing me my glass before downing his in one go. "I could have, if my father hadn't just said yes."

I cursed, but something in Evander's face gave me even more pause.

"What else?"

"This is twice now he's baited me into publicly disagreeing with my father. I can't tell if this is a general tactic to undermine me so it's easier for him to get his way, or..." He sighed, massaging the bridge of his nose with his forefinger and thumb. "Something else."

The prickling along my spine intensified, and I glanced warily out of the large, bay window. Sure enough, sinister black clouds skated in from the distance.

It felt like more than that, though.

It felt like an omen.

CHAPTER THIRTY-FIVE

ROWAN

W e didn't have to wait long for the other shoe to drop.

We had barely begun to pour another serving of vodka when an unearthly shriek sounded from the hallway.

Evander and I exchanged a single look before we both bolted for the door. We emerged into the hallway to find Ava trembling and pale, only held up by her guard.

Dread trickled through my limbs, numbing me from the inside out.

We weren't the only ones who had come to investigate. Mikhail and Inessa's father were in the hallway as well, both staring at Ava with apprehension.

"What's happened?" the Viper lord asked.

"I went to the sauna," she answered in a shaky voice. "And when I returned, I found him..." Ava trailed off when she saw Evander and me.

"This was you," she said, venom coating her tone.

Evander didn't even stop to acknowledge her. He just barreled past, into Aleksander's room. I followed fast on his heels, hearing the dukes shuffle in behind us.

It shouldn't have been surprising, given that there were few things that it would have made sense for Ava to be so upset about. But the sight still stole my breath.

Aleksander lay on the bed, unmoving, unblinking, as blood dripped from the mattress, staining the bearskin rug on the floor.

Evander came to a dead stop several feet from the bed, and I moved to stand next to him.

His gray eyes were wide, his lips parted, but it was more than shock. There was an edge of fury, and perhaps even panic, as he wordlessly stared down at his father…and the dagger protruding from his throat.

My mouth went dry, and the room spun.

Not just any dagger.

My dagger.

My heart pounded in my chest, a halting, blaring rhythm that echoed in my ears.

It was you, Ava had said. Not to Evander. To me.

A gasp sounded behind us from one of the dukes, and Iiro's voice floated down the hallway.

Just what we need.

I placed a hand on Evander's shoulder, noticing the way his entire body thrummed with pent-up tension as Iiro burst into the room. Theo was right behind him, but he halted in shock when he beheld Aleksander's body.

Evander pried the golden and jewel-studded dagger from his father's body before covering him over with the rest of his blankets. His hand lingered on Aleksander's shoulder uncertainly, and an ache went through me.

In spite of who Aleksander was, he was still Evander's father. Before I could open my mouth to offer condolences or say anything remotely useful, Ava's shrill voice assaulted my ears.

"It was her. That's her dagger," she exclaimed, her bony finger pointed at me.

I thought back to the day at the sauna in Bear, when she had clearly been rifling through my things. Whatever her purpose had been, she had to have seen the dagger.

The extremely recognizable, one-of-a-kind blade she knew I had on me at all times.

And then it had gone missing.

I glared at her as Iiro looked from me to the blade in question, still held in Evander's hand, still dripping with Aleksander's blood. There was a pause before Iiro spoke.

"There will be an investigation immediately," he snapped. "Everyone is to adjourn to the throne room."

He held out a hand to Evander expectantly. "Give me the weapon."

Evander was unnaturally still as he stared back at the king. His narrowed eyes were the only thing that gave away the intense rage I knew was coursing through his veins.

His eyes swept the room, landing on the three other dukes, his stepmother, and finally, me. Reluctantly, he handed over the weapon.

Then we made our way to the throne room, though I couldn't help but think that every measured step felt more like walking toward the gallows.

Each of the clans stood at the front of the throne room, with their soldiers filling the rest of the space.

Inessa sat behind Iiro to his left, her eyes darting between her husband and me with disquiet.

Her small throne was elegant, made of the same obsidian stone as the palace, with a curved back and smooth, polished crystals that dotted the armrests and each leg.

Still, it paled in comparison to Iiro's.

His was a massive, imposing black structure, carved and polished to perfection. The wide back had nine pointed black crystals rising up from it. It was obviously the most important feature in the room, demanding even more attention than the pretentious crown that sat on Iiro's head.

"Lady Stenvall," Iiro began, interrupting my thoughts.

Ava and I both looked up, and he clarified. "Lady *Rowan* Stenvall. Do you confirm this is your dagger?"

Evander tensed at my side, but he refrained from speaking for me.

"Yes, but it went missing this morning," I said.

Iiro's smile was frigid.

"How convenient. I assume you reported this to someone." His smug tone said he knew damned good and well I hadn't.

"No," I gritted out. "But--"

"Brother," Theo cut in. "Surely you aren't suggesting that the princess bested a seasoned warrior with no more than a dagger."

I would have glared at him for that if he hadn't been trying to help me. Murmurs of agreement sounded through the other dukes, the whole misogynistic bunch of them.

Iiro let out a condescending chuckle. "Naturally not."

Arsehat.

He had literally watched me take out members of the Unclanned, though admittedly, that had been with a sword. I supposed it hardly mattered as long as he wasn't accusing me.

My shoulders sagged in relief, until his gaze landed on Evander.

"But someone else had easy access to Lady Rowan's dagger," he said, just barely able to keep the glee from his tone. "Only one person, in fact. Someone who had ample motive to want Sir Aleksander out of the way."

And too late, I realized Iiro's game.

Evander's eyes snapped up to the self-proclaimed king's, burning with pure murder.

"If I wanted my father out of the way," Evander growled, having apparently found his voice. "Why would I wait until I was in your castle, surrounded by potential witnesses?"

"Because he was about to help me enact a law to feed our people, one you staunchly disagreed with." Iiro's tone was matter-of-fact. "We all heard how you felt about that."

He made an encompassing gesture.

To my horror, the other dukes appeared dubious. Well, Mikhail looked downright giddy, but even Inessa's father was clearly being swayed.

"And why would I use my wife's dagger?" Evander challenged.

"Poetic justice?" Iiro suggested. "You appear to have grown

rather fond of her for reasons unbeknownst to me, and he did order her flogging, did he not?"

"He did," Ava said like the lying, despicable wench that she was.

"If he's fond of her, that hardly seems a reason to implicate her in his father's murder," Theo said.

There was something like warning in his tone, and I shot him a grateful look.

"You said yourself, Brother, no one would believe someone Rowan's size could take down the duke." Iiro waved a dismissive hand. "She was never in danger."

"Then why implicate myself that way?" Evander growled.

"A clever misdirect, obviously," Iiro said.

"Your Majesty." Theo's voice was tightly controlled. "I'm sure no one here believes that Lord Evander would murder his own father and the duke of his clan."

Iiro sent Theo a withering glance. "And can you vouch for his whereabouts between dinner and the time Sir Aleksander's body was discovered?"

"You know that I cannot," Theo all but snapped. "As I was with you."

I suspected he realized at the same time I did how calculated that was, taking the only person who might have been on our side enough to provide an alibi out of the picture. He shook his head in quiet disbelief.

Inessa's eyes narrowed with more emotion than she usually allowed herself to show. Suspicion of Evander? Of her husband? Of me?

Iiro, on the other hand, looked more satisfied than I had ever seen him, and why wouldn't he be? He had just gotten the unpredictable Duke of Bear out of the picture and eliminated the one real threat to himself in one go.

Disgracing Evander was a happy bonus, and it punished *me* as well.

I barely breathed, trying to count the spaces between one racing heartbeat, then another, in an effort to calm myself. Evander's features were the most terrifying part of all. For a man who usually had a plan followed by several contingency plans, he looked furious...but also bitterly resigned.

Iiro had played his game well, and entrapping Evander while he was still processing the shock and grief of Aleksander's death was probably the only way he could have successfully managed it.

I opened my mouth to tell the room Evander had been with me, for all the good it would do, when another voice rang out.

"I can vouch for their whereabouts."

CHAPTER THIRTY-SIX

ROWAN

Inessa's voice was quiet and demure as ever, but it nonetheless echoed on the dark stone walls.

I tried to wipe the shock from my features, which was more than Iiro was managing to do. His jaw dropped, his eyes widening as he slowly turned his head to look at her.

"If that's true..." He said the words like he suspected it wasn't. "Why not speak up sooner, my dear?"

Her gaze darted calmly from me to Evander, then back to her husband. "I confess, it was a matter of propriety. Lady Rowan reached out to me with questions of a delicate nature, and I visited her rooms to answer."

"And you spoke of such things in front of Lord Evander?" Iiro tilted his head in disbelief.

"He was unwilling to leave." She shrugged a slim shoulder.

That sounded exactly like Evander. So much so that not a single person would question it.

But of course, it wasn't true. None of it was.

She was lying to her husband, her *king*, for us, and I couldn't for the life of me imagine why.

A life debt, for the time I had saved hers? Or was she as horrified by her husband's actions as the rest of us were?

"And how long were you there?" he asked.

Inessa didn't hesitate. "I had only just left when we heard Lady Ava's cry."

Her features were so neutral, I would never have guessed it wasn't the truth if I hadn't known.

And Iiro...even if he suspected, he could hardly publicly accuse her of lying. He may not love much in this world, but he loved Inessa, and he would never let her be punished for that.

Even if he had been willing to let that happen, one look at her father's face said he would never stand for it. Besides which, Iiro would look weak for not controlling his own wife.

She had played him even more effectively than he had played us.

A savage part of me appreciated that it was his own underestimation of women that led to his plans being ruined. It was Theo he had bothered to get out of the way, never once suspecting Inessa might be the chink in his armor.

But I wasn't quite ready to be relieved yet.

Iiro turned his enraged gaze on me. "And what did the two of you discuss?"

If he couldn't blame Evander, it appeared he would settle for humiliating me. Oh, well. I had embarrassed myself for far less important reasons than this.

"I was inquiring after herbs for my...moontime pains," I said it quietly, like it bothered me.

"And that conversation took the better part of an hour?" Iiro demanded.

"One thing led to another," I said vaguely. "If his majesty wishes to be informed of every detail of a conversation about my...delicate female matters, I would be happy to oblige."

Let's see him respond to that one.

Sure enough, his features darkened. "I'm certain that won't be necessary."

Theo gave me the faintest of smiles, and Inessa's father cleared his throat before speaking up. "It seems the investigation will need to continue."

"Indeed." Iiro's voice could have cut solid diamond.

"In the meantime," Evander said in an equally hard tone, "I

need to return to Bear with my father's body to see that the funeral rites are followed. Unless, of course, you have an objection to that."

I knew from Mila that funeral rites were sacred for dukes, and there was no possible way the king could refuse that request.

"Of course not," Iiro bit out. "You may leave immediately."

It was more of an order than a suggestion, but one I was all too happy to follow.

A glance around the room showed that the only person more furious than Iiro was Ava. A flurry of thoughts and questions ran through my mind all at once.

Had she killed the duke herself? It didn't seem likely, since she was a far cry from a warrior, but she was certainly soulless enough to murder her own husband.

And it wouldn't have been hard to embed a dagger in his throat if he were sleeping, unsuspecting.

My mind snagged on that for a moment, with one question drawing out all of my other thoughts.

What could have possibly motivated her to kill the man who kept her untouchable? She had more power when he was around. She could manipulate him into carrying out her wishes. She could hide behind him.

A look passed between her and Iiro, and a suspicion formed in the back of my mind. Then Evander's hand closed around mine, and I realized that was something I could consider later.

For now, we just needed to get the hell out of this castle.

We needed to get home.

CHAPTER THIRTY-SEVEN

EVANDER

I stared back at Iiro, meeting his enraged gaze with my own. My blood boiled in my veins, and even a lifetime of schooling my features was threatening to fail me now.

He had orchestrated this.

I wasn't sure how, but the amount of anger rolling off of him when his wife lied for us was telling. But he hadn't been alone.

My gaze found Ava, still staring furiously at Rowan.

Funny, how my father's widow seemed more angry than sad.

How she was the only one to have seen him before she went to the sauna, then happened to find him when she returned.

She was certainly capable of murder, but I had to wonder what she could possibly have gotten out of this arrangement. Of course, I couldn't prove any of it, which meant she would be headed back to Bear with us.

That was just as well. She had no power left, and I wanted to keep an eye on her. Besides, there were more important things to worry about right now, like getting Rowan safely away from here.

"Kindly return my wife's dagger as well," I said, taking a step closer to the dais. "It is a family heirloom."

Iiro's eyes narrowed even further. He glanced from me down to the blood-stained blade in his hand, making a show of examining it.

"It's a shame your father was killed with something so vulgar," Iiro commented.

I didn't respond, because I wasn't sure I agreed. Instead, I stepped forward to take the proffered blade.

"I expect we'll be updated on what's sure to be a very thorough investigation," I said pointedly as I dipped into a shallow bow, maintaining eye contact with him.

A bitter smile pulled at his mouth, but he nodded for his audience.

Turning my back to the king, I walked directly to Rowan and took her hand. She entwined her fingers tightly with mine, and we strode out of the room.

After a few quick words with Kirill and Henrick, things were set in motion for us to leave. Ava stayed in the main room with Iiro, while Rowan and I went to the room where Samu was still holding vigil over my father's body.

I reached for the silks the maids had brought up with numb fingers, preparing to wrap my father's body as it was customary for the heirs to do.

What wasn't customary, or expected, was Rowan stepping on the other side, reaching her hands out to help. While my relationship with my father was complex, hers was not. He had only ever been cruel to my wife, her people, and her family.

"You don't have to–" I began.

"I know," she said resolutely. "But I want to. You're my husband, and he's your father. So tell me what to do."

Her bright green gaze connected with mine, holding nothing but determination, so I reluctantly walked her through the motions.

When we were done, I painstakingly washed each droplet of blood from my hands and nails while Rowan did the same.

How many times had I cleansed someone's blood from my skin? How many times had I wished it was my father's?

And yet, I felt hollow.

I had grieved him a long time ago, but that didn't take away the sinking realization that he was gone. Or the twisted part of my soul that felt nearly as much sorrow as relief.

I was still scrubbing at phantom residual droplets when a smaller pair of hands came over mine.

"They're clean now," Rowan said, gently guiding my hands out of the bowl to a nearby towel.

She was right, I realized. They were red and raw and free of blood, as far as the eye could see.

But I could feel my father's blood, nonetheless, staining my skin and my mind and my soul.

CHAPTER THIRTY-EIGHT

ROWAN

W e left with significantly less fanfare than when we had arrived, embarking on our long, somber journey back to Bear.

Ava stayed away from us whenever we stopped. Her features became harder and more withdrawn each time I saw her.

I tried in vain to decipher her motives, but they remained murky. Then again, the type of person who was willing to flog a child and abuse her only daughter for years wasn't really a predictable person to begin with.

We took turns resting our horses and ourselves, never staying anywhere for longer than necessary. Though the temperatures were dropping by the day, we were still traveling with Aleksander's corpse.

It wasn't a journey that any of us wanted to extend for long.

I knew it was weighing on Evander, too. His father's death, the impending responsibility waiting for him back at the estate, as well as whatever we had just walked away from at the Obsidian Palace.

Iiro was not going to let this go, but we had no way of knowing what his next move would be.

We had just crossed the border into Bear when it hit me.

The telltale tingling along my spine that warned of an

oncoming storm. Only, like before, this felt like a different kind of foreboding.

Evander might not have had fae blood, but it was clear he sensed the wrongness as well. His shoulders were tense and his jawline hard as he surveyed the soldiers through the window.

Neither of us spoke about the foreboding pressing in around us, but we exchanged a look of shared understanding.

The dread pooled in my veins as the hours went on, even when we stopped at midday to water the horses. The sky was overcast and gray, but there were no wind or hail storms that I could sense.

I had been right, then. It wasn't truly from the weather.

While Evander spoke with Kirill, I took the opportunity to stretch my legs. Ava shot me a glare laced with pure malice, and the feeling along my spine intensified.

I returned her stare, realizing a moment too late that I was playing right into her hands.

Because by focusing on her, I had let my immediate guard down.

It happened in an instant.

The soldier next to me wrapped a massive arm around my middle, pinning my arms to my side. Before I could react, his dagger was at my neck.

I froze, my heart pounding in my ears too loudly as I frantically sought out Evander.

His swords were already in his hands, his face a mask of rage deeper than any I had ever seen. Kirill was drawing his weapon as well, both of them moving toward me.

Another soldier stepped in front of them, sword at the ready, but with one quick flash of his sabers, my husband cleanly removed the soldier's head from his body, not so much as pausing in his trajectory toward me.

At least, not until Ava's voice rang out. "Unless you want her to die, Stepson, now would be a good time to stop."

"Don't--" I started, but the dagger pressed against my throat hard enough that rivulets of blood crept down my neck.

Evander lowered his weapon, turning slowly to face Ava

where she stood half-hiding behind Samu. My husband's voice dripped with the calm lethality he had mastered so well.

"What is it that you hope to gain here?" Without waiting for an answer, he turned to the man who had his hands on me. "And you, turning your weapon on a Clan Wife?"

It was Samu who answered, spitting on the ground. "You killed the rightful duke. You have no right to call yourself the heir, and if you are not the heir, then she is nothing."

His accented words echoed through me. That was her game... Since Iiro couldn't actually convict Evander of Aleksander's murder, Ava was just going to turn his men against him.

I scanned the faces of the soldiers around us.

Some of them looked uneasy or had donned the same furious expression as Kirill, their hands resting on the hilt of their weapons. Though, quite a few stood with their arms crossed, clearly interested in what Samu had to say.

It didn't matter, though, that there were more on our side. Because Ava knew and I knew and Evander knew that he wasn't going to risk me getting killed.

Stars damn it all...

Sure enough, Evander held out a hand to stop the men who were going for their weapons. "No one moves while my wife is in danger."

Helpless rage overtook me while his face darkened with fury.

"And we both know I am not the one who killed the duke." He hurled the words at Ava.

The weight of my dagger on my thigh called to me. If I could access it without alerting anyone, I could at least get myself out of this mess, take any concerns for my safety off the table for Ava to use as leverage.

But I suspected the man holding me wouldn't hesitate to kill me if I tried. Ava or Samu would see from where they were poised between Evander and me.

"What is it that you want, Stepmother?" he asked again, his low tone more deadly than the sharpened blades of his sabers.

A slow grin spread over her lips.

"It's not about what *I* want, so much as what the king wants," she said with a shrug. "But I won't deny that this brings me joy."

"And what is it that our illustrious king wants?" Evander asked coldly.

"For you to pay for the sins of your *crime*, of course," she said, playing to the rapt audience.

I wanted to scream.

We had our suspicions about her working with Iiro, but had the man truly orchestrated all of this to get rid of Evander? Was he planning to use him as an example to fortify his power?

"And what do you get out of this?" he demanded.

"Besides justice, you mean?" Her tone was full of false self-righteousness. "Protection, since you and your whore of a wife have both threatened me. A Clan Wife."

Some of the men looked uncomfortable about her accusation, and my mind spun with ways to get us out of this.

"You can't hope to win with a handful of men." I tried to reason with her.

The grip around me tightened, squeezing the air from my lungs as her hateful voice rang out again.

"On the contrary," Ava said, looking far too satisfied with herself. "Evander is going to order his men to stand down. There's no reason to bring the wrath of Lochlann down on us for killing you unless we have to, and my stepson understands that." She turned her attention back to Evander, her cruel smile twisting her features once more. "Don't you?"

Furious tears stabbed at the back of my eyes as Evander's gaze met mine. I saw in that moment that she was right.

He would face death at the hands of Iiro--hell, he would let his men die--just to keep me from danger.

"No." I said the word even though I knew it would make no difference.

"Yes," he countered, turning his attention back to Ava. "Let her go, and I'll come with you. My men will escort her back to the estate, safely."

A vicious chuckle escaped her lips as she shook her head.

"The king wants her back at the Obsidian Palace as well," she said dismissively. "And your men will come, too, to ensure they can be kept in line."

If I had thought Evander's eyes were incensed before, they were pure, unadulterated murder now.

"I'll go," I told her, then turned to Evander. "I'm not leaving you. And she's right, he has more to lose by hurting me than he stands to gain."

His hands flexed around his sword, and Ava shot a look at the man holding me. The soldier dragged his blade along my neck in a jagged pattern, and I squeezed my eyes shut against the pain.

"Stop," Evander said. "I'll do it."

I opened my eyes to see him staring into them, but it wasn't with the resignation I was expecting to see. He was still enraged. Defiant.

"Excellent," Ava said. "Though, there is one more thing."

She turned to look directly at me. "You should have thought twice before threatening me."

I thought about my threat, if she ever so much as breathed in Evander's direction again. And I knew, I knew what she was going to say before she even opened her mouth.

"Samu, I think forty lashes should do it."

My lips parted in a fury more intense than anything I had ever felt.

"Do not touch him," I snarled, not even caring when the bobbing of my throat made the knife cut a little deeper.

Even as the blood trickled down my neck, I made myself a promise.

Regardless of what else happened today, I would kill her for this.

CHAPTER THIRTY-NINE

ROWAN

E vander took one look at me, at the blood pooling along my collarbone, and nodded. Like the decision was obvious.

Tears started spilling down my face in truth, but I blinked them away. He gave me a single, meaningful look before he sheathed his swords and unbuckled his double baldric.

Then he walked toward a tree, calmly unbuttoning his jacket next.

His men moved forward, but Evander held out his hand again. "I ordered you to stand down. Do not make me say it again."

Kirill looked angrier than I had ever seen him, but he reluctantly lowered his weapon.

"You heard His Grace," he told the men.

They also looked furious, but they obeyed. And I knew they hated Ava, but they hated me as well. This was my fault. He was doing this for me.

Because of me.

I watched helplessly as Samu handed Ava a whip. As Evander carefully laid his swords against the ground. As he pulled off first his jacket, then his shirt, hanging them neatly on a branch. As he held his hands out to brace himself against the trunk of the tree.

My heartbeat roared in my ears, my lungs scrambling for short, panicked puffs of air.

But my father hadn't raised me to panic. And Evander hadn't chosen that tree at random. It forced Ava's attention away from me.

Everyone's attention, in fact.

With slow, cautious movements, I reached my hand into my pocket, the one that was always left open for easy access to my dagger.

Crack.

Evander didn't even flinch as the first lash sliced across his back. Blood poured from the wound, and it took every ounce of self-control I never knew I possessed not to scream, not to lunge for my dagger, not to do anything that might bring attention to me.

Instead, I forced myself to go slowly, even as another crack rang out. I kept myself calm with visions of Ava's head being severed from her body, as my hand crept so, so carefully toward my thigh.

My fingers wrapped around the siren hilt, and I slowly slid the weapon out of its sheath, hating myself for masking the sound with yet another crack of the whip.

By the fifth lash, Evander's back was taut with pain, his muscles seizing. But he still didn't cry out.

And neither did I.

The man behind me shifted, and I froze, but he didn't seem to notice anything out of the ordinary.

My dagger was nearly clear of my pocket now, so I stared at Kirill until he returned the look. Shooting him a single significant blink, I only had a second to hope he understood before I plunged the dagger directly into the gut of the man holding me.

The soldier's arm twitched reflexively, his fingers unclenching from his weapon as I dragged my blade upward through his flesh. Kirill wasted no time raising his sword, turning on the nearest dissenter.

Chaos broke out.

Ava froze at the same time Evander turned, already going for his sword. Which was good, because Samu was halfway to my husband, his own weapon drawn.

But Kirill was already fighting his way there, and I only had eyes for Ava.

The despicable coward turned to run, but I was faster. I ducked and twirled my way out of the trajectory of clashing steel until I caught up to her, yanking her back by her hair.

She hit the ground with a solid thunk.

Before she could even consider trying to escape my grasp, I moved over her, straddling her waist while I pinned her arms beneath my legs. Her eyes widened in terror, her lips trembling.

It might have been my favorite expression she had ever worn.

"Beg." My voice was emptier than I had ever heard it, issuing that one-word command.

My heartbeat thundered in my ears, one fractured beat after the other. Each measured breath I took was a cacophony, but they weren't loud enough to drown out her single breathless question.

"What?" she said.

All I could hear was her mocking Evander about begging. I saw her standing over a child with that same whip she had used just now. Saw her hurting my husband and using me against him.

Cold, unrelenting fury washed over me.

Vaguely, I registered Samu falling beside me, registered stillness in the air around me that probably meant the rest of the fighting was over with.

"I want you to beg for your life." I bit out each word with more vitriol than the last.

Ava swallowed back whatever vestige of sick pride she had left, nodding. "Please, don't kill me. I *beg* of you. We're family."

Perhaps it should have been harder to look into her eyes, eyes that were nearly identical to my sister's, my father's, my aunt's...and want so badly to see them empty and lifeless.

But this woman...

"You don't deserve to be anyone's family," I said in the same calm deadly tone I usually heard from Evander's lips. "And I want you to know, when you die, that you were completely alone. That everyone despises you. That when I tell your daughter and your grandchildren how you died begging and screaming, they will be nothing but satisfied to hear it."

She bucked and kicked, but I had been training every day for weeks, and she was as weak on the outside as her despicable, cowardly insides.

I plunged my dagger into the sensitive skin at her elbow, long enough to hear her scream and make my prediction of her death entirely accurate.

Then I stabbed it through her throat.

CHAPTER FORTY

EVANDER

The clearing was silent as Rowan's words rang out.

I want you to beg for your life.

My eyebrows rose, somewhere between impressed and concerned. I had always known ruthlessness lurked within her, but it was still shocking to see it unfold, especially when I knew it was on my behalf.

Kirill moved to intervene, but I held out a hand to stop him. This was her decision, her way of carrying out whatever threats she had made, and she wouldn't thank us for intervening.

Rowan muttered something so quiet, I could only make out the words *die begging and screaming,* and then she stabbed Ava. Twice.

Blood spattered on her dress, her face, but her features didn't waver. I walked over to where she straddled Ava's body, still staring coldly down at it.

My eyes flitted over the body of the woman who had made it her mission in life to make mine a living hell, and just as quickly, I looked away. She hadn't deserved a second thought while she was alive, and she sure as hell didn't now.

Instead, I looked at my perfect, gorgeous, slightly savage wife.

"Lemmikki." I closed the distance between us, extending a hand.

The motion tugged at the wounds on my back, but it was far from the worst lashing I had ever had. The way it overlapped old scar tissue, I hadn't even felt all of them.

What I had felt was the weight of Rowan's tearstained face. And her fury.

Her love, as she ordered me not to do this for her.

Her fierce protection, as she took her vengeance, not because of what Ava did to her, but because of what Ava did to *me*.

The darker part of my soul couldn't help but be grateful, and a little bit proud.

Rowan looked up at the sound of my voice, placing her hand in mine.

"Your Grace," she responded, getting to her feet in one fluid motion.

Her tone was casual, like we were conversing at a dinner party and not over the slain body of a woman we both hated more than words.

I gently dropped her hand to see to the execution of the few remaining traitors. It was a swift process that left no doubt in the rest of their minds what would happen to anyone who dared to hurt my wife, or to threaten me.

When we were finished, we piled the bodies in the center of a sparse field and left a few trusted men to burn their corpses. There was no sense in leaving evidence of what exactly had transpired.

As soon as we were in the carriage with the curtains drawn, Rowan turned to me, her features still distant and cold.

"Your back," she said, digging a medical bag from under the bench.

Her voice, at least, had been strong outside, but it was hollow now.

"Your neck," I countered.

I had avoided looking at the blood smeared across her throat, her collarbone, knowing how close it had come to taking her from me.

She narrowed her eyes. "It's nothing. It's already stopped

bleeding, which is more than I can say for you. You'll stain the carriage seats."

There was forced nonchalance in her tone, but it was easy to see she was precariously close to...something.

So instead of arguing, I turned to give her access to the wounds.

She used my flask to clean her hands before silently pouring the remaining vodka over my wounds as well. I winced as it burned my open flesh, but it was nothing compared to the solution she applied next.

It burned like every kind of hell.

I forced myself not to flinch, taking slow breaths as it bubbled away on each of my seven lashes.

She hissed an apology under her breath before gently applying a salve. Afterward, she wrapped a muslin bandage around me several times, but by the last wrap, her hands were starting to shake.

I pulled my shirt back on, turning to tend to her neck. I made quick work of her wounds, which were deeper than she let on, and tried not to show my rage all over again.

She avoided my gaze the entire time, her fingers quivering a little more with each passing moment. When I was done, I took her slim hands in mine. They were freezing and trembling, all of the adrenaline from the battle leeching from her body.

"Lemmikki?"

She shook her head.

"Rowan?" I tried again, using her name softly.

Finally, her eyes met mine, glistening with unshed tears. Something inside me broke apart at the rare sight, and I squeezed her hands a little tighter.

"I almost lost you," she whispered, her tone low and insistent to the point of sounding panicked. "And I--I don't want to be in a world where you're not."

Her words landed like blows to my chest. As well as I could read her, she kept her emotions on a tight leash most of the time. It was one thing, knowing that she loved me, but this...it filled me with a mix of elation and pure terror.

Because I was a soldier, and the reality was that my life had been on the line more than once and undoubtedly would be again.

"Don't ever say that, Lemmikki," I growled. "Whatever happens to me, you're a survivor."

Her features hardened, her furious green eyes boring into mine.

"No." She shook her head again. "You don't get to walk willingly into that evil woman's clutches, put your life on the line, and then tell me I can't feel the same way."

Then the tears started spilling down her face in truth, and I pulled her against me, cradling her against my chest.

I didn't respond, because there was nothing honest I could say, so I only pressed my lips into her hair while I ran my hands in comforting lines up and down her back.

I understood her panic better than I wished I did.

It was the way I had felt tonight watching that dagger bite into her throat, like if I lost her, I would lose every part of myself that mattered, too.

Like there was nothing in the world I wouldn't do to stop that from happening.

CHAPTER FORTY-ONE

ROWAN

I spent the rest of the journey with the sick, twisting feeling that this wasn't over. That we had only just begun to see the hell that would be unleashed.

When we arrived back at the estate, that feeling only intensified. Though we had sent word ahead of us, what greeted us beyond the gates was shock and chaos.

Soldiers and local villagers alike crowded around the courtyard as our carriages pulled to a stop, each of them mirroring the same fearful expression of the person beside them.

Evander stepped out first, turning back to assist me down from the carriage. We walked toward the doors before he faced the crowd.

My grip tightened on his arm, but he didn't show a single trace of anxiety as he addressed his people. His voice was smooth, his words careful, and I could see all over again the honesty in what Luca had said about Evander making a strong leader.

I was a little surprised when he told his people the truth about what happened. His words clearly implicated Iiro, and he didn't bother to lie about Ava's involvement, though he continued referring to her as Mairi.

Then he said some kind words about his father that were decidedly less true, and promised everyone who was listening that he would not step into this new role lightly. Just as he had always done, he would continue to protect them and care for them as best as he could.

Now that Aleksander was dead, I think more than a few of those in attendance knew that would be true.

As soon as the funeral rites were over and Aleksander was buried, Evander was officially sworn in as Duke.

It should have been a relief, not having to tiptoe around the castle, not having to worry about either us or the people of Bear suffering needlessly at the hands of Ava or the former duke.

But like everything in our lives, this, too, was tainted by Iiro and his insatiable need for power.

Evander's first act as Duke was to send an official letter refusing Iiro's tax law, as well as revoking the support of Clan Bear for Iiro to be king. It was a bold move, but a necessary one.

Now three clans opposed Iiro's rulership.

It stormed that day, hailstones and lightning falling to the ground in perilous waves, destroying everything in its path, but even when the storm passed, the feeling of encroaching calamity didn't.

"What happens next?" I asked Evander, though part of me felt like I already knew the answer.

"Either he peacefully abdicates." My husband's face looked as dubious as I felt about that possibility. "Or there is war."

"War," I echoed.

The one thing we had all been trying to avoid.

He met my gaze solidly. "We'll certainly prepare for that, but there is still hope for diplomatic measures."

I took a moment to think about that. It was possible, since Iiro had been content to do things with minimal bloodshed in the past. But he also had a lot of pride, and this was sure to rankle it.

Evander sent Taras and Mila to Lynx to talk to Arès about

possible ramifications. He sent messengers to Crane and Wolf as well, so they could be prepared.

Then there was nothing to do but wait for word back and try to adjust to our new roles within the clan.

The latter of those two things came far more easily to Evander than it did to me, which was probably in part due to the strict laws of succession and in part because he had been the primary face of authority for so long already.

That didn't stop the whispers, though. The hushed conversations around corners about the fact that we left with the duke and his wife but returned with both dead.

That Evander and I had conspired to get them out of the way.

Perhaps if that were true, I wouldn't spend so much time questioning everything that had happened and wondering who the hell I had turned into in those last moments with Ava.

And what war would make of me yet.

CHAPTER FORTY-TWO

ROWAN

For the next few weeks, I saw less and less of my husband. As much as he was handling before, Evander managed to be busier than ever as the actual duke. Or perhaps that was the war preparations.

Every day, Evander and I went to the training rooms in the morning, and in the afternoons, when he went to a series of meetings, I familiarized myself with the responsibilities of Clan Wife that I was still learning.

I slowly realized the luncheons and teas were for far more than the superficial association they had appeared to be at first.

The ladies of court would often come to me to mention issues they were facing, but either weren't allowed to present in front of the council or were too nervous to ask.

They also brought bits of information from their estates, rumors about what was happening in the outer villages and territories, all things they hoped I would be able to assist with or take to Evander.

And I did, glad to be helping, but also to be steadily quashing the residual rumors over the fate of the former duke and his wife.

As far as the nobles were concerned, things seemed to be going fairly well, but there was still the rest of Bear.

Back home, the villagers came to the castle once a week to petition my parents for aid or to settle a dispute, but that wasn't the case in Bear. Or at least, it hadn't been under Aleksander's rule.

"Kirill?" I poked my head outside my door to speak to him. "How do you think the villagers would take to a visit?"

Opening my senses up, I could see the day promised to be particularly beautiful, cold and crisp and still.

He paused, a thoughtful expression crossing his features. "I think it might be good for them to see the wife of Bear."

I tilted my head to the side, allowing him to see the disbelief in my eyes.

"Cursed hair and all?"

Kirill laughed then but nodded. "Cursed hair and all."

I thought about that for a moment before deciding to go for it. I wanted them to see that I was more than a princess of Lochlann. That I could help them. That things could change from how they were before.

That I was not Ava, and that Evander was not his father or the monster they believed him to be.

With that, we gathered Yuriy and a few other soldiers before loading a wagon with food from the castle larder and heading out into the crisp morning air.

When we arrived at Hymi, the nearest village to the estate, everyone who was walking through the streets scrambled out of the way at the sight of the carriage, terror evident in each expression.

It wasn't any better when I emerged with my red curls and my more comfortable black Socairan gown.

They dipped their heads in a bow, not one of them making the superstitious sign to ward off evil. But right now, that was from fear, and that wasn't what I wanted from them.

I uncovered the wagon and had the men help me pass out the food. Kirill and Yuriy both stayed close to me, their expressions open and comfortable.

By the time the wagon was empty, the villagers were far less suspicious of my presence in the village.

A few of the people dipped into lower bows as Kirill and I walked the streets, buying things from the small shops or the street vendors. The baker was amazed when I purchased an entire tray of pastries to share with the women and children outside.

We spent the next several hours like that, purchasing what we could from the sellers and sharing much of it back with the people.

And slowly, slowly, the expressions the villagers wore shifted from fear to wariness, and eventually into something almost like hope.

When we finally returned to the castle, I had hoped to feel better than I had before we left, but that wasn't the case. There was still an oppressive weight to the air that weighed down all that I did, everything I felt.

I made plans to follow up with as many villages as I could, offering the same support and assistance as I had in Hymi. Maybe if I poured myself into helping them, it would help me ignore the impending sense of doom that hovered over us like a thundercloud, waiting to break apart.

In spite of filling my days with lunches and teas and food distributions, or seeing to the immediate needs of the castle, I still struggled to sleep through the night.

Most nights I woke to the sound of Evander's quill scratching from the other room. I never told him that was what woke me, not when he had so much on his plate as it was.

I missed him, though. And it didn't escape my notice that he wasn't sleeping, either. Instead, he was throwing himself into everything he could possibly find to do, late into most nights.

Tonight was no exception.

I threw my dressing gown on and padded barefoot to his study. He didn't turn when I entered, but I knew it was more because he was finishing his thought than because he didn't hear me.

He was always aware of his surroundings.

I crept behind him, putting my hands on the tense muscles in his shoulders and gently kneading them. He lifted his head, groaning softly and letting his quill drop to the desk.

"What time is it, Lemmikki?"

I leaned down, placing a kiss against the side of his neck. "Late."

He reached his hand up to cover mine, tugging me gently until I was standing in front of him. Heat flooded his gaze when he took in my loosely tied black robe and the nothing that was underneath it.

He raked his eyes all the way down my body and back up before pulling me in closer, pressing his mouth against the bare strip of skin of my stomach. A shiver ran through me, and his lips skated lower.

Deft fingers untied the sash of my robe, pushing the silk fabric out of the way, and he worked his way down to the indentation inside my hip bone, eliciting a gasp from me.

He moved his mouth over until he was just below my belly button, his gaze sliding up to meet mine.

"I'm afraid I've been neglecting you in truth this time." He murmured the words against my skin, his warm breath sending delicious tendrils of fire all the way down to my toes.

If I could have spoken, I would have told him I didn't blame him, not when he had lost his father and gained the full responsibility of his clan overnight, but he had effectively robbed me of my ability to form words.

He didn't wait for my answer, sliding his papers and quill aside without looking at them. Then he picked me up with a firm hand on each of my hips, setting me on the empty space on his massive desk.

He kissed his way back up my body, bracing me with one solid arm behind my back. My entire body pulsed with need.

"Evander." I breathed his name, a mix between a demand and a plea, and he froze with his mouth on my neck.

"Der'mo, Lemmikki," he growled. "Do you have any idea what the sound of my name on your lips does to me?"

I shivered again, arching further into him.

Probably the same thing the sound of the words *Der'mo, Lemmikki* did to me. But once again, I had no capacity to articulate that, or anything.

And really, there was no need for words, anyway.

CHAPTER FORTY-THREE

EVANDER

Rowan wasn't sleeping like she usually did.

After last night, I resolved to be back in our bed earlier. Even if I didn't get any more sleep, at least she would.

My mind swam with the never-ending list of things to deal with, not least of which was Iiro's uncharacteristic and ominous silence.

Crane had sent back word that they would stand with Bear, and Wolf did as well. I had been concerned on that last front, since Nils had been fonder of my father than he was of me, but he had stood by his loyalty in the end.

Taras and Mila would be back any day with word from Arès. I suspected he would stand with us as well, since he had never signed off on Iiro's monarchy to begin with.

Not to mention the fact that this was his daughter's clan now.

In theory, everything was falling in line.

Then why do I have the feeling I'm missing something?

I thought that I would feel freer with my father gone, but his ghost still walked these halls, reminding me of everything I had ever done for him. Because of him.

Reminding me that no matter what the people thought or

how much they were forced to submit to me, half of my clan still cowered in terror when I walked into a room.

With good reason.

Which made Rowan all the more spectacular. Not only had she never truly been afraid of me, but day by day, she was reminding the people of our humanity, as she had with her snowball fights in the villages.

The court was warming up to her, even if most of the lords still didn't know quite what to think, and the villagers were beginning to love her. Not only because she brought them food, but because she brought them laughter, something that they sorely needed after the dark reign of my father.

Tonight, she raised her eyebrows when I slid into bed well before midnight. She was still awake, which was telling in and of itself, and the firelight illuminated a pensive expression on her perfect features.

I held out an arm, and she eagerly nestled herself into me. Gently, I trailed my hand from her shoulder down to her wrist and back again. She sighed, equal parts relief and something I couldn't quite identify.

"Lemmikki," I said quietly. "What is it?"

"Do you think that I'm a monster, for the way I killed Ava?" she said the words quietly, shifting until she was laying back on her pillows and staring at the canopy overhead.

A huff of air escaped me.

"Well, no," I said dryly. "But you've watched me execute, brand, and on one notable occasion, mildly torture someone, so if you're that concerned about it, we should probably find someone less biased to ask."

Rowan let out a surprised laugh. We both knew the list of things that made me a monster was far more extensive than that, but there was no sense in bringing that up now.

"*Are* you concerned about it?" I asked in a more serious tone.

She shook her head, not so much a denial as a confirmation. "I've killed before, but I've never *wanted* to kill someone...wanted to hurt someone, as badly as I did that day." She let out a slow breath, continuing.

"It wasn't defense," she said. "It wasn't even an execution. It was revenge, pure and simple. I made her beg, Evander. I made her scream. And then I killed her anyway."

A whoosh of air escaped my lungs. "Do you think she sat up at night racked with regret for the people she hurt?"

She thought that over for a moment, but her brow was still furrowed.

"I think the worst part is that I don't regret it...not really. I just feel like I should. But every time I picture..." She trailed off, but I knew what she was going to say.

In some ways, I think Ava whipping me that last time haunted Rowan far more than it did me.

"When I picture her hurting you," she picked up, "I just wish I could bring her back and kill her all over again."

I thought about my father's death, about the strange mix of satisfaction and grief that coursed through me every time I pictured his lifeless features.

"Death is complicated when it happens to a terrible person," I finally said. "My father was..." The sentence trailed off because there were no real words to describe him, the complex relationship we had.

"I hated him most days," I filled in. "I spent the better part of the last decade wishing he would die so I could take care of our people without him standing in my way or outright hurting them. And then he finally did."

She reached out her small hand and tucked it in mine, still not looking anywhere but toward the ceiling. It was easier this way, I realized, for both of us to talk. Here, in the dark, without the weight of each other's scrutinizing gaze.

I ran my thumb along the top of her hand, feeling the same connection I always did with her.

"And now you don't know how to feel," she said, an observation more than a question.

"Now, I feel like I'm glad he's dead. But what kind of person does that make me?"

"A decent one," she said. "One who cares more about your people than anything else in the world."

I looked at my wife, then, and at the features I had come to know as well as my own. I didn't want to fight with her, not tonight, so I didn't make the response out loud.

But in my head, I knew she was wrong to think I cared more about Bear than anything else in the world. And in my head, I told her the truth.

Not *anything*.

CHAPTER FORTY-FOUR

ROWAN

After our late-night conversation, it finally felt like Evander and I were moving on from everything that had happened.

Sure, we were two broken souls with violent tendencies when it came to protecting the people we loved… But at least I knew he didn't think less of me for it.

As the days passed, there was still no news on the Obsidian Palace front.

In spite of the vague distressing feeling in the back of my mind, I let myself sink into some version of a normal life here.

Though I remained cautiously pessimistic about our future, there was no reason to not enjoy the time we had now.

I was still in a good mood from visiting nearby villagers the day Mila and Taras finally returned. Having skipped tea with the ladies for this, I impatiently waited for her carriage in the courtyard.

Snow was falling in big, puffy flakes, settling on the already-thick blanket that covered the ground. So, naturally, I reached down to make a quick snowball, throwing it at Evander's unsuspecting face. He laughed, dodging it easily, which made me wonder if he had let me hit him in the village all those months ago.

I narrowed my eyes, and he gathered a snowball in response.

He pulled me toward him, making a movement like he was going to smash it in my face. But just as I braced myself for the freezing cold snow, he dropped it, pressing his mouth against mine instead.

How was he still this warm when it was so cold outside?

I leaned into him, our small snow battle forgotten for the moment. No sooner had I pressed my body against his than the carriage finally came ambling up the road.

Evander let out a low growl when I released him. Shivers of pleasure raked down my skin at the sound, but I still bounded off to greet my friend.

I had so many things to catch her up on with the court, which was an odd switch of our usual positions.

A footman stepped forward to open the carriage door, and Mila came tumbling out with decidedly less grace than she usually displayed. I moved forward to catch her, and she pitched toward me...promptly vomiting all over the hem of my dress.

"Are you unwell?" I asked as Taras hurried to put a protective arm around her.

"Sorry, Row," she croaked, standing straighter. "And I'm fine. Just...well, carrying a little extra these days."

Taras' gaze softened, a frown tugging the corners of his mouth downward as he stared at Mila with concern.

My gaze flew to her stomach, and she nodded, giving a wan smile. I tried to gauge whether she was excited or terrified, but she seemed happy enough.

So I tried to be happy, too... Tried to ignore the way my mind told me this was just one more person we stood to lose if things went badly with Iiro.

Still, I wanted to be optimistic, for her sake. I leaned in and hugged her and congratulated her and pretended that I believed everything was going to work out for the best.

But Taras' wary eyes met mine over her shoulder, and I knew he was thinking the same thing.

Worse still, it only took seven hours for us to be proven right.

CHAPTER FORTY-FIVE

ROWAN

The bird came in the middle of the night, an urgent message from Crane scrawled in hurried, slanted script.

Forces from the Obsidian Palace had surprised them, overwhelming their contingent at the southeastern border.

And now Iiro's men were marching on Bear.

CHAPTER FORTY-SIX

ROWAN

Evander had only said a single word when we received the letter, the lines of his face etched in a calm, detached fury.

Der'mo.

After that, it was a flurry of orders to the soldiers in our hallway, a rush for us to both get dressed, and then we were out the door.

He led us down an unfamiliar hallway to a room I had never been to.

The war room.

A map was etched into the rectangular table, and small, painted figurines were scattered across the top, each representing a different clan animal.

No wonder Evander had taken to Dominion so quickly. This was just a more realistic version of that board.

Several lords joined us, including Taras.

Evander took a moment to tell me how many forces each piece represented. I remembered what he had said back in Lochlann, that Bear had the single largest military force in Socair.

It hadn't been an exaggeration. There were nearly twice as many black pieces on the board as any other clan had, though Elk was close to rivaling Bear, and Wolf wasn't far behind them.

Going to a drawer, Evander grabbed a velvet bag and spilled out a pile of purple crowns, then started moving them around based on the vague intel we had received from Crane.

His hands went to the black pieces, and Taras listed out numbers and locations until Evander had those placed as well.

"We can assume he has forces from Eagle and Viper," Evander said, moving those in a line.

"Ram?" Someone asked.

His eyes flickered to a lord at the opposite end of the table.

The man shook his head. "We haven't heard from our spies."

"And now we know why," Evander muttered. "Mikhail is a coward, so if he's joining Iiro's forces, it won't be until the last minute. He won't pit them directly against Bear. That will buy us time."

"And Elk?" I asked.

Evander's hand stilled over the map, and he met my eye. "Iiro is likely in charge of Elk forces."

The truth of his words hit me like a stone. It made sense, of course, but still…it meant that Theo would be on the other side of this battlefield.

"And what about our allies?" I asked.

"Crane's forces are clearly depleted, but they will step in once they aren't walking into a slaughter," he confirmed. "Lynx is…less militant than some of the other clans, but their size will be an attribute. Still, it will take them time to mobilize."

"Wolf?" I glanced at the canine-shaped pieces on the board, noting there were quite a few of them considering the space.

"Their forces aren't as well positioned to help, but they will be crucial in holding the eastern line at the border." His eyes slid down to the territory southwest of Wolf. "And Bison is still anyone's guess."

Evander surveyed the map before sliding several of the minuscule black bears along the southwestern border of our territory.

"We'll send a sizable contingent to the Ram border to intimidate them into staying out of this fight. The troops we sent to the south should be sufficient for now, but we'll mobilize a cavalry to bolster them, and leave the western forces where they are to guard the border and the estate."

Of course, he had already sent troops to prepare for this possibility. I couldn't help but shoot him an admiring gaze. The man really did think of everything.

"When do we leave?" Taras asked.

There was no trace of fear in his tone, only the determined tone of a soldier prepared to do his duty. As far as I could tell, Taras was the Socairan equivalent to a Lochlannian Captain of the Guard. Leading the troops to battle would normally fall on his shoulders.

But Evander looked at him for a long moment, long enough that I knew what he was going to say before he said it.

And I knew why.

Judging by the protest in Taras' eyes, he knew also.

"*We* don't," Evander said shortly. "I do. I need you here to guard the estate."

Meaning, *I refuse to let you leave your expectant wife unless you have to.*

Taras opened his mouth, then shut it with a wary glance around the room. He would not contradict his duke in the middle of the war room, but it was clear he wasn't happy.

Which made two of us. Because I couldn't help but notice that Evander said *I.*

I also refrained from opening my mouth to argue, but my husband must have sensed that I wanted to. He glanced at me, his gray eyes assessing the flinty look in mine before giving a sharp nod.

"Lady Rowan will accompany me," he declared casually.

My mouth dropped open, but he had already returned to issuing orders.

"Gather the soldiers. We leave at dawn."

And just like that, we were headed to war.

CHAPTER FORTY-SEVEN

EVANDER

I braced myself for my cousin's ire on top of the spectacular quagmire today had already been. Sure enough, he followed Rowan and me down the hall instead of going back to his own room.

"It's my duty to lead the soldiers to war, Van." His voice echoed off the cavernous walls.

I didn't hesitate before responding. "You have a duty to your wife and your child as well."

"Yes, and it's to keep them safe," he fired back, taking a few steps closer.

"Which you can do from here," I reminded him.

He opened his mouth to argue again, and I held up a hand, effectively silencing him. "Depending on how this war goes, you may yet need to go charging into battle, Cousin. But that time isn't now. And as your duke, it is my prerogative to decide if and when you do."

His features hardened.

"For what it's worth," I said in a softer tone. "I'm not doing this just to keep you out of the line of fire. You know as well as I do that one of us needs to go, and one of us needs to stay. Right now, it makes sense that the one of us who stays would be the one with the expectant wife."

His lips parted, likely to form another argument, when Rowan chimed in beside me.

"Shall I tell Mila how hard you're pushing to leave her right now?" She raised her eyebrows, her tone politely inquiring.

His mouth snapped shut.

"Ready the soldiers, then go back to your wife, Taras." I sighed. "I'll send word if anything changes."

He clenched his jaw, but nodded, reaching out a hand to clap me on the shoulder.

"May the stars light your path and may the mountains tremble in your wake, Cousin."

I nodded in response to the soldier's farewell as he turned to leave. Heading to a warfront without Taras at my back wouldn't have been my first choice, but there was no one I trusted more to care for the clan in my absence.

When Rowan and I finally made it back to our rooms, we had barely shut the door before she finally asked what I knew she had been dying to know.

"You're really not going to put up a fight about me coming?" Her tone was laced with suspicion.

I leveled a look at her. "Lemmikki, short of locking you in this room, do I have any real hope of stopping you?"

She didn't hesitate. "No."

"Then I'd rather you be with me than traipsing around Bear where I have no way of knowing if you're safe." *Or alive.* "Seven weeks of that was more than enough," I added.

Besides, it wasn't like we would be fighting on the front lines, either of us. My job was to command all of the troops, and I had to stay somewhere neutral to effectively do that.

For now, she was safest at my side. And if that changed...that was a battle I would fight if and when it occurred.

Rowan closed the distance between us, putting her hands on my face and guiding it until I was looking directly at her.

"What does this war realistically look like for us?" she asked.

I mentally surveyed the map we had just left, putting it together with what I knew of my own forces and Iiro's mentality before responding.

"If we get there fast enough, we can end this relatively quickly. We outnumber him, and the Bear army truly is the most skilled in Socair. With Crane and Lynx boxing him in and Wolf halting his progress on the western side, I don't anticipate problems."

Her shoulders relaxed slightly.

"But, what if we don't?" she asked quietly. "Get there fast enough, I mean."

"Then we can still keep him at bay...but the cost will be substantially higher," I admitted. "My guess is that he will maneuver something in an attempt to force us into a surrender, to recover his pride and his power over Bear."

Taras was already sending a bird to the troops on that side to head Iiro off at the border and move the villagers in toward the estate, but it still may not come soon enough.

Rowan met my gaze with nothing more than a steely determination. "Then I suppose we should get going."

CHAPTER FORTY-EIGHT

ROWAN

I t took us two and a half days of hard riding to reach the border.

Two-and-a-half days of riding in the freezing, sleeting wind. Once again, I cursed the weather knowledge that only allowed me to have a keener awareness of just how miserable we would be all day, rather than actually do anything about it.

The trip had been fairly quiet with constant talk of strategy and precautions we would need to be aware of.

When the large camp came into view, I was relieved that we had finally made it and eager to get to work with whatever needed to be done. Not to mention grateful to see the many fires burning, chasing off the bitter chill and melting the snow on the ground around them.

We left our horses with a group of soldiers, giving them a much-needed break before heading into the large war tent.

"Report," Evander ordered.

One of the men looked up from the map on the table. He stood abruptly when he realized who was addressing him, and the rest of the men in the room quickly dipped their heads in a respectful greeting.

"The king has nearly double the forces we were anticipating," he said. "Crane and the few from Bear that could make it in time held the line, but they lost a lot of ground and sustained significant casualties."

His jaw tightened, and his fists clenched at his sides. It had only been a few days since the battles began, but they had clearly taken their toll on the men here.

Evander nodded, his features hard as he walked over to look at the pieces on the map. It was a cluster of black with a few scattered yellow pieces for what was left of Crane, but mostly, purple, brown, and green dominated the battlefield.

"What of the villages on the border?" I asked.

The soldier appeared startled to have a woman questioning him, but Evander stared at him pointedly until he answered.

"Some he left alone, but any who resisted…" He paused. "He made an example of."

The air whooshed from my lungs. It wasn't difficult to imagine what sort of an example he was referring to.

Evander told the man he would be back later to strategize before we headed over to our tent.

Voices reached us from the south of camp where weary soldiers were half dragging themselves in. Some of them marched on their own two feet, and others were being helped along by another.

But far too many were being wheeled in on wagons, their bodies piled on top of one another in a heap.

The cavalry rushed past us, ready to take their place in the raging battle just a few miles south of here. We watched them until they disappeared over the hills in the distance.

If Evander was frustrated about not joining them, he didn't show it.

The first day of the war camp was an unending barrage of troubling reports and wounded soldiers. Evander never ceased to amaze me with the way he took constant decisive action, the way he organized the facts in his head and carefully took them into account every time something new was brought to his attention.

As dire as things appeared, we were winning, technically speaking. Even if it sure as hell didn't feel like it.

I had deduced quickly that I would be the most useful helping with the wounded. That is, as soon as the male healers got over themselves.

I was by no means an expert, but I could tend to a battle wound as well as the next person. It was appallingly apparent after a few hours that we didn't have anywhere close to enough hands to handle the vast quantities of injured soldiers.

So, I requested Kirill's company and rode my horse the short distance to the nearest village while Evander dealt with the local lord. It wasn't difficult to find the main inn, which, if Socair was anything at all like Lochlann, was where I would be able to accomplish the most.

From there, I used a combination of my halting Socairan and the common tongue to explain to the aging innkeep what I needed: young, strong women to help me at the war camp.

The balding man was not receptive, but he knew who I was. Who Evander was. So he nodded tersely, fetching his daughter for me.

She shook her head when I told her why I was there.

"It is not done, My Lady," she said in Socairan.

"It is now," I told her, my voice more encouraging than commanding. "Your clan needs you."

If that didn't work, I wasn't above leveraging the villagers' fear of my husband and my hair to get what I needed. But something in my expression must have swayed her, because she had a group of ladies gathered within the hour.

All told, twelve women came back to the camp with me, which was frankly, more than I could have hoped for.

Evander was standing outside the war tent as I strode into camp. His face was carefully neutral when he caught sight of me, but intrigue shone from his pale-gray gaze.

I asked the women to wait a moment while I went to speak with him.

As cold as it was, his nose was barely pink compared to the way I knew my entire face was likely red. Only Evander could look handsome in the middle of a frigid war camp. Damn him.

I didn't even want to know what I looked like, with the melting sleet no doubt frizzing up the curls around my face.

My husband raised a single, dark eyebrow as I strode over and peered tentatively up at him.

"I could use your assistance with something." Because the healers were absolutely not going to go for this.

Already, the women were garnering suspicious looks.

"Oh?" he asked, his assessing glance landing on the group of women huddled at the outskirts of camp.

"Really," I clarified. "I just need you to stand next to me and look authoritative."

A smirk tugged at the corner of his lips. "I can do that."

My smile widened.

It didn't escape my notice that he didn't ask me what this was for. Perhaps he had guessed, but the fact remained that he trusted me enough to lend his support without asking.

And that...that meant everything.

CHAPTER FORTY-NINE

ROWAN

The healers took to the new arrangement about how I expected them to, though Evander's glowering presence certainly helped.

They recovered quickly when they saw how useful the women were, though.

Johanna, the innkeeper's daughter, was a particularly quick study. She had a fire that resonated with me, one that allowed her to be forceful enough with the soldiers to tend their wounds, but kind enough to reassure them.

"We have many wounds at the inn," she told me in Socairan.

At least, I thought that was what she said. My knowledge of the language was woefully underprepared for war, and I belatedly realized, overprepared for requesting all manner of food.

Karina, the youngest of the village women, busied herself with bringing the men water, and I instructed the others on how to clean a wound to prevent infection. One of the healers even took to teaching them.

It was well past midnight when I dragged myself back to my and Evander's tent after seeing the women were comfortable in theirs.

He looked up from the parchment he was examining, taking in my blood-spattered gown.

"We need to get you an apron, Lemmikki," he said.

I huffed out a low, humorless chuckle, stripping off my dress and going to a barrel of water in the corner of our tent. Using the clean cloths set to the side, I scrubbed at my hands, my face, my chest, everywhere my dress hadn't been covering.

At least it was warm in here, a small fire burning in the middle of the tent with the smoke escaping through a hole in the top. There were far too many wounded for the healer's tent, so I had spent most of my day in the elements trying to keep the men warm as well as alive.

Still, the water itself was freezing, doing nothing to thaw my frozen skin.

"What you did today..." Evander began.

I turned slowly, wondering if he was about to chastise me.

"The healers say you reduced the casualties by more than half." Pride shone from his gaze, and a small, exhausted smile crept onto my lips.

"Some of the men were dying from ridiculous, preventable things." I shook my head. "There just weren't enough hands, and I knew there were no able-bodied young *men* to be spared, so it was the next logical choice. The only option, really."

"How did you convince the women to come?" he asked curiously as I dried myself off with a fresh cloth.

"Oh, I just told them we had the finest knitting needles in all of Socair, and a big strong husband at the end, to boot." I gave him a tired smirk. "And they gleefully came skipping after me."

He let out a low chuckle, putting his arms around me and pulling me down onto the pallet next to him. *Warm.* He was so warm.

"Did you tell them the only thing you knew how to do with those knitting needles was stab someone?" he asked casually.

"That felt like unnecessary information to share." I stifled a yawn before adding more seriously, "I need to organize everyone into shifts."

"That would be wise," he agreed, kissing me on the forehead. "But it can wait until tomorrow. You look exhausted, Lemmikki. For now, rest."

I nestled further into him, putting my icy toes on his warm calves, which he valiantly did not complain about.

"Only if you rest, too," I countered, knowing he was likely to stay up half the night going over and over strategies in his head.

It was an empty threat, though, because I was asleep before my head even fell against his chest.

The days continued to pass in a haze of blood and injuries and death.

I had seen men die before, in battle and otherwise, but nothing on this scale. Every day, we pushed the line a little further back, but every day, it came at significant cost.

More women arrived to help as word spread, and I wanted to feel happy about that, but I mostly just felt exhausted from the constant slew of injuries that necessitated their presence.

When I wasn't with the wounded men, I was in the war tent, listening to reports with Evander. He rode back and forth to the battlefront, alternating between seeing things for himself and getting the information secondhand.

Everything was going as planned, he said, but wars took time.

And death.

So much death.

I couldn't imagine how my Aunt Isla had done this day after day while she was pregnant with twins. The never-ending smell of infection and blood made my head swim and my stomach churn, even when I was decidedly *not* with child.

It was well into the early hours of the morning when the head healer, Aapo, forced me to leave and get some rest. A bone-deep exhaustion gnawed at me, each step weighed down with lead as I dragged myself into our tent.

Evander was unsurprisingly still awake, standing near the bedroll and pulling his shirt off and over his head. Neatly folding it, of course.

He looked up when I entered, pausing at whatever he saw in my features.

"Lemmikki?" He said the word in a quiet, concerned tone.

I think I surprised us both when I wordlessly crossed the distance between us and leaned my head against his chest. Though Evander had offered comfort a handful of times, I rarely sought it out.

But tonight...

His arms came around me as he pressed a kiss against the top of my head. We remained standing like that, unmoving, while I greedily soaked in the strength he always seemed to lend me.

"I'm just so tired of watching people die," I finally said, letting out a shallow breath.

He heaved a long, slow sigh. "So am I, Lemmikki."

And though there was nothing either of us could do about it, that shared moment of understanding was enough. It was more than enough.

CHAPTER FIFTY

EVANDER

I thought that my father's reign had taught me everything I needed to know about the brutality and unfairness of death and battle.

I was wrong.

This war was on another level, with men younger than I was dying in numbers I could hardly process. Every other day, I rode to the battlefront, watching the wounded men be carried away.

Then there was Rowan, holding their hands and tending their wounds and training the assistants for the healers.

Every night, she came back spattered in blood and exhausted. And every day, she woke early and went straight back to the healers.

They had long since stopped complaining about having women help them, partly because they realized how much help the women could give, but mostly because everyone was stretched to their limit and they had no other choice.

My only consolation was that this would be over soon. Crane and Lynx were finally mobilized on the other side, and Iiro's forces were weakening surprisingly fast.

Almost too fast, truth be told. For a man who started a war, he wasn't fighting it with the vigor I had been expecting.

Then again, he may not have been prepared for Lynx to step

ROBIN D. MAHLE & ELLE MADISON

in as well as Crane. Something about that felt false, but I hadn't been able to come up with a better explanation.

I should have trusted that instinct. I should have thought harder about it.

I should have done a lot of things, but I didn't quite realize the magnitude of my mistakes until the day the messenger arrived.

I was surveying the camp, mentally tallying the supplies we would need to secure before the week's end, when Pavel approached me.

"There's a man outside the camp to see you," he told me uncertainly.

"Send him in," I ordered.

Pavel hesitated. "He says he needs to speak with you in private."

I glanced over to where Rowan was unflinchingly stitching a wound in a man's chest, deciding it wasn't the best time to interrupt her. Besides, this was...suspicious, to say the least.

Kirill was watching over her, as he always did without complaint, so I left her to find out who this man was and what he wanted.

I recognized him immediately as an Elk soldier. My fingers were already twitching toward my sabers when he raised his hands in front of him.

"Sir Theodore sent me with a message," he said quietly.

"About what?" I asked, hearing the steel behind my words.

He met my gaze evenly, begrudgingly raising my respect for him. "Wolf has betrayed you."

Cold dread seeped through my body. *Nils.*

The man continued. "Their forces, along with Elk's, march toward Bear as we speak."

"He's both alerting me of an invasion and facilitating it?" I asked, suspicion lacing my tone.

"Iiro still controls Elk's forces, and Sir Theodore's attempts to sway him have been...unsuccessful."

"If Iiro controls Elk's forces, why are you here?" I asked. "Betraying him?"

The man lifted his chin. "Because I am loyal to Sir Theodore. And to your wife."

That last part gave me pause, given the earnestness with which he said it.

"What possible loyalty could you have toward a Lochlannian princess?" I demanded.

And storms help this man if it had anything to do with her relationship with Korhonan.

Once again, he met my eyes without hesitation. "Your wife saved my life during the Unclanned attack. I had never shown her a single shred of kindness, and she picked up a dead man's sword and killed a man who was about to kill me."

He sounded sincere, and that certainly sounded like Rowan.

Taking him at his word was dangerous, though.

If we abandoned the front here, Iiro could overwhelm Bear from the southwest. But if the man was telling the truth and forces were coming from the southeastern border, they could march straight for the estate.

If they captured that, the war was over for Bear, and there was no hope of victory for the other clans without us.

Worse still, we had no allies on that side. Lynx and Crane were trapped fighting on the other side of this battle.

Bison remained completely neutral in this conflict, and Lochlann, even if I was willing to call for their aid and King Logan was willing to give it, would take weeks to arrive through the tunnels.

Even with the defenses of the estate, it would be a slaughter if we didn't bring in extra forces.

Still, we couldn't move everyone from the line here without adding the substantial line of troops Iiro had on this end to that attack.

Hell, even if we did move most of our troops there, if Wolf

and Elk attacked together, they would easily overwhelm the castle.

If the man was telling the truth.

He examined my features, then slowly reached toward his jacket. "I'm only going for a note," he said.

I nodded, and he pulled out a folded piece of parchment, handing it over to me. The handwriting was familiar from all the letters Korhonan had written Rowan.

For everything I had ever thought about him, I didn't honestly believe he would betray anyone on this level, or...as much as I hated to admit it, put Rowan in any kind of danger.

He did love her, and I couldn't actually bring myself to hate him for that right now. Not when I read his note.

It was a hastily sketched map with X's drawn for where the troops were, something any soldier learned how to do, and then a single line of words.

He wants revenge on both of you.

That explained why he was warning me, aside from just basic decency. Rowan was a direct target of this attack, which I could have guessed. But having it confirmed...

I took several tense breaths through my nose, then turned my attention back to the man.

"I assume you're returning to him, to report?" I asked.

He nodded.

My brain worked furiously, weighing the very few options I had before landing on the only possible choice.

"Then I need you to give him a message as well."

CHAPTER FIFTY-ONE

ROWAN

I knew something was wrong the moment Evander walked back into camp.

Quickly, I finished giving the man I was tending to a swallow of sleeping tonic, then gave Johanna a hurried instruction to see to his sutures once the draught kicked in.

Pocketing the vial and wiping my bloody hands on a towel, I finally made my way to Evander.

"What is it?" I asked.

He examined my face, his dusty eyes more haunted than I had ever seen them, while the rest of his features were almost eerily calm.

He tilted his head toward our tent, and I followed him to where we would have more privacy.

"Nils has betrayed us," he said, running a hand over his unshaven jaw. "He's marching on the estate."

My mouth dropped open. I had seen the sheer volume of wolf pieces on his section of the map back at the estate, but then, Bear had significant forces as well.

"So we go to head him off," I said, which I was sure he had already planned. "Join the soldiers you already have stationed there."

He gave a terse nod, and my stomach sank as I filled in the

rest of my thought. "But...taking too many will leave this part of Bear open for the taking."

Evander nodded. "We'll move the soldiers around in a cascading pattern from the Ram border and just hope they don't decide to join the fight."

He sounded like he didn't actually believe that, and I didn't blame him.

Not after this devastating news.

"We'll leave within the hour, in advance of the soldiers," he added after a moment.

"Of course. I'll give some last-minute instructions to Johanna, then pack my things."

Evander squeezed his eyes shut, wordlessly pulling me against him before taking a deep, steadying breath.

I wrapped my arms around his torso. "We'll get through this. The estate is a veritable fortress, and you said yourself, Bear soldiers are the best."

It wasn't a lie, either. I understood now that was largely due to Evander, the way he personally chose trainers and walked through his men with his unparalleled observation skills.

His soldiers were the best because he had made it so.

My husband leaned down to kiss my forehead. "We should get moving."

There was enough on his plate already that I didn't bring attention to the fact that he wasn't actually responding to me.

But I sure as stars noticed.

We rode until well after nightfall before stopping at an unfamiliar inn where we stayed in a two-room suite on the top floor. It was different from the soldiers' lodging Evander normally chose, but I wasn't complaining because there was a sizable bathtub.

It was impossible to relax knowing that forces were marching toward my pregnant best friend and toward our estate, knowing that Iiro had found yet another way to make our lives miserable and our people pay for his unending quest for power.

But neither was I complaining about the opportunity to be truly clean after weeks in the tents, or truly warm.

And of course, there was the bonus of the added privacy, when we had been in a thin canvas tent surrounded by soldiers for longer than I cared to think about.

Once Evander and I were both clean, he didn't wait for me to get dressed before he tugged me gently over to the bed, sitting down and pulling me in between his knees. That still just barely put us at eye level.

His kiss was slower than normal, deeper. Instead of the current that usually zapped through me, this one sent a gentle heat spreading across every inch of my skin.

He took his time, running his hands over my body like he was memorizing the way I felt under his fingertips. It was slow and sensual and utterly terrifying, because for the first time, I realized how concerned he was about this upcoming assault.

I returned his touches with urgency, gliding my fingers through the short, silky strands of his hair, then down across his freshly shaven jaw. My fingers clutched his shoulders, pulling him more tightly against me, like I could keep him alive, keep us in this moment forever just by willing it so.

At least I was here, with him. At least he had kept his promise to remember that we were in this together.

That would be enough. It would have to be.

CHAPTER FIFTY-TWO

EVANDER

I t took everything I had to pry myself away from Rowan's perfect, warm body.

But this was the only way.

I tucked the blankets in around her, keeping my arm around her shoulders until I could be sure she wouldn't stir. Leaning in, I gave her a kiss on the forehead before I dressed silently and went to meet Korhonan in the hall.

She was a sound sleeper when she wasn't having nightmares, but I knew she would wake soon after I left. That's why I had waited until close to dawn. I had minutes, at best.

My lungs seized, my entire body rebelling at leaving her this way. Without a goodbye. Without explaining anything.

But I only barely found the strength to leave her at all. If she argued, I would cave.

Then she would die in the attack, or worse, by Iiro's hands.

Korhonan was right where he said he would be. He looked troubled, but then, everything about this situation was a mess.

"Thank you for coming." It might have been the nicest thing I had said to him in years.

It was impossible to feel any kind of ire toward the man who was saving Rowan's life, at great risk to himself.

He nodded. "Of course."

I checked down the hall to be sure we weren't overheard, conscious that we had very little time.

"Tell me about the forces," I said quietly.

So he did, giving me updated numbers and locations, each one twisting the knife deeper into my gut. Somewhere in the back of my mind, I had held on to hope that this wouldn't be necessary.

That I could walk back into the room and climb into bed next to her and pretend that none of this ever happened.

But we would need a miracle to survive this, and I wouldn't bank her life on that.

I thanked Korhonan again, then handed him one note for him and one that I had written Rowan while she was in the tub.

"The top one is for Rowan," I told him. "When she wakes up."

His lips parted. "You didn't tell her?"

I didn't verbally respond, but something in my features must have given me away.

"Because you couldn't have left her." He heaved a deep sigh. "You truly do love her."

"More than my life," I said, turning to walk away.

More than everything else in this world combined.

CHAPTER FIFTY-THREE

ROWAN

Lightning zapped along my spine.

I expected to wake up cocooned in Evander's warm embrace, but the bed was cold.

And Evander wasn't here.

My heart pounded, even as I told myself how unreasonable it was. He probably just went to fetch breakfast.

A glance out the window showed it was nearly morning, gentle rays of sun poking through hostile storm clouds that had nothing to do with the current shooting through every nerve in my back.

I ordered myself to be calm, hastily tossing on a clean dress and throwing open the door to the small sitting room.

A figure sat stiffly in one of the chairs, and for the smallest fraction of a second, relief coursed through my veins.

But where I should have seen black locks and a sardonic smirk was a white-blond head and an earnest, troubled frown.

"Theo," I breathed out. "What are you doing here? And where is my husband?"

My voice was a jagged shard of ice by that last question, and Theo actually winced.

"I was the only one who could get you safely across the enemy lines," he said quietly, evenly, as if he had rehearsed the line several times.

"I don't need to be across enemy lines," I bit back, panic rising in my throat. "Where. Is. Evander."

He sighed, sitting forward and taking two agonizingly long breaths.

"He left," Theo said.

My heart dropped into my stomach, sinking rapidly like a boulder hurled carelessly into a pond.

"What? No, he wouldn't do that." But even as I said the words, I knew they weren't true, not if he thought I was in danger.

Hadn't he said that more than once?

Theo reached into his jacket and pulled out a piece of parchment. I crossed the distance between us and snatched it, turning to read the familiar, elegant script.

I told you there was nothing I wouldn't do to keep you safe, Lemmikki. I love you with every last broken piece of my soul.

Evander

Fury rippled through me. *How dare he.*

I moved to walk toward the door, but Theo held out an arm.

"Rowan."

My dagger was in my hand in an instant, precariously balanced against Theo's throat. "Help or get out of my way."

"I won't help you march to your death," he said calmly, wrapping one solid hand around my wrist.

"We're moving the soldiers. It will be fine," I said, reluctantly forced to let my hand drop.

"No." Theo shook his head sadly. "It won't. Iiro controls Elk's forces. They are marching with Wolf. They will come in at an angle to cut off the other forces, and there is no help to be had on the eastern front."

Theo's normally calming presence couldn't touch the sheer horror creeping in on me. He held my gaze with his golden green eyes, like he was trying to will me to understand.

"Clan Bear will fall," he said bluntly. "And when it does, my brother will be sure to make an example of those who thwarted them."

That was said with a significant look at me, but all I could think of was the person who had made Iiro look the weakest.

Evander.

"No." I shook my head in denial. "You don't get to tell me my husband just waltzed off to his death and then expect me to just go back to Elk with you and wait for it to happen."

My mind was reeling, terror and panic and rage beating thunderously in my eardrums.

"No," Theo agreed. "I have men to take you to the tunnel, to take you home."

"This is my home," I snarled.

Evander is my home.

Or he was, before he left me here. Before he took my choice from me and subjected me to the thing I was the most terrified of in the entire world.

Losing him.

I took a deep breath, clenching my shaking hands in an effort to steady myself.

"They're your men," I hissed. "Find a way to fix this!"

The silence that filled the space between us was palpable. A tangible, evil thing that said far more than he could.

"Rowan," Theo finally spoke again. "There is nothing I can do. There is nothing anyone can do. The men answer to Iiro, and Bison has refused to come. There are no more soldiers to call."

Something niggled at the back of my brain when he said that, but his next words effectively distracted me from whatever it was.

"Evander obviously knew that, or he wouldn't have…" Theo wisely did not finish that sentence, but it didn't matter because my brain filled it in anyway.

Or he wouldn't have left you here.

Was it possible to break apart from the inside out? My chest physically ached, like it had been cleaved in half with a sword. Two things kept repeating on a rote in my head.

Evander left me.

Evander went to die.

"I'm sorry," he said. "But we need to leave quickly. I will be missed soon, and we will lose our chance to get you out safely."

I was only half listening to him, because the thrumming on my spine had started up again, and it seemed to be pulling me toward the bedroom. I spun on my heel and walked away, shutting the door behind me.

The tingling was more intense here, shooting bolts of lightning down through my body in time with my stilted heartbeats. And it grew worse, the closer I drew to the saddlebag that held...

The box.

Rayan had said I would know when I needed it.

And sure enough, I did.

CHAPTER FIFTY-FOUR

ROWAN

P rying open the box was surprisingly easy. Somehow, I had expected it to weigh more, but the wooden lid swung open on smooth hinges.

Folds of black velvet filled the entire rectangular space.

My heart managed to race even faster in my chest.

Will whatever is in here help me save Evander?

With trembling hands, I reached for the top, feeling the outline of a sword.

It was a black saber, made of the same material as Evander's, but smaller. Black diamonds winked at the hilt, and the cross-guard came down in two wicked points. The second wrapped bundle held its twin.

They were beautiful, to be sure, and lightweight the way all of Rayan's weapons always seemed to be, but I knew they weren't enough to be what he had warned me about.

Setting them aside for now, I dug through the rest of the box to find...a set of armor. Small, black pieces of metallic stone woven into the fabric that interlocked in a perfect shield, accented with white swaths of fur and bits of obsidian.

The pressure along my spine intensified, and I knew this was it.

Whatever *it* was.

As soon as my fingers touched the obsidian, the tingling stopped.

Or rather, it focused.

My awareness of the clouds, the wind... It was as though I could sense each individual raindrop poised to fall at any moment. The pressure of the oncoming storm felt tangible, somehow, present.

So I pushed back.

Raindrops spattered against the window, a few at first, then more and more.

Surely not...

I stared at my hands on the armor, felt the sensation that buzzed through my fingers and pulsed along my skin. Then I looked back at the sky, pushing harder until the downpour made it impossible to see through the glass at all.

What the actual stars-blasted hell?

Why had Rayan given me this?

I knew he had some ability with stones, and he had spoken of the amplifying effects of the fae and certain crystals... But my weather senses were fairly useless, and a little rain wasn't going to help me fight a war.

A knock at the door startled me, and I dropped the armor. The thrumming returned, but not as strong as before, like the energy had lessened...or been used.

"Rowan," Theo's voice sounded through the solid wood. "We really do need to leave."

I looked from the armor to the door.

Even if my "woo woo powers" as Davin called them were mostly useless, this armor wasn't, because it brought my sister's words to mind.

You are Rowan Pendragon, second-in-line to the most powerful throne in the world, and daughter of the Warrior Queen.

I was Rowan Stenvall now, and Clan Wife of Bear. But her words rang true, nonetheless.

Do not let them think they hold all the cards here, she had said.

I thought about Evander, having the nerve to leave me here

without so much as consulting me. Theo, ready to cart me back to Lochlann against my will.

And most of all, Iiro, who was killing countless thousands in his quest for power. For revenge. For his pride.

Who wanted to hurt the person I loved most in the world.

No, Avani. I won't let them think that at all.

I clenched my jaw, determination and fury battling within me. I didn't know how Rayan's armor would help, and I didn't know how I was going to do it, but I was damned well going to find a way to stop him.

And I would save Evander.

Aalio that he was.

CHAPTER FIFTY-FIVE

ROWAN

There was only one problem with my plan.

"Evander said you would try to escape." Theo heaved an exasperated sigh while I fumed about him tethering our horses together.

It was barely past dawn, and apparently we were already late. The plan was to make it to the tunnels before the end of the week where I would be escorted back to Lochlann.

Even when I told him I would gather my parents' forces and come right back through, I knew the threat was useless. By the time I made it to Chridhe and then we moved the militia back through the tunnels, it would be too late.

Theo knew that, too, and he was intent to make sure his plan--Evander's plan--for me succeeded.

He wasn't alone, either. There were three guards, all loyal to him, all equally committed to ensuring I cooperated.

"And you're just fine with taking me against my will?" I demanded in a frigid tone. "*Again?*"

Theo flinched, but I wasn't done. Not even close.

"Last time, you at least had the relative excuse that I had broken your precious laws, but what is it this time?" I pushed. "Or do you just truly believe that women aren't entitled to free will?"

He shook his head, his features shuttering.

I wasn't actually sure who I hated more right now, my husband or the man currently treating me like a prisoner. Both were taking my choices from me.

But only one of them had promised me we were in this together, had held me like I was his entire life, and then left me in the middle of the night with nothing more than a stars-damned letter.

I decided there was plenty of fury to go around.

It didn't help that it was freezing again, traveling quickly by horse in the dead of winter.

"What I believe," Theo said in a growl, "is that you are still as reckless now as you were then. If you won't come for your own sake, then ask yourself this. Do you honestly believe that Evander can concentrate on defending Bear when you are in danger?"

All the air whooshed from my lungs. Unbidden, memories came to me of Evander walking to that tree trunk to be flogged. Of him ordering his men to stand down.

Is that what I am? A liability? Is that the real reason he left me here?

Tendrils of doubt crept through me, but then, I thought about that day. I had freed myself from the man holding a dagger to my throat.

I had killed Ava.

Before that, I had fought at Evander's side with the Unclanned, fought for him with the rebels in Lochlann.

So, no. The problem was not me.

I narrowed my eyes at Theo. "I thought you said there was no hope for Bear, so it hardly matters, does it?"

He sighed, running a hand over his weary face. The fight was leaving him as soon as he heard the bitter resignation in my voice.

"There is always hope, Rowan," he said sadly. "If the men break through the western line in time to help. But it's a slim hope, and I won't bring you back only to die."

A slim hope.

But hope, nonetheless.

One I could find a way to capitalize on, if I could get away from Theo. The vial I had accidentally taken from camp was still in my saddlebags, and I had the feeling it could prove quite useful, under the right circumstances.

I just needed to time it right.

CHAPTER FIFTY-SIX

ROWAN

We made our way through Bear territory, presumably toward the heavily armed border that Theo and Evander had devised a way to sneak me through.

It hadn't taken me long to come up with a plan to get free, but I still didn't know what I would do after that. The part of my brain that was as reckless as Theo accused me of being wanted to leave anyway.

But I remembered the game of Dominion I had played with Evander in Lochlann. Another pang lanced through me at the thought of him, but I ignored it, focusing.

Sometimes winning requires patience, Lemmikki. And an actual plan.

I spent the morning in silence, forcing myself to come up with one.

Slowly, something vague started to come together in my mind, but I didn't see the full picture until well after our break to water the horses.

Until we spotted an enormous band of the Unclanned passing along the other side of the river. Most of them kept their heads down, but others glanced in our direction, some with curious gazes and others with eyes full of resentment.

What was it Evander had said?

All of the Unclanned were soldiers once.

I knew they were willing to work for money, since Ava had paid them, but my father had always said that mercenaries were worth less than half of a soldier fighting for a cause.

And these men had been ostracized, forced to live off nothing. They would never see a reason to fight for Bear. They needed something else.

Hope.

Turning to Theo, I forced myself to speak to him again.

"What offenses lead to Unclanning?" My voice was still hollow, but at least it didn't come out half as hateful as I felt.

He looked at me askance, but he answered, probably grateful that it appeared I was on the path to being *reasonable* about this.

"As you know," he began, "blood spilled at the Summit. Treason against the duke is the most common one, any kind of offense in the military. But in certain cases, thieves will get Unclanned as well."

I nodded thoughtfully. "What about your everyday murderers? Rapists?"

He shook his head. "No. We execute for that. To allow someone like that to roam freely with nothing left to lose would be unconscionable."

So there were bands of trained soldiers that, in all likelihood, were guilty of no more than speaking or acting out against authority.

Following my gaze, Theo sighed. "Rowan, each of those men knew what they were doing when they got Unclanned. Don't let yourself forget how dangerous they are."

"Dangerous?" I said softly. "You mean like a man who kills thousands for a power trip? Surely, we're past that kind of judgment now, Theo."

His eyes darkened, and he pursed his lips. When he spoke, he sounded so defeated that I actually felt a little guilty for bringing it up.

"All those times Evander accused him...I never truly believed my brother was capable of this."

There was nothing I could say to comfort him, not when I felt the way I did about Iiro, so I settled on an observation instead, one that felt like it applied to so much more than Theo's arsehat of a brother.

"I suppose you never really know what someone is capable of," I said quietly.

For better or worse.

We stayed at a soldier's inn where Theo insisted on us sharing a room, though he felt very clearly uncomfortable about it.

I tried not to look at the two beds and remember the first night I had argued with Evander about my propriety, the way that even then, he had made my heart race for all the wrong reasons.

Tried not to think about the journey to the cabin that last time, when he had settled on the small bed with me to stop my nightmares.

Tried not to think about him at all.

Instead, I waited until Theo disappeared into the hallway to ask the guard about dinner to dump half the vial from my dress into my flask of vodka. When he returned, I did my best to look contrite, or at least not enraged.

"Do you have a deck of cards?" I asked, pretending to take a swig from my flask.

"I'm sure my guards do," he said hesitantly. "Why?"

"I just...need something to get my mind off everything." I gave him a wan smile.

He nodded in understanding, and I almost felt guilty before I remembered that he had conspired with my *aalio* of a husband to trick me into going back to Lochlann.

"I'll go ask," he offered.

"Oh, we'll need the guard as well," I said. "It's a game for at least three people."

Theo reluctantly nodded and brought his guard in, along

with a deck of cards. This was not the right audience for Kings and Arselings, so I taught them a milder game.

But it was still a drinking game.

"Oh, that means you have to take a drink," I ordered when Stefan, the guard, laid down the wrong card.

The guard looked around, and I pretended to take another swig from my flask before helpfully handing it out to him.

He chuckled and took a sip, nodding at me. He would need at least three more for this to work, and then there was Theo. Fortunately, I was an expert in making up card rules.

It wasn't long before they had each consumed about half of the flask and I had faked several more sips. Giving a huge yawn, I announced it was time for bed, and the guard excused himself.

He stumbled a little on the way out, and Theo narrowed his eyes.

"Guess he's a lightweight." I shrugged, infusing my tone with more playfulness than I felt.

Or it was the double dose of sleeping draught he just unwittingly consumed.

He stifled a yawn, not responding, and I settled into my blankets. Then I counted down the seconds, slowly, until I heard his soft snores.

On featherlight feet, I crept from the bed, going to gather what I needed from my pack as quietly as I could. There was a low fire burning in the hearth, but it was enough for me to see by, enough to scratch out a quick note.

Theo,

I thought if anyone could understand drugging someone or conspiring to leave them in the middle of the night with no more than a note, it would be you.

Sincerely, though, I appreciate what you tried to do, even if your methods leave much to be desired. Stay safe.

And don't come after me.

. . .

I didn't sign the note, conscious that someone else might see it. Placing it on my pillow, I eased my way out of the room and stepped over the guard who was in a drugged sleep against the wall near my door.

That had been the trickiest part of my plan, making sure the other two didn't discover him, but I had guessed correctly that they would try to get all the rest they could for their own shifts.

I put up the hood of my black fur-lined cloak to make my way downstairs and out to the stables. It was the same stableboy on duty as earlier.

I gave him my most innocent smile, my heart racing a thousand miles each second.

"My Lord asked me to take the clydesdale out," I said softly, handing him a coin.

The boy looked from it to me as if considering what he should do. I pulled one more coin out of my purse and slid it in front of him to sweeten the deal. If he didn't cooperate, that would be a problem, one I really couldn't afford at the moment.

When his ice-blue eyes took in the copper and the silver piece in front of him, he nodded eagerly. Quickly pocketing the coins, he ran to fetch the horse without stopping to question why I needed it at midnight.

Fortunately, he saddled the large mare quickly, so it was no time at all before I hitched on my pack and led her around to the side of the inn. I waited several stilted heartbeats before mounting her, making sure that the boy hadn't decided to come back or send out a cry of alarm.

When it was safe, I urged the horse forward into the icy night air, a churning mix of emotions propelling me forward.

I would be damned if Evander had chosen to go to his death in this battle and leave me behind.

The thought made me spur the horse to go even faster, back in the direction we had come from and toward the band of Unclanned I had seen earlier.

Energy coursed through my veins, filling me with a stone-cold determination.

No matter how I had tried to avoid or deny it, there was no escaping what Evander and I had.

The kind of love you go to war for.

And that's exactly what I intended to do.

CHAPTER FIFTY-SEVEN

EVANDER

Taras rushed out to meet me as soon as I rode up to the estate. I had sent a bird ahead about the attack, but not about...

"Where is your wife?" Panic crept into his tone.

I steeled my expression, shutting down the swell of guilt and the stabbing sense of loss that threatened to overtake me.

"I sent her back to Lochlann."

His mouth dropped open, a rare display of emotion for him. "You what? And she just...went?"

I blinked, climbing down from my horse and walking him into the stables. "Not exactly."

He ran a hand over his face and wariness crept into his gaze. "What happened?"

"I did what I had to do," I said simply, handing the horse off to the stableboy before heading toward the castle. "Tell me about the preparations here," I ordered before he could question me further.

My cousin nodded hesitantly, keeping pace with me. "We're as prepared as we can be, but the forces just aren't here."

I thought back to the battle map and how woefully underprepared we were for this sort of betrayal.

"I know," I admitted, running a hand through my hair. "But it should buy us a couple weeks."

If we were lucky.

He dipped his head again, knowing as well as I did that we had no hope of withstanding a siege with the numbers they were talking about. We had to bank on Crane and Lynx getting through the western front, and on our holding out until they could--*if* they could.

It was a strange feeling.

As long as I had been alive, Bear had been all but untouchable. But this... Iiro's underhanded methods may finally pay off for him.

At least he wouldn't get his hands on Rowan now.

If there was one thing I could trust Korhonan with, it was Rowan's life.

My cousin glanced at me like he could hear the thoughts playing out in my head, but he didn't speak again until we were inside, away from prying ears. I headed to the war room, realizing there was no part of me that was ready to face the rooms I shared with Rowan.

They probably still smelled like her, like amber and citrus and something uniquely *Rowan*.

"Tell me what happened," Taras said quietly once I shut the door.

I paused, steeling myself as I met his glare with my own.

"I left her at an inn with Korhonan." I said the words far more casually than I felt them.

My cousin blinked in disbelief, and several beats of silence passed between us until he finally breathed out one single word. "Der'mo."

"She was going to be a target for Iiro, and Korhonan was the only one who could get her across the border. And," I admitted reluctantly, "the only one I trusted to keep her safe."

He shook his head in disbelief. "That's certainly an interesting turn of events."

My cousin paused for a beat, then looked back up at me. "What did she think of the plan?"

I ran an uncomfortable hand over the light stubble on my jaw. "Well, I...left her a note."

Taras' brow rose as he digested that information. Finally, he shook his head silently before a small, dry laugh escaped him.

"I wouldn't want to be Korhonan right now. Or you, at the end of this," he tacked on.

A bitter, only slightly amused huff of air left me. But, while my wife excelled at *getting* angry, she didn't generally stay that way for long. Besides...

"Assuming I even live through this, at least she'll be alive to be mad," I responded. "You would do the same thing for Mila."

Fortunately, even Iiro wouldn't allow the noblewomen to be harmed. Except my wife, of course.

His head tilted to the side as if he were weighing the truth of my words. "I would tell her, at least."

I shot him a look, raising one eyebrow. "That's because Mila would still go if you explained it. Have you met Rowan?"

"Yes." He sighed, rubbing the bridge of his nose between his thumb and forefinger. "Yes, I have."

CHAPTER FIFTY-EIGHT

ROWAN

The brisk winds and scattered freezing rain made the ride interminable. I still had at least another hour to go to reach the village I needed, if, of course, I was headed in the right direction.

I shivered and burrowed further into my cloak as I scanned the hills and trees for any sign of familiarity. I had never been terrible with directions, but going in the opposite direction in the dead of night made it difficult to recognize landmarks.

There was no one to ask, of course. No one to collaborate with on this half-arsed plan of mine. No sister, no parents, no cousin, not a single overbearing Socairan.

I was more alone than I had ever been, though there was, at least, a freedom in this.

Which was more than I could have said a few hours ago.

When I finally passed by the patch of trees that were all leaning sideways, ones that Theo had explained were that way because of the constant windstorms, I breathed a sigh of relief.

Occasionally, I reached into my saddle bags to touch the armor, experimenting with the strange energy I could feel so much more clearly with the help of Rayan's stones.

Each time my fingers even barely grazed the material, awareness came crashing over me in an overwhelming wave. It stole my breath, sending shivers running up and down my skin until I adjusted to the new heightened ability.

But other than honed senses, I hadn't discovered anything terribly helpful.

I could divert the wind to a small extent, which made sense, in hindsight. That storm that hit on the way to the Summit should have swept Theo up, too, but the wind had seemed to stop right where he was.

Other than that, with the help of the armor, or the stones and crystals it contained, I could make a tiny gust or get the rain to fall a little sooner.

Which, of course, reminded me of the conversation I had with Evander back at Lochlann. In his rooms, just before…

The wave of fury and panic and betrayal that hit me every time I thought his name crackled through me with an intense energy this time.

A bolt of lightning shot down in the clearing next to me, close enough to scare my horse. I took several minutes to calm her before I contemplated the meaning of that.

So.

Emotions, it would seem, played a crucial role as well.

I removed my hand from the armor and sagged in my saddle, whatever just happened having taken a significant amount of my energy. It was an effort not to fall asleep on my horse, but every time I started to doze off, I pictured Evander's forces getting overwhelmed at the estate.

Pictured his obnoxiously perfect features still and unmoving.

And I damned well found the strength to keep riding.

When I arrived at the village, I paid the stable boy extra to care for my horse before checking into an inn for a few hours of desperately needed sleep.

I didn't bother to hide my hair. Evander was past here by now, and Iiro's soldiers were coming in from the south. By the time anyone cared where I was, I would be gone.

The innkeeper clearly recognized me, but he didn't comment, just gave me a key and directed me to my room. I wasn't concerned for my safety here, with the shrouded protection of being a Clan Wife.

It was the Unclanned I would need to worry about.

Still, I locked my door, pushed a chair up against the handle to secure it, and kept all of my weapons within reach while I slept.

I was as safe as I was going to be, and eventually, I managed to fall into a restless semblance of sleep. Even if the bed felt empty and cold and like a betrayal in and of itself.

It was well after noon when I groggily pulled myself out of bed, and I kicked myself for even sleeping that long. I threw on my most casual, functional dress before smoothing out my curls and grabbing a quick lunch downstairs.

On my way out of town, I stopped by the market and the bakery to see what little they may have to spare in the way of food. It wasn't enough, but it would have to do.

I was finally ready to make my way to the Unclanned.

The camp I had passed with Theo was a short ride from here, nestled into the snowy hills on the other side of the field.

Not nearly enough time to prepare my jumbled nerves.

If this didn't work, I was well and truly out of options. I would still go back to Evander, it would just likely be to join him in his death sentence whether he stars-damned-well liked it or not.

Or perhaps I could find a way to cart him away from the battle and protecting his people and see how much he enjoyed that.

On that enticing thought, the camp came into view.

There were mostly men, with a few women and children scattered throughout. Every one of them looked up when my horse's hoofbeats sounded on the frozen ground.

Bundled in furs and tattered cloaks and blankets around small campfires, they stared at me with each step we took forward.

A tremor of fear shot through me. I was relatively unarmed,

knowing that a couple of swords wouldn't do much against more than forty seasoned warriors.

Perhaps I am still as reckless as I ever was.

But this was my only chance.

Dismounting, I walked half the distance toward the nearest men, waiting for them to come the rest of the way to me and hoping fervently they didn't decide to kill me on sight.

Sure enough, two of them walked toward me. The man on the left had black hair and hazel eyes, where the one on the right had locks so pale they were almost white, and curiously colorless eyes.

But they were both tall, both sporting the telltale *B* branded into their foreheads. Both thin to the point of being gaunt.

And both surveying me with wary, haunted expressions.

I lowered the hood of my cloak, and the men stilled at the sight of my cursed hair waving in the wind behind me.

"You know who I am." I didn't bother to phrase it as a question, but they nodded anyway.

"What's your name?" I asked the dark-haired man, speaking in the common tongue.

His eyes widened, and I wondered when the last time someone had bothered to ask that was. Did anyone treat them as human?

The man looked back at the group behind him before turning and finally answering. "Andrei."

I looked at the man next to him.

"Maxim," he offered with a grunt, suspicion lining his eyes.

I had given a lot of thought to who the Unclanned really were, what they wanted, and some of it was as simple as restoring their basic dignity and humanity.

"Well, Andrei and Maxim. I am Lady Rowan Stenvall." I dipped my head in respect, the way that all nobles greeted one another before gesturing to my horse. "I brought food, and if you'll allow me to distribute it, I would very much like to speak with you all."

They glanced at each other, then back at me.

It was a gamble that they wouldn't just kill me and take the food anyway, but I was banking on curiosity and the oddity of someone showing up, offering them something and then asking for their permission about anything, to stay their hands.

Somehow, it worked.

A relieved whoosh of air escaped my lungs as they nodded in unison.

Now, I just had to convince them.

CHAPTER FIFTY-NINE

ROWAN

Convincing them was not going well.

I explained what I wanted, and what I had to offer in return.

They would fight for me, and in turn, I would make every effort to have them reintegrated into society here. In the event I couldn't accomplish that, or that they didn't want to stay, they could come to live on my vast holdings in Lochlann.

Da' had said the land was mine to do with as I wished. I doubted seriously this is what he had in mind, but I also knew he would respect this decision. Because the men in Lochlann didn't discount the decisions the women made.

Unlike here.

Unlike my husband.

The Unclanned spoke among themselves, and I would have known what they were saying even if I hadn't caught snippets here and there.

Who was I, a woman, to ask this of them? To promise them a different life? To deliver on any of those promises?

When they returned, it was with a decisive *no*.

"We don't swear fealty to women, milady," Andrei said. "But we will fight for coin, for food."

That wasn't good enough. We would already be outnumbered. Out-armed. I needed more from them.

My heart sank, but I wasn't ready to give up yet.

"Thank you for your time," I said simply. "I'll be back tomorrow with more food."

I rode hard to the next village, purchasing whatever little surplus of food they had, then set out to locate the next band of Unclanned.

And promptly got the same answer.

Frustrated, I headed to the blacksmith's, needing to at least accomplish something. These men had agreed to fight for food and coin. I told myself that was better than nothing, even if it didn't feel that way.

A woman looked up when I entered.

"Is the smith in?" I asked in Socairan.

"My husband has gone to the war efforts, milady."

I took in her stature, her strong build and the burn scars on her arms. It was becoming apparent that Socairan women did plenty, they just didn't do it out in the open.

Or get credit for it.

I walked to the counter, putting a high stack of gold coins in front of her. As usual, my *aalio* of a husband had thought of everything, but at least this time, it worked in my favor.

At least if he had planned every aspect of ditching me in the middle of the night, I could use the substantial amount of coins he had left in my trunk toward my own ends.

"I need swords. As many as *anyone--*" I stressed the word. "--can make in the next week."

I held her pale-blue gaze with my own until she gave me a definitive dip of her chin.

"I'll return in one week," I said, leaving as quickly as I had come.

I revisited the same bands the next day, and again, the next.

Every day, their answer was the same. But they were wavering. By the third day, they let me stay longer, or at least, they didn't appear to be uncomfortable about my presence.

I approached a group of children standing in a circle throwing sticks at a pile of sticks, but it took me a moment to register the game. *Gorodki.* Instead of the weighted pins and bats that Theo had used, these children were making use of what they had around them.

"Do you know how to play?" one of the girls watching the game asked me in Socairan, and I nodded.

"A little," I told her in the same language.

A shy grin tempted the corners of her mouth, and I couldn't help but return it. She looked younger than the twins, with pale blond hair that was braided back and knotted at her nape. Her rich brown eyes held all of the excitement that my sisters had at her age, and it tugged at something inside of me.

She deserved better. All of them did.

Not a life of wondering when they were going to eat again or whether or not the next storm was going to wipe out half of their camp.

I needed their help, but I also wanted to help them.

The girl led me to the outskirts of camp near a small section of trees where we collected sticks of our own to play a round of *Gorodki.* When we found what we needed, she taught me how to set them up the right way.

We soon had a few more children who were ready to join in.

Again, I considered who these people were. They wanted their lives back. More than that, they wanted to belong to something again.

I saw it in the way they banded together, the way their faces held wary hope when I brought up the possibility of a new start.

Instead of going back to the inn, I stayed and played with the children, sat and talked with the men, listened to the women and the horror stories of how hard they had to fight to survive.

On the fourth day, I didn't bother sitting down.

"We are running out of time," I told them.

Already, reports were coming of the soldiers marching this way to box the western side of Bear in. I didn't know how far they would go, if we would be trapped on the other side, but it wasn't a risk we could take.

"We've told you, milady, we'll fight for coin," Andrei said again.

"And I have told you that I want more than your skills," I said definitively. "I want your loyalty."

Andrei shook his head and a few of the others let out sardonic chuckles.

"You expect us to be loyal to a Clan that was never loyal to us," Maxim spat.

"No," I shook my head. "I expect you to be loyal to *me*."

That gave them pause, but I continued on.

"Not to your Clan Wife," I clarified. "But to the woman who wants something different for you."

"It isn't done--" Andrei began, but I saw the temptation on his face. The desire for something more.

I cut him off, speaking in a voice loud enough to carry.

"I know that Socairan traditions run deep," I said. "In the past, you have not sworn fealty to women. In the past, you have been removed from your clan, some of you for something as simple as refusing to murder a child."

My gaze wandered the crowd, meeting each of their eyes in turn.

"But that doesn't have to be your future," I told them. "You don't have to be Unclanned anymore. You don't have to be *Besklanovvy.*"

There it was. Hope, in several of their faces. It bolstered me to go on.

"Swear fealty," I continued, "and from this point forward, you belong to me. Swear fealty, and we will forge a new path forward. Together."

I waited the several heartbeats it took for them to respond, wondering if they would laugh at me, turn and walk away. If they would tell me what I already knew, that I had no idea what I was doing.

And then it happened.

One by one, the men dropped to a knee.

One by one, they became *mine*.

CHAPTER SIXTY

ROWAN

Word of mouth spread quickly among the Unclanned.

Once I gained the first band, it was surprisingly easy to gain others. Thank the stars that Andrei had influence, even outside of his own group. Whenever I mentioned his name, the people sat up a little straighter and listened a little closer.

Of course, there were still those who refused, but they were by far the minority.

I left my room at the inn and moved into Andrei's camp. We were in this together, and my leaving them each night to stay somewhere else didn't encourage that unity I was working so hard for.

It wasn't like I was getting sleep anyway, in the cold, empty bed that reminded me of everything I stood to lose.

Everything I already had lost.

I kept busy enough not to think about that, though, because our camp grew by the day. Eventually, the bands of *Besklanovvy* started coming to us. Our party of fifty quickly became one hundred, then two and three before I lost count.

I used the ample coin I had to purchase the little food available in the villages while we supplemented it by hunting and fishing each day.

Well, the men hunted and fished.

They did try to teach me to do those things as well, but they were not skills that came naturally to me, as they required a person to be very still and very quiet, neither of which was my strong suit.

Mostly, I learned how to survive on much, much less than I was accustomed to. Surrounded by the too-thin faces of the Unclanned and their families, though, I certainly wasn't complaining about that.

While I was out securing what meager food I could wrangle, I also made my way to every village blacksmith I could find.

Andrei had stepped in as the spokesperson for the entire group, and soon, he was coordinating with some of the men to send runners back and forth to report on the battle.

The news was not promising.

Bear forces were moving toward the estate in droves, but so were Wolf's and Elk's. Ram had finally joined the fray, fighting Bear's forces on the west.

Was it too much to hope that Mikhail was the one leading his troops? I doubted the aging, portly man would fare well in a battle. The thought almost made me smile.

Lynx and Crane were still barred on the other side of the battle. The line at the Crane border was holding, if only barely, which was about the only positive news we had.

On the sixth day, a man came to tell us the estate was officially under siege.

My heart seized in my chest. It wasn't only Evander I stood to lose.

Mila.

Taras.

Yuriy.

Kirill.

Henrick.

I had made friends there, and every single one of them was in danger now.

We sat around the campfire that night, trying to devise a

strategy that might actually work. It was strange, the combination of deference and familiarity with which they treated me.

I had learned that no one here would ask for your story until you were ready to share it. There was a comfort in that acceptance, in the way that not one person had asked me why I was out here in the middle of Bear without my husband or a single guard.

"We have hundreds of men to their thousands, no horses, and are severely under-armed," Andrei said bluntly.

"I'm...working on that last one," I countered. "And the enemy's forces are being depleted."

Though, so were Bear's.

"The element of surprise might be enough to turn the tides," Maxim added.

I nodded, musing aloud. "But how do you sneak up on an army? There are trees around the estate, but there are sure to be scouts as well."

Either way, time was running out. We needed to start making our way to the estate tomorrow, after the women and I went to pick up the swords. The men couldn't go, largely because they were the ones with the very obvious brands on their foreheads.

Hopefully, we would amass more forces along the way.

I spoke with the men late into the night, but we didn't manage any solid solutions.

When I got back to my bedroll, I pulled my armor close to me, as I did every night. I hadn't put it on yet, but touching the stones seemed to be enough.

There was no storm for me to experiment with tonight, for all the good it had been doing me. It was freezing this far from the fire, with the dusting of snow that was quietly settling around us, and I wished my abilities could extend to making it warmer.

Instead, I played with little fog clouds, using miniscule bursts of wind to move them around while an idea formed in the back of my mind.

We needed a way to hide. A distraction.

Fog.

Lightning.

Maybe what I could do wasn't so useless after all.

CHAPTER SIXTY-ONE

EVANDER

The siege was going about how we had expected it to. Only worse.

Wolf's and Elk's troops came in with deadly force, bolstered by the news that the western front was failing and Ram was advancing by the day.

We would be lucky to survive the week.

Red lined my vision as I thought over the few options we had left. I would kill Nils for this, if I survived long enough to do it.

The only thing I had to be grateful about was that Rowan was far, far away from all of it. She would be nearing the pass soon and well on her way back to Castle Chridhe by the end of the week.

Even if there wasn't a single place in this storms-blasted castle that didn't remind me of her.

Even if I couldn't go five minutes without picturing her wicked smirk or the way her body felt pressed against mine.

Even if I could hardly look at Mila without realizing how deeply I had let myself want that with Rowan, how I had imagined the flat planes of her stomach growing round while her substantial temper grew even worse.

But we would never have that now.

The days passed in a blur of blood and death. We lost Pavel.

Hell, we lost half our regiment. The men coming in from the west weren't going to be enough to stop this when more troops were arriving from the south by the day.

The castle walls had nearly been breached a handful of times already. Even as I employed every single tactic I had ever thought of or read about, the day came when we needed every man.

I met Taras in his rooms. Mila stood stoically while my cousin clasped on his baldric, crossed at the front like mine was.

"I want you to stay," I said.

It was an *aalio* move saying it in front of Mila, but I had hope that she would help me convince him. Despite the sadness lingering in her eyes, though, she only shook her head in defeat, looking at me like I should have known better than to bother with that.

"Not a chance," my cousin responded without bothering to look up.

"Iiro needs subjects," I argued. "He isn't likely to take out everyone, and you can speak for Bear when..."

When I'm not here to do it.

"Van." He finally looked at me. "As my duke, you could ask anything of me, and I would comply. Except this."

I shook my head in frustration. "You don't need to give up your chance to meet your child for a fight we can't win."

"I am your second-in-command," he hissed, a rare bit of anger entering his tone. "I couldn't even look my child in the eyes if I didn't fight at your side."

Mila put a consoling hand on his arm, giving me a sideways glance. "If you were that concerned about him fighting, surely you could have found an inn somewhere to lock him against his will."

She had not been happy when she found out where Rowan was.

"Would that I had," I muttered. "And for the last storms-blasted time, I didn't lock Rowan anywhere."

"Oh?" she pressed. "So she was free to go?"

I let out a slow breath through my nose.

"She was freer than she would have been when Iiro got his hands on her," I reminded Mila. "Would you rather I had brought her back here, when she's all but got a target painted on her? She wouldn't have stayed out of this fight, and she wouldn't have survived it."

I didn't say the rest, that Mila was already losing her husband and the father of her child without adding her best friend to the roster, but her eyes flashed like she heard it anyway.

She didn't back down, though. "Need I remind you that I am in the process of outfitting *my* husband and the father of my child to walk out on a battlefield that I am nowhere near naive or uninformed enough to believe he will return from?"

A bitter huff of air escaped her lips.

"So don't you dare condescend to me like I don't understand what's at stake here." She shook her head. "I know, just as Rowan knew, just as you and Taras know, but I don't see either of you running away like you forced her to."

She scowled before turning back to Taras, but my cousin looked at me in sympathy.

"Mila," Taras said softly. "The risk for Rowan wasn't the same as it is for me. Death on the battlefield would be preferable to what Iiro could do if he wanted to make an example of her."

Mila stilled, her gaze landing on me. I watched the realization dawn on her features that Rowan wasn't the only one Iiro wanted.

She surprised me by closing the distance between us and wrapping her arms around me in a brief, solid hug, her firm bump only slightly getting in the way. I reflexively returned it, taking comfort in her sisterly presence.

"I suppose there are no good choices in war," she acknowledged quietly, backing away.

Nodding mutely, I left to give them the privacy to say goodbye. I needed to make sure our battalion was ready, convince them that we hadn't yet lost this war.

I needed them to fight like there was hope, even if I didn't feel that myself. In one more hour, we would be heading to the battle.

They at least deserved to feel like there was a chance we might come back.

CHAPTER SIXTY-TWO

ROWAN

The trek to the estate was relatively smooth, considering I was discreetly traveling with a large group of Unclanned across a war-torn territory, with highly recognizable hair and wanted by the dubious King of Socair.

The Unclanned knew how to travel off the main roads, though, and no one usually looked twice at them anyway. Or rather whoever was around fled if the Unclanned were near, imagining that somehow just because they had been abandoned by their duke and their people that they had turned into monsters overnight.

Not that I could judge them, when I had let myself fall victim to the same prejudices, but I didn't even see the brands when I looked at my men now.

Traveling with them made it easier to see the way it affected them, too, how they tried not to wince each time someone ran away in terror. But still, they kept marching.

We made camp in the forest near Hymi, the closest village to the estate. Every day, I made up excuses to my men not to attack yet because the clear, sunny sky was not at all conducive to my needs.

We were careful to avoid town. When we needed supplies, we sent the unbranded wives and daughters with my purse to get whatever little excess there was.

It wasn't nearly enough, but it was more than they were used to having, so I forced myself to be content with it as well.

And again, I promised myself they would live a different sort of life soon.

Each moment was more tenuous than the last, and I found myself holding my breath more often than not. Waiting for the moment the sky darkened, or for the soldiers to discover us and ruin the element of surprise we so desperately needed.

Every now and then, we would see Elk or Wolf soldiers making trips back to Hymi for one reason or another. So, I found myself scouting and constantly checking in with the sentries to be sure none of them were getting too close.

Their attention was fixed solely on the estate. On getting through the walls. Still, I kept my hair hidden and my hood pulled low. We couldn't take any chances.

But every day we hid and waited to strike, another piece of me broke off and shattered.

Every day, I heard about the death toll and wondered who was counted among those bodies, and every day, I wondered if we would be too late. If I was making the right choice.

But we only got one shot at this.

Finally, I felt the prickling of an oncoming storm.

Finally, it was time to don my armor.

Marita, one of the wives, helped me to fasten it in all the right places.

Energy thrummed off each stone as it connected to my skin. It hummed against my body, sending waves of warmth through me as it amplified every sensation that the oncoming storm had ignited.

I was acutely aware of how heavy the storm clouds were, the freezing rain that was desperate and ready to break free from them, how fast the wind was moving, and even the lightning that crackled through the sky, ready to strike.

Wearing the armor was entirely different than merely touching the stones had been. Now they connected to my skin in several places at once, and I didn't think the placement was random.

The stones hovered over pulse points and nerve endings at my neck, my wrists, even my ankles, like they were connecting whatever awareness was in me directly to the elements outside.

It was an effort to focus past the sensation to this moment, but eventually, the weather faded to the back of my mind.

When she was finished with the last clasp, I rolled my shoulders to get a better feel for the armor. It was a testament to Rayan's skill that it was practically weightless. The metal tunic and pants appeared to blend together seamlessly as if they were one solid piece.

A long stretch of black fur wound like a sash around my left shoulder, tying at my right hip, making the effect both feminine and powerful in addition to the necessary warmth it offered. I buckled my double baldric into place and sheathed my new, impressive sabers.

Marita braided my hair in the long fishtail style that she and the other women with the Unclanned favored. A warrior's braid, she called it.

When she was finished, she handed me my helmet. It was sturdy, but flexible, fitted around the top of my head and coming down to cover my nose and cheekbones, with spaces for my eyes.

When I looked in the river at my reflection, I barely recognized myself.

I felt strong. Untouchable.

Furious energy coursed through my veins, more than just the hyper awareness of the storm. It was the sure knowledge that after everything, I was finally here, going into battle.

I only hoped I wasn't too late.

CHAPTER SIXTY-THREE

ROWAN

I t was still hours from dawn when I crept through the forest ahead of my men. They were coming in from all angles, moving silently even on the brittle pine needles and icy forest floor.

As I stared at the battlefield below, it wasn't hard to dredge up the emotion I would need to make this work. Even in the darkness of the bleak cloud covering, it was plain to see that Wolf and Elk had breached the gates.

The castle would fall. And with it, my friends. *My husband.*

My stomach twisted as I pictured each of their faces in turn before I pushed that fear away. It wouldn't help me now.

Instead, I focused on the dense layer of clouds in the sky, willing gusts of wind to bring them closer to the ground over the enemy soldiers. Then I counted slowly to a hundred, waiting for my men to emerge from the covering of the trees.

Unleashing every ounce of my rage and hoping like hell I had practiced enough to get the placement right, I called down a bolt of lightning right in the middle of the Elk and Wolf soldiers.

A bright light stretched through the air before the sound of something breaking echoed through the battlefield.

Then the screaming started.

Men cried out as their fellow soldiers flew backward or

forward or sideways into them. The smell of burnt hair and skin wafted through the air, bringing with it a cacophony of chaos.

My knees threatened to give out beneath me, between moving the vast amounts of fog and the raw energy needed for the lightning. I took several slow, even breaths, recovering myself.

That was the only bolt I would be able to direct without passing out, but it had served its primary purpose. The men were scattered, injured, and distracted.

And that's when my army attacked. It was an impressive sight to behold.

Arrows rained down in wave after wave, felling enemy soldiers one by one. It was a drop in the bucket, for now, but this was only the beginning.

While the opposing troops were still confused about an attack coming from the wrong direction, still lost in the layer of fog so dense they couldn't see through it, my men were already at their backs.

Every part of me begged to join them, but I wasn't quite finished here. The fog needed to go now that they were in the immediate fray. Using the smallest gusts I could, I lifted the mist enough for my men to be able to discern friend from foe.

Confused orders were called out, and it took the Elk and Wolf soldiers too long to register that they were being attacked from behind. Which is exactly what we needed.

Or more to the point, what Evander needed. Assuming he was the one in charge of this battle, I knew he would take advantage of this opening to turn the tides from his side.

Once I found my bearings again and my hands stopped shaking, I drew my sabers and finally joined them in battle.

I lost myself in ducking and whirling and lashing out with both blades. For all that Rayan's skill had been impressive with the first sword he made me, these were something else entirely.

They were lighter than air, perfectly balanced, functioning like extensions of my arms. They cut through the enemy soldiers like a hot knife through butter.

The obsidian scales on my armor seemed to absorb the light

rather than reflect it, so I moved about like a wraith on the battlefield, slashing and fighting my way to the castle.

To Evander.

If he was still alive...

Panic gripped my insides, but I harnessed it, using it to fuel the adrenaline that was the only thing keeping me going.

He had to be alive. I would feel it if he had died. I would know, somehow.

A sword glanced off my torso with a bruising impact but didn't penetrate my armor. I brought my left blade up to fend off that attack, simultaneously whirling my right one to the side.

When the man in Wolf colors caught a glimpse of my long red braid, it was enough to distract him so that I could run my saber through the tender skin at his neck.

He gasped in surprise before falling to his knees with cold, unblinking eyes.

I left him to fight the next man and the next and the next until my armor was stained nearly as scarlet as my curls, sticky and coated with other people's blood.

Still, I didn't falter. I couldn't.

Hours passed, enough time for the sun to peek over the mountains and bathe the crimson field in a golden, gory glow. And what it revealed was...impossible.

We were winning.

Bear's forces had been able to advance while we kept the soldiers distracted from the other side.

The enemy soldiers must have seen the same thing, because the sound of a horn rang out along with an order to retreat. I raised my arm, shouting for my own men to fall back.

There was no need for anyone else to die if the defeated troops were leaving.

There were tense moments while they fled, but I had eyes only for the Bear soldiers on the other side of the field.

For one of them, in particular. It didn't take me long to spot him, my eyes drawn to him by the same force that always seemed to tie us together.

It wasn't until I actually saw Evander, though, removing his helmet and running a hand through his midnight hair, that I realized part of me had believed I never would again.

My heart seized in my chest as I stared at my husband. He hadn't noticed me yet, tucked behind several of the towering Unclanned.

I had a moment to soak in the sight of him, to reflect on how, even exhausted and blood-spattered, he was gorgeous.

To feel an intense, knee-weakening relief that he was alive.

Then that moment was gone, and a cold, quiet rage washed over me.

Because I might have never seen him again, if he had anything to say about it. Because he had left me without a voice, without a say, without so much as a single stars-blasted goodbye.

He had left me, after I had told him I didn't want a love that could break me, that I didn't want to live in a world where he wasn't.

Despite my bone-deep fatigue, I stalked across the field. My fury propelled me forward, one leaden step at a time.

I couldn't tear my gaze from his face, so I registered the moment Evander noticed me.

His lips parted in a rare display of shock and what might have been awe as I picked my way across corpses and severed limbs to stand directly in front of him.

Churning gray eyes met mine in disbelief. Amazement. Confusion.

My gaze burned into his, and my heart beat furiously in my chest. Plunging one of my blades into the ground, I took a step toward him.

"Lem--"

But he didn't get to finish the word, because I reached up my hand and slapped him. Hard. Right across his perfect face.

While he was still stunned by that, I turned to pull my blade back out of the ground and stepped around him to enter the castle.

CHAPTER SIXTY-FOUR

EVANDER

I knew it was over when they breached the walls.

The fortress of Bear Estate hadn't been penetrated in over a century, but here we were, less than a year into my illustrious reign as Duke.

Still, I wouldn't stop fighting as long as my men were, even if we all knew a lost cause when we saw one. On the off chance that we could win and save my people from Iiro's tyranny, I would keep going.

But then the strange fog came and the odd bolt of lightning, and I should have known.

On some level, perhaps I did, when the contingent of soldiers I thought were coming to back up the enemy started fighting against them instead.

But it was impossible. Or, at least, it should have been.

Whatever it was, I took advantage of their distraction to switch up tactics, relentlessly going on the offensive.

I had been fighting without respite for nearly eighteen hours when the sun finally rose and the soldiers retreated. My eyes were bleary, my vision swimming with fatigue, and I began to wonder if I was hallucinating the entire thing.

Especially when I saw that the soldiers who had come to our aid were the *Besklanovvy*.

Especially when *she* emerged from amongst them.

The dawning sun lit the courtyard in an ethereal glow, adding to the unreal feel of the figure striding across the battle-field in pitch-black armor, a saber in each of her hands.

And I knew it was Rowan, even with half of her face covered. Those soft lips, that pointed chin, the long tendrils of crimson curls escaping to blow in the gentle breeze…I would know them anywhere.

Had I been injured after all? Was this all some elaborate trick of my imagination, a way for my mind to comfort me in the minutes before I succumbed to death?

She stopped in front of me, and all I could do was stare mutely, my breaths forming a fog in the freezing cold air between us.

For all I usually read her so well, the cold, hard lines of her face were unfamiliar to me, and again, I wondered if she was even here at all, even as she stuck her sword into the ground.

Then her eyes met mine, and the unrelenting fury burning in their bright-green depths was enough to bowl me completely over. I knew then that this had to be real. There was no version of her in my imagination that would look at me like that.

"Lem--"

A lightly gauntleted hand connected with my cheek before I could finish the word.

I was stunned into silence. By her presence. By the literal weight of her rage. By the fact that she had shown up at my castle with an army and the miracle we needed.

While I was still reeling from all of that, she yanked her sword out of the ground and walked into the estate.

"Lemmikki." I belatedly followed her, but she didn't slow down until she got to one of the young squires who was waiting inside the door.

"Please see that these are cleaned and returned to me." She handed him her blades with hands that trembled slightly.

He nodded, looking nearly as overwhelmed by her presence as I was.

She took off her helmet as she turned to a second squire.

"I need you to fetch Lord Taras for me," she told him.

The boy nodded, taking off at a run.

"What do you need with Taras?" I asked, confused.

"I need someone to take care of a few things for me," she said without looking at me.

I bristled in spite of myself. "And you don't think the duke of the entire clan could help you with that?"

"I'm sorry." Sarcasm laced her tone. "What I meant was, I need someone I can trust."

The words were like a punch to the gut. Perhaps I had misjudged her capacity to stay angry.

My lips parted, but before I could respond, she spun around to head toward the East Wing. Where our old rooms were.

She paused only long enough to ask a maid to send Taisiya to her room, clarifying that they were the ones in the East Wing. I opened my mouth to ask her about it when Taras' voice sounded behind us.

"Rowan?" He didn't sound surprised, but then, he had probably seen her trek across the battlefield.

And the way she slapped me.

"Could you kindly walk with me to my room, Taras?" Her voice was all cold efficiency, in a way I had never heard it before.

Something uncomfortable churned in my stomach. Not quite dread...but close.

"Of course, My Lady." He stepped around me with a single wary glance in my direction.

Naturally, I followed.

"I'm sure you noticed the men who came to your aid today were Unclanned," she began.

He nodded.

"They are under my protection and my care." She sounded more commanding than I had ever heard her.

Taras looked at me, and Rowan let out an irritable breath.

"Not as a Clan Wife," she clarified. "Since that position obviously does not afford me the luxury of having an actual voice."

She might not have been acknowledging my presence, but the words were clearly meant for me.

"Lemmikki," I interjected to argue, but she barreled over me.

ROBIN D. MAHLE & ELLE MADISON

"They are under my protection as the princess and second-in-line to the throne of Lochlann. A man named Andrei is one of their leaders. You can deal with him. They can be fed from my dowry, and Lochlann will replenish the stores from my holdings." Her tone was matter-of-fact now.

"*I* feel as though they have more than earned their reintegration to society," she continued.

My cousin's eyes widened in shock, and she held her hand up.

"But as it has been made abundantly clear that my opinion is neither desired nor given any consideration, if that cannot be arranged, I will settle for them being taken care of until such time as they can accompany me back to my holdings in Lochlann," she finished.

Rowan stopped so suddenly outside her door that I nearly ran into her, my exhausted mind belatedly processing the last thing she said.

"You're going back to Lochlann?" I asked.

To escort the Unclanned? To visit her family?

To stay?

She didn't respond, holding Taras' gaze. "Will you take care of that for me?"

"Yes, My Lady." His tone was quiet, troubled, but I didn't think it was about what she had asked for the Unclanned.

"Lemmikki?" I pushed.

"Thank you," she said to him, still ignoring me.

Taisiya appeared at Rowan's side, reaching behind her to open the door. My wife turned to head inside, and I reached out to grab her arm.

"Rowan," I growled.

She turned very slowly, meeting my eyes at last. The fury in hers was gone, replaced by a colder kind of rage.

"Just leave me alone, Evander. You're good at that."

It felt like she had slapped me again.

I stood frozen as she tugged her arm out of my unmoving grasp and slammed the door in my face.

Taras only raised his eyebrows and let out a low whistle.

"Can't say I didn't see that coming, Cousin," he said drily.

Then he clapped me on the shoulder and took off down the hall, presumably to see to Rowan's orders.

I groaned internally before knocking on her door.

"Lemmikki," I called. "Talk to me."

Had she ever refused to speak to me? I thought back to our long line of arguments, everything from the first time we had danced to our more recent fight about the council room.

She always had something to say. Sometimes I had wished she didn't, but this...this was infinitely worse.

I tried a couple more times before finally walking away. Going in her rooms when she asked me not to would only make things worse.

Still, a sick, sinking feeling twisted in my gut with each step I took further from her. But, considering what she had done, I knew she needed rest.

Hell, we all did.

There was no telling how long this reprieve would be.

Besides, I needed to see to my men. None of them had believed we would live to see the dawn, and against all odds, we had.

We had won.

Even if it didn't feel that way right now.

CHAPTER SIXTY-FIVE

ROWAN

"Lemmikki," Evander's voice called through the door. "Talk to me."

I deliberately did not think about how much I had missed that voice. How it tugged at every single part of me that had felt empty and broken since he left me in that inn.

Damn him for putting us both in this position.

And I didn't want to talk to him.

Or, more accurately, I couldn't.

What was I supposed to say?

Remember that time you said you wanted to share your life with me? Remember when you promised we were in this together? Remember when you handed me off like a piece of property to my former betrothed without bothering to consult me?

Taisiya helped me remove my armor while my thoughts raced.

While I tried not to let months of bloodshed and death and betrayal physically drive me to my knees.

Though, the fatigue was likely to do that. I had been exhausted before I even joined the battle, from the lightning bolt. From the marching and the effort it took to gather the men, from the not knowing what we would find when we even reached the castle.

Then I had fought for hours.

Then I had seen Evander.

His voice came through the door again, with a more insistent knock this time.

"Lemmikki."

I hated that word.

I *loved* that word.

It would be so, so easy to open the door. To let him come in and put his perfect lips against mine and disappear into a place where none of this mattered.

But what happened the next time he thought he knew best?

The next time I was in danger?

Something inside of me cracked a little more.

Again, I ignored him. Not unlike he had ignored me, when I said I thought I would have a voice here.

When my armor was finally off, I climbed into bed without bothering to bathe or clean off any of the lingering blood and death that coated my skin.

My soul.

Taisiya closed the canopy around me, and the last thing I heard before I succumbed to oblivion was Evander's voice floating through the solid wood of the door.

My head was pounding when I awoke, and my mouth was dry enough to make me wonder just how long I had slept. Gentle shafts of light filtered through the slats in the velvet canopy, but that didn't tell me much.

I felt hollow and sore and even emptier than I had before.

Motion next to me on the bed gave me pause.

Stars.

I was not ready to talk to Evander. To look at him. To think about him. To drown in his perfect storm-cloud eyes and forget all the reasons I couldn't let this go.

I shifted around with a sigh, the movement pulling at the many bruises coating my body.

But it wasn't Evander.

"Scarlet Princess." Mila usually sounded excited when she greeted me that way, but this time, her voice was thick with emotion.

She was laying on top of the plush white blankets, facing me. I reached out until I felt her hand, taking it in my own.

How much did she know about what happened? I couldn't quite bring myself to ask her, not when the answer would lead back to Evander. I couldn't seem to say anything at all.

"So…" She saved me from my own awkward silence. "Do you want to tell me how you managed to raise an Unclanned army and slay your way across the battlefield like some goddess of lore and save all of our arses?"

I chuckled softly and mulled that over for a moment. "I'd rather hear about the tiny, unbearably gorgeous baby you're growing."

She gave a small laugh, but I wasn't kidding. Taras was a beautiful man, and Mila was one of the most attractive people I had ever seen. Their child was going to be the cutest thing in the entire world.

"Well, I'm past the part where I vomit on people's dresses without warning, which is nice." She took my hand and moved it to her small, round bump. "And look, Baby Lehtinan is moving."

Sure enough, something shifted under my hand.

"That's amazing," I said quietly. "I can't believe how much has changed in just two months."

"Well, nearly three now," she amended.

My brow furrowed.

"No. That can't be right." I did some quick math in my head, staring at the ceiling. "It took us less than a week to get to the front. Then we were there for…" I realized I didn't actually know.

Everything had blended together.

"When…Evander--" She said his name hesitantly, like she knew how much it would hurt me to hear it out loud. "—got here two weeks ago, you had already been gone over two months."

Panic shot through my body, because if that was true…

"Mila?" My casual tone likely wasn't fooling her.

It certainly wasn't fooling me.

"What is it?" she asked hesitantly.

"Erm." I cleared my throat. "Completely unrelated to everything you just said, how did you know when you were...with child."

She went still. For several heartbeats, there was only the sound of our breaths.

"Well, my moon time was missing," she began. "I had random headaches and couldn't get through a day without napping. And then the vomiting started."

I didn't say anything, still trying to count backward, trying to remember if I had taken my herbs on time.

Those weeks were a blur, though, and I had no way of knowing for sure. I did, however, know that my moon time was also conspicuously absent, by at least a week, but I had none of those other symptoms.

Avani sometimes was weeks late for no reason at all, and I knew stress could play a role.

Something I've had an abundance of.

Still, my breaths came faster.

"Rowan," she began. "Do you think you might be?"

"I'm not sure." My tone was a quiet hush. "I don't have headaches or queasiness, and I battled for hours this morning, so--"

"Row, time is not your friend today," she said gently. "That was yesterday. You've been sleeping for more than a day."

"*Stars,*" I muttered. "I need to go check on my men."

I rolled out of bed with a groan, throwing on the dressing gown Taisiya had left near the bed.

"What you need is a bath." Mila wrinkled her nose. "You're covered in blood. Taras and--" She cut off. "Taras made sure they were taken care of. You can spare an hour to care for yourself."

My stomach growled loudly at that exact moment.

"Fine," I relented, heading toward the door to ask one of the guards to get Taisiya for me. "I'll ask for breakfast and a bath first."

"Erm..." Mila made an uncomfortable sound, and I turned slowly back toward her. "You should probably know that Evander won't leave your hallway. It was all I could do to get him to not come in here."

I heaved a long, slow sigh, but she moved to get out of bed instead.

"I'll ask," she insisted, much to my relief.

"Have I told you how much I love you lately?" I sighed.

When she stood, I got my first decent view of her protruding belly. It was perfect.

And in another life, one without war and bloodshed and husbands I couldn't even bring myself to talk to, I would have been elated to be right there with her. We could have been like Mamá and Aunt Isla, having our babies only months apart and raising them to be close.

We could have given our children what I had with my cousins, a bond I wouldn't trade for anything.

But this was not that world, and I hoped fervently that stress was the only thing causing...*this*.

Mila padded to the door, only a little less graceful than usual, and poked her head out while I hid behind my bed curtains like the adult that I was.

"Since you insist on standing out here, you may as well make yourself useful and send for a bath and breakfast."

I nearly laughed out loud. *No one* talked to Evander that way, but obviously Mila had gotten plenty comfortable with him.

Or had been plenty irritated.

"She's awake?" Why did his voice have to be as perfect as the rest of him? Except for his *aalio* personality and his penchant for acting like a caveman when the mood suited him. "Is she all right?"

His concern did not warm any part of me. At all.

"Yes and yes," Mila answered. "But in need of a bath and breakfast, as I said."

Before she shut the door, I caught a brief glimpse of him and his tousled midnight waves and silver gaze. Then he was gone, and it was once again just me and Mila.

Whatever she saw in my expression had her own drawing tight in sympathy.

"Are you going to talk to him?" she asked.

"I...don't know." I admitted, leaning back against the black damask wall.

"Are you truly going back to Lochlann?" Her voice was barely a whisper.

Taras must have mentioned that to her.

I heaved out a sigh, considering. I would need to go long enough to escort the Unclanned who wished to go back to my holdings. But beyond that... Could I really leave Evander?

Could I really stay if he was going to spend the rest of our lives making decisions for me *for my own good*? Where he might leave me again whenever he deemed it necessary?

Was any amount of love worth that?

I had told him once that I had resigned myself to that life with Theo, one without choices. It was clear to me now that I never could have actually lived that way.

And what if there was a child involved?

"I don't know that, either," I finally answered, my voice even quieter than hers had been.

I knew Mila was a true friend, because in spite of her wrinkled nose and the fact that she had just told me I was covered in blood and grime, she threw both of her arms around me, tugging me against her.

"For whatever it's worth," she whispered, "I don't blame you for being furious. I'll support whatever you decide to do."

"But..." I asked, pulling gently away to see her expression.

Her features were drawn in sympathy. "But, as stupidly as he went about everything, he was trying to save you from being killed, or worse, by Iiro. If nothing else, it's obvious to anyone with eyes that Evander loves you."

"I know that," I told her. And I did. "But what is love without respect?"

And could I really stay without both?

CHAPTER SIXTY-SIX

EVANDER

I hadn't left the hallway outside of Rowan's door in hours.

I had forced myself to leave yesterday, wanting to go talk to *Andrei* myself. One thing had been immediately apparent. These were, indeed, her men. They had no particular love of me, of Bear, of Socair at all, really, but they had a clear loyalty to my wife.

But then, that was Rowan's way.

Kirill had taken to her immediately, and I would never forget the first time I saw her playing cards with Yuriy. Even Taras had been protective of her, in spite of himself.

If people respected me for my strategic mind or feared me for my position, they had something else entirely for her. Rowan inspired people.

As impressed as I was by her, though, the predominant emotion I felt when I left my conversation with Andrei was something I was altogether unfamiliar with.

I wasn't used to feeling...stupid.

Twice now, I had missed the obvious. I hadn't expected Nils to betray us. Then when he did, we had needed more men, and I was convinced there were none to be found.

But Rowan, who had never bothered to live her life by anyone else's rules, had seen what the rest of us hadn't.

Though, in fairness, I wasn't sure they would have even

fought for me, at least, not as anything more than mercenaries. But if I had thought of it, if I had thought we had another chance, would things have been different?

I nearly slammed my fist into the wall in frustration. With myself. With Iiro. With Nils.

With every storms-blasted thing that led us here, to me standing outside my wife's rooms wondering if she was going to speak to me today. If she was going to forgive me, ever.

I never would have left Rowan if I had believed we might actually survive this assault. But given the information I had, I would make the same choice every time.

There was no version of myself that could have brought her back here to die when I had another option.

I just hoped she could understand that one day.

If there was one thing I knew about Rowan, though, it was that she didn't take well to being pushed. I would have to wait her out, even if it killed me.

Even if I almost stopped breathing when she finally stepped into the hallway.

My gaze roamed over her face, from the guarded set of her eyes to the slight bow in the lips that I had missed more than I could stand to think about.

Yesterday, she had looked ethereal and deadly, wearing armor and spattered in blood.

But today, she just looked like...herself. Gorgeous and perfect and *mine*.

I flinched, realizing that the last part was far more tenuous than I wanted to admit.

CHAPTER SIXTY-SEVEN

ROWAN

When I was clean and fed and feeling almost like a human, I finally found the strength to step out into the hallway where I knew Evander was waiting.

Sure enough, there he stood, looking heartrendingly gorgeous with his pristine military coat and his freshly shaven face and his perfectly swept-back midnight hair.

Tension crackled in the air between us, thick and cloying and achingly familiar.

I sort of wanted to slap him again.

He opened his mouth to speak, but I cut him off. "I need to see to my men."

He nodded once. "I'll escort you to them."

I was a little taken aback that he didn't argue, but relieved, all the same. My shoulders dropped slightly, and I gestured for him to lead the way.

"Your men have been fed and the wounded tended to," he told me in a neutral voice.

I glanced up at him in surprise. Not because my requests had been seen through, but because he had referred to them as *my* men and had clearly overseen their care himself.

"Casualties are still being tallied," he went on, ignoring my look. "But Andrei estimates you lost close to two hundred men."

That was a staggering number. I squeezed my eyes shut.

"I would imagine it would have been far higher, had the fog not hidden their approach and the lightning distracted them." Evander said the words casually, but it was evident he knew I had done those things.

And that he was offering me comfort.

Of course, he had always *seen* me...until he chose not to.

I gave him a dip of my chin, and we walked the rest of the way down the stone halls without speaking. It wasn't the comfortable silence I had come to enjoy with him. This one was weighted down with everything we weren't saying.

Everything I couldn't quite bring myself to ask.

Did he regret leaving me there?

Did he understand how very wrong it was?

Or did he justify it, the same way he did everything else, as a means to an end?

The truth was, I already knew the answer. He wasn't a monster. I saw remorse stirring behind his eyes, even as he kept the rest of his features under control. It had probably killed him to leave me, the way that it had killed him to Unclan Vasily.

But that didn't mean he wouldn't do it again, if and when he deemed it necessary.

Some part of me couldn't quite handle hearing him admit that right now, knowing that it would feel like hammering the final nail into the coffin of everything we were supposed to be.

And I couldn't help but be furious with him for that.

So I said nothing.

The former Unclanned and their families had all been brought into the keep.

Surprising me again, Evander actually hung back, giving me space to talk to my men. I went around to check on a few, visiting with the women and hugging the children, before I finally found Andrei.

He put a fist on his heart when I approached, the Socairan version of a salute, and I nodded in return.

"I hear we have sustained high casualties," I said without preamble.

"Yes," he replied somberly. "Maxim fell."

"I'm sorry." The ineffectual words were barely a whisper.

Andrei leveled a look at me. "I wondered if I would live to regret following a woman into battle."

I suppressed a flinch, but he went on.

"But you were a sight to behold, Highness," he said with a trace of awe. "If the men hadn't rallied to you the way they did, we would have lost far more. We all knew the risks coming into this, and it was worth it, for the life you promised. My family's belly was full this week for the first time in years, but you gave us more than food."

He met my eyes solidly. "You gave us hope."

I nodded, a little stunned. All I could do was put a hand on his arm, but I hoped it conveyed my gratitude at the words I desperately needed to hear.

Clearing my throat, I returned to business.

"And the wounded, they were tended to?" I verified.

"Very thoroughly." Something like amusement crept into his tone. "Some of the men were quite reluctant to leave."

I shot him a questioning look, and he walked me next door where the sick bay was.

My eyebrows climbed in surprise. There were...women. Everywhere. Getting water, stitching wounds, holding vomit bowls, everything. And not just village women.

I recognized several noblewomen as well, including Lady Katerina, her sleeves pushed back to her elbows and a determined frown on her face as she cleansed a particularly nasty wound.

A smile tugged at my lips when I realized what Andrei meant about the men being reluctant to leave.

"Everything seems to be in order for now, then," I said. "I'll get more information and check back in the next couple of days. In the meantime, send word if you need anything."

He put his fist over his heart again. "Thank you, Highness."

"Thank *you*, Andrei," I told him sincerely.

In spite of everything, I left him feeling like I might be able to breathe again someday.

CHAPTER SIXTY-EIGHT

ROWAN

E vander waited for me near the entrance to the Great Hall. As always, he observed everything with an impassive face.

Or rather, he observed me.

If I didn't know any better, I would say he looked impressed. But if he found me so stars-damned impressive, he wouldn't have hesitated to let me fight for our people the same way he did.

"Noblewomen in the sick bay?" I asked, feeling like it was the most neutral topic.

"After they saw what you did, they wanted to help," he explained.

That was...unexpected. *Amazing.*

I started to walk back toward my rooms when Evander gestured in the other direction.

"We're meeting in the war room next."

I wasn't sure if he meant *we* as in he and his lords or as in he and I, but I was definitely going.

"Good," I nodded. "Consider me the Princess of Lochlann in that room since that's the only way I'll have a say."

He let out an irritable breath. "I'll consider you my wife in that room, and the Clan Wife of Bear. And you will have a say."

"Oh?" A bitter laugh escaped me, in spite of my attempts at

nonchalance. "Like you did when you left me, naked, in an inn room with my former betrothed? Tell me, is that standard practice for wives these days?"

His features darkened. "I believe standard practice for wives is doing everything you can to ensure they don't get captured and tortured and killed."

My lips parted. I couldn't honestly believe the arseling was standing by that.

"Right, because they couldn't possibly do that for themselves," I bit back. "Tell me, were you planning on handing me over to Theo when you traipsed back here to die? Did you have a pact for him to take over our marriage so he could take care of my delicate person once you were gone?"

A muscle twitched in his jaw.

"Lemmikki." He said the word like a warning, his voice carefully controlled. "Kindly refrain from referencing marrying another man. Ever again."

I could lie to myself from here until the end of the world and still not be able to deny the way his low growl set my every nerve on fire.

Not for the first time, I reflected on how easy it would be to give in to him. To let this go and pretend it had never happened, to move on and be grateful we were both alive.

And not for the first time, I realized that there would come a day where I would regret not fighting for this, no matter how much I loved him.

Craved him.

Missed the hell out of him.

We reached the war room, and he held open the door, gesturing for me to go in first.

When I entered, I came to an abrupt halt. The table was full this time, the lords seated along both sides of the rectangle and the far end.

But I didn't have to worry about where to sit, because at the head of the table where there had only been one chair before, there were now two.

"Lady Stenvall," Evander said casually, gesturing to one of the chairs.

I held his gaze for a long moment, wondering if he was actively trying to make me cave or only genuinely showing me respect. He had said before we left for the front that he was changing things, and he had, in fairness, shown it along the way.

The problem was that he chose when he felt like doing that. But still...this was no small thing.

I took my seat, and he took his. Taras nodded respectfully, but a few of the men gasped. Evander looked up sharply.

"Surely no one is objecting to your Clan *Wife*." He emphasized the word, and I knew it was for my benefit. "Being here. The woman who raised her own army in less than two weeks and used it to take down the forces who, I might remind you, had breached our walls. What she did was nothing short of a miracle, and if you don't think that's earned her a seat at this table, now would be the time to leave."

No one spoke or moved.

"Excellent." Evander continued as though nothing had happened. "Reports."

A man at the far end spoke up. "Iiro's forces are retreating to his territory, from here and the Crane border. Ram's troops slunk back as soon as Iiro's did, and what was left of Wolf and Elk have returned to their territories as well."

"And our men?" Evander asked.

"We lost nearly half of the men stationed here," Taras said with a small shake of his head. "A fifth of those on the southern line, and a couple hundred men from the western forces."

Evander's features didn't twitch, but I knew those numbers gutted him. In spite of everything, in spite of what he had done and where we were, I couldn't help but surreptitiously put my hand over his.

His eyes widened, but he squeezed back without hesitation.

The gesture brought back so many memories that tears threatened to stab at the back of my eyes, so I pulled my hand back to my lap. He swallowed but didn't otherwise react.

"We can assume they're regrouping for now," Evander said. "What we don't know is for how long."

"They'll have wounded as well," Taras said. "They will need time to recover."

"And Mikhail is a coward," I added. "He was beaten once and retreated. Now that Lynx and Crane aren't tied up with Iiro, I doubt he'll risk joining the assault again."

Evander nodded in approval, and only a few of the men looked at me like I had grown a second head.

All in all, the meeting went as well as could be expected.

Except for the part where I was left feeling more confused than ever.

CHAPTER SIXTY-NINE

ROWAN

I retreated to my rooms as soon as the meeting ended.

There was too much on my mind, an endless maelstrom I couldn't quite process.

Evander had insisted on moving into his old rooms as well, which I supposed was more space than I had thought he would give me. But the knowledge that he was right next door was slowly driving me mad.

I couldn't avoid this conversation forever.

Finally, unable to bear my own relentless thoughts any longer, I threw on a dressing gown and stormed down the hall. Not bothering to knock, I pushed open his door to find him sitting casually in a chair by the fire.

"Lemmikki." He looked up without a trace of surprise, lifting a glass of what I assumed was vodka to his lips. "I wasn't expecting you to come barreling in here tonight."

Then the arrogant arse gestured at the glass of chilled vodka already waiting on the table beside the other chair.

I was tempted to turn right back around, but I couldn't actually handle the idea of another night without a single answer to my questions. I stalked over to the leather chair, sinking into it and taking a long, long sip of that vodka.

Evander assessed me, waiting for whatever I had to say, but I think we were both surprised by the first thing that popped out of my mouth.

"You said you wanted to share your life with me." Every word was an accusation.

"Yes, Lemmikki." He met my gaze solidly. "My *life*. Not my death."

I scoffed. "You don't just get to pick the parts you want, Evander. Either you're all in, or you aren't."

Evander shook his head, his black locks swaying where they had fallen on his brow. "I will never be all in if it means you needlessly dying."

"Fine." I spread my hands out. "If you were so worried about that, why didn't we both go to Lochlann?"

"I had a clan to protect." He said it like it was obvious, and I reared back as if he had slapped me.

"Whereas I just had my next tiara to pick out?" My words hung in the air between us for a long moment.

A muscle worked in his jaw. "It's different, and you know it."

"I don't, actually," I countered. "Explain it to me."

He gritted his teeth. "The difference is that I swore an oath to protect my people, and you didn't."

"And what about the promise you made to me?" My voice rose with each syllable. "That we were in this together? Or did you conveniently forget about *that* oath?"

"I also made a vow to protect you," he growled.

"We made a vow to protect each other!" I shot back. "But you didn't even give me the option of fulfilling mine when you left me in the middle of the night with a stars-damned note!"

He outright winced that time.

"I knew that if I told you, you would try to talk me out of it, and because it was already destroying me to leave you, I would cave. Then you would die." He ran his hand through his hair in frustration. "The *Besklanovvy* never occurred to me, and I didn't see another way to keep you safe."

"And what if there hadn't been?" I countered. "If I hadn't been able to get the Unclanned? What if you had died, and I hadn't even gotten to say goodbye?" My voice cracked, and I looked away, staring into the crackling flames in the hearth.

"Then I would have been grateful I did everything I could to keep you from that same fate." His tone was gentle, but insistent.

We were going in circles. Draining my glass, I got to my feet.

"You know what kills me, Evander?" I said quietly, meeting his eyes once again. "That you knew--you *knew* that losing you was my worst fear. I told you I didn't want to live in a world where you weren't. And still, somehow you see no problem with the fact that you resigned me to that life without a second thought."

"It wasn't without a second thought." He leaned forward in his chair, speaking more forcefully now. "It was the *only* way. I couldn't have handled it if something happened to you."

"Do you even hear how selfish that sounds?" I demanded. "What about what *I* could handle? Do you honestly think there is any part of me that would want to go on living if you were gone?"

He squeezed his eyes shut, remorse clouding his features.

"I never wanted to hurt you. And I *am* sorry for that." His voice was quieter then, thick with emotion that nearly brought me to my knees.

"I don't want an apology, Evander. I want you to say that you'll never do it again."

"Lemmikki, I would do anything for you. *Give* anything for you." He took a breath, his silver eyes boring into mine. "But you cannot ask me to sit back and watch you die when there is something I can do to stop it. I am not capable of that."

How could a set of words be so perfect and so wrong at the same time?

"Even if that's my choice?" I clarified.

He held my gaze for what would have been several breaths, if I had been breathing. "Even then."

Shaking my head silently, I spun around and left his room.

There really was nothing left to say.

CHAPTER SEVENTY

ROWAN

The next morning, Evander was once again waiting for me. His eyes were bloodshot and hooded, a matching set to the dark purple rings underneath mine.

Sleep had clearly not come to either of us.

I only wished that this exhaustion, this hurt, was enough to stop the energy that thrummed between us, the constant awareness and longing I had for him.

I supposed I would have to settle for ignoring it.

With a sigh, I took off toward the war room, where we had yet another meeting. We didn't speak a single word on the way there.

"Lady Rowan," the elder Lord Lehtinan addressed me once I sat down. "What of your men?"

"We can't honestly be thinking to let Unclanned fight--" Another lord interrupted him.

"They are not Unclanned any longer," I spoke over the lord. "They belong to me now."

"However..." Evander countered, and I barely resisted the urge to glare at him. "They will be offered the chance to rejoin society in exchange for their fighting for Bear."

He glanced at me. "I think they've more than earned it."

It was an echo of what I had said the night I arrived.

"I quite agree," I said quietly, resisting the small, traitorous smile threatening at my lips. "You were saying, Lord Lehtinan?"

"Will they continue to fight with us?" he asked.

"Yes," I answered. "They stay with me, and I don't plan on going anywhere until this war is won."

The men chuckled like I had made a joke, but Evander looked sharply at me, fully aware of how I meant the words. I didn't acknowledge him.

"What will your men need?" Taras asked.

"Most of them are in need of new boots. Weapons, obviously."

"There are plenty of spare weapons and boots to go around right now," Taras said darkly. Of course there were. We had lost hundreds of men just in the last battle.

I nodded my thanks to him, then something else occurred to me.

"Oh, and the use of the training yard this afternoon?" I added.

Taras exchanged an uncomfortable look with Evander before turning back to me.

"Our men won't train with them," Taras said.

Of course, they wouldn't.

I looked at Evander, and he raised his eyebrows the smallest fraction, letting me know this was my decision.

We were in the middle of a war, and we needed all the soldiers we could get. Evander was upholding what I had told the Unclanned, even though he didn't have to. He was going up against his lords for this.

So, I could make an issue out of it, try to change a lifetime's worth of Socairan ideals overnight. Or I could be patient and work with what we had.

I turned back to Taras. "They don't need to train together. These are my men, anyway. Perhaps the Bear soldiers could vacate the training yard for a couple of hours?"

He nodded, as much in agreement as approval. Out of the corner of my eye, I saw Evander do the same.

Not that I cared, obviously.

When the meeting was done, I practically fled the room without looking back.

I went to find Andrei, telling him about the plans to train and getting his input. We talked for a while about who might make the best trainers, trying to choose someone from every band.

The men were raised as soldiers, but it was important to hone those skills if more battles were coming.

Finally, Taras came to let us know the training yard was free.

Before sparring myself, I walked around assessing them and sorting them into groups. They weren't as militant as Evander's men, not as used to moving in sync as a unit anymore, but they fought with an unrelenting vigor that made up for it.

A surge of pride went through me. It was no wonder we had been as successful as we had in the battle.

I felt Evander before I saw him, just as I always did. He strode across the grounds, his scrutinizing gaze landing on the men, and then me.

"Skilled and brutal. It's a good combination for war." It was a compliment, so I nodded.

Then, steeling myself, I turned to him. "Spar with me."

He raised his eyebrows, this time in a question.

I sighed. "I want to get better with both blades. And not to make that giant head of yours any bigger, but we both know that you're the best person for that job."

Sure enough, his lips tilted up into a milder version of his usual arrogant smirk, though it was still shadowed with everything that was between us.

I hated that this was hurting him, too.

As if he sensed the thought, his eyes shuttered, but his mouth was still pulled into a half grin when he responded.

"I am ever at your service."

CHAPTER SEVENTY-ONE

EVANDER

Sparring with Rowan was either a very good or a very bad idea.

On the one hand, she was right. I was the best person for the job.

On the other, I had meant what I said last night. I would support her in literally anything that she wanted to do, except die. It wasn't that a part of me couldn't understand what she was saying about choices.

It was that there was *no* part of me that could stand back and do nothing while she was in a position to be hurt.

I didn't know where that left things, except that there was an endless chasm between us, one that was infinitely more painful whenever I was near her.

Then again, being away from her was just as excruciating. Hence, the mixed feelings on sparring.

Rowan took a moment to stretch, and my mind flew back to the first time we did this.

Her crimson braid had been messier than it was now, her jade eyes not nearly as guarded.

It was impossible to forget how breathtaking she had been, standing in a sparring ring in a dress meant for dancing, staring me down without a trace of apprehension.

How she had taken me off guard with her bawdy joke. How

desperate I had been to know her better, even as I searched in vain for reasons to hate her.

How even then, I had wanted her to improve, because even then, the thought of something happening to her had filled me with unreasonable, unbridled panic.

Wrenching myself back to the present with considerable effort, I went on the attack without warning, as I always did.

And as she always did, Rowan reacted instantaneously. Her reflexes were quick, and her instincts were solid. If she had been the size of a man, she would have been better than most of my soldiers.

But she wasn't, so she had to be faster and more skilled to make up for it.

Just as I opened my mouth to tell her she was too high on her left, she attacked with the same kind of unrelenting fury I had seen from her men, only far more intense.

What had she said when we sparred before? *I had a lot of anger to work out.*

That was clearly true now as well.

She may have wanted me to train her, but part of me wondered if she also just wanted the chance to come at me this way.

I had to work harder than usual to keep up with her, and twice, she hit me on the side.

Hard.

The second time she came in with too much force. I used the momentum to pull her to the ground, putting my blade to her throat.

"You're letting your emotions get the better of you," I told her. "Nothing will make you lose your fight faster than that."

I moved my blade, offering her a hand up. Heat spread from every place her gently calloused fingers touched mine.

When she got to her feet, she was standing closer to me than I realized she would be. She dropped my hand, but she didn't step back. She only looked up at me, her eyes burning with passion.

"You're wrong about that." Rowan's tone was low, but no less fervent for it. "You can't just take the emotions out of a situation. Sometimes they're all you have. Sometimes they're what keep you going long enough to win."

She shook her head in disbelief. "You asked me how I raised an army in two weeks, Evander. It sure as hell wasn't by leaving my emotions out of it. Perhaps the problem is that you should put your emotions *into* things."

I thought about the things I had done because of my father. The only way I had lived with myself was by a careful, logical accounting of the greater number of lives I could still protect.

Then there was my stepmother, who had thrived on seeing another person's pain.

"Not everyone has had the luxury of living their lives that way, Lemmikki," I said flatly.

Her eyes flared with the same intense protection I had seen from her before.

"Maybe not before," she allowed, taking her stance to start another spar. "But it isn't too late for us to live a different sort of life."

She launched into a series of attacks before I could respond to her comment.

Which was just as well, because, for a rare change, I had no idea what I would have said.

CHAPTER SEVENTY-TWO

ROWAN

A week passed in much the same manner.

There was no time for returning to my tea with the ladies, since most of them were still helping in the sick bay, but I did visit them there and lend my assistance whenever I could.

Other than that, my days were filled with war room meetings, training with my men, sparring with my husband. Though, our banter was conspicuously absent, since I had told him we didn't have to live in his past anymore.

Maybe he disagreed. Maybe he just didn't know how to process that concept.

In any event, my moon time had even come and gone, so I had been right about it being attributed to stress. Which was for the best, obviously, since Evander and I were barely speaking, and our clan was in the middle of a war.

So I knew how unreasonable it was, the sinking feeling I got whenever I thought about it. But I didn't quite understand why until Mila asked me.

We had just finished our luncheon in the vast room where we usually held tea with the ladies, and she was working on mending some of the men's uniforms while I reluctantly helped her with my mediocre sewing skills.

I was mid-stitch when she broke our comfortable silence with the question.

"Did you ever find out if you were..." She looked significantly at my stomach, and it dawned on me.

How badly I had wanted to hold on to this dream. How saying the words out loud effectively killed the last part of me that saw a future with babies and laughter and my and Mila's children growing up together.

With Evander and I being whole again.

Maybe it didn't make any sense to mourn something you never had, but here I was, barely forcing the words out.

"I did," I said quietly. "There's no baby. Just a mountain of stress, as it turns out."

Her brown eyes carefully scrutinized mine, and she didn't say any of the things that would have been difficult for me to hear. In fact, she didn't get a chance to say anything at all before a different voice sounded behind us.

"You thought there was a baby, and you didn't think to tell me?" Evander's low voice echoed in the cavernous room, coated with an emotion I wasn't sure I had ever heard from him before.

Mila abruptly realized she needed to be somewhere at that very moment and left the room without so much as a backward glance.

Reluctantly, I got to my feet, turning slowly to face my husband. His expression was...shattered. Maybe like me, he realized just how far we had come from when we had lain in our bed with his hand on my abdomen, talking about the children we would have one day.

My chest tightened, each breath coming in more strained than the last. Still, I kept my features neutral and my tone even, trying to hide the defeat that was steadily creeping its way into my soul.

"Let's not pretend we have the kind of relationship where we tell each other everything, Evander," I said in a low tone.

His features went distant, hardening into a version of his usual mask.

"So because I kept something from you, you would have,

what, taken our child to Lochlann and never told me?" He huffed out a disbelieving breath.

"Of course not." I didn't bother to hide the offense in my tone. "I would have told you when and if it became relevant, which is, by the way, more courtesy than you have shown me. But there's really nothing to concern yourself with, because there is no baby."

And I...I had thought that saying the words out loud to Mila were the final straw, but I could see now this was infinitely worse. A solid lump formed in my throat, but I forced myself to speak past it.

"There never was," I continued. "So, that's a relief, right?"

Evander held my gaze for a single, stuttering heartbeat. "Yes. A relief," he said coldly.

Holding myself together with the last vestiges of my self-control, I nodded to Evander and walked calmly from the room.

CHAPTER SEVENTY-THREE

EVANDER

I stood stunned in the empty tearoom after Rowan walked out.

A relief.

It should have been, perhaps.

But all I could see was my wife lying in our bed while I traced circles on her flat stomach and wondered if it would ever grow round with something that was entirely ours.

All I could hear was her telling me she wanted our children one day, and how it had been enough to steal my breath.

And now.

Now we were here, at a point where she wouldn't even tell me that was a possibility. What the hell had happened to us?

Even as I asked the question, I knew.

I had happened to us.

I had pushed her so far that she went from sleeping in my arms every night to saying it was a relief we didn't have a child to worry about.

Spinning on my heel, I took off in the direction of her rooms.

She had told me on my balcony just how badly she didn't want to be in love at all, for fear of losing that person. *Who in their right minds would want to go through what Avani went through?*

Then in the carriage. *I don't want to live in a world where you're not.*

ROBIN D. MAHLE & ELLE MADISON

I had known those things, on a logical level, but...

I walked faster, a rare bit of panic overtaking me because I was starting to wonder if I had already lost her.

Even in my rooms, she had said it again. *You knew that losing you was my worst fear.*

When I got to her room, I pushed her door open without knocking.

"Lemmikki, I--" The words died on my lips when I heard the hitching sound of a sob.

Opening the door the rest of the way, I stepped inside to find her curled up on her bed, shaking with the weight of the tears she so rarely shed.

"Go away," she choked out between sobs.

I hesitated for less than a second before I shut the door behind me, kicking my boots off and crossing the distance to her.

"No," I said quietly, settling onto the bed and wrapping my arms around her. "I never should have left you to begin with, and I'm sure as hell not going to do it again."

She huffed out something between a bitter laugh and a sob. "No matter what I want, right?"

I stilled. "Do you want me to leave, Lemmikki?"

If she said yes...I would force myself to go. But it would take everything I had to do it.

Another wave of tears assaulted her, and she buried her face in my chest, her fists clinging to my shirt. "No."

It was the only word she could get out. She was breaking. And I--I had broken her. Pain lanced through my chest, like it was cracking open.

"I'm sorry, Lemmikki. I'm so sorry." I pressed my lips into her hair, and she cried harder.

"Were you really relieved?" she asked me.

She didn't have to clarify what she was talking about. And I could have given her the rational explanation, all the reasons this would have been terrible timing for a baby.

Instead, I gave her another jagged piece of my soul.

"No, Lemmikki," I breathed out. "I wasn't relieved. I wanted that—want that, more than anything. A child with you. A life with you."

She pulled back, examining my features through a cloud of tears. "Then why don't you care enough to respect what I want?"

I opened my mouth, then closed it, not sure exactly how to explain this to her, how to make her understand that I saw it now.

That I had assumed she was angry, not realizing just how broken she felt over this.

But I understood it now.

And for everything I had thought and said and did, I realized in this moment that if me finding a way to change was the price of keeping her from feeling this way ever again, then I would damned well figure out a way.

CHAPTER SEVENTY-FOUR

ROWAN

I didn't push Evander to answer, because I could tell he wasn't avoiding the question this time. He wasn't hesitating before he told me something he knew I didn't want to hear.

He was considering his response, and that gave me the first surge of hope I had felt in a while.

Part of me knew I should back away, should give myself physical space and a clearer head, but I wasn't nearly strong enough to let him go now that I finally had his arms around me.

At least, not until I knew what he was going to say.

"Before the Summit," he began, then paused.

It surprised me. Evander rarely talked about his life before, and I couldn't imagine why he was bringing it up now.

But I wasn't about to interrupt him.

"Before the Summit," he started again, "I was living my life like it was someone else's. The things I had to do, the people I had to kill and brand and Unclan, the person I had to be to keep up a show of strength so that no one might guess my people were vulnerable under my father's rule... All of it was slowly turning me into the monster everyone thought I was."

"You were never a monster," I said earnestly.

He only shook his head silently before continuing.

"Everything I did, I did for the sake of the clan. For the people my father was trying to hurt. The rare times we went to the cabin were the only times I felt human, and even then, we had all but stopped going."

His words sliced at something inside me, but I didn't interject again.

"So you weren't wrong when you called me a broken shell of a person," he said with a bitter breath.

I winced at the words I had hurled at him in the sparring room, what felt like a lifetime ago.

"That's exactly what I was." He shook his head, the motion rustling my curls. "Living each day waiting for the next horrible thing I had to do to my people, *for* my people, and wondering if all the good I was trying to do would ever be enough to make up for the bad. I was starting to believe it wouldn't."

I couldn't help but run a comforting hand up and down the arm he had wrapped around me. Evander squeezed me tighter before continuing.

"I was starting to believe none of it mattered," he said quietly. "And then..."

He paused, and I held my breath, sure he wasn't about to say what I thought he was. But he did.

"And then I saw you." His gaze bored into mine.

Another two tears tracked down my face, and he brushed them away gently.

"I thought that I had lost my capacity to be surprised by anyone. Or anything, really," he added wryly. "Yet there you were, with your acerbic wit and your dangerous temper and your unending fearlessness."

Was that how he had seen me? When I had felt weak and out of sorts at that Summit, entirely at the whims of everyone around me and desperately clinging to whatever I could?

"And the truth is," he went on. "You were right, too, when you called me selfish."

My chest felt crushed by that admission.

"I don't think you're selfish, Evander," I hastened to clarify. "I said that what you *said* sounded selfish. I have seen you time after time put everyone and everything ahead of yourself, including me."

"Until I didn't," he countered. "The thing is, that it had been months since I even felt like smiling, and suddenly, I found myself resisting the urge to laugh at every turn. I felt...whole when you were around, even then."

The air whooshed out of me. In hindsight, it was easy to see I had felt the same, how quickly I had become out of sorts as soon as he wasn't near. *Inevitable*, Theo had said, and it was true.

"Der'mo, Lemmikki." He let out a disbelieving breath. "Part of me honestly wonders if I would have called in that blood debt even if you hadn't been about to marry Korhonan. I think I might have done anything to make you mine, no matter the consequences."

Maybe I should have blamed him for that, but I couldn't quite bring myself to. Not when I understood the deep need that drove me toward him time and again.

When I didn't say anything, he kept talking. "Then, I was selfish again when I kissed you, knowing that it wasn't something you could possibly consent to under the circumstances. I knew I held power over you, and I promised myself I wouldn't take advantage of that."

On some level, I had known he felt that way, but I still hated to hear it out loud. That kiss...that kiss had been everything, and it had existed outside a world of blood debts and captive princesses.

I managed to refrain from interrupting him to tell him that, but only because I was desperate to see where he was going with this.

Evander let out a slow breath. "But every part of me was drawn to every part of you, and I had never wanted anything in my entire life as badly as I wanted you that day in the cabin. I hated myself for that."

"Don't make that something it wasn't." Heat crept into my tone. "I already loved you then, and I wanted you, too. More than anything."

"But the entire situation was convoluted by you being a prisoner," he said gently. "So yes, when your father came, I told you to go. It was, perhaps, the first unselfish thing I did where you were concerned. You did need that time, Lemmikki. You needed space to heal and process and consider what you really wanted."

Though it was frustrating, he wasn't entirely wrong. I had been indecisive the day I left, confused, and terrified to leave him. But if I had stayed, would we have ever gotten to where we were right now?

"I can concede to that," I said.

His eyebrows rose in surprise, but he nodded. "So, I told myself I would give that to you, even if it meant that you went back to Korhonan. That I would respect whatever decision you made."

A small smile bloomed on my lips, in spite of myself.

"How did that work out for you?" I couldn't help but ask, considering he had come to forbid me from marrying Theo.

The corner of his mouth tilted up in response.

"I hardly remember deciding to leave," he admitted. "I got Korhonan's bird about marrying you...and I didn't think. I told Taras I was going instead of him, and I threw a trunk together, and I left. I knew that there would be consequences for Bear, and I still left."

For a man who had done anything and everything for his clan, that was...unthinkable. I moved closer to him, almost on instinct, and he pulled his arms more tightly around me.

"Even when we found out what Iiro had done," he said in a quieter tone, "I couldn't honestly bring myself to regret it when it meant I had you."

I tried not to let his words fill up every empty piece of me...and failed. Because what he was saying, the fact that he was saying it, was everything.

"So yes." He trailed his hand from my shoulder to my wrist, like he was convincing himself I was still there, real and in his arms. "I have always been selfish where you are concerned. You said I should try putting emotion into the things I do, but that's all I seem to know how to do with you.

"Logically, I knew that you wouldn't want to go back to Lochlann. That you would hate me for that." He met my eyes with so much honesty in his that I could hardly breathe.

"But I felt such blind panic every time I thought about something happening to you, that I convinced myself it would be better for you to be alive and unhappy than dead. I thought you would move on someday, have a life, still be this amazing, fiery light in an otherwise dark world, and I couldn't handle the idea of that light being snuffed out."

I understood that. And I even appreciated it. I really, truly did, but I was sincerely hoping that he was about to caveat it, because knowing where he was coming from did not solve the central issue between us.

"And now?" I asked, hardly daring to hope.

"Now..." He gently moved a strand of hair back from my forehead, running his thumb along the side of my face. "I still can't handle it. But I can't handle seeing you like this, either, and I sure as hell can't handle losing you."

"What are you saying?" I needed to hear him utter the words out loud.

He swallowed. "I'm saying that if what you need from me is to know that I will never again take that choice from you, then...I won't."

"Even if my life is in danger?" I pressed. "Even if you think there's no other way out?"

He squeezed his eyes shut, visibly warring with himself. "Even then. But can you at least tell me you will try to be careful?"

I reached my hand out to his lightly stubbled cheek. "Evander, I will always fight to make my way back to you."

"All right." He opened his eyes again. "I promise you, even if your life is in danger, even if I believe there is no way out, I will always be honest with you. I will respect your decision...whatever it is." He linked his hand in mine, as he had on both of our wedding days. "I swear it on my life."

"No." I shook my head, and he widened his eyes. "That just

means the next time you think you're going to die, you won't see the need to uphold it. I want you to swear it on *my* life."

He paused, taking a single, shaky breath. Slowly, his hand squeezed mine.

"I swear it on your life, Lemmikki."

CHAPTER SEVENTY-FIVE

ROWAN

For several silent minutes, I let Evander's words sink in, pulling them close around me and using them to soothe the battered parts of myself.

His gaze never left mine. We lay inches from each other, our shallow, waiting breaths the only sound in the hushed room.

There was no doubt that he meant what he said. In the past, when I had tried to elicit this promise from him, he had always hedged or staunchly insisted that he was in the right.

But now, he was willing to make this change, for me. For *us*.

And that was more than enough.

I melted into him, letting his warmth envelope me. "Can we go back to our room now?"

His entire body eased as he leaned in and pressed a kiss to my forehead. "I thought you'd never ask."

Pulling me out of bed with an almost laughable speed, he only dropped my hand long enough for us to both put our shoes on. Then he quickly encompassed it with his own again. A slow smile spread across my face as we made our way down the several hallways that led to our rooms.

When we stepped into the open, airy space, I took my first deep breath in weeks. He shut the door, and I turned to him, burying my face in his chest and inhaling the scent of everything that he was.

Mine.

He pressed soft kisses against my hair, then my forehead in slow, gentle motions that were almost reverent. Heat spread through me, and I tilted my face upward to meet his, stepping back against the door.

He covered my mouth in a deep, exploratory kiss, like he was cherishing the way I felt, memorizing it. I slid my tongue between his lips, entwining it with his and savoring his familiar taste, letting it consume me.

Slowly, he dragged our linked hands up until they were over my head, pinning them against the door behind us. My heart raced a wild, unrestrained beat that echoed in my ears.

Stars, I had missed him.

His mouth skated down to my neck, then he paused.

"Lemmikki, did you take your herbs?"

I nodded, not trusting my voice. I hadn't been ready to give up on us yet, hadn't been convinced I wouldn't need them. And no matter how I felt about the potential pregnancy, I didn't want to bring a child into this world with Evander by accident.

I wanted it to be a choice we made.

He resumed his almost worshipful kissing of my neck, but it was slower this time. One more time, he stopped, pulling back to look at me.

"Do you think that when this war is over, you might want to...abstain from taking them?" His face was carefully neutral, but I remembered what he had said earlier.

I want that more than anything.

"Yes," I breathed, nodding.

A rare genuine smile broke out on his face, with none of the sardonic lilt it usually had.

Then his mouth was on mine again, hot and urgent and fitted perfectly against me. He kissed me like I was the other half of his soul in truth, like I might disappear if he stopped. Shivers ran through me, my breath coming shallower in my chest.

My hands went to the buttons of his uniform. It took every bit of patience I had to undo them one by one instead of ripping the entire thing off.

I wanted to feel his skin against mine again, to feel like we were both here and alive and *together*.

It was a mark of how much he wanted the same thing that he didn't even die when I shoved his jacket off his shoulders and let it fall in a heap on the floor.

Instead, he removed my clothes in deft, hurried movements before he picked me up and carried me to our bed, our bed that I had missed nearly as much as the man in it.

It smelled like him, like us.

"Der'mo, Lemmikki," he growled in my ear. "I missed you every second of every day."

His capable hands roamed my body as he, in detail, expounded on each part of me that he had missed. Awareness coursed through me, stealing my response.

Evander nipped at my shoulder, and I let out a gasp.

"And I missed that little sound you just made," he murmured against my skin.

His fingers moved in a tantalizing pattern up and down my thighs, and I arched into him.

"Evander." It was more of a demand than a plea, and he let out a low chuckle that undid me entirely.

I realized in that moment that if he had deprived me of this, of us, forever, with his stubborn *aalio* mentality, I would have killed him myself.

CHAPTER SEVENTY-SIX

ROWAN

I had fallen asleep to Evander's kisses, and I woke up that way, too.

He was doing a valiant job of making up for lost time, and I had no real complaints about that. Except...

"We should go start training," I said halfheartedly.

"No." It was one clipped word, and I let out a small laugh.

But I didn't argue. There wasn't much to be done on the warfront while all of the things we set in motion were going forward, and there was no part of me that wanted to leave our bed.

So, we spent the day there, talking and laughing and focusing wholly on one another. I wondered if this was Evander's way of making sure I didn't think back to when I had woken up without him, but I was more than ready to put that behind us.

We had each of our meals delivered to our room, along with a small side of maple bacon for Boris, who seemed uncharacteristically pleased that we were all back in our room.

He lay at the foot of our bed, soaking up the rays of sunshine that streamed in from the window, purring whenever I offered him another bite of food.

I had just sat back against the pillows when Evander's voice sounded over Boris' gentle murmurings. "At the risk of bringing this up...how did you get away from Korhonan?"

"I...drugged him," I said nonchalantly. "And his guard. After tricking them into playing a card game with me and lacing my flask."

Evander threw his head back and laughed, a rich sound that warmed every part of me. "Storms, Lemmikki. You are savage when you want to be."

I shrugged. "A fact you would do well to keep in mind."

"Oh, I do," he assured me. "Though, for the record, I never would have fallen for that."

"No," I agreed, running my hand along the powerful ridges of his arm and shoulder. "I would have had to seduce you instead."

"Now that...that, I would have been powerless against." He pressed his lips against mine in another lazy kiss.

Then he wanted to know all about how I got the Unclanned, so I told him about meeting Andrei, about traveling to the villages and asking for help from the women behind the blacksmiths, and about the clans falling to their knees when they were offered a second chance.

He listened patiently, something like awe taking over his expression.

"You are truly remarkable, Lemmikki. What you did that day, for Bear--"

I put a finger on his soft, full lips, silencing him.

"Let me be clear about something," I began. "I love Bear. I love our people. But I don't know that I could have done what I did for them."

His brow furrowed, and I shook my head, looking for a way to put into words what I wanted to say.

"I did that for you, Evander," I finally said. "All this time, I was worried about having the kind of love you go to war for. I thought it made you weak and selfish and reckless. And I don't know, maybe those last two things are true, but I do know that the way that I love you...it makes me stronger, not weaker."

Evander's lips moved like he wanted to respond but couldn't find the words. He settled for pressing another reverent kiss against my forehead.

"And I heard what you did in the battle here," I added. "I wasn't the only one doing remarkable things."

His face darkened then, and he told me about the battle, how they were outnumbered five to one, how he had to pull out every military tactic he had ever learned or read about just to make it the several days they did.

"And then you came." He scrutinized me for a moment. "Are you going to tell me about the storm?"

"The armor Rayan gave me, along with the swords--"

Evander held a hand up for silence.

"Wait, have I told you how incredibly sexy you looked striding across that battlefield with those swords? I mean, until you slapped me in the face." The corner of his lips tilted up in the barest hint of a smirk. "Which, by the way, no one has ever actually done before."

"Then you were clearly overdue." I shrugged, and he laughed, pulling me closer and lowering his lips to mine again.

He kissed me like we had all the time in the world, and I greedily soaked it up.

Even though we both knew it was a lie.

CHAPTER SEVENTY-SEVEN

ROWAN

Finally, the next morning, we forced ourselves back to the war room.

Though it was slow progress, since Evander insisted on "helping" me get dressed, which was not actually helpful or conducive to my clothes staying on at all.

"Why hasn't he made a move yet?" I mused aloud on the way to the war room.

I didn't have to explain who I meant.

"I can't say for sure, but I'd be willing to bet he lost a lot of support when they lost the last time." Evander looked at me, pride in his expression. "You did that, Lemmikki."

I had managed to explain about the armor and weather the night before, in between many, many kisses.

"*We* did that," I amended. "I knew the men I brought wouldn't be enough to turn the tides, but I also knew that if I distracted the enemy soldiers, if you were...still alive..." I had to swallow back the wave of emotion that always came when I remembered those weeks when I hadn't been sure if I would see him again.

"I knew if you were still the one commanding, you would take advantage of that," I said. "And you did. If you had reacted any less quickly, it wouldn't have mattered what I did."

A look crossed his features, somewhere between bafflement and gratitude. "You had that much faith in me, even then?"

"In your brilliant mind?" I clarified. "Yes. In your ability to not be a massive *aalio*? No, I had rather lost that."

He let out a low chuckle. "And now?"

"And now, you're slowly building it back." I gave him a private smile, one that he returned.

I would be lying if I told him I didn't have moments of panic where I wondered if he would change his mind again, but if he was willing to change, I was willing to find a way to trust him again.

Two of the servants opened the large doors to the war room, and we strode through. Taras gave a faint smirk, and I raised an eyebrow in response. Mila was rubbing off on him.

I suspected that he had something to do with Evander and me actually being left alone yesterday, though, and I was incredibly grateful for that.

"Have we heard back from any of the spies?" Evander asked once we sat down.

His hand held mine under the table, his thumb running small circles over my skin, and I forced myself to focus.

"Nothing yet," Taras responded, poring over the paperwork in front of him.

"He has to be plotting something," I said, not for the first time. "He knows once the pass opens, Lochlann will be able to get through, and that will not end well for him."

"Since the pass could open anytime in the next couple of months, he'll be planning something soon, then," Evander said thoughtfully.

"How many forces would we need to take this fight to him?" I asked after a moment.

He shook his head. "More than we have. All the military tactics in the world won't make up for the fact that he's holed up in a veritable fortress, and we have no allies to the east anymore. Crane's forces have been decimated, and our own weakened. Armies on the march aren't exactly subtle, and I suspect we wouldn't get further than the border before we were summarily slaughtered."

"Well, that's...promising," I muttered.

"All of this is assuming he even attacks again," Lord Lehtinan added.

"Iiro is never going to let this stand," I countered.

Something Evander had just said was niggling at my brain. *Armies on the march aren't exactly subtle.*

No, they weren't.

But my men were.

Evander was watching my face closely enough that he saw the moment it dawned on me.

"You have something in mind." He phrased it as a statement more than a question, but I nodded anyway.

"The Unclanned," I said. "They move about unseen."

"But a few hundred men wouldn't be able to overtake the castle, even in a surprise attack," Taras said gently.

Evander looked at me with wariness, though, and I knew he already saw where I was going with this.

"Those were only the men I could reach on the way here, in less than a week, in a small section of Bear. I could probably get...five times that many?" I guessed. "Would that be sufficient?"

I watched the gears turning in my husband's brilliant mind, knowing he was also taking into account whatever small advantage my skill with the weather would bring us. Holding my gaze, he nodded, a single, reluctant dip of his chin.

"Get them how?" One of the lords asked.

"Sir Evander offered reintegration into the clan in exchange for fighting. Surely, that will bring them here," Taras suggested.

I shook my head, but it was Evander who answered.

"They don't trust the clan, or...me," he said with a resigned frown. He glanced at me, visibly bracing himself. "What did you have in mind? Sending one of them out?"

His tone was a hair too casual, like he knew that wasn't where I was going with this. Now was our chance to see if he meant what he said about my choices.

"To some extent, they trust each other, or at least, will listen to each other, especially Andrei. But they won't follow him." I squared my shoulders. "They will follow me."

"You want to go out to recruit them yourself?" he asked, again so, so neutrally.

I nodded.

"Alone?" His voice was tighter now.

"I would take a small contingent of my men," I clarified. "Including Andrei."

He held my gaze for what felt like an eternity before he finally swallowed, a muscle twitching in his jaw. "When do you leave?"

I squeezed his hand, my shoulders falling with relief.

"The sooner the better." A small smile pulled at my lips. "And, of course, you would be welcome to accompany me."

The corner of his mouth tilted up as if to say, *well played*. He knew now I had been testing him. But at least he had passed.

"I'm sure that can be arranged," he replied, looking at Taras. "We'll keep runners in motion and send birds when we can."

"Of course, Your Grace." Taras nodded respectfully, but he, too, looked amused.

Evander spent the rest of the meeting outlining several potential strategies, based on how many men we were able to get. His mind was an impressive thing to behold.

"We still need a way in the gates," he finally said. "But I'll think on that."

After that, he announced that the meeting was over. Everyone filed out except for the two of us and Taras, the latter of which eyed me with interest.

"It seems I was right about the chaos," he commented.

"In fairness," I told him, "I never said you weren't."

"No," he agreed with a smirk reminiscent of his cousin's. "It was Van who kept insisting *everything is under control*."

"Well," Evander began. Then he paused like he wasn't quite sure where he was going with that. "It wasn't."

He turned to me, raising an eyebrow. "Speaking of chaos, Lemmikki, it's time to go get your army."

CHAPTER SEVENTY-EIGHT

ROWAN

We spent the next several weeks on the road, traveling up and down the length of Bear as quickly as we could. Our party was small, with only Evander, me, Andrei, and two others, so we could avoid drawing too much attention to ourselves.

Every day, we gathered more of the Unclanned to our cause and tried to spread word through their network. Our nights were spent sneaking away from camp to test the limits of my ability to manipulate the weather.

Between his careful insights and my natural skillset, we discovered several more uses for what I could do. Navigating straight line winds, icing the ground, and smaller, more targeted bursts of lightning were all possible.

It was exhausting, but with each new drill Evander had me running, it was also exciting to see how my skills were growing.

Overall, our efforts were a success.

More and more of the Unclanned joined us or sent word that they would. The testimony of Andrei and the two others had gone a long way to prove that I meant every word I spoke, that I would do whatever I needed to give them back their lives or help them create new ones.

Though they were still cautious of Evander, they never failed to be impressed, if not wildly intrigued, about the fact that he stood back and allowed me to speak for both of us.

By the time we made it back to Bear Estate, we had rallied over two thousand more men to our side. All that was left was to find a way into the castle, an opening.

But when word finally came, it wasn't at all what we expected.

As soon as we returned, we made sure that whatever food and supplies that could be spared were sent out in small, inconspicuous bundles to the Unclanned that had sworn themselves to me.

And the men who couldn't fight but wanted to help in other ways made their way to the castle to assist in the farming, weapons making, or whatever other role they could fill.

Word was still spreading about the shift in Bear and how the Unclanned didn't have to live that way anymore. The people weren't exactly coming around to the idea, but at least there was less outright hostility than there had been before.

More often than not, we found ourselves in the war room or Evander's study, poring over maps or an endless sea of war reports and losses and strategic assessments for next steps.

Which was what we were doing when Evander's deep voice sounded over the low sounds of rustling parchment.

"We need to get you a desk in here, Lemmikki," he announced conspicuously after I added another report to my rather messy stack. "Really, it's *our* study now."

I glanced from my corner of the desk to his much neater side before shrugging.

"But I have so much more fun sharing yours," I said innocently, batting my eyelashes up at him. "It can be *our* desk now."

He eyed the papers strewn across his normally pristine workspace and cleared his throat. "Yes, well, getting you your own would be so much more practical."

I resisted the urge to laugh, opening my mouth to come up

with a reason why it wouldn't be practical, mostly just to irritate him.

But a knock on the door interrupted us.

"There's someone here to see you both," Taras called through the door.

I was the closest, so I rose to open it.

"Who is it?" I asked.

Taras looked between Evander and me, pitching his voice low when he spoke.

"It's Sir Theodore."

CHAPTER SEVENTY-NINE

ROWAN

I exchanged a surprised glance with Evander.

"Korhonan?" Evander asked quietly, more to himself than to Taras.

"Bring him here?" I suggested.

Evander nodded, and Taras disappeared.

"Why do you think he's here? Do you think he's heard about what we're doing?" I asked, and Evander shook his head.

"Unless Iiro has spies within the Unclanned, that wouldn't be possible..." He trailed off, and I knew we were both thinking the same thing.

Isn't that what Ava had done? Paid off the Unclanned for information on my whereabouts with a bonus for whoever brought her my head?

"No," Evander said in answer to whatever he had been thinking. "No, Iiro is too prideful and clings to the old ways. He would never *lower himself* in that manner."

I nodded as the door swung open once again, this time with Taras leading a hooded figure inside. Theo lowered his hood, dipping his head in greeting.

Whatever this was about, it was clearly important if he was willing to risk coming into Bear, let alone seeking us out to speak in person. I moved to the decanter and poured three glasses of vodka, placing an ice cube in each one.

Theo eyed his warily. "At the risk of giving offense, my Lady, I'm not sure I'll be drinking anything you pour any time soon."

"Technically," I clarified, "I didn't pour anything last time."

Evander chuckled, taking a healthy swig from his glass. "If it makes you feel any better, she slapped me in front of my entire squadron."

I was a little surprised by that show of camaraderie, but then, they had been friends once, and I knew that Evander was grateful for Theo's forewarning...and his dubious assistance in getting me to safety.

Theo's somewhat horrified gaze landed on me, and I shrugged.

"Let's not pretend you didn't both deserve what you got and more, but if it helps..." I took a healthy swig of the vodka before holding it out to him again.

He took the glass, but still didn't drink from it. I didn't really blame him, since I had pretended to drink before.

I gestured for Theo to take a seat on one of the plush sofas in front of the fireplace, sinking down onto the one opposite him.

"What brings you here?" Evander asked, taking his seat next to me.

"We needed to speak, in person," Theo answered flatly.

Evander eyed him warily, but he gave a dip of his head for Theo to continue.

Now that I took a moment to really look at him, the lines of his face were drawn in exhaustion. His hazel eyes were blood-shot, and a rare bit of pale-blond stubble lined his jaw.

More than all of that, though, he looked...sad. Resigned.

"Things cannot continue as they are," he said.

"If you're here to tell me to bend the knee—" Evander began.

"That is not why I'm here," Theo interrupted him. "I'm here because I know you are planning something, and I want in."

I turned to look at Evander, but his eyes remained fixed on Theo, his features remaining completely neutral. Part of me couldn't help but be suspicious, wondering if this was a test or a trap. But I knew Theo better than that.

His honor was the most important thing to him. He would

never be so underhanded as to lie to us like this. Then my mind leapt to another, more exciting conclusion.

If Theo joined us, it would be the opening we needed.

Unreasonable hope flitted through me and was dashed just as quickly.

"I will never be able to convince my men to fight against their allies, nor their former duke, now king."

"You didn't come all this way just to say that," Evander stated plainly.

"No, I didn't," he agreed. "I can't convince them to fight on your side...but they will stand down if I order it. They were not happy, being led into a slaughter."

I winced at the term. If there had been a slaughter, Evander and I had been the butchers.

But then, they had attacked our people, on our land. Still, there were no real victors in war. Only those who suffered slightly fewer deaths.

"However," Theo continued, "I have two conditions."

His tone was enough to tell me that whatever they were, we weren't going to like them. I gestured for him to continue.

"I want you to spare Inessa," he said.

"Of course," I responded quickly. "You have to know we would never intentionally hurt her when she's been innocent in all of this."

He nodded, then met Evander's eyes solidly. "And I want you to spare my brother."

My husband looked thoughtful, but my jaw dropped of its own accord.

We would never be safe if Iiro was alive. We would spend our entire lives looking over our shoulders waiting for the day he decided his pride couldn't handle us being alive and out from under his thumb.

"You want us to spare Iiro after all of the people who died because of him?" I demanded.

Theo looked pointedly from Evander to me. "I'm quite certain there is no one in this room who doesn't have blood on their hands."

A flush rose into my cheeks. "Perhaps not, but there is also no one in this room who has started a war lately."

"Though I seem to recall your actions coming perilously close," he reminded me.

My lips parted in ire.

"Because of a situation the brother you so desperately want to live put us in," I snapped.

Evander put a hand on mine, presumably his subtle way of telling me to calm myself.

"You're suggesting imprisonment of some sort?" he interjected.

Theo nodded. "At Elk Estate."

"Where he can regroup and do this all over again in a couple of years?" I asked.

"No, where I can ensure that he is sequestered and unable to act again." Impatience crept into Theo's tone. "Besides, it took him years to garner support for this, and once he is dethroned, he will not be able to again. He will see that."

I wasn't sure any part of Iiro would accept defeat, but he had, admittedly, been cautious in the past.

Cautious and patient and ruthless and calculating, in a way that put my entire family at risk. In a way that put *Evander* at risk.

My parents had left Ava alive, and every one of us had paid for that.

Would this be the same? Iiro biding his time until he could hurt Evander again?

"You have not historically been the best person to recognize when Iiro is scheming," I reminded Theo, drinking down the rest of my vodka before pouring another round.

When I sat down again, Theo met my eyes, defeat dulling his own. "Rest assured, Rowan, the days when I was able to harbor any illusions about who my brother is or the things he would do are far behind me."

In spite of myself, I softened at his words. No one wanted to feel that way about their own family. I looked at my husband, who had donned his aloof mask.

It was impossible to tell what he was thinking, even for me.

"I assume you're staying at least until the morning?" Evander asked.

Theo nodded again.

"Then, we can discuss this over dinner," Evander suggested.

"We can." Theo got to his feet. "Though, you should know these are not terms I will negotiate on."

"Understood," Evander replied.

And just like that, all of our plans began to take shape, with one monstrous, asinine, and completely ridiculous caveat thrown in.

CHAPTER EIGHTY

ROWAN

Dinner was brought into our private dining chamber. If the staff saw anything strange about the fact that we asked for serving utensils to fend for ourselves for the evening, they didn't say anything about it.

Instead, once they made sure we had everything we needed, they dutifully left us alone. Evander brought Theo in from the office through the private door, gesturing to the chair across from me.

We helped ourselves to bowls of stew and a basket of bread rolls, eating in silence.

"What did you have in mind?" Evander asked after a few minutes.

"Something that will hopefully cause less bloodshed than another all-out war," he said. "You need a way into the palace, and I can convince Iiro to invite you."

That was exactly what we needed. It was easy to forget that Theo, too, had been raised to be in the military, to be a strategist, because of his blind spot where Iiro was concerned.

We went back and forth for the better part of the next few hours until we had a firm plan in place.

"And what about you?" Evander asked after a moment. "What happens when this is over?"

Theo met his gaze before shifting to meet mine.

"Then we go back to the way things were," he said. "I didn't want the throne before, and I sure as hell don't want it now."

Evander and I nodded our agreement.

We were just wrapping up dinner when a knock sounded at the door and Taras ducked his head inside to ask for a word with Evander in the hall. With a reluctant glance in my direction, Evander nodded and joined him, leaving me alone with Theo for the first time since our unfortunate encounter.

"So, this is what you've been up to since I saw you last? Becoming a proper Socairan lady while planning wars and treason?" Though his tone was light, there was a weight behind his hazel eyes.

"Well, a girl's got to have her hobbies, and my knitting skills leave much to be desired," I said flippantly.

A chuckle escaped him, brightening his face incrementally. "Of course. It was clearly the next logical choice."

"It was either this or cooking lessons. The options for women these days are so limited." I smiled up at him, and he returned it before looking back out the window once more.

"I hope you can understand why this is important to me, Rowan," he said after a moment, that heaviness seeping back into his tone. "Why I can't lose the only family I have left."

I swallowed hard. I had been so focused on the political and personal manipulations, along with Iiro's death toll, that I hadn't thought about the parts of him that someone would miss.

Seeing the sincerity in Theo's gaze, I knew my answer was important to him.

"I do," I responded softly, and the tension in his shoulders eased a little. "But my understanding will run its course if he tries to hurt my husband again."

He closed his eyes, nodding once. "That's fair."

There was a beat of silence when we both stared out at the stars before he spoke again.

"Regardless of how this ends, I am not your enemy, Rowan. I never could be."

Something in my chest eased, and I looked back at him.

"No, I don't think you could be, either." I said earnestly.

Then, the corner of my mouth twitched up. "Not unless you serve us borscht when we come to visit, of course."

"I would never," he assured me.

"Oh," I added. "And you're going to have to remove kidnapping me from your list of potential plans in the future."

He shook his head, reluctant laughter escaping his lips. "Consider it done."

"Then consider us friends." The word felt right.

It felt like hope for something normal and easy on the other side of all of this.

True to Theo's word, it was only two weeks before Iiro's smarmy-arse letter arrived by bird. Evander brought it over to our desk, waiting until I was right next to him to rip it open.

To my loyal subject; Sir Evander, Duke of Clan Bear and Servant of the Socairan Crown,

I have decided, against my better judgment, to extend one last opportunity for you to do what is right to further a united Socair. In exactly three weeks' time, we will be holding the annual tithing at the Palace. I will expect your presence, along with the agreed upon taxes.

And I am certain you will convince your allies to do their part as well.

After all, no one wants a real war.

His Royal Majesty, King Iiro

I could perfectly picture his smug expression as he wrote the last three lines. There was a clear threat behind his words, which meant he imagined he had the upper hand. Whatever Theo had said to him had worked.

"We have a date," Evander said, crushing the letter in his hand before tossing it into the unlit hearth.

"I'll send word to my men," I said.

"I'll do the same with Lynx and Crane," he confirmed.

"We'll need meet with Andrei directly to tell him the plan," I mused aloud. "I'm sure he's capable of leading the men into battle, and I can find an excuse to get to a balcony somewhere to do my part…"

I trailed off at the speculative expression on Evander's face.

"We need this to be a success," he said, his features taut with tension.

"I know." I placed a hand on his arm. "And your plan is a good one."

"But not perfect," he countered.

"Nothing is perfect." My tone was wry, and I wondered where he was going with this.

He studied my face for a long moment before nodding to himself.

"The men respect Andrei," he said. "But they revere you. And your affinity works best when you are out among the elements."

My lips parted with the realization of what he was about to say.

"You should be the one who leads them into battle." His eyes were a thunderstorm, churning and mercurial, but his voice didn't waver.

It hadn't even occurred to me that I wouldn't be at Evander's side, but he wasn't wrong. Our chances of success were higher this way.

"All right," I said. "If you're sure."

My husband looked very much like he wished he could say he was not sure, but he nodded.

"I'm sure," he said quietly. "After all, we're in this together, right?"

CHAPTER EIGHTY-ONE

EVANDER

I n the two weeks since Rowan had left before me to sneak
through the enemy's territory with her men, I had wanted
to kick myself more times than I could count.

But the strategist in me couldn't deny this was the best plan.
And I did trust her, even if I hated the necessity of being away
from her.

Even if I wondered whether that last night we spent together
would be the last time I ever held her in my arms.

There was no time to dwell on that now, though, surrounded
by enemies as I pulled up to the Obsidian Palace.

I had less than three seconds to climb down from the
carriage before the grating sound of Nils' voice reached my ears.
He didn't bother with a greeting or false niceties.

Instead, he took the opportunity to vocalize his fury at my
presence here, which wouldn't have bothered me on its own. I
had long since grown used to the disparaging way that people
spoke about me.

It wasn't in my nature to want to prove anything to them.

But then he strung together the words *Lochlannian* and *whore*.

Red lined my vision, and I slowly turned to face him, ready
to tear his traitorous head from his shoulders, when a different
face appeared in my line of vision instead.

"Sir Arès," I greeted with a smile that didn't reach my eyes.

"Sir Evander," he returned with a dip of his head. "I thought we might head in together."

I arched an eyebrow, my eyes drifting toward the door where Nils had already retreated.

"If only to keep you from spilling blood on the palace steps," Arès offered a second later, then more quietly, "Iiro will set you up to fail at every turn. He wants a reason to execute you in front of everyone. Do not give him one. Not yet, at least."

He clapped me on the back, and I was forced to acknowledge that he was right.

I turned to speak a few hushed orders to Kirill and Yuriy, making sure that they were on their guard and ready for the signal.

With a sharp nod, they assured me they would be. Then we watched as Iiro's new soldiers, all dressed in the deep purple of the Socairan monarchy, unloaded the food my people needed and carried it into the palace larders.

We had been forced to bring it along, since Iiro wouldn't entertain me for long if he didn't think he had won.

Arès made a sound of disgust as he watched the soldiers unload the food. We both knew that this tax wouldn't benefit the people of Socair. Instead, it would allow Iiro to live the life of excess and luxury that he craved.

And that was just one of the reasons why his rule could not continue.

When I finally couldn't stand it anymore, we followed the sound of music into the palace doors where we would feast and drink with the pseudo-king as if he hadn't brought war to my doorstep before forcing me to spend the evening with my trai-torous former ally.

"Do we have a time?" Arès asked quietly as we entered the Great Hall.

A servant walked past, offering us glasses of medovukha. I took mine, drinking down a healthy gulp before responding.

"Tomorrow morning," I murmured.

Arès took a drink, making a thoughtful sound in acknowl-edgment.

What he didn't understand about the plan was the fact that we were relying, in a very large part, on the morning fog and Rowan's ability to use it to her advantage.

And the fact that she was still alive and unharmed.

I reminded myself that she was safe with her men. Andrei was a loyal captain. From the small amount of time I had spent around him and the others, I knew they would protect her.

Besides, if they had been found out, Iiro surely would have thrown that in my face already. As if the bastard could hear my thoughts, his eyes met mine from across the room and he raised a glass in toast.

Aalio.

He tilted his head curiously before making his way forward.

"Der'mo," I muttered mostly to myself before Arès echoed the sentiment.

"Sir Stenvall, Sir Kostya," Iiro greeted as if he were a casual acquaintance, rather than the man who brought a bloody battle to my doorstep and cost my clan thousands of lives.

I dipped my head in response.

"I had expected your wife to be here with you." He made a show of glancing around the room.

"She had other things to take care of," I offered without an apology, and Iiro's eyes narrowed.

Whether it was in suspicion or in offense, I couldn't be sure.

"Well, do send her our regards," he said flatly. "I am certain that next time, she won't miss it."

He left on that threatening note, while I comforted myself with the reminder that there wouldn't be a *next time* after tomorrow.

I took another long swig of medovukha, gripping the chalice so tightly that my knuckles whitened.

All that was left to do was play the game and bide our time until Rowan's signal. That, and keep my word to Korhonan by not killing his brother the way I so, so desperately wanted to.

"Sometimes I wish I hadn't sworn to let him live," I admitted under my breath, and Arès chuckled.

"Well, I didn't promise anything," he said.

I couldn't tell whether or not he was being serious, but there was no time to clarify before Iiro made a grand, sweeping gesture, effectively ordering everyone to take their seats at the table.

And the game officially began.

CHAPTER EIGHTY-TWO

ROWAN

The fog rolled in right on time and with it, two of the caravans from Bear.

That should have been a good sign, should have given me a modicum of hope, but my spine tingled with alarm bells that had nothing to do with the storm-cloud hanging overhead.

I couldn't shake the feeling that no matter what happened today, we would pay a steep price.

My stomach churned, my meager breakfast threatening to make a reappearance.

Looking at the men around me, from Andrei to where the others were nestled out of sight in the trees, I wondered how many of them would be left standing at the end of this.

I wondered if I would.

If Evander would.

But there wasn't time for thoughts like that now. We had made a plan, and it was time to see it through. Evander was trusting me to do this, and half of Socair was depending on me doing it well.

I centered myself, taking all of the fury I felt toward the tyrannical monster who had made himself a king, and channeling it out in increments to help me move the fog.

A thick, gray blanket of mist clung to the castle, obscuring the view of the guards.

Andrei looked to me, and I shook my head. It wasn't time yet. I wasn't quite finished with my part.

He nodded his understanding. True to their form, not a single one of my men had ever let on that they knew what I could do, but they damned sure had to realize it wasn't a coincidence that lightning struck when I was around.

And if they hadn't realized it before, they certainly would now.

Evander had reasoned that if I could move clouds of fog, I could move storm clouds as well. So, I had effectively brought one with me, a particularly charged little nebula that I had moved along with bursts of wind, in case there were no storms nearby.

I could have, in theory, also pulled the fog from what mist was around us, but it would have taken all I had. Again, I reminded myself that things were going as well as could be expected.

I pushed the charged cloud forward until it was hanging directly over the castle, blotting out the sun. Then I called down two small bolts of lightning, one right after the other.

With a deafening crack, the two palace guards in the posts closest to us were flung from their towers.

The other two were Elk. They should look the other way. They should remain silent.

Should.

It was more tenuous than I wanted it to be when every single life here was on the line. But we had no choice, so on we went.

As soon as we heard the groaning of the portcullis opening to allow one of Evander's many "waylaid" food wagons through, the first round of soldiers crept through the gates. I held my breath for it to close once again, for this to be a trap...

But, true to Theo's word, it remained open, and the Elk guards stationed in the watchtowers sounded no alarm as they turned their backs to allow my men through.

Andrei took the lead while I stayed behind with most of our

army, waiting to send them in as needed. Theo had warned us that there would always be soldiers inside the courtyard, so we knew what to expect.

Still, my heartbeat thundered in my chest, a slow, powerful rhythm fueled by adrenaline and dread.

And then several voices cried out in surprise before they were abruptly cut off. Footsteps crunched along the loose gravel paths as more of the Palace or Clan soldiers ran over to the sounds of fighting, and I sent another twenty men into the mists to help.

Though I knew that holding on to the fog gave my men the upper hand, I couldn't help the feeling of uselessness as I stood back and waited for the fighting to be over.

But, I had promised Evander I would be careful. That I wouldn't take unnecessary risks. As I stared through the mist, I knew trying to fight in it would be exactly that, not to mention compromise what we were trying to do.

My stomach twisted as I counted off the sounds of dying men, hoping that none of them had belonged to us.

Every so often, I glanced up at the watchtowers, waiting for the Elk soldiers to go back on their word. But they continued to stand still as statues with their eyes focused on anything but the battle below them.

Eventually the sounds of the fray were over, and a figure moved in the fog, coming toward us until finally Andrei's face came into view.

Relief coursed through me. While he was covered in blood, none of it appeared to belong to him.

He brought our injured men outside of the gates, lining them up against the walls while I ordered a soldier with medic training to tend to them.

"The courtyard is clear, but we should move quickly in case more come," Andrei whispered beside me, and I agreed.

My pulse quickened as the rest of the soldiers followed us into the gates. The ground was wet from either the mists or blood, so we picked our way carefully toward the palace entrance, stepping over bodies of Palace and Clan guards along the way.

Two of my men shoved open the doors to find six guards lining the hallway that led to the throne room.

Half of them were Elk, but the other three wore deep purple.

Thud.

I barely heard the whisper of steel against flesh over the sound of my own heartbeat, barely registered the blood pouring from the throats of the enemy soldiers as my men backed away.

The bodies fell to the floor with a low thump, the guards silenced before a cry of alarm could be raised. Three pools of crimson marred the pristine black marble, and I looked away, examining the remaining soldiers.

But the Elk guards didn't move. Didn't speak. I nodded to them, not breaking my stride toward the obsidian double doors.

Our muffled footsteps mingled with the gasps and shouts of the servants before they turned to run. We let them go. By the time they brought help back, we would already be barred in the throne room.

Halfway down the hallway, I gestured to Andrei. He nodded, sending his second-in-command up the stairs that would lead to the upper level of the room, along with a contingent of men.

Then finally, we stood outside the gleaming black doors that led to every reason I was here.

To stop Iiro.

To keep Evander safe.

To protect Bear.

All of it relied on what would happen in that room.

With a single dip of my chin, two of my men went to open those doors.

To seal our fate, for better or worse.

CHAPTER EIGHTY-THREE

EVANDER

I had given up on sleep several hours after midnight, resigning myself to pacing the room and relentlessly reviewing every detail of what should have been a nearly flawless plan.

But when my entire clan was at stake, when my wife was at stake, *nearly* wasn't good enough.

So it took more effort than usual to will my features into a haughty, careless mask as I made my way down the hallways to the throne room. Kirill and Yuriy were at my back, as I was chronically incapable of trusting Iiro.

Arès clearly felt the same way, since he was waiting outside the door for us rather than going in. Danil Uitto, the Duke of Crane, joined us moments later.

He bore a solemn expression as he approached. With the losses he had suffered, Crane had more reason than even Bear to hate Iiro and his rule.

"Danil," I greeted, with Arès following suit.

He nodded in return, fixing his features into neutrality before we entered the throne room.

The first thing I did was carefully assess the surroundings. Guards lined the room, the allotted ten each clan was allowed to bring plus the hundreds from Elk and the Palace.

I would have been frustrated by his clear favoritism in

allowing his brother to bring an actual regiment if it wasn't working in our favor.

Iiro perched on his gaudy throne, predictably wearing his oversized crown, ridiculously ornate robes, and that obnoxious, arrogant expression he favored.

Even knowing how this day would end for him, I could still hardly stand to look at his face.

He had a smattering of Elk guards around him, but more than half were his own, which was unfortunate. At least Korhonan had apparently been successful in convincing him Inessa would be better off holding tea this morning, since she was nowhere to be seen.

"My good dukes," Iiro began, gesturing to the room. "Thank you all for attending our first annual tithing."

Arès and Danil shifted uncomfortably on their feet, and they weren't the only ones. The dukes from Bison and even Viper looked just as uneasy about being here. Bear's taxes might have been the worst, but no one was coming out of this unaffected.

My gaze shifted from them to the window, looking for the telltale sign that Rowan was close, but still, nothing. When I caught Kirill's gaze, he subtly shook his head to confirm he saw nothing from his vantage point either.

I didn't look at Korhonan, not wanting to give his brother any cause for suspicion.

Without preamble, Iiro got straight to the point, his gaze locking on me and the dukes at my side.

"Sir Stenvall," he said in an overly pleasant tone. "Why don't we begin with you."

He gestured for me to stand before him, and I resisted the urge to roll my eyes. Instead, I nodded, casually sliding my hands into my pockets as I stepped forward.

We had known that he would likely single me out first, to make an example of me. To encourage the others to bow to his whims once he forced me to do the same.

Before Iiro could utter a single word, a dense mist settled over the palace, obscuring the morning sun that had lit up the room only moments ago. A few of the dukes exchanged startled glances at the abrupt wave of fog uncharacteristically high in the air, but there was no real alarm.

Until a burst of light flashed through the air, punctuated by a sharp crack directly over our heads. Iiro barked a few orders for the guards stationed near him to make sure that no major damage had been done, shooting cautious glances out the window.

"You were saying," I prodded, wanting his attention on me and not the courtyard, just in case.

He slowly turned back to me. "Yes. I assume you're ready to accept the taxes on imported goods, for the betterment of our great kingdom."

I pretended to consider it while I took several steps closer to him. His guards had been well trained, though. They stepped in as well.

"Tell me," I said conversationally. "Will you be collecting nearly half of all dowries going forward, or is that treatment limited to Bear?"

Iiro's eyes narrowed. "When those dowries are moved in from another kingdom, I will."

It was the wrong answer. Even the dukes on his side murmured in disagreement.

But I didn't really care what he said, just that we conversed long enough for me to be the closest one to his throne, and that he remained distracted until Rowan got here.

"I see." I let a facetious note enter my tone. "And the taxes on food, what do you plan on doing with the surplus?"

Iiro huffed out an irritable breath. "I hardly see how that is relevant for you to know."

"I would like to know as well," Arès spoke up. "Surely you believe the clans have a right to be told where their tithes are being used?"

Ignoring their back and forth since it would hardly matter in a few minutes, I took the opportunity to survey the room again. Everything was as we expected it to be.

There was no reason for anything to go wrong. Except…

Except that anything could go wrong in a battle. My wife was more than capable, but as she was fond of saying, it only took one good opening for someone else to best you.

Panic threatened to seize my chest, and I locked it away. It would accomplish nothing, and I needed to keep my head.

Vaguely, I registered Iiro directing a snide comment toward me just as the doors to the room burst open and the very woman in question strode into the room.

And she was...stunning. Covered nearly head to toe in her black armor, a wicked saber in each hand, and her eyes burning with resolve.

But it wasn't just her that everyone was looking at. The army of *Besklanovvy* at her back had their rapt attention. As if on cue, the soldiers from Elk stepped back.

Iiro's eyes widened with betrayal, but I didn't give him time to process what was happening before I advanced on his nearest guard. Arès and Danil had drawn their weapons as well, and I had a moment to be grateful for the deeply traditional nature of Socairan laws.

The king couldn't disarm his dukes. All he could do was bolster himself with guards, but unfortunately for Iiro, nearly half of his were already against him.

I registered the sounds of fighting around me as I cleanly defeated the first guard, then the second. By the time I felled the third, Arès and Danil were taking care of the others.

Iiro drew his weapon, realizing it was down to him and me. I had known on some level that we would wind up here from the moment he betrayed me to Ava, all those years ago.

It really was a shame I couldn't kill him for that.

CHAPTER EIGHTY-FOUR

ROWAN

There was a single beat of silence when we entered the throne room, just before all hell broke loose.

Evander went straight for Iiro on the dais, as we had planned.

Still, I cursed under my breath. I wanted to be fighting at his side, not stuck across the room and separated by our makeshift battlefield.

I told myself he would be fine.

He had to be.

Besides, he wasn't alone. Arès was at his side with Danil and a few of the soldiers from Crane as they took on what was left of the private guard.

Everyone was moving, dodging a blow or delivering one themselves. The upstairs level was bedlam, and this floor wasn't faring any better.

Palace soldiers, along with Ram and Wolf were headed straight for us and the handful of Bear soldiers that had been allowed into the meeting.

Lynx and Crane were quick to spring into action, defending our men and fighting off as many of the others as they could, while the other clans seemed to be watching and waiting.

The cowards likely wouldn't join in the fight until they were more confident in who the victor would be.

That twisting, inauspicious feeling came roaring back to life as I met the blade of a Ram soldier charging straight for me. Deflecting his cutlass with one saber, I used every ounce of the strength I had to run the other through his stomach.

His eyes widened as he groaned and fell to the floor. I had barely removed my sword from his body before the next man was charging forward. This time, it was a joint effort to take the man down, with Andrei coming in for the kill while I dodged his blade again and again.

The fighting had broken out before the majority of my men could enter the room, leaving far too many of them bottlenecked at the door. If they pushed forward now, they would likely trample us in their quest to stop the other soldiers.

For the moment, they could only slowly wait to join the fight whenever room was made for them.

All around us, cries rang out above the clashing of steel. I could barely see as I pushed and fought my way through the men trying to trample me, desperate to reach the front of the room where Evander was.

An unexpected blade bounced off of my armor with a bruising impact, and I winced. When I spun to face my attacker, I found Andrei instead. His back was to me, and his hand shook as his sword held off the blade of a Wolf soldier.

Then Andrei's blade wavered, a tremble that seemed to resonate all the way through me.

I flung forward as he lost his grip on his hilt before falling to the ground at his attacker's feet, but I wasn't fast enough. Andrei's hand gripped his abdomen, doing nothing to staunch the steady stream of blood spilling from his gaping wound.

His body hadn't even hit the ground before I went on the attack. The soldier's eyes were feral as he drew his sword high in the air once more.

I neatly dodged it, slicing mine across his thighs before doing it once again across his neck. Then I brought my boot up, kicking him backwards into the melee behind him.

My attention slid back to Andrei, to where his lifeless eyes stared blankly ahead. Bitter bile crept up my throat.

We had all known the stakes when we marched on the palace, but somehow, I hadn't expected to count him among the casualties. An unreasonable part of me still wanted to go to him, to check for some sign that he was still alive.

But the attacks were relentless.

And the reality was that even if I had been able to get to him, I had spent weeks in the sick tent at the battlefront. I knew what death looked like.

There was nothing to be done for him.

My stomach twisted, but this battle was far from over.

I forcibly averted my eyes when other soldiers stepped on and over Andrei's body in an effort to get to me, taking out every ounce of fury I had on each and every one of them.

Lightning flashed and thunder roared just outside the windows, rattling the panes with the intensity of the storm I had unwittingly called, as I stood, ready to unleash one of my own.

CHAPTER EIGHTY-FIVE

EVANDER

Korhonan was lending his hand to the fray, but the other dukes were milling about, looking uncertain.

I only had eyes for Iiro. For the blade he was drawing in his right hand as he reached for that of his fallen guard with his left.

I was at a disadvantage here since I had promised to keep him alive, but I was also the far better swordsman. Still, I wasn't naïve enough to be off my guard.

I advanced without hesitation.

"Tell me, Iiro," I said, going on the offensive with a strike he parried. "Did you know who my stepmother was?"

He sneered. "It wasn't hard to guess."

"Then why help her?" I wasn't sure why it mattered after all these years, but I found myself asking anyway, told myself it was my way of distracting him.

"With your father's mind already going, I assumed she might prove useful one day." He managed to shrug and attack at the same time, a lightning-fast movement of his sword that reminded me of the many duels he had won before he stopped going in the ring. "Which I was right about."

And of course, he hadn't cared about the collateral damage, not when he was laying careful, long-term plans for his rule.

"By getting my father to sign off on your monarchy, then later killing him?" I asked.

He didn't answer, but his silence was confirmation enough. Bolstered by a new wave of ire, I attacked with a relentless speed. There was no more room for conversation amidst a blur of strikes and parries.

Iiro might have been a masterful swordsman at one point, but he had gotten lazy. Sloppy. Arrogant in his rule.

And in the end, that was his undoing.

He faltered under the nonstop slew of hits I was delivering his way, overstepping in his dodge, and I used the momentum to send him flying to the ground.

With both of my blades at his throat, he had no choice but to drop his weapons. I kicked them far from his reach.

Lifting my eyes to survey the battle, I immediately spotted my wife, fighting like I had never seen before. Her blades whipped through the air, slicing through her enemies with an unmatched speed and precision.

She was death itself, dealing swift judgment with each of her blows.

I forced myself to look away from her, meeting Iiro's gaze once again. Lowering my sword to his throat, I pressed the tip of the blade into his skin, enough to draw a single drop of blood.

I wasn't going to kill him, but he didn't know that. Still, he only glared at me, refusing to show fear, even on the brink of death.

I could almost have respected him, if I didn't so deeply despise him.

Looking back out at the crowd, I raised my voice loud enough to break through the clashing steel and cries of pain.

"Enough!" I yelled. "We have the king."

Slowly, the sounds of battle died down as the soldiers realized I had their king.

Iiro lay silent as a stone, staring mutely ahead while I spoke to the crowd.

"The fight is over," I said in a more moderate tone. "Hand

over your weapons now, and you will suffer no further repercussions."

The soldiers all looked around suspiciously before dropping their swords at the feet of the Unclanned.

Backing away, I allowed Iiro to stand, though I didn't lower my blades.

I opened my mouth to speak again when motion caught my attention. Arès gave a brief, curt nod to one of his soldiers, just as the man hurled a throwing knife.

"No!" I ordered, but it was too late.

The blade sailed toward Iiro, toward the part of his chest where his heart would have been, if he had one. It was everything I had wanted for years, to see this man bleed out in front of me.

But I had made a promise to Korhonan that his brother would live. I had sworn it. I refused to be no better than the man I was currently de-throning.

That was the only excuse I had for what I did next.

I leapt in front of Iiro, just in time for a sharp, stabbing pain to bite into my chest. I fell to the floor, unable to bear the weight of it. Pain was nothing new to me, but this held a new level of intensity.

It radiated from my chest, through my shoulder and back, spreading out like tendrils of fire.

I distantly registered vibrant green eyes and an ominous crack of thunder before the world went black.

CHAPTER EIGHTY-SIX

ROWAN

Two heartbeats.

That was all it took for Evander to fall after the knife pierced his chest.

Time slowed down, like I was wading through mud, trying to get to him. Iiro stood, stunned, and Theo was already on his knees beside my husband.

I finally made it to Evander's side, in time to see crimson blooming across his pristine coat. I had the illogical thought that he would hate that, the mess it was making.

His face was so, so pale, his eyes wide.

Like Andrei's had been, just as he—

No.

No, no, no.

Distantly, I heard myself shout for a healer.

Panic surged in my chest, and wind battered the windows around us until one of them shattered, spilling shards of glass like jagged raindrops all around us.

I tried not to read into that, tried to ignore the macabre feeling that fate was toying with us, showing me that Evander and I began and ended with broken glass.

No.

We were not going to end this way.

Theo tore off his coat to staunch the wound, and I turned

away just long enough to glare at Arès, who was looking uncertainly at his men.

"You will not make a mockery of this," I hissed at him. "Detain Iiro like we were supposed to do in the first damned place."

Lightning crackled just outside the space where the window used to be, and I tried to rein in my fury, turning back to my husband.

"Don't you dare die on me now, Evander," I ordered, pleaded. "You're going to be fine. The healer is coming, and everything is going to be all right."

I repeated some rambling version of those words over and over again, though I didn't know if he could hear me, if he believed me.

I didn't even know if I believed me.

Evander still hadn't woken up.

The healer said it was anyone's guess as to whether he would, given the amount of blood he lost.

I refused to believe that, though.

Even though hours upon hours had passed.

Theo had sent a runner to Lochlann for me, to Gallagher, but I knew it wasn't entirely reasonable, knew that it would take him weeks to get back.

I lay next to my husband, tracing the uncharacteristically pale lines of his face and talking about everything and nothing. Begging him to hold on, to come back to me.

But hours turned into days, and still, he didn't stir.

A slew of faces came to check on Evander, including Arès, though he left quickly at my glare, making excuses to visit the rest of the injured.

Evander wasn't the only one in a sickbed. Kirill had been

reprimanded by the healers for leaving his to check on Evander. I had barely recognized him with his face hidden beneath a swath of bandages.

There were others, too. Others who had made it out of the battle with minor injuries, simple flesh wounds.

They would be able to heal and go home to their families, which was more than I could say for Andrei. He hadn't even been given that much.

Tears pricked at the back of my eyes as I remembered the first day he took a knee in front of me. The day he thanked me for giving him hope.

What did that hope mean now that he had died anyway?

When Theo came to tell me the dukes were discussing next steps with the monarchy, whether to disband it or set up a successor, I told him I didn't care.

And I didn't.

The only thing I cared about right now was lying lifeless in this bed.

The healers came to administer blood replenishing tonics, to check his wound for infection. They listened to his heart and felt for his pulse and told me a whole lot of nothing every time before they left.

A waiting game, they said.

But *hell* felt like a more accurate term.

On the third day, Evander's eyelids fluttered.

His cheeks looked less pallid than they had, if only barely. He might have been merely sleeping, if not for the fact that I couldn't seem to wake him.

I thought about that first day in his carriage, how he had casually rested his head against the wall, his eyes closed. How even then, he had sensed me, my movement as I was going for my dagger.

And I realized that although he had told me our story as he knew it, I had never given it back to him. So I did, and all I could do was hope that somewhere in his brilliant mind, he could hear me.

"It isn't ridiculous," I began. "To think that we were connected from the first time we danced. I look back and I realize you were all I could see. The rest of the room, the world, fell away, and it was only you, and your stupidly beautiful, frustrating face."

I choked on a sob.

"Then you took me, and even when I wanted to hate you, I couldn't. Because you saw me. And I saw you, too." My eyes roamed over his features, remembering how I would scrutinize them for the smallest reaction in those early days.

"I saw every last, jagged edge of who you were and loved you more for each one. Maybe it's because they resonated with the broken pieces of myself, or maybe we always would have been this way, perfectly fitted for one another." The latter felt true.

That in a thousand possibilities of our lives together, every version of me belonged with every version of Evander.

"You said that you didn't like who you were turning into when I came along," I went on, my words tripping over themselves with urgency. Like he needed to hear this, like he would wake up if he did.

"But you weren't the only one. I was barely living my life, barely feeling at all, and then there you were. Making me furious." Something between a laugh and a sob escaped my lips. "Making me feel things. Making me want to take a chance on something impossible."

I brushed one of his careless locks away from his brow, my fingers skimming the skin that wasn't nearly as warm as it should have been.

"So I need you to come back to me, because we did it," I told him. "We did it together, just like we said we would. We took that impossible chance, and even with all of the odds stacked against us, we won."

Tears tracked down my cheeks, and my voice was rough with emotion.

"And it does *not* end like this. So wake up," I demanded. "Wake up and smirk at me and call me Lemmikki."

But he didn't stir, aside from another fluttering of his eyelids.

I leaned over him, burying my face in the crook of his arm and trying to muffle my broken sobs. I thought about Avani and wondered how she even found the strength to open her eyes every morning.

Because if Evander didn't survive this, I didn't think I would either.

Lemmikki.

I must have fallen asleep that way because I was dreaming. Evander was calling me in a soft tone, and it sounded so perfect, so right, that I didn't want to wake up.

I forced my eyelids shut tighter, trying to stay trapped in that moment for as long as I could before I had to face reality.

Lemmikki, wake up.

It sounded so real, another sob escaped my lips.

Then the arm I was sleeping on moved, the hand I was clutching so desperately squeezing mine in return.

Finally, I lifted my head, slowly, still terrified to hope. But Evander was there, his storm-cloud eyes tired, but open, and staring at my tearstained face in concern.

The sight of it only made me cry harder, my limbs going weak with relief. I pressed my lips against his mouth, his forehead, his cheeks, my tears spilling on his face.

"I love you," I said between hitching breaths. "With every last broken piece of my soul, and when it's whole, and everything in between."

His hand gripped mine tighter.

"I love you, too, Lemmikki." His voice was low and rough with disuse and still endlessly perfect. "Always."

Lemmikki undid me all over again, but finally, I calmed down enough to move back, calling for the healer.

"How long have I been out?" he asked, his voice cracking.

Moving to get the glass of water next to me, I held it to his lips, making sure he drank as I answered.

"Nearly four days," I told him.

He nodded, then winced with the movement. "Is Iiro…"

"Imprisoned," I supplied. "He's here until Theo takes him back to Elk."

Evander gave another short dip of his chin. Even exhausted and in pain, his sharp eyes processed and analyzed the information as it came.

"And you, Lemmikki?" he asked in a softer tone.

"Now that you're awake?" I answered. "I'm perfect."

The corner of his mouth twitched up in the barest hint of a smirk. "Well, you were always perfect." Then, he managed to raise one sardonic eyebrow. "And Lemmikki?"

I shot him a questioning look.

His gaze bored into mine, but there was a teasing glint in his eyes. "You made me feel things, too."

CHAPTER EIGHTY-SEVEN

EVANDER

T hough I normally would have had no complaints about staying in bed with my gorgeous wife for days on end, this situation was decidedly less fun than it could have been.

Yuriy brought me reports, and Korhonan came by more than once to express his gratitude and see how I was faring. Arès stopped by as well, though Rowan's furious countenance chased him from the room rather quickly.

But I couldn't just sit here while the other dukes discussed the future of Socair. By the third day, I demanded to be brought to the council room, and Rowan, of course, adamantly insisted that I stay in bed.

Despite the healer's many reassurances about my steady improvement, my wife remained convinced I might die at any moment.

I couldn't blame her, not when I remembered what it was like to be on the other side of this. We hadn't even really belonged to each other when the fever threatened to take her from me, and it had still been a few of the worst days of my life.

Still, I needed to get out of this room.

She finally relented, albeit reluctantly, so I slowly made my way downstairs, with a detour to Kirill's room.

He looked even worse than I felt, but he still had a smile on his lips. My gaze lingered on the bandage over one of his eyes, or rather, where the eye used to be, according to Rowan.

I sank into a chair, the short walk tiring me more than I wanted to admit, and surveyed my friend with concern.

"Don't give me that look, Van," he said flippantly. "Though your wife clearly prefers pretty men, mine likes the rugged type, so she'll be thrilled with this turn of events."

I smiled, shaking my head, and Rowan chuckled softly next to me.

"Pretty?" I demanded.

"It's the eyelashes," she said drily.

Kirill shrugged smugly, and I pretended to take offense before forcing myself back to my feet. With a brief farewell, we continued our trek downstairs.

It was even slower going down the stairs to the council room. Each step jarred the wound in my chest, but I pushed the pain away before Rowan could see it on my face.

Finally, we made it to the room where the eight dukes were sitting, plus Yuriy, who had been acting in my stead as the next-highest-ranking member of Bear present.

Except for Rowan, of course, but even if the men would have allowed it, she refused to leave my side.

Yuriy jumped up from his seat. I settled into it, glaring at Mikhail until he vacated his own chair in favor of one further down so my wife could sit next to me.

I knew something was wrong when all eight sets of eyes settled on me warily. Nine, if I was counting Yuriy's hesitant glances. My eyebrow raised of its own accord as I met each of their stares in turn.

"We've been discussing the next steps," Korhonan said, hesitation clear in his tone. "Technically, by succession, the crown would fall to me..."

Now both of my eyebrows shot up. He had told Rowan and me in no uncertain terms that he wouldn't be taking the throne.

If I was being honest with myself, Korhonan wouldn't make the worst ruler, but I wasn't convinced he had the discernment or the strategy necessary to unite Socair.

Nor was there any world in which I wanted to be in subjection to him.

"But I don't want it," he finished up before I could say any of those things.

"All right," I said evenly, "so we go back to the way it was, as we discussed."

Arès cleared his throat. "We believe that Socair would benefit from a more united front."

Rowan shot him a look, but I didn't think that was in response to his words as much as her general lack of forgiveness. I bit back a smile at her characteristic ruthlessness before returning my attention to the matter at hand.

"You have made it abundantly clear on more than one occasion that you don't believe the monarchy should be reinstated," I reminded the Lynx duke.

"Under Iiro," he agreed. "But if someone else were to take up that mantle..."

"Someone like...?" I asked, waiting for him to supply his own name.

"Someone like you," Korhonan answered. "You are the one who defeated the king, after all."

I blinked several times rapidly, sure I had misheard him. Once again, I surveyed the dukes at the table. Mikhail and Nils looked decidedly disgruntled, but everyone else appeared... thoughtful. Hopeful, even.

"You're the logical choice," Arès said. "I've observed your strategy myself, the way you form alliances, securing trade and food for the first time in a generation."

"In spite of your father's rule, those under your command consider your decisions to be fair, and you have been a loyal ally," the Duke of Crane added.

"And you are already peacefully tied to our only potential enemy," Andreyev from Viper chimed in.

It was clear they had discussed this at length already.

Korhonan pushed a crisp sheet of parchment in front of me. I briefly scanned the contents of what appeared to be a contract to rule, written in elegantly lettered script...with eight signatures already on the bottom.

"It's only missing yours," Arès pointed out, nudging a quill and ink across the table toward me.

My mind reeled with the possibilities. Was this even something I wanted? I certainly didn't want anyone else doing it, not when I didn't trust their interests, but was a monarchy even necessary?

And what about Rowan?

I met her eyes solidly. They were wide with surprise, but also affirmation.

Her hand came over mine. "Think of your plans for resources. Think of everything you could accomplish."

In spite of myself, I contemplated what they were asking. Socair would continue to suffer if the clans couldn't band together. Hadn't I thought that more than once?

Then I considered Rowan, how she had already changed things with the Unclanned and the women tending the injured, just in the short time she had been here.

How the balance of power had been off between us from the first day we met, and how many problems that had caused.

How she couldn't even sit in on council meetings in my stead.

"I'm afraid I'll have to decline to sign this document," I said, shoving it back toward Korhonan.

Several mouths opened, no doubt to argue with me, when I raised my hand for silence.

"If, however, you feel so inclined to draw up a new contract for the monarchy," I said casually. "One that includes my wife as an equal ruling partner, I could be convinced to sign that one."

Gasps rang out across the table, but Korhonan nodded like he had been expecting that. Nils and Mikhail started speaking at the same time in clear opposition when Arès' voice silenced them.

"Need I remind you both that we are generously deciding not to sanction your clans for your part in the war, nor to deprive Sir Nils of his head for his betrayal of an alliance."

Their mouths closed so quickly, it was almost comical.

"It isn't done," the Duke of Viper insisted quietly.

Remembering what Rowan had said to the bands of Unclanned every day for weeks when she was recruiting them, I let a haughty smirk take over my features.

"It is now," I told him.

Korhonan spoke up as well. "I might point out that until last week, it was also unheard of for a woman to lead an army of *Besklanovvy*, but if Lady Stenvall hadn't done just that, we would all still be under the rule of a tyrant king."

He barely even stumbled over the description of his brother.

"Not to mention…" Arès gave my wife a look far fonder than the ones she had been giving him. "She has been raised for this, as second-in-line to her own throne, trained to rule the same as the dukes at this table."

Reluctantly, Andreyev nodded, along with the rest of them. Except Mikhail and Nils, who still glowered silently.

I smirked at the latter. If I couldn't kill him, subjecting him to the rule of the woman he insisted on being prejudiced toward was a solid consolation prize.

Then I turned to my wife, who actually appeared to be stunned into silence for a change.

Think of everything you could accomplish, she had said.

"We," I corrected her.

She raised her eyebrows in question.

"Think of everything *we* could accomplish," I said, squeezing her hand.

A slow smile spread across her lips.

"Well, then," she said, entwining her fingers with mine. "I believe this calls for some vodka."

EPILOGUE

ROWAN

Six Months Later...

Evander and I finally returned to our rooms at the Obsidian Palace after yet another long day of trying to get the kingdom in order. It was going more smoothly than expected, at least on my husband's end.

His natural talent for ruling and the practical plans for food and resources he put in place were well received across the board. Whereas my ideas were generally more...controversial.

It started with the Unclanned becoming my official Queensmen. When push came to shove, none had elected to return to my holdings in Lochlann. They stayed here with me, trying to face this brave new world.

Then I implemented a law that ensured women would be considered for the same apprenticeships that men were, at which point I could practically hear the sound of several thousand Socairan men clutching their pearls and clinging to their outdated ideals.

At least I could still put my armor to good use, gently persuading the weather to calm down for the sake of the crops nearby.

It was possible that sometimes I also utilized the stones to make it rain on Mikhail's head when he visited, conveniently timed so that he would first leave his carriage without any covering and then find himself drenched by the time he reached the palace doors.

But mostly, I put it to good use.

Evander walked over to his dresser and set his crown neatly on its stand. It was one of two simple bands of obsidian with low, evenly spaced points that he had commissioned to replace the originals. I removed my nearly identical crown, setting it haphazardly next to his.

There was, technically, a third matching crown as well. It was much smaller and outfitted with a leather strap to ensure it wouldn't fall off.

But Boris refused to wear it most of the time.

Iiro and Inessa remained at Elk Estate. And while I still sometimes daydreamed about casually visiting to murder him, I was glad that neither Theo nor Inessa had been forced to grieve him.

The cost of the war had been high enough, and I couldn't actually bring myself to wish there had been any more deaths. Usually.

Since Inessa wasn't confined to the estate, she had been emboldened to open an orphanage for those left without parents during the war. Theo was busily heading his clan, though he no longer seemed in any immediate hurry to marry.

And of course, Mila and Taras were both horrendously sleep-deprived and deliriously happy when they came to visit with their son, Wilhelm. I called him Wil, obviously, because no one calls a baby *Wilhelm*.

My family had started to take turns visiting me after Gallagher's emergent trip, bringing an extra dose of life and laughter to the recovering kingdom.

So all in all, things were finally calming down.

Except the way I craved Evander. That never stopped. Never wavered.

Even now, I crossed the room to him as he neatly removed

his jacket. I tugged on his shirt, and he raised his eyebrows before taking it off.

My fingers went to the knotted skin on his chest. Just like always, I had an obsessive need to make sure it was really healed.

"It isn't going to come back, Lemmikki," he said softly.

Instead of answering him, I pressed my lips over the scar before skating them up to his neck.

His breath hitched in his throat, and the sound filled me with a heady, delicious pleasure. Then his hands were on my waist, and he was picking me up against the wall, bringing my face level with his.

Evander leaned in, his mouth covering mine, his tongue teasing my lips until I let out a soft groan. He pressed himself further against me, kissing his way over to my ear with an intensity that made my toes curl.

"Lemmikki?" His low tone sent warmth spreading to every part of my body.

I murmured some sort of questioning response that wasn't remotely coherent.

"Did you take your herbs?" he asked.

"No," I breathed, nervousness and excitement coursing through my veins.

"Good." He smiled against my skin.

I reached up to run my fingernails through his hair, bringing his mouth back to mine and gently dragging my teeth along his bottom lip.

"Der'mo, Lemmikki," he growled.

I chuckled softly, still basking in the decision we had made, in the improbable happiness we had found together, and the life we were going to create.

It was perfect, even when it was chaos.

After all, chaos was my specialty.

Pronunciation Guide

Rowan	ROE-an (long O)
Davin	DAV-in (short A)
Theo	THEE-oe
Iiro	EER-oe
Avani	ah-VAHN-ee
Mila	MEE-lah
Venla	VEN-lah
Inessa	in-ES-ah
Evander	ee-VAN-der
Socair	soe-CARE
Lochlann	LOCK-lan
Chridhe	CREE
Hagail	ha-GALE
Borscht	borsht
Lemmikki	lem-EEK-ee

Clan Elk
Duke: Iiro
Colors: Navy & Tan

Clan Bison
Duke: Ivan
Colors: Orange & Gray

Clan Ram
Duke: Mikhail
Colors: White & Red

Clan Viper
Duke: Andreyev
Colors: Green & Gold

Clan Wolf
Duke: Nils
Colors: Gray & White

Clan Lynx
Duke: Arès
Colors: Teal & Gold

Clan Crane
Duke: Danil
Colors: Yellow & Black

Clan Eagle
Duke: Timofey
Colors: White & Brown

Clan Bear
Duke: Aleksander
Colors: Black & White

A MESSAGE FROM US

We need your help!

Did you know that authors, in particular indie authors like us, make their living on reviews? If you liked this book, or even if you didn't, please take a moment to let people know on all of the major review platforms like; Amazon, Goodreads, and/or Bookbub!

(Social Media gushing is also highly encouraged!)

Remember, reviews don't have to be long. It can be as simple as whatever star rating you feel comfortable with and an: 'I loved it!' or: 'Not my cup of tea...'

Now that that's out of the way, if you want to come shenanigate with us, rant and rave about these books and others, get access to awesome giveaways, exclusive content and some pretty ridiculous live videos, come join us on Facebook at our group; Drifters and Wanderers

ROBIN'S ACKNOWLEDGMENTS

There are so many people to thank with not only every book, but especially the completion of a series, that I don't even know where to begin here.

The first thank you goes out to my bestie/co-author. Elle, when I came to you with the idea to demolish our entire line-up in favor of a brand new series and a brand new story based on a random scene I saw in my head at three o'clock in the morning, you were just crazy enough to say yes.

And I love you for it.

More than that, you saw it, too, and together, we made the most amazing characters and couples we have ever created. Rowan is you and me and our bad choices and our ridiculousness and our stubbornness and our sarcasm, unfettered, and I am so eternally grateful that we got to go on this journey with her.

Jamie, you deserve all the whiskey in all the world for your unending patience with us and this project, not only for your amazing edits but also the encouragement and feedback and general love and awesomeness you send our way. Thank you, always, always, always!

To Jesikah, who very legitimately saved this story and our arses. I will never be able to thank you enough for taking the time to help us craft this story when your own schedule was hectic and insane. I would have quite literally lost my mind without you. You are now my whole heart. The end.

Sophies, Habitha, bestie-besties, and general purveyors of gloriousness. Thank you for your support and most importantly, your friendship and your understanding when we were nonresponsive lumps. It means the world to us, and so do you guys. <3

To Amanda and her ample bosoms, I sometimes think we wouldn't still be on this writing journey at all if it weren't for you. And if we were, we would be doing it badly. You made it possible for us to get our books out into the world, to get them seen, and you became one of our dearest friends in the meantime. All the love <3

Emily, we would be so, so lost without you. Your careful management of our whole lives, your cheerleading, your reminders to sleep and hydrate, even when we ignore them. You are everything we never knew we needed in authordom, and I honestly don't know how we ever survived without you, but suffice it to say, we never want to again.

Beta Babes, you know that we live for our chat, your hilarious commentary, and your GIF summaries of our books. Most importantly, our stories would suck and be riddled with inconsistencies without you. We appreciate you guys more than you will ever know!

ElBin's Street Team, you guys have ROCKED it with these books. We have given you tight deadlines and very little wiggle room and you 1000% made it work, and seriously, it means everything to us!

Drifters and Wanderers, this is our social media safe space, and you guys help keep it that way. We love the interactions, the memes, the polls, and the general hilarity and support you bring every day.

Overall, we got through this grueling release schedule by the grace of our author friends and supportive readers and very patient families. I'm sure there are so many people I've left out of these acknowledgements, but as always, I'm going to close with my family.

To my husband, who first came up with the idea to write a book, who helps me work through plot holes and never wavers in his faith in me, I love you and our family more than everything else in this world combined.

ELLE'S ACKNOWLEDGMENTS

This is it. The end of the series and a whirlwind couple of months!

Thank you to everyone who supported us and encouraged us and cheered us on from all over the world. Especially our beautiful readers who have craved more and more Rowander and Lochlann in general.

We are far from done with this world. We love these characters and their stories so very much and cannot wait to share what else we have in store with you!

Onto our list of amazing supporters and our writing and editing team that made this possible!

First and foremost, Robin. We did it. We ACTUALLY did it!

In spite of all the curveballs and health scares and surgeries and family issues and brain fog and ridiculous deadlines, we finished this series. And it's the one I am the most proud of. Every inch of these books is filled with us, our ridiculous selves, our quirky personalities, our sarcasm and black humor and most importantly, our friendship.

I have loved working on this project with you and I am so so happy that we returned to Lochlann after the past year we've had. It really is our happy place! Thank you again for being such a rockstar and pulling more than your fair share of work when my body decided to rebel and send me into the hospital. You are super woman <3

Jamie Whiskey-Drinking Holmes - There are never enough words to express how much you mean to us. We absolutely adore you and are so incredibly grateful for your friendship and your editor's eye. You help us refine our story so that it's ready for public consumption and we are so so thankful for that.

Thank you for being so flexible with this book, and well, every book we write. Thank you for being on our team and always cheering us on. We love you <3<3

Jesikah Sundin- The other half of my potato-faerie loving heart. Thank you for being an amazing friend and stepping in to save the day! We literally could not have finished this project without you! <3

Emily Prebich, aka The Best PA ever! - What can I say that we haven't said a million times before??? You are quite literally the best thing that has happened to us. You keep us in line, on track, sane-ish, and relevant. Thank you so much for never being offended when we fail to communicate, for reminding us of our responsibilities and to hydrate, and for being an amazing human that we literally cannot live without. We love you so much!

Sophie Bobcat Davis - You girls have no idea how much you mean to us. You came into our lives and are now stuck here. Thank you for checking in on us as we trudged our way through these deadlines, for sending us Mountain Lion Gifs to make us laugh, for sharing in our insanity in the wee hours of the morning and for just being the bestie besties we could ever ask for. <3

Amanda Buxom Steele - Can you just move out here so I can hug you all the time?? Do you even know how vital you are to us as a team, as individual humans, and as secret raccoon shifters that sometimes indulge in too much trash??? We can never thank you enough for your support, your encouragement, your feedback and your bosoms. Thank you for taking us under your wing and for letting us stay there. (We're never leaving)

Beta Babes!!! Sarah, Hope, Erin, Rachel, Michelle and Ali!!!

What would we do without you??? You girls are the absolute best and have been instrumental in EVERY SINGLE BOOK WE'VE WRITTEN THIS YEAR!!! I cannot believe we haven't driven you away yet with all of our insane deadlines and our incessant questions and late night additions to chapters you've already read 5 times over!

Thank you for sticking around and being the best beta team we could ask for!

Thank you to our **Street Team and Drifters and Wanderers** for being the best readers we could ask for! Your constant support and cravings for each new word we write is what fuels us to keep going <3

Thank you to my amazing husband who dealt with all of the chaos while I hid in my writing cave trying to meet impossible deadlines while acting like a rabid bear trying to hibernate. Thank you for leaving snacks and wine while I stayed up all hours of the night trying to get these characters to cooperate. And mostly, thank you for taking amazing care of me when I had to go into the hospital. You really are my knight in shining armor and I love you more than all the brownie batter in the world <3

And finally, thank you to **Reginald**, the mountain lion who decided to live outside of my house for a few months, providing me with endless amounts of terrifying and amusing stories.

ABOUT THE AUTHORS

Elle and Robin can usually be found on road trips around the US haunting taco-festivals and taking selfies with unsuspecting Spice Girls impersonators.

They have a combined PH.D in Faery Folklore and keep a romance advice column under a British pen-name for raccoons. They have a rare blood type made up solely of red wine and can only write books while under the influence of the full moon.

Between the two of them they've created a small army of insatiable humans and when not wrangling them into their cages, they can be seen dancing jigs and sacrificing brownie batter to the pits of their stomachs.

And somewhere between their busy schedules, they still find time to create words and put them into books.

ALSO BY ELLE & ROBIN